CW01464443

ASCENDANT
BOOK 3

ASCENDANT

BOOK 3

EmergencyComplaints

Podium

All rights reserved. No part of this publication may be reproduced, stored in a retrieval system, or transmitted in any form or by any means electronic, mechanical, photocopying, recording, or otherwise without prior written permission from Podium Publishing.

This is a work of fiction. Names, characters, places, and incidents are either products of the author's imagination or used fictitiously. Any resemblance to actual events, locales, or persons, living, dead, or undead, is entirely coincidental.

Copyright © 2024 by David Sherman

Cover design by Iromonik

ISBN: 978-1-0394-4687-8

Published in 2024 by Podium Publishing
www.podiumaudio.com

Podium

ASCENDANT

BOOK 3

EmergencyComplaints

Podium

All rights reserved. No part of this publication may be reproduced, stored in a retrieval system, or transmitted in any form or by any means electronic, mechanical, photocopying, recording, or otherwise without prior written permission from Podium Publishing.

This is a work of fiction. Names, characters, places, and incidents are either products of the author's imagination or used fictitiously. Any resemblance to actual events, locales, or persons, living, dead, or undead, is entirely coincidental.

Copyright © 2024 by David Sherman

Cover design by Iromonik

ISBN: 978-1-0394-4687-8

Published in 2024 by Podium Publishing
www.podiumaudio.com

Podium

ASCENDANT

BOOK 3

EmergencyComplaints

Podium

All rights reserved. No part of this publication may be reproduced, stored in a retrieval system, or transmitted in any form or by any means electronic, mechanical, photocopying, recording, or otherwise without prior written permission from Podium Publishing.

This is a work of fiction. Names, characters, places, and incidents are either products of the author's imagination or used fictitiously. Any resemblance to actual events, locales, or persons, living, dead, or undead, is entirely coincidental.

Copyright © 2024 by David Sherman

Cover design by Iromonik

ISBN: 978-1-0394-4687-8

Published in 2024 by Podium Publishing
www.podiumaudio.com

Podium

ASCENDANT
BOOK 3

CHAPTER ONE

Nym's first impression of Shu-Ain was that there were a lot of people with much darker skin than him speaking in a language he didn't know. Even on the outskirts of the main city, the streets were packed. A great number of people lived there, or at least were visiting today.

The language barrier wouldn't be a problem, Nym hoped. There was a spell he'd picked up specifically for the occasion, a third-circle translation spell that worked by establishing a telepathic connection between him and the person he was speaking to and altering what each of them heard into something they'd recognize. It wasn't perfect, and its biggest flaw was that it worked best on an individual person, with the spell becoming significantly more expensive to maintain the more connections he included in it.

It would hopefully be enough to help him get directions to a money changer and find out the current exchange rate. He didn't have much else he needed to do in Shu-Ain, but he thought he might explore the city a little bit anyway before he left. He'd never been in one that didn't restrict the public usage of magic, and he was hoping to see a few interesting spells before he left.

Unlike most cities he'd visited, Shu-Ain didn't have walls. Back in Delvros, almost every town did, or at least those on the west side of the country did. Thrakus was the only city he'd ever seen without one, and even then, it had been heavily garrisoned and patrolled. The only reason it lacked walls was all the farmland butting up against the city.

Nym supposed living on an island where humanity had thoroughly extinguished the competition meant that there was no need for walls. Most threats would presumably come from the air or, he supposed, from other people. People meant magic though, and walls were of limited use against mages. In the end, it always seemed to come down to money. It was cheaper not to build walls, and there was nothing for them to protect the city against, so they didn't.

On the bright side, it did mean that Nym could just walk right in or, rather, that he could fly right in. There were hundreds of people flying through the air at different heights, some weaving through the buildings, which often got up to three or four floors in height, others taking to higher altitudes and skimming over the roofs.

Nym flew around for a bit, trying to get a feel for the layout of Shu-Ain, but he mostly just discovered that their culture wasn't big on city planning. Buildings were rarely uniform in size or height, although he did find some districts that would have a distinctive style of construction or clothing. Sometimes the people living there would have markings or tattoos that seemed culturally important in some way. There were also a lot of piercings, often in places that looked extremely sensitive.

A lot of people wore a lot less clothing than he was used to, which was how he noticed some of those sensitive piercings. Shirts weren't exactly uncommon, but not wearing them wasn't uncommon either. Most everyone had something covering their loins, though he did fly over a group of four old men, all completely naked and . . . hanging out . . . around a pond outside the city proper while they fished.

Nym had had a lot on his mind over the last year, and he hadn't really given any thought to situations where he would see other people naked. It was definitely a bit of culture shock to see so much exposed flesh, and his rapidly aging body's hormones had things to say about some of the prettier and more athletic people he saw. He did his best to keep from ogling anyone, but he wasn't sure how well he succeeded.

Analia was a lot more relaxed now than she'd been when he'd first met her, but she was going to have a fit when she saw the state of general undress the natives of Shu-Ain did their business in. Nym grinned at the thought. He'd have to make sure he stuck around to watch her reaction.

As distracting as it was to see so many people so exposed, Nym was, as always, more interested in the magic. He didn't stumble across any great secrets, of course. There were a lot of people using magic in its most basic forms: as tools to assist them in whatever they were trying to accomplish.

He spied a potter using telekinesis to form an extra set of invisible hands that helped him shape clay. Nearby was a girl who looked to be his own age using a sustained elemental-air spell to create a strong breeze over a line of wet clothes. A new mother sang to her baby, and her voice had a soothing, almost hypnotic quality to it as arcana infused her words. Opposite her sat a man that Nym assumed was the father, smiling as he listened and deftly weaving cloth over and through a large, complicated-looking wooden frame to form a collapsible canopy for his family to stay cool under.

There were little things like that everywhere, and while nothing was revolutionary to him, it was nice to see magic freely used. Nym had forgotten how restrictive it was to have to hide his magic use in every dinky little town he passed through. Honestly, as he'd gotten stronger, specifically after breaking into the third tier, he'd stopped really bothering.

Most of those small towns didn't care to check if he was licensed anyway. It was only if he encountered one with a mage guildhall that he even considered being circumspect. But down in Byramin they didn't care about that. It was refreshing. Nym could get used to living in a place with unfettered magic usage.

Then he flew over the slave auction and saw people being herded up onto blocks, shackles on their wrists and ankles. Men and women were sold one at a time after the auctioneer gave an accounting of whatever crime they'd been accused of that had landed them in a slaver's pen. Some of the crimes might even be true, but Nym doubted it.

It served as a stark reminder that Shu-Ain was not necessarily a safe place, and Bildar's warning that slavers liked to target foreigners echoed in his head. Nym flew away in a hurry, lest he tempt fate. It did seem that trouble found him in new cities more often than not, and he wasn't interested in dealing with that again.

Eventually, he found something that looked like a market and landed on the street. He put the translation spell into effect, felt it connect to a nearby merchant, and said, "Excuse me, can you point me to the money changers?"

"I change money at you," the merchant told him. "What coin value want you change much?"

It took him a second to unravel that. He could only assume he'd done something wrong when casting the spell but through some fluke had gotten it close enough to correct that it was still functioning. He wondered what the merchant was hearing on his end.

"I just need to know the exchange rate," Nym said, brandishing a silver shield.

"Daksuun for Delvrovian shield," the merchant said.

Nym had no clue what a daksuun was, or even if they'd understood each other right. "Oh, okay. Thank you."

He broke the translation spell's connection and walked away. Immediately the merchant started speaking to him in rapid-fire native Byramese. Nym could cast the translation spell again, but he figured he should also make an effort to actually learn the language. Whatever the merchant was saying, he sounded upset. Nym decided to practice with someone else.

He did eventually find a money changer's stall a few streets over. It was open-air but was guarded by three large men with bulging muscles and thick, sturdy clubs hanging from leather straps around their wrists. The money changer himself was a thin, reedy man with skin that was far lighter than almost anyone else around them, though still darker than Nym's. He had a wispy beard poking out of his chin and, unlike his guards, was wearing both pants and a shirt.

"Oooh, what's this? A foreigner from the northlands," the money changer said.

"Oh, you speak my language? That's good. My translation spell doesn't seem to be working right."

"They never do," the money changer told him. "Even the third-circle versions cause problems. They're better than nothing but not as good as learning the language yourself. But! That's not what you're here for. You want some daksuun? Or maybe just dakvol?"

"Dakars, actually. What's the rate now?"

"Five and a quarter for a Delvrovian crest, minus a tenth for my fee," the money changer said.

"Uh . . ."

"You give me four crests, I give you twenty-one dakars, minus two and a single daksuun as the fee."

"I'm not familiar with the local currency," Nym admitted. "Which I realize is probably not a great thing to admit to a money changer, but . . . Daksuun and dakvol?"

"One dakar is ten daksuun. One daksuun is ten dakvol. Simple enough."

"Oh good. That'll make things easier. It steps up the same way as the currency I'm used to."

"Yes, it's a good system. Very easy to do the math. That's why Delvros stole it from us and modeled their own currency off ours."

Nym laughed. "Well, if it's not broke . . ."

"Indeed. So, my young friend, how many dakars are you needing today?"

"Let's just say one crest's worth today," Nym said, fishing the coin out of his pack as he spoke. The money pouch was buried at the bottom, but thanks to a bit of telekinesis, he had worked the coin up to the top while they spoke. He handed it over, and the money changer gave it a cursory inspection.

"Solid gold all the way through, edges haven't been shaved. Very well."

The money changer reached into his shirt and pulled out his own money pouch, which hung from a string around his neck. Nym made a mental note to get one of those, as it seemed convenient and difficult to steal from. The money changer pulled out a handful of strange coins. They were all gold, and all significantly smaller than the crest Nym had handed over.

The largest one was slightly fatter than a crest but not even a quarter its size. The money changer separated four of those, followed by seven more than were maybe a tenth the size of a crest and half as thick, and finally two more that were barely the size of Nym's pinkie nail and so thin that he thought they might bend if he squeezed them.

"Here you are, my friend. Four dakar, seven daksuun, two dakvol. Or five and a quarter, minus my tenth as a fee."

"Ah, thank you. Before I go, could you perhaps point me in the direction of a good meal?"

"If you are eager to give money right back into my hands, I would recommend my brother's restaurant two streets over and a little bit south. It is called the Saecharou. He does not speak your language so well as me, but if you tell him I sent you, he will treat you very well."

"Oh, thanks! I'll give it a try. Um . . . I did not get your name."

The money changer laughed again. "It is Taiduuk. Now get on out of here, young man. Go and fill your belly while you empty your purse!"

Nym found himself laughing with the money changer. "Thank you, Taiduuk, I think I will."

It was easy enough to find the Saecharou, and Nym treated himself to a dish he'd never heard of, made with ingredients he had no words for, but which nonetheless were quite tasty. Taiduuk's brother told him what it was called multiple times, but by the time he left, Nym was forced to admit he still couldn't remember it.

His business concluded, Nym pulled in arcana and teleported out of the city.

CHAPTER TWO

Nym eyed the trunk doubtfully. "Why don't I come back for it later? We don't want to haul this around all day."

"Then I'd need to pay for another day's lodging," Analia pointed out.

"Might be doing that anyway. There's no guarantee we'll find a place on the first day," Cern told her.

"I know a team of contractors who could put a place up pretty fast," Nym said.

"I don't think we have the funds to have a workshop built."

Nym and Analia both started laughing. "Maybe if you paid them in baked goods," she said.

"Please! I saved their lives. Surely that's worth an afternoon's labor."

"We'd still need to pay for some labor to make the interior functional. I'm not living inside a stone box."

"What are you guys talking about?" Cern asked.

Nym explained who the Earth Shapers were and what his relationship with them was. The longer he talked, the shrewder the expression on Cern's face got. By the time he was done, the alchemist was literally rubbing his hands together in anticipation.

"This is a much better idea than renting or buying a workshop. Hrmm, we'll still need to buy land though, and it's expensive in Byramin. Go figure, it being an island nation. What was the exchange rate again? Five and a quarter?"

Nym nodded and the alchemist started doing calculations. He had no hesitation at all about claiming all Nym and Analia's money for the project either. When they'd mentioned it, he'd told them that they could always get more and to think of it as a business investment that would pay them back many times over anyway.

The first part was true enough, at least. Master mages were extremely rare, and third-circle spells were such a huge step up from second that the only real problem with finding new work was that he wanted to keep a low profile. It was kind of pointless to leave the country if he just started advertising himself as a powerful mage looking for work in the next city. He didn't want the people who made Archmage Veran look like an amateur finding him before he was ready to fight back.

Truth be told, the better he got at magic, the less he cared about money. He needed it for food and shelter, but anymore, those were minor obstacles. He wasn't so enamored with the high life that he cared about staying in the finest inns and eating exquisitely prepared meals. If it came down to it, Nym was confident he could live out in the wilderness in relative safety and comfort.

This was mostly an exercise in helping Analia refine her alchemical skills and helping Cern bounce back from losing his shop. Between the undead destroying all of Zoskan and mysterious unknown looters scavenging the wreckage, there hadn't been anything of value left. Nym had no doubt army staff had picked through it and collected anything the bolder refugees hadn't managed to scavenge first.

"I don't think we can afford it," Cern said. "Unless I'm dramatically overestimating the price of land, it would take almost everything we have, with nothing left over to furnish a home or workshop, let alone purchase the supplies we need to get started."

"I do have some equipment already," Analia said.

"Yes, but not what we need and not on a scale we need to go commercial. No offense, but you have a hobbyist's kit, good for making some stuff at home in small batches. Unless you've got another thirty crests you've been hiding away, we'd be better off renting for now until we've built up more capital to invest in a workshop of our own."

"That, and when you're done in Shu-Ain, you'd have to leave it behind," Nym said.

"Not a real issue. Selling a fully furnished and functional alchemist workshop in the birthplace of alchemy would not be a problem. Renting it out would be even more profitable, long term, but that requires a measure of oversight that prohibits actually leaving the city."

"Do you want to leave the city though?" Analia asked. "It's not likely that the forest is going to be fully recovered for a long time. The fighting did a lot of damage, and the army is still doing cleanup. It could be a year or more before people even start rebuilding."

"All true, but no, I am not interested in staying in Shu-Ain long term. They're friendly to short-term tourists who've come to do business and spend money. As soon as it becomes clear that we mean to stay permanently, a lot of that goodwill is going to disappear. And their culture has some nasty practices I don't want to be involved in. Last thing we need is getting kidnapped and sold into slavery down there."

"If it makes you feel any better, I surveyed their slave auctions yesterday, and they don't have anything I saw that can hold an accomplished mage."

"Look closer next time," Cern said sourly. "Mage slaves aren't sold in open auctions, but trust me, they exist. The things they do to those people to . . . ensure compliance . . ."

The alchemist shuddered and trailed off. Nym could well imagine some of the measures an unscrupulous person would take. If his own captors hadn't been interested in a cooperative research subject, he probably would have been placed under an involuntary and much stronger geas. Their desperation to resolve things quickly had probably given him a lot more leeway than he would have otherwise had.

"Maybe living in Shu-Ain isn't the best idea," Nym said.

"Everywhere has problems. Why, I once lived in an area that was overrun by a horde of undead monsters. I lost everything I owned and was lucky to get out with my life," Cern said dryly.

He'd feel better if Analia reached the third layer, but that wasn't likely to happen anytime soon. Even with him trying to help guide her, it was still a process. She got closer when he was assisting but still didn't quite break that barrier. He had already compiled several small journals full of spells for her, just waiting for her to gain the ability to cast them.

He glanced over at her, and she shrugged. "I need to make a living somehow. It could be years before I can reliably cast third-circle spells."

"I guess we're doing this then. Try not to get sold into slavery or murdered or whatever."

"I'm sure we'll be fine," Cern said. "But in regard to our moving plans, I don't think it's financially viable to buy land at this point. It could be something we look into in the next three or four months."

"There's really nothing unclaimed anywhere on that whole archipelago?" Nym asked.

Cern shrugged. "There might be, but it hardly matters for our purposes. We need to be in Shu-Ain so that we have ready access to its markets and supplies."

"It'll probably be a day before you guys can move in either way then. Let's just leave the luggage here for today."

That settled, Nym teleported the three of them into the sky outside Shu-Ain. Under Cern's direction, he flew them to a part of the city he hadn't explored yesterday and followed the alchemist into a building staffed by a pair of men who were seated in front of a detailed city map.

Nym couldn't follow much of the conversation, since it was all in a language he didn't speak. Cern did though and was apparently quite fluent in it. He got whatever information he was looking for, scribbled some notes down on a piece of parchment, and paid the men one of the medium-sized coins. Nym couldn't remember the name off the top of his head.

"What is this for?" he asked once they were back out on the street.

"Alchemy workshops available to be leased," Cern told him. "There's only one furnished option, and they told me the owner is firm on a price that's way too high. I figured we'd start at the cheapest one and work our way up from there. The managers have messaged owners to meet us at each one at specific times, so we're on a bit of a schedule."

Using Cern's notes, they flew over to the first workshop, where they were met by a large man with a wild mane of long dark hair. He spoke in a deep, rolling voice that Nym could swear he felt in his chest. Together, they toured a small workshop. Everything looked fine to Nym, but he would readily admit that he wasn't an expert.

Cern must have thought otherwise because they left without coming to any sort of agreement. Once they were back up in the air, he asked, "What was wrong with that one?"

"Too small, couldn't do half of what I wanted with the space available. Was missing some of the built-in workbenches the listing said it had. No attached suite to live in."

"Ah. Well, it's a good thing we have options."

They breezed through the next two locations, which Cern rejected for various reasons that eluded Nym. He traded looks with Analia, who just shrugged and whispered, "He's the master alchemist. He knows what he wants."

On the fourth spot, it seemed like they'd found a winner. Cern had his negotiating face on, and Nym didn't understand the language anyway, so he just blended into the background while the alchemist talked to the owner, a remarkably thin woman wearing less clothing than Nym was comfortable with and covered in puckered scars from what he assumed was being splashed with some sort of acid.

The workshop was three times the size of the first one they'd seen and had two rooms full of built-in benches and tables at various heights. There was a back corner that had a small patch of dirt instead of floorboards, which was important for some reason. Cern's negotiating face melted into naked glee when he saw it, though he quickly regained his composure.

It even had a three-room suite attached to the back of the workshop, which included a bedroom, kitchen, and an office. While Cern and the woman were discussing terms, Nym leaned over to Analia and asked, "So who's staying here, and who's living somewhere else?"

"We'll share the workshop. Since it's not going to be used as a storefront, there's plenty of space. He's the one interested in the business portion of it though, so he'll live here. I'll find a place to rent nearby. I figured we'd do that later."

"Do you speak . . . uh . . . whatever this language is?"

"Nope. Going to make Cern translate for me or use a translation spell. I think it's called Byrat? Byrach? Something like that."

"Wow, we really did our research before picking this place."

"It was going to be a problem no matter which country we moved to. I can adapt to this quickly enough. And you can teleport now. We're not investing too heavily into Shu-Ain; nothing that we can't afford to lose. If it comes down to it, we'll leave."

"Looks like he likes the place, at least."

"Yeah. I wonder if he's just going to cancel those other appointments."

They didn't, and even though there was a nicer workshop, the price wasn't as nice. They ended up going back to the one owned by the skinny woman with the scars and paying thirty dakars for a deposit and a month's rent.

"Okay, let's get started," Cern said, rubbing his hands again and looking around. "We'll grab the stuff we left behind, then I'll start pricing out the rest of the equipment we'll need, and we can make a supply run to get the initial materials."

"Before that, I need a place to live," Analia said firmly. "There's no room for me here."

"Oh, yes, yes. Of course. So . . . You'll do that first, and then we'll get started."

"Oh no. You're coming with me. I need you to translate."

Cern's face fell, but he nodded. "Yes, of course. I should make sure you're not going to get scammed."

"Among other things. Come on then, let's see what we can find."

Analia pushed Nym and Cern out the door, barely giving the alchemist time to lock it behind him.

CHAPTER THREE

With Analia comfortably settled into her new home, a two-room house a few blocks away from the workshop that was costing her seven dakars a month, Nym left the pair of them to their work and returned to Archmage Veran's sanctum. His own studies were progressing somewhat smoothly, though he was still failing to bore through the fourth layer. He could, if he wanted, pull in the arcana, though it was practically unusable in its base form.

There were techniques to learn how to process it, but material was scarce on the subject. Those few humans who'd reached the fourth layer universally agreed that it wasn't worth it. Based on the brief communication he'd gotten from his own past self, it seemed that ascendants also backed that philosophy.

So Nym did not spend time learning to harness fourth-layer arcana. Instead, he sharpened his willpower with practice and researched some of the more esoteric physical and mental alterations he could make to assist him in pushing his conduit to the fifth layer. Archmage Veran was a considerable help in both planning out a set of enhancements and helping him implement them.

Nym spent so much time working on his own progress that he became something of a hermit, with days or weeks going by between visits to his friends. They were all weathering the winter months in relative comfort thanks to the southern climates, and though snow piled up in Abilanth, Thrakus, and a dozen other northern cities, Nym was perfectly comfortable in his room.

His life could only remain warm and uneventful for so long, of course. One day while he was poking through some of the upper shelves of the library, Archmage Veran appeared in the room and peered at him. "Nym, I need a favor," he called up.

He shelved the book he'd been flipping through and flew down to the floor. "What's up?"

"I need a capable combat mage to chaperone a class at the Academy. They're going on a field trip to Glacial Valley to get some experience with elemental water using an ice-aspected filter. It shouldn't be too dangerous, but there are some hostile creatures living in the area, and we'd like to keep our students alive."

"Glacial Valley . . . That sounds familiar."

"The region is rather famous as one of the best training locations for water mages seeking to learn ice magic. That's why we take classes out there regularly."

"No." Nym frowned. "Something else. I can't remember what though. I guess it's not important. So I just meet the class there and keep an eye on them to make sure they don't get eaten by an ice worm."

"Ice worm? Hmm? Oh, you mean a tecula? It's possible, but I consider it unlikely. We had a hive south of here last winter, which is the first time that's happened ever, as far as we're aware. It was a once-in-a-lifetime occurrence."

Nym snorted. "Lucky me," he muttered. "What kind of threats are you worried about then?"

"Bighorn yetis are the most common nuisance. They're difficult to spot with sight alone, and they're voracious meat eaters. Fortunately, they're territorial and solitary outside of mating season, which this isn't, so you're not likely to encounter more than one. Professor Lakton knows what to look out for, so your job will mostly be to attack any dangers she points out."

"Seems easy enough."

"I'm glad you think so. The class leaves tomorrow morning from the Academy teleportation grounds, and the trip lasts three days. I suggest dressing warmly and bringing something to do. If all goes well, you'll be bored out of your mind the whole time. The Academy itself will provide food and shelter for everyone."

"I'll have to do a bit of shopping. I don't think I own any warm clothes anymore," he said. He'd kept five crests back from the funds he'd given Analia and Cern, more than enough to cover the costs. Usually he just used a thermal barrier if he needed to go out in the cold weather, and most of his time outside the sanctum was spent far to the south.

Nym teleported himself to Abilanth. Technically he still didn't have a license, which he supposed he should take care of at some point, though he'd more or less lost interest once Ebalsan had collapsed and the whole region had descended into lawlessness. With no one around to call him out for unlicensed use of magic, he'd started using it for anything and everything.

Going to another country that didn't restrict magic usage hadn't helped with the casual mindset, so when he appeared in Abilanth in front of the mage guildhall, he momentarily forgot that the laws were different there.

A nearby man flinched so hard he bumped into the woman he was walking next to, practically knocking her into the snow. "Hey!" he demanded, tossing a glare at Nym. "That was incredibly rude!"

"I'm sorry," Nym said. "I didn't mean to scare you."

"See here," the man said, completely ignoring his companion, who was still climbing back to her feet and was covered in snow. "Do you even have a license, a kid as young as you?"

That didn't take long to get busted. Before he could say anything, the woman grabbed hold of the man and hissed, "Shut up! Teleportation is a third-circle spell. He's a master mage!"

The man's face paled, and his attitude instantly flipped. "My apologies, sir. I didn't realize. It was wrong of me to question you."

Bemused, Nym nodded along. "It's fine. Really. I should have appeared higher up so I didn't startle anyone. That was careless of me."

"No, no, not at all."

"Here, let me at least get you cleaned up." Nym grabbed hold of the snow coating the woman with hydrokinesis and swept it away. "There we go. Now, if you don't mind, I have somewhere else to be."

Nym hustled away from the pair, extremely conscious of their eyes on his back. Before he turned the corner, a mage stepped out of the guildhall and started talking to them. Nym wasn't looking to chat with anyone, especially after his unlicensed use of magic. If he could have, he would have preferred to teleport in somewhere else, but the guildhall was the only place in the middle ring he was familiar enough with to teleport to, and he didn't want to deal with the district gate checks.

It took a bit of looking around to jog his memory, but he did eventually find a tailor's shop. He couldn't remember if it was the same one he'd originally visited over a year ago, not that it mattered. They had a fine selection of winter clothes. Nym purchased two outfits, had his measurements taken, and tipped extra to have them done before the shop closed for the evening.

Then he found a leatherworker and bought new shoes and a coat trimmed in fur. Shoes were a constant pain to him, something he spent more money on than anything else, it seemed. He'd grown so much that he'd had to replace his shoes four times already, and he'd spent half his time barefoot! Getting new shoes was a familiar process, and he at least saved a bit of money by selling his old ones back. Since they were barely worn, being only a few months old, he got a decent price.

He returned to the sanctum late that evening, a new pack hanging from a strap off his shoulder. In it were two winter outfits, a book on advanced rune sequences, and a second book detailing some of the rarer plants that grew in extremely cold climates and were prized by alchemists. He didn't expect to find anything since he'd have to stay close to the class, but it didn't hurt to know what to look for, just in case.

His own library was pitiful compared to the grand thing that made up two whole floors in the archmage's sanctum. Honestly, it was pitiful compared to just about anything, being only a single shelf with nine books on it. Nym placed the rune-sequences book on it, up to ten now, next to the other two he had devoted to the craft, and settled down to begin reading about winter plants.

"Is the sun even up yet?" one of the students groused, peering up at the cloud-covered sky.

Nym agreed with the sentiment, but he kept his mouth shut. Some of the students here were older than he looked, and more than a few had shot curious glances at him. They were all dressed in Academy-standard winter robes with slight color variations, though Nym hadn't worked out quite what that signified.

He, on the other hand, was wearing a plain if well-made set of clothes with none of the ornamentation or heraldry a wealthy mage usually sported. His hair was long enough after a year without getting it cut that he could tie it back, though he knew he really should see a barber. At this point, he was only resisting a haircut because it was starting to drive Ophelia up the wall.

A woman in her thirties or forties appeared from a nearby building and marched over to the group. Arcana swept the path in front of her, pushing any snow off to the side and leaving her with a clear stretch of stone. As she walked, her eyes scanned the assembled students, then turned to Nym.

"You are the chaperone?" she asked, stopping in front of him.

"I am."

"My name is Professor Lakton."

"Nym."

"It is a pleasure to meet you, Nym. I'll be honest, normally I'd have a lot of reservations about someone so young, especially someone who isn't even Academy trained, but when the headmaster personally vouches for you, well, you take it on faith."

It certainly didn't seem like she was taking anything on faith, considering all the divination spells he could see in her aura, but Nym let it pass. He knew what he looked like, and he was just happy that people had stopped questioning him at every turn. Just six months ago, it had been a never-ending struggle to get an adult to take him seriously. Now they were just a bit skeptical.

"We'll talk more later," Professor Lakton said. "For now, I've got to get this lot moving before we miss our time slot."

Without waiting for an answer, she strode over to where the students were huddled against the cold and raised her voice. "Everyone is here? Good. Start heading to the teleportation platform. We'll be outbound in ten minutes."

The entire class trudged through the snow in the predawn shadows to a squat building on the north end of the courtyard. It had a formidable set of wards on it, already active. If Nym understood them correctly, they were designed to siphon arcana to power the teleportation platform, which seemed like a roundabout way of doing things, but he supposed if they didn't have dedicated operators to power them, it made sense.

Once inside the building, he could feel the wards tugging at him, looking for arcana. The sensation was mildly unpleasant and apparently prevalent enough that even the students could feel it. Almost immediately, arcana auras sprang up in the crowd. The wards snatched at them, pulling away long strands as the students let them loose and funneling them to the largest platform Nym had ever seen.

It was a twenty-foot circle, probably with about four times the surface area of the standard platforms he'd used in the past. With something that big, it made sense it had a ward scheme designed to pull from multiple sources. An average person would run themselves dry trying to power it.

Nym let out his own stream of second-layer arcana for the wards to catch, and within thirty seconds, the platform came to life. The professor's eyebrows shot up, and she gave Nym a covert glance before ushering the students and their chaperone onto the platform. Then she activated a set of runes inscribed on a control panel, and the whole thing started humming.

Three seconds later, the world pinched around him, and everything went dark. When sight returned, they were standing on an identical platform in a room made of blue stone.

"God's shriveled sac, it's cold!" someone cursed.

Once again, Nym wholeheartedly agreed with that sentiment, and he immediately put up a thermal barrier. Even with the new clothes, he suspected he'd be using that spell frequently for the next few days.

CHAPTER FOUR

Since Nym wasn't at the glacier to get in touch with his inner icicle, he saw no reason to suffer. The others could shiver and cope; he'd already done his time with that. Professor Lakton had probably done this trip quite a few times, and she already had a personal-heating spell going before Nym even turned to look at her.

She was also already cutting through the complaining her students had started up. "Get used to it," she said, raising her voice. "This is why you're here. Internalize that feeling of cold. Accept it and reflect upon what it would mean to never be warm again. Craft your intent from that.

"But that's for later. For now, there are thirty dorm rooms available, more than enough for everyone. Pick one, deposit your stuff, and meet in the main lecture hall in half an hour. Check the rooms before you just walk in to make sure nothing else has moved in."

"How do we know where that's at?" one of the students asked.

"What do you mean moved in?" another one asked at the same time.

"This facility is unmanned when not in use. It should be sealed against any invasive animals entering the building. Confirm this in your dorms, which you can find by following the signs. That is all. Dismissed."

The grumbling didn't subside completely, but it dropped in volume, and the students trudged off the teleportation platform. Nym and the professor followed them out of the room, though they went straight down the hall instead of turning into the dorm area. Nym sent a scry anchor to sweep the area and make sure it was clean while they walked.

He got the layout of the building and confirmed it free of vermin, not that he was surprised. The kitchen was already stocked, and he was betting someone had come through in the last few days to prep it for habitation. The front door was locked and barricaded and thick enough that Nym doubted he could brute force it open with a second-circle spell.

Professor Lakton led him to the faculty wing, which was six suites, each one much, much larger than the student dorms. "Take whichever you like," she said. "We'll be the only ones here for this trip."

Nym didn't have much use for a full suite. At least, that was his initial thought. Once he got inside and had a chance to examine it, he realized it had rune sequences in it to keep it warm, to cook food, for the bathroom, and even to heat the bed specifically. It seemed the faculty was not as willing to rough it out in the frozen northlands as they were to put their students through it.

It was still far more space than he needed. He wasn't actually an instructor, so he didn't need to set up an office to work out of. Everything he'd brought with him was in a pack that he unceremoniously dropped on the floor. After a few minutes examining the rune sequences, which also all linked back to a control panel near the door, he returned to the hall.

Noise-dampening wards were active around a different suite, one he assumed Professor Lakton had claimed. Rather than waiting for her to come back out, Nym flew through the building to the front gate. If his primary job was going to be keeping everyone safe, he figured he needed to know what kind of protections the place offered.

It didn't take long for him to conclude that the door was actually more secure than the walls that surrounded it, and those were foot-thick blocks of granite magically locked together in a kind of tongue-and-groove pattern that was actually impossible to separate without reshaping the blocks. The work was professionally done, though it was very, very old. Newer builds used the same principle but a completely different pattern that was more stable while building.

There were also rune sequences and wards waiting to be activated that would temporarily brace the door with a plane of force while simultaneously repelling invaders. It was a formidable defense, though it seemed designed primarily to keep out things that relied on nothing but physical strength. There was very little in the way of defenses against magic.

He supposed that's what he was there for. A set of wards, no matter how intricate, would never be half as flexible as a living mage. Things that wouldn't be stopped by the door would require an active effort to capture, expel, or kill. He could handle that. The list of things small enough to fit inside the training facility but deadly enough to force a retreat was vanishingly small.

His scry anchor at the lecture hall showed him students entering in groups of twos or threes. The professor had turned up at some time too and was standing at a podium, waiting for the rest of the class to show up. Nym spent a few seconds studying the room, noted the empty space around the podium, then teleported himself there. He even took the extra time and effort to work on his precision so that he showed up already standing on the floor.

There were a couple surprised shouts at his entrance, but he ignored them and asked Professor Lakton, "What's the plan here? Do you want me standing guard at the back of the lecture hall? Should I go to the front door? Patrol the surrounding area to catch threats before they materialize?"

He could probably do all three with enough air golems acting as mobile scry points that he could cycle through, but he figured it was better to just do whatever the Academy's faculty wanted him to. It was their field trip, after all, and there was no reason to reveal all his capabilities. His teleportation spell would hopefully be enough to reassure everyone of his status as a third-circle mage and keep anyone from questioning him.

"Er, whatever you think is best," the professor said, clearly taken aback.

"Okay. What's the schedule like? Is everyone going to be in here for the next few hours?"

"Only for long enough to give out instructions before we go outside."

Nym gave her a sharp look. "What's wrong with in here? Seems cold enough to me."

"No." She shook her head. "There are a few places nearby that have always been very . . . inspirational, let's say. The class will visit one each day for a few hours, then come back here to reflect on what they felt there. I'll be available to help them refine those thoughts into intent filters."

"I see," Nym said. "I guess this is why you wanted a chaperone then. This place is secure enough to sleep in, but you're going out into the wilds with twenty kids and need to make sure nothing sneaks up on us."

He was fully aware of the irony of calling the students kids. Most of them were at least as old as he appeared to be, and there were three or four that looked to be in their early twenties. Only one was around thirteen. That put Nym solidly in the middle, age wise. He had no doubt he'd be a topic of gossip among the students during their free time.

Damn the archmage's sanctum for having such a good library.

After giving everyone their instructions, Professor Lakton led them out into the biting cold. Unlike the facility they were sleeping in, there were no walls to protect against the wind and snow being driven up into their faces. Some of the more prepared students had scarves that they pulled up to cover themselves with. Others were less fortunate and had to suffer through the sting of snow and ice pelting their exposed skin.

Nym had no such protections, but other than the physical sensation of the snow hitting him, there was no cold behind it. He could ignore that easily, and in fact barely even noticed it with his attention on the chain of scrying spells he was cycling through to get a look around him. As soon as he'd found out where they were going, he'd created an air golem and sent it to check the route. Now he was doing a more thorough investigation of all the little caves he'd spotted and scanning as far up a trail leading higher into the mountains as he could.

Nym was almost positive it was a bighorn-yeti trail, but he hadn't actually spotted one yet. Still, it was six feet wide, and the snow had been flung as much as twenty feet away from the trail when it had been broken, which he guessed was within the last day. If it wasn't a snow yeti, he wasn't sure he wanted to know what else it could be.

Either way, if it got too close, it was getting a lightning bolt to the face.

He followed along behind the students, who were for the most part flying over the snow, albeit not very well. Their flight was unstable, and few of them could keep it up for more than a few minutes. The ones who'd cast some sort of reduced-weight or water-alteration spell to walk on top of the snow were performing far better.

It was getting harder to keep an eye on everyone as the group spread out, with the stragglers getting farther and farther behind. Professor Lakton was at the front, and Nym was sure she was competent enough to keep her students alive long enough for Nym to fly over and assist her, but if they were attacked from both sides, it would be a disaster.

He lifted up the half a dozen students at the back and started flying them forward, though he had to grab one three times when he kept squirming and breaking the air cushion around him. Nym plopped them back down solidly in the middle of the line and moved forward so that he was behind the slightly faster students that were now at the back.

"I don't suppose you could do that again?" one of them called up.

"Every time I have to group you back together because you're moving too slow, I'm going to talk to your instructor about lowering your grade for this class. Are you sure you want me to ferry you around?"

"You don't have to be a jerk about it," the student said.

"My job is to keep you safe. It's hard to do when there's a half a mile between the ones at the front and the ones at the back."

The group quickly overtook the ones Nym had moved anyway, since they still weren't moving any faster, but by that point the lead students had reached their destination: an ice cave that supposedly glowed brilliantly when the sun hit it from certain angles. The theory was that the striking tableau would help cement the memory in their minds, a visual representation of how cold they'd felt when they saw it.

Nym's air golem was already there and scanning the interior. It only went a few hundred feet into the glacier, and there didn't seem to be anything dangerous living there. He'd still keep a careful watch, of course. He was concerned about something invisible in there, something he wouldn't see until he checked the place himself and confirmed there was no arcana in there.

He was probably being overly paranoid, but he wasn't going to take the job lightly. If anything happened, he would feel ridiculously vindicated for all his scrying. He was spending a ton of effort on it, after all.

That was probably the reason he was so damn annoyed when a rumbling sound filled the air and a small avalanche came barreling down the mountain above them.

CHAPTER FIVE

Nym's first thought was to use hydrokinesis to divert the snow. It couldn't be that heavy, after all. Then he watched it obliterate a fully grown tree on the way down and decided that it could in fact be that heavy and that the better course of action would be to get everyone out of the way.

He flew straight up and used greater telekinesis to grab seven students who were walking on the snow. Panicked yelling filled the air, though it was barely audible over the rumble of the avalanche. The other students flew higher, all of them flocking around Professor Lakton. Nym brought the group he'd pulled up over to join the rest, and together the whole class watched snow wash away the trail they'd been following.

It took a minute or two for the snow to pass by. While they waited, Nym said, "This happen often up here?"

The professor frowned down at the rushing snow. "It does seem awfully suspicious. Avalanches happen, but the timing on this one . . ."

Nym cast perfect sight and scoured the mountain side. He wasn't sure what he was looking for exactly, but a casual glance was all it took to spot dozens of humanoid figures gathered together in the snow above where the avalanche had started. "There's something up there. I can't quite tell what they are."

"We can't go after them now," Professor Lakton said. "We have prior business to attend to."

"The lesson?" Nym asked, surprised. "You're not going to take everyone back to the facility?"

"It's a tight schedule," she said, her face pained. "If we had more staff, I'd say go take care of them, but if there's more of them that attack from another direction, I'll need your help to defend the students."

Nym didn't like it. Something had attacked them, something smart enough to work in a cooperative group and with enough magic to drop an avalanche on their heads. The attack had been easy enough to foil, but whatever the creatures were, they were going to slink away to come at them from another angle.

Nym spun up an air golem and sent it out to scout the creatures. He linked his scrying to it and watched it get closer to the shadowy creatures while he moved the rest of the class into the cave. A team of them were working on excavating the snow out of the mouth, at least far enough to get people in. Once they were safely inside, he turned his full attention to what his golem was seeing.

There were twenty-eight of them gathered together, arguing violently with one another. They were tall, taller than any human could be at least, and broad shouldered, but with gangly limbs and thin, wrinkled chests covered in patchy white hair and loose skin flaps. Horns came out of their heads, glossy blue and green to match their skin.

Nym's golem didn't transmit sound back to him, but it was obvious the things were arguing with one another. It was a fight of words punctuated with periodic fisticuffs. Not a one of them was without a broken nose or black eye, but even as he watched, their noses shifted back into place and bruised skin faded back into blue-green to match the rest of their bodies.

The regeneration was impressive, but what was really curious about it was the way the creatures moved. When one attacked the other, their attacks always managed to either perfectly predict how the target would dodge, or it was completely off, oftentimes lashing out in the opposite direction of the way they needed to strike.

Nym couldn't make heads or tails of it, but he was sure the creatures possessed some kind of snow or ice magic that had allowed them to start the avalanche. Their position was too much of a coincidence to be anything but the cause of the disaster.

"Professor Lakton, I've got a scry on the attackers. I don't recognize what they are, but maybe you might?"

He started to describe them to her, but she immediately cut him off. "They're trolls. Tribal creatures, very territorial. Meat eaters, but they don't mind it cold or even frozen. No doubt they saw an opportunity to reinforce their larders with some fresh human corpses. They're probably arguing about whether or not to try again."

"Trolls," Nym said. "Hmm. I think someone told me about them once. They can see the future?"

"That's right. It's what makes them dangerous. They're very difficult to fight against when they do attack, but at the same time, they almost never attack unless there's a strong chance they'll win. They must have misjudged something in their divination."

Nym assumed it was because of him. He wasn't sure why exactly, other than to pin it on general ascendant weirdness. That professor who'd examined him a year ago hadn't had any problems seeing his future, so he wasn't sure what would trip up the trolls. Maybe he'd see if Archmage Veran could cast some of those spells on him, just so they could see how weird the results were.

"There aren't that many. I could be up there, fry the lot of them, and back inside of five minutes."

She considered for just a moment, cast a glance at the assembled students filing into the glacial cave, and nodded. "Don't let yourself get drawn into a prolonged encounter, please. I'll station myself at the entrance and keep everyone safe."

"Anything I should know about trolls? I was planning on hitting them with light-ning, but if you think something else would work better, I'm open to suggestions."

"It might work, but you'd need repeated blasts for each one. If it were only a few, that would be a winning strategy. For as many as you say are there, widespread fire would be a better choice. Trolls in general aren't fans of open flames, and glacial trolls hate it even more."

"Why's it always fire?" Nym muttered. "Just once, could it be something else?"

Fire remained, as always, his weakest element. He'd put a lot of effort into improving it, had even learned a few third-circle spells, but his intent filter just wasn't correct. It was close, he thought, but still missing something. Maybe he ought to find a place like Glacial Valley—except for fire—and study it, or whatever it was the kids were supposed to be doing.

Nym put both parts of his partitioned mind to use multicasting spells. He started with a camouflaging sphere, similar to Archmage Veran's disc, except fully enclosing him. Then he teleported to the spot his golem was stationed at using a variant spell that brought active magic along with him. Once he was there, he cast out an immense thermal barrier in a bubble encircling the surrounding trolls.

He didn't want what he was about to do to trigger a second avalanche, so that barrier was the most important part. The last thing he needed was to have to dig out an entire Academy class that he was supposed to be protecting. At the same time, he didn't want the trolls escaping either, so he added a selective kinetic barrier to the area as well. Anything that ran into it from either side would bounce off, hopefully keeping the trolls contained.

A hyperkinetic barrier would have been stronger but also vastly more draining since he had to keep the entire area powered at all times. He wasn't sure he could manage that even without doing anything else, so the kinetic barrier would suffice. If nothing else, it should slow down any troll and allow him to tag it with a greater telekinesis before it got away.

The last spell was the kill shot. He flooded the interior of the thermal barrier with third-layer arcana, as much as he could channel over sixty seconds. And then he ignited it into a flash fire, burning it all up in an instant and raising the tempera-ture inside the barrier so high that he couldn't contain it. Plumes of superheated air jetted out the top, thankfully into the open sky, without disturbing any snow.

The trolls trapped inside went berserk, at least the ones that survived the initial conflagration. No longer blue-green, they instead were a charred black without a single tuft of hair left. Weirdly, the ones that were still alive were now hornless, and gray, slimy blood ran down the sides of their skulls. A chorus of raging wails came up from the group, but Nym was hidden from sight, and they didn't know where to direct any sort of counterattack.

He resealed the thermal barrier as best he could and watched the heat slowly cook them. A part of him almost thought he should feel bad, but then, they had tried to kill him first. That he wasn't actually in any danger didn't change the fact that if they'd had the power to do the job, he'd be buried under twenty feet of snow and freezing to death.

Still, he did have a class to get back to. He flooded the area with arcana again, ignited it, and left their corpses cooling on the now-blackened and snow-free mountainside.

It took the class an hour or so to get everyone calmed down from the attack, despite Professor Lakton's best efforts. That did mean Nym had plenty of time to get back and got to observe the entire lesson. It was kind of weird, at least to him. Mostly she just gave a normal lesson on intent filters, adding aspects to arcana, and how to most efficiently partition and channel it into the soul well.

While she was lecturing, the students were watching the shifting light patterns come through the ice ceiling of the cave and shivering. Unlike him, they were allowed no magic to protect themselves from the cold, and no amount of clothing was going to get the job done. They were huddled together, obviously miserable, and occasionally shooting hate-filled glances at Professor Lakton.

She definitely noticed them but, if anything, seemed perversely amused. In fact, the longer the lecture went on, the more Nym got the idea that she was subtly encouraging them to glower in her direction. Every few minutes, the professor would say something to egg them on, to rub in the fact that they were shivering in the cold and she was not.

Nym was reminded of the flight lessons he'd joined in on when he'd first met Brogan, and his own tactics of verbally berating his students. At the time, Nym had thought the man was just a hard teacher and a bit of a jerk, but personal experience had shown him that emotions could help cement an intent filter in place. It was just one more thing to tie that memory back to the intent they were trying to develop.

That did not stop him from noticing no less than four different students cheating and casting warming spells on themselves. Nym considered saying something, but it wasn't his job, they weren't his students, and if they wanted to cheat themselves out of the classes they were paying thousands of crests for, that was their problem.

When it was time to go a few hours later, Nym sent out two different air golems to canvass the area for more trolls or for any other threats. Everything came back clear, and the trip back to the Academy's Glacial Valley training facility went smoothly, or at least as smoothly as it could go with a bunch of teenagers who had trouble keeping themselves moving forward.

It was a long, slow trip, one that grated on Nym's nerves as he constantly scanned for threats that never materialized. It was only after they were safely back behind magically crafted and reinforced walls that he let himself relax.

"Looking after a bunch of people is stressful," he said to himself. "But only two more days."

CHAPTER SIX

After they returned, Professor Lakton directed the class to the lecture hall to discuss internalizing the memories of the ice cave so they would associate it with the intent filters they were trying to create. Nym sat in the back of the hall, several rows behind the students, and tuned out the lesson. It was not new information to him, and he was much more focused on the air golem he had patrolling outside the facility.

There was no guarantee that the trolls would attack again, or even that they knew where the Academy's Glacial Valley facility was. They obviously had access to at least second-layer arcana though, and if he assumed what the professor who'd tried to help him recover his memories had told him was correct, they were a prognostic species.

The class only had two more field trips to do though, and then he'd be back at the sanctum with free access to Archmage Veran's fat, juicy library. Little jobs like this were a small price to pay for all the ways the archmage had gone above and beyond the strict terms of their agreement. Nym wouldn't say he was friends with the old man, but he appreciated he had a generous mentor.

He'd positioned the air golem in various spots, trying to get the broadest slice of the valley that still included the trail leading back to the building. The unfortunate truth was that due to the secluded nature of where they'd built the place, the trail wound around a lot. Even from the sky, Nym couldn't find a good angle to see the whole thing, let alone the valley opening up beyond it.

If he wanted to dedicate two air golems to lookout duty, it was possible to do what he wanted, but that meant double the arcana usage and triple the headache of having to process three sets of eyes at the same time. He supposed he was probably being too paranoid about the whole thing, but he knew he'd feel awful if anyone died when it was his job to keep them safe.

He didn't realize the lecture had ended until students started leaving. Even then, he wasn't paying a lot of attention until two of them sat down next to him. One was a boy, the other a girl, both around fifteen or sixteen in age, and close enough in looks that he guessed them to be family. "Hi there," the boy said. "I'm Phan. This is my sister, Risa."

"Hello. I'm Nym," he said, bringing more of his brainpower back to what was going on around him. The sensory input from the air golem was regulated to the partitioned portion of his mind, which would make it difficult to multicast, but he didn't think he'd need it at that particular moment. "Need something?"

"We just wanted to thank you for the save earlier. Neither of us are good fliers, and when all that snow came down on us, we just kind of froze. Pardon the pun."

Risa groaned. "Don't pardon it," she told Nym. "He did it on purpose."

"Nothing wrong with a good pun. They're a great way to break the ice," Nym said.

"Oh God, save my poor immortal soul, there's two of them now," she said, staring up at the ceiling and clasping her hands together.

"Ignore her. She likes her theatrics," Phan said. "Like I said, we wanted to thank you. We'd probably be dead without your intervention."

"Don't worry about it. It's literally my job. I'm just glad you guys were clumped close enough that I could grab everyone at once."

"Ah, yes. Also thanks to you. I'm a bit slow with elemental water." Risa's face flushed, and Nym stared at her blankly for a moment before realizing she'd been part of the group he'd hauled forward.

"Don't worry. Everyone's got their strengths and weaknesses."

"Not likely," Phan said. "You're our age and already a master mage. That's crazy. You've got to be a prodigy at like . . . everything."

"I'm really not," Nym said dryly.

"Master mage but not Academy trained. Definitely a prodigy, tough in a fight, friendly with us lowly second-circle mages, and cute too," Risa said, ticking things off on her fingers. "Total package."

"I . . . Er— What?"

She laughed. "Easy to fluster though. I guess you're right about everyone having weaknesses."

"Go easy on the poor guy," Phan told his sister.

"What would be the fun in that?" she said, leaning forward until her lips were close to Nym's ear. "I heard that the instructors get full soundproof suites. I would love to see one. Perhaps sometime tonight."

Nym's face heated up, and he pulled back from the girl. "I— I'll consider it."

She laughed again and stood up. "You do that," she said and walked away. Her hips swayed back and forth with each step.

Phan buried his face in his hands and sighed. "She has no shame," he muttered.

Nym had to agree, but she was very pretty, if perhaps a little too forward with someone whose name she'd just learned a few minutes earlier. He'd bet she knew every single spell in that book he'd gotten his shaving spell out of, possibly a few more that weren't in the book too.

"Thanks again," Phan said, standing up to follow Risa out. "You seriously saved us both, and a lot of my friends besides. It was impressive. You want to join us for dinner?"

"Dinner? Oh, no thanks. I've got some work to do tonight."

"Fair enough. Invitation is open if you finish up early."

"Thanks," Nym said. "I'm afraid it's going to be an all-nighter though."

"Mm-hmm. Work to do. All-nighter. Just don't let her break your heart, man. And for God's sake use a contraceptive spell. She's kind of airheaded sometimes and will probably forget."

Nym felt his face reddening again. "Not that kind of work. Also you know way too much about your sister's sex life."

Phan gave a long-suffering sigh. "We share a dorm room. Parents couldn't afford housing for two."

Since he had no idea how big those rooms were, he didn't know how cramped it would be sharing a one-person room, but at a guess, he'd say very. "Sorry to hear that."

"Nothing new," Phan said. "Little sis has been tagging along in my life since I was two. I've been accommodating her whims for more than a decade. I'm just glad that *you* have your own room so I don't have to go find somewhere to be. But alright, I've got to get going. We'll be in the dining area for the next hour or so if you change your mind."

"Thanks, maybe tomorrow," Nym said.

The teenager left, and Nym settled back into place. There was no way he was getting the coverage he wanted with one air golem. It was driving him mad. There had to be a way, but he just couldn't find the angle. He was so close. It was tempting to just go out there and collapse the switchback that was blocking his setup from working.

Risa was really cute too. Nym jerked in place and shook his head. Where had that thought come from? "Come on, pay attention," he scolded himself. He had a job to do here and bigger problems that he was on a clock to solve.

"Do you have a moment, professor?" Nym asked that night.

"Of course. What do you need?" Professor Lakton said. He'd caught up to her in the hall leading to the instructors' suites, thanks mostly to his scry anchor flitting around keeping an eye on things.

"I was hoping you could show me the other two spots the class will be visiting. I'd like to scout them out early this time."

"Ah, yes. I can help with that. I should have thought of it. Normally the chaperones already know them. They've been with the Academy for a while, or possibly were students who went on this field trip themselves. Here, come with me. I've got a map of Glacial Valley in my office."

She led him to her suite and ushered him in. The front room looked just like his: a standard office. Hers was a bit more lived-in though. Where he'd had no use for the room, she'd obviously spent hours in it talking to students and had set it up with quite a few of her own personal possessions. Included in that was a large map of Glacial Valley pinned up on one wall.

It showed the facility in the southwest corner with red dotted lines marking the trail they'd take to get to each location. The ice cave was clearly marked at the end of one line, and the other two led to a frozen waterfall and what looked like some sort of field full of flowers. The waterfall made sense to him, but the field seemed out of place.

"What is this?" he asked, tapping the field on the map.

Professor Lakton smiled. "It's one of the wonders of the world. We call it the Garden of Winter. I have no words to do it justice. The pixies tend to it, keep the flowers blooming. It may be the single most beautiful thing you'll ever see in your entire life."

"Huh. Interesting. I'll look forward to seeing it." He studied the trails they'd be taking for a moment and added, "Will your class be alright with just you here? I'd like to fly these two paths tonight and get a feel for what's out there."

"We'll be fine. This facility is well defended, and now that it's occupied, I've activated some of the dormant wards to fortify it even further. However, will you have time? The waterfalls are two hours away from here, and the Garden of Winter is an even longer trip."

"I fly fast," Nym said. "I'll prioritize tomorrow's journey first and only do the second trail if I have time."

"If you're sure," Professor Lakton said. She frowned, shook her head, and said, "It's very hard to think of you as a master mage. You're very young. I keep wanting to treat you like a student."

Nym was used to that. For as long as he could remember, adults had been underestimating him and treating him like a child. Admittedly, they did sometimes have a point. He'd made enough stupid mistakes to be cognizant of the fact that he could use some advice every now and then.

"I get that a lot. I do appreciate your restraint," he said. "Thank you for showing me the map. I'll be back in a few hours."

A few hours ended up being more like six. He flew the trail to the frozen waterfalls at a slow speed, wanting to thoroughly scry the landscape around it. There wasn't much to find, but he noted a few places where a troop of trolls . . . Pack of trolls? Clan? Gang? Whatever they were called, he found a place where a group of creatures capable of performing elemental-water magic could bring down snow to wash out the trail.

He did spot his first yeti, more as a fluke than anything. He'd already scried the area and completely missed it when it exploded out of a mound of snow and tackled a full-grown elk that was walking by. The rest of the herd scattered in panic while the nine-foot-tall bipedal monster ripped the elk's throat out with its teeth and dragged the carcass back under the snow with it.

"That is . . . terrifying," Nym whispered as he watched from the sky. That was going to be a whole new kind of nightmare to watch out for, and he made a mental note of which mound the yeti had popped out of. Fortunately, it was a good quarter mile from where the students would be passing by.

There wasn't time to fly the second trail, not if he wanted to sleep. Nym teleported back to the area outside the Academy facility and let himself back in, a time-consuming process that involved weaving through the wards on the door to get them open. It was much easier with the key the professor had, but Nym hadn't taken it with him, hadn't even asked. He wasn't sure Professor Lakton would have given it to him if he had.

He flew to his suite and walked in, only to hear something crumple under his feet. He looked down to the floor and spotted a folded-up piece of paper that had been slipped under the door. Nym picked it up and opened it.

I guess my brother wasn't joking when he said you'd be busy all night. I ought to be offended that you aren't here, but you're cute, so I'll give you another chance tomorrow.
—R

"Oh God," Nym said. He wasn't sure if he needed to make sure he was gone all night again or if he needed to make sure he got everything done early.

CHAPTER SEVEN

The class set out in the early-morning hours, fully expecting to spend upward of three hours traveling through the ice and cold. It was a bright, clear day, the kind that Nym hated to fly over snow during. Even with a perfect-vision spell active, he quickly found himself with a headache from the glare. He wished he still had his old flying goggles, but the destruction of Ebalsan had taken those from him.

Unfortunately, he lacked the ability to create glass. He suspected he could find a spell like that in an advanced-earth-magic spell book somewhere, but it wasn't something he'd ever thought to look for until he was flying high over sunshine on snow and scanning for threats. It was possible that he might be able to modify perfect vision to account for the light, but he didn't have the time to play with it.

In the end, the solution he ended up using was to filter everything through his air golem. Since the sensory link went straight to his brain, his eyes weren't forced to suffer from all the brightness going into them. Nym decided to stick closer to the students and leave the golem to drift above them high up in the air as a long-range lookout.

The downside to that was of course that several of them started trying to talk to him, and Risa was included in that group. Nym was incredibly awkward around her, and after about half an hour of exchanging pleasantries and dodging questions about where he'd learned and how he'd gotten to third circle at such a young age, he finally hit upon a solution.

"Please, I'm trying not to be rude, but I'm not a student," Nym told the teenagers flying near him. "I have a job to do here. I need you all to stop distracting me. What if there's another avalanche and I don't spot it in time?"

That did the trick, for the most part. The small group that had gathered around him dispersed, most of them going back to walking on top of the snow. Risa waited until everyone else had left, looked Nym directly in the eyes, and said, "I would love to talk more later when you're off duty."

"That . . . might be okay."

She smirked and let herself fall down to the snow where she switched from the extremely shaky flight spell she'd been using to one that hardened the snow under her feet in a small radius. It worked, but she didn't have near enough endurance to keep it up for miles of walking. That was how she'd ended up in the back of the line yesterday.

The group stopped for a break at the halfway point. They were coming up to where he'd seen the bighorn yeti the night before, so Nym took the opportunity to scout ahead with both a second air golem and a scry anchor. The scrying itself was still short-range, but it was the only spell he had that allowed him to see through solid objects, and he was hoping he could find the yeti with it.

He wasn't expecting to find it, both because there was no reason to suspect the yeti was still lurking in the same spot and because of the range constraints, but luck was with him, and he spotted it a few hundred yards down the trail nestled in a small stand of pines and buried under a foot of snow. It was only a hundred feet or so from the trail, probably far enough away for the students to pass by without an issue.

That wasn't a chance Nym wanted to take though. He flew over to where Professor Lakton sat, perched on a bare rock that she'd scoured of snow with a blast of wind. "There's a yeti lurking up ahead, just off the trail," he said in a low voice.

"How far off the trail?" she asked. She took a bite of her sandwich and chewed thoughtfully while he pointed out the trees it was hiding in. "That might not be a problem for now. We'll be a little outside its ambush range even if we don't make adjustments, and we can definitely go around it. My concern is that it'll move closer to take a crack at us on the way back."

"I don't suppose our numbers would discourage it," Nym said.

"Possibly, but I wouldn't count on it. It might be best to dispose of it now so we don't have to worry about it trying something later."

"You want it killed?"

"Do you have a way to subdue it for hours and hours without killing it?"

Nym shrugged. "Sure. Blindness. Paralysis. I could entomb it in ice or earth. I could just teleport it miles away and let it make its way back on its own."

"Oh, well then. That's certainly quite a few options. You're certain you could restrain it? I could give a brief lecture on bighorn yetis with a live specimen."

"Let me see if I can capture it first. I'm not expecting any trouble, but if it resists the magic, I'd rather do it when it's just me there than give it twenty other targets to go after."

"Perfect. We'll wait for you to capture it before we start moving again."

Nym flew ahead the thousand feet or so he needed to get within range of the yeti. He watched it through his scrying spell as he approached. If it noticed him at all, it didn't react. Considering how far he was in the air, Nym thought it was more likely that the yeti lacked the ability to see that far away from its hiding place. He didn't know the limit of its sensory system though, so he decided to play it safe and approach cautiously.

The plan was simple. He was going to grab it with greater telekinesis and blast it with as strong a paralysis spell as he could muster. If that didn't work, he was going to trap it in a block of ice reinforced with stone. He was less confident about the backup plan. The yeti's pure physical might was unknown, but he was betting it was more than strong enough to break through stone.

Nym floated directly over it, perhaps fifty feet in the air. The bighorn yeti was well within range of his greater-telekinesis spell. Nym wove it together and sent it down through the snow to grab the yeti blindly. Without being able to physically see it, he had to approximate its position, but that was countered by just casting a wider net.

A loud, angry roar echoed through the valley as Nym ripped the yeti out of its hiding place. It kicked and flailed at the air, but he had it around the trunk. There was little it could do to get free, at least physically. The yeti must not have been stupid because it realized that quickly and shifted tactics.

Snow burst into the air in a wave around the yeti, spiking up to an impressive thirty or so feet straight up. It was more than high enough to reach the yeti, and with a burst of unfocused arcana, a huge volume of it clung to the thing's fur. Its weight nearly tripled, and Nym lost sight of it inside the massive snowball it turned itself into.

In some ways, that made things easier. Nym wasn't about to engage it in a spell duel where he tried to take control of the snow back away from it. Instead, he just peppered it with a dozen arcana injections. Its aura spasmed wildly, and the snow started falling off in clumps. As soon as it was visible again, he hit it with the paralysis spell he'd prepared, then added blindness to the mix as well.

He didn't have a dedicated sleep spell; it turned out that flicking that switch in something's brain was quite dangerous. But he was able to fully restrain it. Nym used a burst of air to clean a section of the trail and brought his catch down, then started building up literal tons of ice to secure the yeti.

The creature was held upright, paralyzed, blind, and suffering from arcana poisoning. "All clear!" Nym yelled back down the trail. He floated in the air about twenty feet away from the yeti and waited for the class to catch up.

A few minutes later, they arrived and spread out into a semicircle while Professor Lakton approached. "It's still alive?" she asked.

"Yes. I've blinded and paralyzed it, though it can still hear and I assume smell us. I also overloaded its soul well with a series of arcana injections when it tried to use a form of hydrokinesis against me."

"Very well, thank you, Nym." Professor Lakton turned back to her class. "We have a rare opportunity today. Before you is the elusive bighorn yeti. Note the pelt coloring, how it blends in with the snow. The yeti is an ambush predator that buries itself in mounds of snow and waits for fresh meat to wander by. Then it leaps out and attacks with lethal intent before dragging its prey back under the snow to consume it raw."

She stopped and looked around at the class, paying particular attention to a few that were constantly straggling behind. "This sort of danger is just one of the reasons that you need to remain close together while we travel."

There was a sentiment that Nym agreed wholeheartedly with. There were some that just couldn't travel fast enough to keep up, but there were also some that were just too lazy to work hard. And then there were some at the front that the professor had to keep from ranging too far ahead.

"Can anyone tell me what kinds of magics we can expect from an adult snow yeti? Yes, Ms. Lorezi."

One of the older students spoke. "The snow yeti uses primarily self-enhancing and camouflage magic to hide itself and burst out with explosive and overwhelming force upon its prey. It also has some mastery over elemental-water magic, specifically relating to snow and ice, that it uses to move around quickly when needed."

"Correct. The snow yeti is notable for its water magic in that it is one of the rare monstrous species capable of using second-layer magic despite its notable lack of intelligence."

"Looks pretty monstrous to me," one of the students snarked.

Professor Lakton pinned him with her eyes for just a moment, and the student ducked his head. Then she continued as if the interruption hadn't occurred. "Our chaperone was nice enough to capture this one for us and has given it a heavy case of arcana poisoning in addition to restraining it, so we're safe enough here, but what are some good strategies for escaping a hungry yeti if you were to encounter one out in the wild by yourself?"

"Run away," one of the students announced immediately, to the snickers of his peers.

"Fly away," a different student corrected.

"Fire blast it in the face."

"Whatever spell Nym used on it."

"Alright, alright. All good ideas, though if I'm not mistaken, at least one third-circle spell was used to restrain it, so I don't know that I'd recommend trying to repeat this capture," Professor Lakton said. She looked questioningly at Nym.

"A personal-scry variant I developed to find it and greater telekinesis to restrain it until I could layer the other spells on it. Everything but greater telekinesis was second circle."

"Seriously? You found and caught that thing with almost nothing but second-circle spells?" a student asked him.

Nym shrugged. "Not everything requires overwhelming force. There might be more threats today I need to be ready for."

"An excellent lesson in restraint," Professor Lakton cut in. "Now, I wonder if anyone can tell me whether this ice by itself would be enough to imprison a snow yeti."

The lecture continued for another twenty minutes, with the professor pointing out the jaw musculature that allowed the yeti to open its mouth so wide, and the scoop-like hands it used to propel itself under the snow with the aid of its magic. Finally, she exhausted her knowledge of the topic, and Nym flew the yeti several miles off the trail before releasing it. It cast him a hateful glare and burrowed down into the snow immediately.

Nym didn't really blame it. He was the one who'd attacked it after all, but he also knew that if the situation had been reversed, it wouldn't have thought twice about attacking him and eating him. That made it hard to feel sorry for the bighorn yeti and served as good motivation to hurry back so the class could continue its journey under his protection.

CHAPTER EIGHT

Their path ended in a box canyon with a massive frozen waterfall at the north end. Smaller falls blanketed the walls, anywhere from ten feet in height to over two hundred at the very end. The walls themselves were thick ice instead of stone, and they walked on a frozen lake where the wind had blown the snow up against the canyon walls.

Professor Lakton set her students loose to explore, to "make memories forever associated with the brisk coldness of the environment," in her words. Nym could admire the natural beauty, but he had more than enough memories of being cold to draw on already. He spent his time comfortably sheltered inside his thermal barrier while the students walked around, looking at the waterfalls and shivering.

"I am freezing," came a familiar voice behind him. "Maybe a hug would warm me up."

A pair of arms latched on to Nym before he could react, only to pull back in confusion. "What the . . . ? You're just as cold as I am," Risa pouted. "How are you not affected by it?"

"Different spell," Nym said, making a point to step back from her. "I'm blocking all heat transfer both ways instead of warming myself up against the cold."

She sighed and hugged her arms close to her chest. Nym tried not to notice what that did to said chest, even through her coat. "Look, I'm just going to give it to you straight here. I know that you're way out of my league, and it'll be a brief thing before you get back to your life of magical glory and money. I'm not trying to get anything out of it other than some company. I'm honestly not sure if you're interested or not though. If you're not, just tell me, okay?"

"Magical glory and money?" Nym echoed. "What are you talking about?"

"I don't know. You just . . . You know, you're a master mage at sixteen? I figure your family's got to be loaded, and you know . . . Just. Never mind. I don't know what I'm trying to say. Hey, don't laugh at me!"

Nym started chuckling about halfway through. "My family's got to be loaded," he repeated. "God. I don't even have a family. I have an adoptive sister who rescued me and lives in a two-room shack on the coast. I didn't go to the Academy because I was way too poor. I think you have the wrong idea about me."

"Well sorry! You don't need to make fun of me though."

"No, I'm not trying to make fun of you. It's just, you don't know me at all. And

I don't know you. How about instead of . . . whatever this is . . . we have an actual conversation?"

"Yeah. Huh. That's not usually how this goes for me," Risa said. "I don't really know what to say?"

"How about something about yourself? How long have you been a student?"

"I'm in my third year," she said. "Were you serious when you said you didn't go to the Academy at all? I mean, you must be because I think otherwise people would be talking about you still, even if you graduated before I started."

Nym wanted to give his full attention to the conversation, but he was distracted by all the sensory information coming in from two air golems and his own scrying spell. Specifically, he was distracted by a movement in the snow, but it was just some sort of animal. Risa must have noticed his hesitation, but before she could say anything, he told her, "Sorry. I thought I saw something out there with a scrying spell. No, I never went to the Academy. I came to Abilanth to join, but the price was too steep.

"I made it to the third layer through a lot of self-study and a bit of advice from some other mages. I never took any classes and only recently got access to a full library for an extended length of time. That's actually why I'm out here now, doing the headmaster a favor so I can keep poking through his books."

There was that movement again. The snow was obscuring whatever it was. Something was burrowing, but it was far too small to be a yeti. Just because it wasn't eight feet tall didn't mean it couldn't be a threat though, so he ordered one of the golems to divert over to give him a better view. While he was piloting it to the spot, he realized he'd missed what Risa had just said.

"Could you repeat that?" Nym asked. "I'm sorry again. It's probably nothing dangerous, but something is moving around there, and I'm having a hard time keeping it in sight."

"It's fine. I said it's pretty amazing that you got this far on your own. But you've got some work to do, and I should probably get back to my assignment. Lakton's been just glaring at me for the last few minutes anyway."

"Yeah . . ."

Risa stood up to walk away, but before she took a step, Nym grabbed her hand. "Maybe we could talk some more later, after we get back?"

"I'd like that," she said. Then she winked and added, "Maybe in your room though."

"One step at a time," he told her. He really hadn't worked out how he felt about all of that. The whole idea of being intimate was kind of scary in a couple different ways. Even if he ignored the actual age difference between them, he wasn't sure if it was something he was interested in, especially since he doubted he'd ever see Risa again after tomorrow.

Nym shook his head and went back to scrying for danger. It was easier than trying to decide what to do about his personal life.

* * *

Decisions couldn't be put off forever. Even avoiding Risa was a decision in and of itself, considering how little time there was left on the job. He found her and Phan in the dining hall, sitting with another two of their classmates. After getting himself a meal, he sat down across from them.

"How's it going?" he asked.

"Oh, you know, enjoying the high-quality frozen food up here," Phan said. "Nym, these are my friends Trebon and Narshim. And I believe you are . . . already acquainted with my sister."

"Not as acquainted as I'd like him to be," she muttered, purposely pitching her voice so that everyone at the table heard her.

Phan rolled his eyes, and Trebon laughed, but Narshim looked distinctly annoyed. Nym did not miss the dirty look he got from the boy, and it didn't take much to connect the dots on that one. That kind of drama wasn't something he was interested in, but he reminded himself again that they had one place left to visit tomorrow, and then he was leaving anyway.

"Hello, Trebon and Narshim," he said. "How are you guys liking the field trip?"

"Colder than my old man's heart," Trebon said. "And he's a ruthless bastard through and through."

"Not like you'd know," Narshim added. "With all the fancy magic."

Nym turned in his seat to face the student mage fully. "Is there a problem here?" he asked softly.

Narshim didn't answer. His eyes flicked around the table, looking for support. Trebon made a show out of scooting his chair a few inches away, Phan just shook his head slightly, and Risa gave him an exasperated look. Seeing no one willing to side with him, Narshim hunched his shoulders and stared down at his plate. "No problem," he mumbled.

"Perhaps I should find somewhere else to sit," Nym said. "I really shouldn't be spending my time socializing anyway. I still have a lot of work to do tonight."

"Again?" Risa asked, a sigh in her voice.

"I'll just be checking the path to tomorrow's destination for dangers, things like that snow yeti that was lurking near today's route."

"You can scry all that from your room?" Phan asked, surprised.

"Oh, no. God no. I'll be out flying it, then teleporting back if it's too late to make the return trip."

"That's . . . That's a three-hour-long trip," Trebon said.

"Probably a bit more if I'm taking my time to check everything over," Nym agreed.

"Well, I think you're crazy, but I do appreciate your dedication to our safety."

"That's what they pay me for."

"How much does this job pay?" Phan asked curiously.

"No idea. Archmage Veran just asked me to do it, and I said yes. I'll probably still owe him money considering how much of his food I've eaten." Nym leaned forward, a glint in his eyes. "Just between you and me though, I'm not planning on paying him back."

The table dissolved into laughter, even Narshim. "That's ballsy," he said. "Stealing from the headmaster like that."

"Well it's not like he can expel me."

"No, just melt you into a little puddle of goo."

"Probably," Nym agreed. "But I like to think he's fond of me."

"I can see why," Risa said, batting her eyelashes.

Next to her, Phan groaned. "You're coming on a bit strong, don't you think?"

"Please. Boys are dumb. None of you would recognize anything subtle."

"Your interest is officially recognized," Nym said. "Would you like to go for a moonlit flight with me?"

"Are you asking me on a date?" she practically purred.

"I suppose I am, but if you're not interested . . ."

"Oh no. I am! But . . . um, I'm not very good at flying. Fire is actually more my thing."

"I think I can handle the flying for both of us," he said.

"Well then I suppose I'll bring the heat, if you take my mean— Eeep!"

Phan shoved her out of her chair midflirt, causing her to flop onto the floor, or rather onto a thin air cushion Nym tossed out to break her fall. "Jerk!" she said, kicking the leg of his chair and toppling it over. Nym caught him too.

The rest of the meal was filled with pleasant conversation, though Nym ended up setting up a scrying anchor to watch around him, specifically to keep an eye on Narshim. The boy was obviously not happy about recent developments and became sullen and withdrawn. He sat there, picking at his food and shooting Nym dirty looks when he thought no one was watching.

A few other students came over and introduced themselves. Some just wanted to say hi, others asked for tips on spells, and a few wanted to thank him for the avalanche rescue. Nym made polite chitchat with them, though by the end he was starting to get annoyed. The frequency of visitors was making it difficult to finish his meal before it got cold. Well, colder.

The dining hall emptied slowly, and eventually his table excused themselves. "I have a bit of work to do," Risa said. "Come find me in an hour or so?"

"Of course," Nym replied.

He went back to his own suite and cleaned himself up while scrying outside the Academy facility. There wasn't enough time to start any new projects, but that didn't mean he couldn't sweep the area again. As expected, he found nothing, but he left a golem on sentry duty right outside the door.

A second golem hovered in the hall outside the dorms, stationed there specifically to let him know when Risa was ready. Nym kept himself distracted with work, if only to keep his nerves under control. It was just astounding to him that he couldn't keep himself calm now but had no problem flying into life-and-death combat with a legion of undead.

Eventually, it was time.

Nym traveled the facility halls quickly and found Risa a few minutes after she'd left the dorms with a coat thrown over one arm. "Ready to go?" he asked.

"Very much so." She sounded a lot less confident herself.

"A bit nervous?" he asked. At her nod, he added, "Me too."

"I don't go on many dates," she admitted.

That was surprising to hear. She was very pretty, very outgoing, and just judging by the way she interacted with her classmates over dinner, she was well-liked. He wasn't sure how good she was at magic, but he was looking forward to finding out.

"Shall we?"

"Let's."

CHAPTER NINE

Nym sat a thousand feet up in the sky, surrounded by a shell of arcana that held both him and Risa aloft without so much as a stray breeze to ruffle their hair. In the soft light of the stars and moon, he could see the valley stretched out for miles below. Risa sat next to him, a soft smile on her lips as she shared the view.

"It's incredible," she said. "How much arcana would it take to duplicate what nature made here? Would it even be possible?"

"Not for a human, I don't think."

"It helps keep it all in perspective. That's something I think all mages struggle with. We get so used to having power over everything around us that we forget sometimes that we're just people too."

"I suppose so," Nym said. He didn't feel like he had power over everything, though he could see her point. When Niramyn started influencing his thoughts and actions, he did start to judge everyone by how much they could be worth to him, how best to exploit them, how much power he could exert on them.

Nym was afraid to let that side of him out again, afraid of what he might do that he couldn't take back before he regained control. It was another good motivator to get stronger on his own. If he wasn't forced into desperate situations, Niramyn wouldn't have to come out to play.

"How did you get to where you are, if you don't mind me asking?" Risa asked.

Nym blew out a long sigh and laughed slightly. "Lots of trial and error, lots of mistakes and lots of recoveries, and probably more luck than any single person deserves to have."

"That's not really an answer."

"I woke up on a beach with no memories, about to be carried out with the tide into shark-infested waters. A woman saved me, adopted me as her little brother. Then some guy tried to murder me, but I had magic, and he didn't. I was just starting out, could barely cast three spells, but I survived. I had to kill him to accomplish that. If that happened today, he wouldn't even be a threat to me. At the time though . . ."

"God. That's awful. How old were you?"

Nym shrugged. "Ten maybe? I'm not really sure how old I am, and I'm cursed anyway. My body's aging faster than normal."

Risa scooted back and looked him over. "You look like you're my age. How old do you think you are?"

"I woke up on that beach last summer. Back then, everyone agreed I looked like I was ten."

"You're just a little kid?" She looked confused. "But, your magic . . . How? You're already probably the youngest master mage ever."

"It's one of the things Archmage Veran is working on breaking. At the rate things are going, I figure I've got maybe twenty years before I die of old age."

"That's messed up, but I'm sure an archmage can fix it."

Nym leaned back to look straight up at the sky. "Yeah, I hope we can figure something out. No luck so far, but we've only been working on it for a few weeks. There was too much other stuff going on before."

"It feels kind of weird being on a date with an eleven-year-old."

"Am I eleven? Physically, mentally, I'm older. Trust me, all the normal changes happened, and over the span of maybe two months. It was . . . uncomfortable."

That wasn't even counting however many years he'd lived prior to being regressed to the form of a child and locking his memories and personality away to protect him from other ascendants. Time and age were kind of nebulous concepts to him at this point.

"How about you?" Nym asked, wanting to change the subject. "How has your journey on the path of magic treated you?"

"It's . . . It's been tough. How much do you know about the Academy?"

"Not much, just that I was too poor to attend."

"Truthfully, I'm in the same position. It's worse though because my brother and I both displayed enough talent to go. My family are merchants, but not that rich. They took out a lot of loans to pay our tuition, so the pressure to succeed is high. They need us to both become strong mages and come back to help the business. Except they were based out of Ebalsan, and everyone knows what happened there."

Nym winced. "Yeah . . . Ebalsan was bad. That's where I was when everything went to hell."

"Did . . . Did you lose anyone?"

"No, but it was a close thing. I guess I'm lucky that my entire social circle is all mages. We all managed to escape."

"That is lucky. Both my parents got out, and my oldest brother was away at the time, but you know the whole town was flattened. The business is ruined. There's no way my family can pay tuition going forward. It's going to be a miracle if no one ends up in debtor's jail."

She shook her head and said, "But that's not what you asked about. The magic itself I really like. I'm really good at fire magic too. I'm only taking this class because Phan won't shut up about rounding out my skill set. I'm kind of glad I did though, just for this field trip. It's freezing up here, but there's a lot of beautiful stuff to see."

"There is," Nym agreed. "Do you want to look around?"

"Did you have somewhere in mind?"

"Not really. I figure we're already seeing the best spots as part of the class, but this way it won't be work, and you can just enjoy them."

"Plus getting to see them in the moonlight and with fine company," she said. "Take me to the top of the glacier, Nym."

They flew together, still safely wrapped in a shell of air and pleasantly warm. They went at a sedentary pace and enjoyed the landscape rolling by beneath them, but it was still only the work of ten minutes to reach their destination. While they traveled, Nym scried ahead to make sure there was nothing nearby and switched to his special short-range scrying to peek under the snow and ice once they were close.

Nym sculpted seats for them out of ice and layered them with thermal barriers to prevent the cold from seeping into their butts. They sat next to each other, staring out over the valley and not saying anything for a little while. Risa stretched out a hand to hold his.

"This is nice," she said eventually. "Not what I was expecting, but I like it. These chairs could be a little closer together though, or maybe one big chair."

Nym's chair slid to the left and the arm rest dissolved. "Better?"

"Much."

"What do you think you'll do once you're out of school?" he asked.

"Try to get my license, I suppose. I'm three years in; that should be enough to fake it, right? There's no rule that says you have to graduate to get a license. Then . . . I don't know. With everything that's happened, there's no family business to help anymore. Probably go military. They say there's always room for another fire mage in the military."

"Better brush up on your flying then," he told her. "They like their mages highly mobile."

"Yeah, but they have training camps for that stuff. I'm going to focus on things I can only learn at the Academy for now."

Nym nodded. "That's a good plan."

"What about you? What are you going to do in the future?"

"Try to get my missing memories back. I'm close. I know I am. Break this aging curse before it kills me. Spend time with my friends and my big sister. Spend time with you, maybe. Travel whenever and wherever I want. See whatever I want to see."

"Already planning a second date, huh? You think it's going that well?"

"I think it's going pretty good," he said.

"Yeah, I guess it is," she replied. Then she leaned over and kissed him. It was a good kiss. That was really all his brain could come up with at that particular moment to describe the kiss. It was . . . good.

"Mmm. Yes, I'd say a second date is definitely on the table," she told him.

Nym felt his mouth curl up into a silly little smile, one he couldn't seem to stop even if he wanted to. He put an arm around Risa and pulled her closer. "How will I find you once you've left the Academy?" he asked.

"That won't be for a few months. I hope you're not planning on waiting that long."

"No, of course not."

"Then you can always send a letter to me until then. I'll send one to you too. Where are you staying?"

"With Archmage Veran right now, though maybe not for much longer."

"You're so formal. He's not even here, but you always use his title." She laughed a little, a quiet thing that he found far more charming than was reasonable. "I can't even imagine sending a letter to the headmaster himself addressed to the boy I like."

"He's a pretty nice guy once you get to know him," Nym told her.

"It's still weird. But I think I can get over that if it means I get to see you again."

"I can probably get a postal box set up somewhere. I'm not quite sure how. Nobody's ever needed to send me a letter before."

"Then we'll keep in touch, go on a few more dates. I'd like that."

"Yeah," Nym said, "me too."

The conversation turned to lighter things then, funny stories about things Risa had seen happen in various classes, mishaps that had blown up in Nym's face when he was working on new spells, trading tips and discussing which professions paid the best. Nym told her about his friends down south working in earth-magic construction. She talked about her parents' business exporting lumber and rare alchemical herbs.

The product was still there, but they'd lost so much when the warehouses had been destroyed, lost so much manpower when the whole region collapsed, that they were never going to financially recover. "That's why I'll be joining the military, I think. Phan is going to try to work with them directly, but I'm just going to send home shields and crests as fast as I can get them," she said.

Nym made a mental note to speak with Cern about Risa's family, to see if he knew them or if he thought there might be a beneficial connection to be made. He didn't mention it to Risa only because he didn't want to get her hopes up. Cern might have already made other arrangements, or there might not be a need for that kind of business. If he could help though, he wanted to. He couldn't help everybody, didn't want to try, but if he could help his friends, that was enough for him.

After an hour or so, Nym flew them back to the Academy facility. Once inside, he told her, "I had a good time tonight. I would like to do it again if you still want to."

"I very much do."

"When do you have time?"

"I'll be busy with classes for probably two weeks?" she asked as much as she said. "I'll have to look at my class schedule. Next time I have a full day off, maybe we can have a longer date. Tonight was fun, but we didn't have nearly enough time."

She leaned forward again and put her hands behind his head, then pulled him down into another kiss. Then she ran one hand down to his chest and whispered in his ear, "Unless this date isn't done?"

Nym's hormones lobbied for an enthusiastic yes to continue, but he did after all have work to do. He'd delayed it for the date, but if he slacked off, people could die. Glacial Valley was a wild place full of predators and natural hazards. He needed to be more familiar with tomorrow's route so he could make sure nothing went wrong.

Something must have shown on his face because her hand went to his chest, and she said, "Are you sure?"

"I'm sure," he said, though he was not at all sure. "I do have some work to take care of."

"Too bad, but I do admire that dedication."

They kissed one last time, and she went back to her dorms. Nym flew back out into the night sky to continue his work. He didn't put up the thermal barrier right away though. The cold helped distract him.

CHAPTER TEN

Nym hadn't had to use the stimulant spell he'd learned back in Ebalsan in a long time, but that morning it was necessary. By the time he'd gotten to bed, there had barely been an hour left before the sun came up. Fortunately for him, his suite had no windows. Unfortunately, the field trip started early. He got maybe three full hours of sleep, and that was with skipping breakfast, so magic was very, very necessary.

The class started out with Nym watching over them as he flew overhead. It turned out that all Professor Lakton's estimates on travel time had been short, and their final destination was likely going to be four or five hours of walking, by Nym's guess. If they stopped for multiple breaks and lunch, it would be even more.

Nym had taken care of a few problem spots last night, namely a dangerous switchback in the trail that was only a foot wide and had one side open to the air. He'd solved that problem with a bit of terrakinesis to widen it enough to anchor some ice to it, then hydrokinesis to more than triple the trail's thickness and put it at a slope that would slide anyone who lost their footing into the wall, not over the edge.

There'd also been a burrow of some sort of rabbit creatures that were each the size of a large dog. He wasn't sure if they were carnivorous or not, but they weren't interested in hiding their presence, and all of them had arcana auras surrounding them. Nym was confident that he could find them easily again, but he also created a set of ice pillars flanking the entrance to their burrow to serve as a marker.

He'd made it to the Garden of Winter, or at least his air golem had, but it had been so late that he'd done nothing beyond checking to confirm that he'd found the ultimate destination of the field trip, and then teleporting back to the facility. After that it had been straight to bed, too exhausted to think about the night's events.

If he was being honest with himself, he was anxious to get started. It was his last day, and while the work hadn't been hard, it was stressful. If the garden was as beautiful as it had appeared at first glance though, Nym planned on coming back later to view it at his leisure. In the meantime, it would be interesting to see what the professor had to say about it.

Slowly, in packs of two or three, the students started moving. Professor Lakton paid particular attention to the ones who'd been the slowest over the last two days, exhorting them to get moving far more vocally than the ones who'd shown themselves able to keep a strong pace without oversight. Risa was included in that group, of course.

Nym wasn't sure how he felt about the girl. The date had been nice, and he did want to get to know her better, but at the same time, her life was so much different than his. They appeared to be about the same age, but it was just an appearance, and in three or four years he would look more like her father than a classmate unless they found the solution to the aging curse.

He could accept it as a short fling, enjoy it while it lasted, and move on, but that didn't feel right to him. The relationships he valued most strongly were the ones he'd grown with Ciana, Analia, and the Earth Shapers. The rest were just . . . casual friends, people he saw occasionally and would help if they asked, but he didn't spend a lot of time wondering what they were up to or worrying about their safety.

Risa fell more into that second category, and it felt weird to mix physical intimacy with social distance. The obvious solution was to get to know her better, but that led back to the limited amount of time they had before he out-aged her, and at that point his mind had completed another lap around the circle.

Nym sighed and went to work. At least that wasn't complicated. He built a few air golems and sent them out along with a scrying anchor. They swept around in the patterns he'd perfected over the last two days while his mind split their inputs and parsed it all. If nothing else, it was an excellent exercise to get more comfortable with parallel processing.

Morning stretched on into afternoon, and Nym quickly realized his original thought that they'd be there in five hours had been hopelessly optimistic. It seemed two days of brutal cold-weather travel had exhausted the students. They struggled to keep arcana flowing smoothly, struggled to hold the spells that kept them from freezing in place, struggled to just keep walking.

About four hours and three breaks into the march, Nym flew down to talk to the professor. "At this rate, it's going to be an eight-hour trip," he said. "We're barely halfway there."

"Yes," she agreed with a frown. "The last day is always the hardest one, but this class seems unusually drained. How are you feeling?"

"Fine. Little tired. I was up late last night going over the route."

"I'm sure," she said dryly. "And your lack of sleep had nothing to do with any of my students."

"If it did, that would be between me and them," Nym told her. "It also would not be relevant to this conversation."

"It would be if the master mage who is supposed to be protecting us is too tired to do his job."

"Granted, if that were the case. But it's not."

"I should hope not."

Professor Lakton turned her gaze out on the line of students struggling up a snowy slope. "This class hasn't set any records for excellence, but I'm surprised they're this far behind schedule."

Now that Nym was down on the ground near the class and seeing them with his own eyes, he noticed something strange. Their arcana seemed to be slowly crumbling, little pieces of spell constructs broken off and siphoned away. Every single student was struggling to constantly flush new arcana into their spells, to keep them whole, except one.

"That boy there in the yellow coat, the one with the short brown hair," Nym said. "I don't recognize him. Who is he?"

"What . . . yellow coat? I don't see anyone wearing anything like that."

"No? That's interesting."

Nym narrowed his eyes and started really looking at the boy's arcana constructs. It was kind of difficult to tell from so far away, but he was reasonably sure whatever they were, there was nothing for walking on snow or keeping warm in there.

There was something else in there, something he couldn't quite place. Bits and pieces of it looked familiar, but the overall spell was unlike anything he'd seen before. He was assuming it was what was keeping the people around the boy from recognizing that he wasn't supposed to be there. Nym himself probably wouldn't have noticed if he hadn't been able to literally trace the arcana trail leading to him.

It was some sort of obfuscation or illusion spell, something to distract or redirect attention. Whatever was hiding behind those spells could be dangerous. Nym needed to isolate it from the nearby students before he moved to engage it, just in case it was too strong for him. He wasn't expecting it; so far nothing in Glacial Valley had been a challenge to beat, just to find. But he also wasn't willing to bet anyone else's life on it.

"Get everyone moving again," Nym said without looking back. "Let them spread out. I want to get as many students away from this thing as possible before I move on it. It's been lurking in the crowd for hours unnoticed."

"What's lurking?" Professor Lakton asked waspishly.

"I don't know. It's got some sort of attention-deflecting spell going on. Even now I'm having a hard time keeping track of it. Do you remember me pointing it out to you a minute ago?"

"I . . . don't. No." She scowled, but her expression was tinged with fear. "Whatever it is, it's very strong."

"That's what I'm afraid of. It'll probably stick with the largest clump of students it can, but if they're spread out, we'll at least reduce its pool of potential human shields and hostages."

"Right. God help us all. I'll get everyone moving. You go back to patrolling like everything is normal."

"Once the line is spread out, I'll start ferrying the ones in the back toward the front. We'll say we're just trying to get there faster. When I get to the group with Yellow Coat, I'll grab it and pull it back to the empty trail behind us."

Their plan decided, Nym flew back up into the sky to continue going through the motions of scouting ahead. While he was up there, he pondered the best way to handle the situation. A hostile teleport was an option, but he was concerned the thing hiding in the students' midst would resist it and lash out at everyone around it.

Nym didn't dismiss the plan outright. He could bring a lot of arcana down at once and probably overpower the resistance, but it wasn't the best use of his resources. Whatever plan he went with, he needed to pick apart those constructs hiding it, if only so he had a better idea of what he was dealing with.

Except that all the planning was moot. As the line started moving again, the students being harried by Professor Lakton in large groups, the boy in the yellow coat just stood there, staring up at Nym and grinning.

He felt his stomach drop when he realized what had happened. The creature had heard the whole plan, despite being well over a hundred feet away. Nym hadn't seen any sort of sensory-enhancement spells in its aura, so it was likely whatever it was had naturally keen senses. It was confident too, just letting all its potential hostages trudge away from it.

Talking seemed like the way to go then. Nym put up a hyperkinetic barrier, readied a lightning bolt, and dropped out of the sky to land in front of the boy, who just watched it all with an amused grin. He didn't make any moves or say anything; he just stood there, waiting.

"How long have you been following along?" Nym asked.

"Oh, just the last two hours or so," the boy said, proving that he could talk after all.

"What are you?"

"That is a fascinating question. I'll make you a deal. I'll tell you what I am if you tell me what you are."

"I'm a person, obviously."

The boy clicked his tongue. "This is going to be a very short conversation if you're just going to lie. You are not a person, not a human one at least. But you're not an ascendant either. I've never seen anything quite like you."

"It's . . . complicated. I'm something in the middle right now. Either way though, I *am* still a person. And you clearly are not."

"Fair enough." The boy laughed. "Let's let the rest of them get a bit farther away, shall we? Wouldn't want to scare the children."

"Why, what are they going to see?"

"You're too impatient, little half-scendant. Savor the anticipation."

Nym found he wasn't willing to play the game. "Drop the spells or I'll drop them for you."

"That would be a mistake. Mind your manners, lest you be reminded."

The boy's face wasn't so relaxed and easygoing now. In fact, the arcana aura around it was growing bigger and bigger. It couldn't all be the bits it had stolen from the class either; there was just too much. Nym wasn't sure, but he thought it might even be more than he could generate himself.

The air shimmered around the boy, and a face emerged, something with white-and-red fur and a vulpine grin. Then the illusion snapped back into place, leaving the boy in the yellow coat once more.

"Let's talk, shall we?" he said with a smile.

CHAPTER ELEVEN

I don't see where there's much to talk about," Nym said. "You're stealing arcana from the students I'm supposed to protect. You're a threat to them. At the rate you're draining them, they'll die out here."

"That is all true," the boy agreed. "I suppose you're not doing a very good job of protecting them."

Nym's fists tightened. The construct for a lightning bolt was halfway coalesced and could be triggered in an instant. The only thing preventing him from blasting the creature pretending to be a human was Nym's concern about dragging the students into it. The farther away they got, the better off they'd be.

"Would you like me to rectify that for you right now?" he asked icily.

"You are welcome to try, of course. But you'll fail, and I just want to talk anyway."

"Fine. What are we talking about?"

The boy looked around and saw that all the students were slowly disappearing down the trail. He nodded to himself, and the glow of arcana faded. "You know, the thing that always annoyed me the most about you ascendants is your eyes. I can deal with the smugness, even that insufferable arrogance the ones at the top have, but your damn eyes seeing every illusion, even if you can't see past it . . . It's infuriating."

"Is that why you stalk humans and eat their magic? Too hard to take a good bite out of an ascendant?"

The boy threw back his head and laughed. "Ha! You're no better than the rest of your kind, little half-scendant. I think you need a lesson in minding your betters."

The boy vanished, and in his place a white-and-red fox sat on the snow. His head came up to Nym's chest, and a thick, bushy tail flicked out behind him. Nym stared at him for a second, then laughed. "You're a mirror fox. Whew. For a moment there I thought you were something dangerous."

Arcana swelled up around them, completely engulfing Nym. Something otherworldly imposed itself over the physical space the fox occupied, something with deep crimson eyes and whirling, lashing shadows fanned out behind it. "I am to a mirror fox what you are to a human, child. And I do mean your true form, not this paltry disguise you've stuffed yourself into."

The words were sharp, frightening even, and the laughter died in Nym's throat. Whatever the arcana was that surrounded the fox, it was different than anything he'd ever seen. It was heavy and dark and filled with hidden dangers. Archmage

Veran's pinnacle spells, as awe-inspiring as they were, were nothing compared to the mere presence of that arcana.

As abruptly as it had appeared, the arcana was gone, and the fox was once again just a fox. "Steady there," he told Nym, the words clearly audible despite there being no way for a fox's mouth to form them. "I apologize. I lost my temper there."

Nym shook himself out of his stupor and regarded the fox warily. The way he saw it, there were only two possibilities. Either the fox really was more powerful than anything else he'd ever met, or he'd been tricked with an especially powerful illusion. Either way, it was bad news. Nym was suddenly a lot less eager to light the fox up with a lightning bolt, knowing that there was every chance it wouldn't do more than tickle.

"I . . . What do you want?" Nym asked. "You've established that there's probably nothing I can do to stop you if you decide to kill all of us, but you haven't killed anyone, so you must want something."

"Did you know that a lot of the bigger mystical creatures can live off of arcana alone? It's practically a biological necessity for us. We would wipe out whole ecosystems within weeks if we needed meat to survive."

"I . . . Yes. I knew that. Creatures at that level of size and strength are rare though and don't tend to live anywhere near human lands."

"You may have noticed we're not exactly in human lands right now."

"I suppose that's true," Nym allowed, "but you didn't answer my question. What do you want?"

"I'm just sampling some unusual flavors. Humans infuse their arcana with intent; it's quite tasty, and it's a nice variety from my usual diet of nothing but cold, cold, cold arcana."

"Are you . . . Are you comparing this class to a trip to the sweets store?" Nym asked.

The fox started laughing. "In a way, yes, I suppose I am. You don't need to worry, little half-scendant. I'm not going to kill anyone. I'm just nibbling, trying all the samples."

"You say that, but . . . These are students. They're still learning the basics, and they're not strong enough to survive this kind of climate."

"Ugh, yes. Fine. Humans are so squishy. What would you like me to do?" the fox asked.

"Stop stealing their arcana from them so we can get to where we're going?"

The fox seemed to think about that for a minute. "You would be better off turning back and going home. The Garden of Winter is not what it was. It was . . . corrupted. It's dangerous to go there now, which is a shame, as it really was quite beautiful."

"Corrupted how?" Nym asked.

"An interesting question," the fox said. "To be honest with you, I'm not quite sure. The garden isn't pure anymore. It languishes in heat that shouldn't exist, like the land itself is fevered. Also it smells awful, which is why I'm staying far, far away from it."

"That's just fantastic," Nym muttered to himself. He shook his head and added, "But still, that's not an answer."

"I see. I will propose a trade then. In exchange for leaving your flock alone, I want you to wear this emblem. It will allow me to see and hear through it. Since you'll be going to the Garden of Not Really Winter Anymore, I'll get to see what's going on without having to smell it. And I do admit that I really am quite curious."

A ring appeared between them, made of some black metal Nym didn't recognize. A fox-head symbol was set into it, with the eyes the same dark crimson he'd seen when the fox had revealed his true form. The band itself was a pair of tails twined around each other.

Nym took it and looked closely at the band. Inscribed inside it was a series of tiny runes, so fine that he couldn't even fully make them out. "Is that all it does?" he asked.

"All you need to know about," the fox said with a sly grin.

"No thanks then," Nym told him, letting it go. Rather than fall to the snow, it started floating in the air again. "I'm not putting this on my finger without understanding exactly what it does first."

The fox rolled his eyes, but there was a glint of approval there. "Cautious, I see. Good. Take a minute to examine the runes fully and you'll understand what it does."

Nym cast a perfect-sight spell on himself and gave the fox a suspicious glance, but he just sat unmoving on the snow and waited. He squinted at the ring and silently read the runes. The configuration wasn't something he was familiar with, but that didn't concern him. Writing a rune sequence on a large, flat object like a piece of paper or a wall of earth-forged bricks wasn't the same as sewing them into the hem of a dress or carving them on a piece of jewelry.

It was easy to find the sensory-connection runes the fox had admitted were there. They took up perhaps a third of the total sequence, right next to something that looked illusion based with a mild mental compulsion in it. If Nym had to guess, he thought the purpose was to hide the ring from casual observation and influence anyone who did notice it to forget about it.

That part was all well and good. It was the last half that he was concerned about. They did something to the wearer's mind, and they were tangentially linked to the sensory-connection runes. It was possible it allowed the fox to control whoever wore the ring, but that didn't seem right. The rune sequence wasn't nearly strong enough to control anybody. It could maybe nudge their emotions a bit, but full mind control wasn't a possibility.

"What is this section here for?" Nym asked, casting an illusion of the rune sequence into the air.

"Communication," the fox said without hesitation.

"Ah, of course." Now that he knew it, it made sense to Nym. "A two-way mental link tied to the sensory-connection runes to give it some distance. How long does it stretch?"

"A few miles, perhaps as many as ten if someone like you is powering it. It will draw arcana from your soul well when you use it, but the amount should be minuscule compared to what you're capable of."

"No arcana battery?" Nym asked.

"In the eyes, but they're quite empty. Feel free to recharge them for me."

Nym snorted. "So this ring will allow you to see and hear what I see and hear and to hold a conversation telepathically with me and hide itself from casual observation while discouraging more targeted scrutiny. And it has an arcana battery that of course is empty, so I'll have to charge it myself or give it a steady feed of arcana to keep it working."

"Yes, yes, it's a very impressive trinket, I know. Now will you put it on?"

Nym looked it over one more time to make sure he hadn't missed anything, then slid it onto his left middle finger. He poured raw second-layer arcana into it, and the runes came to life, giving him the feeling of someone watching over his shoulder.

[You see? It is harmless,] the fox's voice echoed in his mind.

It was uncomfortable but didn't seem immediately dangerous. Nym was more concerned about what he'd agreed to do with it. He'd just barely extricated himself from the last disaster he'd been involved in, and here he was heading toward another area that an extremely powerful mystical fox wasn't willing to directly investigate.

It was fine though. He'd talk to the professor, they'd send the students back, and he'd fulfill his obligations to the fox via some remote scrying. If he was being honest, he was a bit curious as well. That wouldn't have been enough on its own, but ultimately, he didn't think he was in a position to refuse the fox's deal. Sending in a few golems was a small price to pay in order to free the students from predation.

"Alright, I'm going to catch up to the group. Without your interference, we'll make the garden soon. If it's as bad as you've said it is, we'll likely send the students directly back, and I'll see about getting a good look at what's going on for you. You'll leave this group alone in exchange. Agreed?"

"Agreed," the fox said with a grin. "Take care of yourself, half-scendant. You're such a fascinating creature, and I can't wait to see how your story turns out."

The fox started laughing when it saw the sour look on Nym's face. He vanished midlaugh, though the sound echoed in the air for another second before fading away as well. Nym glanced down at the ring once, sent another surge of arcana into it, and started flying after the students.

He wasn't sure exactly how much to tell Professor Lakton. With any luck, he'd be able to convince her that the best option was to turn everyone back. She was a generally reasonable woman; hopefully she'd agree. Teleporting that many people would be exhausting, but it'd be less work than escorting them all the way back. If he could get them to agree to it though, it would make his work keeping up his end of the bargain a lot easier to fulfill.

CHAPTER TWELVE

Nym hadn't been idle while he was speaking with the mystical fox. One air golem had shadowed the class as they moved, and the other had scouted ahead. He knew exactly where everyone was, and now that they were outside the draining radius of the fox's magic, they were progressing much more quickly.

Professor Lakton wasn't at her normal position near the front. Instead, she was somewhere in the middle, close enough to the back of the line to respond immediately, and was repeatedly reminding everyone to stay close together. Some of the students at least seemed to be listening.

"One problem solved, but maybe another one up ahead," he said without preamble.

It was painfully obvious that the nearby students were trying to listen without appearing to be, but at this point Nym didn't much care if they knew. This didn't sound like something he'd be clearing out before they could reach it anyway, so he didn't see the point in being circumspect about it.

"I've got some scrying spells working to give me more information, but I was told the Garden of Winter has been corrupted somehow, or maybe infected with something. I'm not sure yet. It may not be safe to bring the class there."

"Corrupted . . . By what though?" the professor muttered. "This field trip has had far too much excitement. Normally chaperones have an easy few days; nothing much around here tends to bother a full class of mages, at least nothing difficult to handle."

"If you say so," Nym said absently. They were still a bit too far from their destination for his golems to report back. "If I go ahead, will you be okay back here on your own?"

"What happened to that monster you found?" Professor Lakton asked, glancing over her shoulder and looking down the trail. "I didn't even see it. Even after you pointed it out, it was hard to notice it until you got it away from everyone else."

"We . . . We made a deal to keep him from hurting anyone. I'm going to look into the corruption, and he won't eat any more spells. But he's strong. If he's not willing to go into the Garden of Winter personally, it's probably a bad idea to let the class in."

"If that's the case, it's a bad idea for you to go in too," she said in the same tone Nym had heard her use on some of the more disruptive students.

"If there's anyone here who can do it, it's me." He lowered his voice and turned away from the students. "That thing . . . He was like a mirror fox but so much stronger. I don't think I can take him in a straight fight. I don't think the archmage himself could do it. This was what he wanted, and I'm inclined to do it."

"That's ridiculous. There's no such thing as a mirror fox with that kind of power."

"How many mirror foxes have you met, professor? A few, I'd guess." At her nod, Nym continued, "Did you ever have any problems detecting them, especially after someone else pointed it out?"

"I . . ." Professor Lakton trailed off. "I'll keep an eye on everyone here. You go ahead and get a look, then come straight back. We'll decide what to do from there. It's going to be rough on everyone to walk back without ever getting a chance to have a real rest."

"I'll start teleporting people if necessary," Nym said.

"The whole class? That would be quite a feat."

"If necessary," Nym repeated.

Nym shot straight back up and flew as fast as he could without switching to overland flight. For a journey of only ten or so miles, that would be complete overkill, and it wasn't worth the mental strain of an overland-flight spell when it would only take a few minutes to get there by normal means.

He hadn't gotten a good look at the Garden of Winter last night. It was tucked away in its own little basin, split off from the rest of the valley and accessible only by flying or by a single trail that led into a cave system he hadn't spent much time looking at. Perhaps if he'd approached from the ground, he might have noticed something strange, or even if he'd flown over in person.

That was always the drawback of scrying and sensory-link spells. They didn't let him see the arcana like he would in person. Someday he'd find a spell that did, but for now he had to work around the handicap. That meant getting a closer look than he was necessarily comfortable with, which wasn't to say the golem wasn't going in first, just that he thought it was a long shot the fox would be satisfied with what he learned through just that.

Nym approached the garden and looked down at it. At first glance, it looked much the same in the afternoon sun as it had at night. Stone arches were scattered across the garden, lined up in such a way as to give the impression of a trail where there was none. Flowering vines climbed up and down pillars of stone and filled natural trellises, and thorn-studded rosebushes caught in eternal bloom colored the scenery. Ponds were joined together by thin rippling streams of water that passed over stones.

All of that had been painted over with a coating of frost that muted the colors and made the entire garden glimmer in the light. The water itself had a thin coating of ice, so fragile it might break if the smallest mouse tried to cross. Even from a distance, Nym could see the water running beneath the ice. It was as if some powerful mage had set off a flash freeze in a brilliant summer garden.

There were creatures there too but not the ones he would have found in the warmer southern climates. Little flickers of multicolored light flitted from one frozen flower to another, pixies taking the place of bees. Small insects with carapaces made of ice instead of chitin crawled through the leaves and roots of the bushes.

And settled over all of it, invisible to his golems or his scrying spells, was a cobweb of arcana, threaded through every living thing in the garden until the whole thing was a roiling fogbank of arcana, thrumming with power from something hidden deeper within. It pulsed through the arcana like something alive, something all-consuming.

Nym understood the fox's description of that arcana, calling it a corruption, a fever. That was exactly what it was, an invader, something that lacked the clear, sharp purity of winter and didn't belong. It was a blurry, muddled thing, a coating of filth over something clean.

What he didn't know was what it did.

He had probably the better part of two hours to investigate before the class arrived, but he didn't want to leave them alone for that long. Even if the fox kept his word, there were other dangers that might fall on the exhausted students before they found their way to the garden.

"Do you see what I see?" Nym said to the ring. He'd never been on the sending side of a sensory link before. If there was anyone who could construct one that would show arcana the way he saw it, it was that fox who was beyond human magics.

[I do, little half-scendant. Your eyes . . . They do fascinate so. I think I might like them for myself.]

"I'm not inclined to give them to you," Nym said dryly.

[You'd be surprised what I could offer to tempt you. You have an impressive number of curses sealing away parts of your mind, keeping secrets from you. Would you like them removed? I could do that.]

"The only one I care about is the aging curse. If you can do that one, we can discuss a trade that doesn't involve my eyeballs."

[Of course I can. Don't insult me.]

Nym blinked. He hadn't expected that. "You . . . can? Huh. I'll need to think about it. For now, let's talk about what's going on here."

[Oh really. That's something important to you then. That might be more interesting than what's happening in the Garden of Winter. But very well, a discussion for another day. The way your kind can see arcana has always fascinated me. I'll admit that my own attempts to replicate it are a pale thing by comparison. It's more of a scent-based detection than sight, and not nearly as precise.]

"What does it mean though?" Nym asked. "If you ignore the strands of arcana smeared over top of everything, which no one else could even see, it all looks normal to me. I mean, as normal as a place like this would ever look."

Seen through the scrying anchor or by one of his air golems, the Garden of Winter was undeniably beautiful. He had no basis of comparison, but he didn't think anyone else would find anything wrong with the sight of the place. What would happen when they walked into that miasma of red arcana was another matter.

Truth be told, Nym was hesitant to fly over it. It hung over the ground, stretching up maybe thirty or forty feet at the most, but it moved around like a living thing. If it sensed him and lunged up to attack, his only defense would be his speed and sending out strands of his own raw arcana to block it. He was justifiably hesitant about touching the miasma with raw arcana, even if he severed it from his soul well first.

[Something has infected this place with its musk,] the fox said. *[It probably still lingers nearby, wallowing in its own stink as it slowly poisons the land around it. I would like to know what that thing is. Find it for me and I will consider our bargain concluded.]*

"It's a risk, going in there. I don't know what will happen to me if the miasma infects me too."

[Why do you think I avoided going in myself?] the fox asked.

"I'm just saying that's a bit outside what we agreed on. I was supposed to wear the ring and take a look for you. I did that."

[Hardly! You're barely at the edge. Go look at the cause of this, and then we will be settled.]

"You get why I'm not keen to go in there, right? You didn't want to go in there either, and you're . . . strong."

[With a strong nose. It stinks. It's not dangerous. Well, not to me. I don't want to smell the place. I'm not afraid of getting ensnared in it. Even your students probably wouldn't be affected long-term from a short visit, and they're just about as weak as humans can get.]

Nym had to consider the possibility that the fox was lying to him. He wanted something, and Nym doubted he'd care much if someone else got hurt, as long as he got what he wanted. Of course, being the someone else who got hurt wasn't something Nym was fine with. That was why he sent new air golems flying over the garden and watched the miasma's reaction carefully.

As long as they stayed over a certain height, the miasma ignored them. It was only when they dipped lower that it started to rise, sending thin tendrils into the air that lashed around, trying to make contact. Nym manually controlled the golem, keeping it moving around the tendrils. He wasn't sure what would happen if they made contact, and he didn't think he wanted to know.

It was a good thing the one that had scouted the garden for him last night had flown high and relied on perfect vision to look at the place for him. He'd unintentionally dodged a potential disaster through sheer happenstance. Unfortunately, he had a sinking feeling he wasn't going to be so lucky today. The best he could do was circle the outer edge of the garden and hope to spot something.

Maybe that would be enough. A nice, easy, risk-free job would be a welcome change of pace. Somehow, Nym doubted it would work out that way.

CHAPTER THIRTEEN

As it turned out, for once, it actually wasn't that hard and didn't require Nym to put himself in any sort of danger to identify the source of the feverish corruption that had infected the Garden of Winter. He circled around the outside edge to examine the arcana from a few other angles, and it didn't take long for a pattern to start to form, one that pointed not to the middle of the garden, but toward the back.

That was the hardest part because what he was looking for was under an overhang that forced him to actually fly over the garden to get a good angle of sight on it. Even then though, he stayed well outside the range of the grasping tendrils of miasma.

"Do you see it?" he asked.

[Indeed. How strange.]

A gargantuan flower, easily big enough for him to sit on the petals, was growing out of the rocky soil. It wasn't part of a bush or vine or any other plant life. Instead, it was a single flower growing on a stem that shot straight up out of the ground. Nym wasn't an expert gardener, but it seemed . . . odd. More importantly, all the red miasma that coated the Garden of Winter was coming from it.

Nym could see pulses of arcana shoot up through the stem, circulate into the petals, and then rise into the air like gossamer strands carried away on the breeze. Except they weren't carried away. More and more just kept coming out of the flower until the strand touched something, then it solidified into a new connection.

Almost the entire garden was coated, even places that would normally be sheltered from the flower's magic had been tangled up by pixies who'd been snared and carried strands of it around. It wasn't until Nym had to fly over to get the angle on the flower that he realized those miasmic tendrils were actually clouds of pixies attracted to the arcana constructs that made up his magic.

He spared a brief moment to wonder how they detected arcana. It was obvious now that there were plenty of species that could sense arcana in one form or another, though from what the fox had told him, being able to see active spell constructs seemed to be something unique to ascendants. When he considered it in a more limited capacity, even regular humans had magic to enable them to see the presence of arcana.

It was something to consider later though. He was working now. "Are you satisfied now?" he asked the ring.

[Not quite. This plant appears to merely be a conduit to the source of the corruption. You see how the magic rises from below the ground? What is down there?]

"I could scry below, but you won't get the arcana sight with it."

[Why not? What kind of ascendant are you?]

"Uh . . . The kind who can't see arcana through scrying spells?"

[Show me your spell,] the fox said.

Annoyed, Nym swiftly conjured up a scry anchor in front of him. "You see? It doesn't see arcana like I do."

[Of course it doesn't. You don't have a resonance loop integrated into the construct. How would the spell benefit from your own senses if the feedback is only one way?]

"I . . . What?"

A huge part of the construct was designed to send back whatever visual stimulus it received. If he understood what the fox was telling him correctly though, he needed the feedback to go . . . both ways? "How would that help? I already do that when I project sensory-enhancing spells through the golems."

[No, you don't. You feed that spell into them. That's not the same as feeding your own senses to them. You need to think of it as if you were the scry spell and your anchor point is you. Feed your senses to it so that it can see what you see. Then loop its senses back to yourself so you see what it sees with your eyes.]

That made sense, kind of. Nym dismissed the scry anchor and started trying to build a new one, this time with a second sensory-connection bridge that flowed the opposite direction. That proved to be too complex for it, and the whole thing collapsed. He wasn't sure if that meant he wasn't building it correctly or just that he needed to be faster, but he was inclined to think it just wasn't possible the way the spell was structured.

[No, not like that,] the fox scolded him. *[Do you build two bridges for your wagon to cross a river? Integrate both directions into one structure.]*

Nym kept trying, eventually forgoing everything except the linking structure of the spell so that he could iterate it faster. With the fox looking over his shoulder and offering quips of varying degrees of helpfulness, he eventually built something that he thought would do what he wanted.

Integrating it into the rest of the spell was more of a challenge. It was heavier, for one thing, and a bit wider. It forced him to switch around some steps and required both more stabilization portions and a faster cast to get everything in place before it fell apart. He suspected both issues could be solved by using a different intent filter to make the arcana more rigid, but that would cut down on the range of the spell if he did that.

"Alright, this is it," he said. If it worked, he'd be able to see arcana through his scrying anchor. It would be another spell unique to him, since it relied on his own biological eyes to provide the arcana-sensing portion, so there would be no sharing it with anyone else to grant them the ability to see arcana, but it would still be a step forward.

He wove the spell together as quickly as he could and felt it snap into place, and the scrying anchor popped into existence in front of him. It looked down, and Nym grinned to see all the tendrils of arcana wound through the garden below.

"Ha, how about that. I've been trying to figure that out for months."

[Ugh. Congratulations. Very good. Your mastery of extremely basic magical theory knows no bounds. It wasn't tedious at all teaching you to do this.]

Nym laughed. "Yeah, yeah. Go be grumpy somewhere else. Now, let's see what's hiding under that flower."

He sent the scry anchor down, deftly weaving it through the tangled miasma of arcana to the rocky soil. Through it, he saw that the flower itself was connected to a massive underground root system, or maybe *root* wasn't the right word. It looked almost like a branch buried in the dirt so that only the flower part breached the surface.

Nym was about to follow it deeper when he realized something was happening on the surface. He blinked twice, reorienting himself to sight through his own eyes, and looked closer at the motion that had caught his attention. The miasma below was roiling, slowly rising with new tendrils lashing out wildly. Some of them were following the connection between Nym and his scry anchor and arching up to where he hovered in the air.

"Would it be a problem if I ended up killing a bunch of these pixies?" he asked.

[I'm sure someone would care. Not me, but someone.]

"Good enough for me," he said and unleashed a lightning bolt into the miasma.

The pixies didn't take that well. They lit up red both in his regular sight and as they started to glow with arcana. They swarmed up from the ground, trailing red miasma behind them, and there were far too many for him to target individually, thousands maybe, so he pulled out another old trick he hadn't used in a while.

Nym activated his aura spell in conjunction with lightning bolt to create an electrically charged area around him. Anything that entered got fried with lightning immediately, and that included every single pixie that got within five feet of him. They fell by the dozens every second, a little localized shower of glittering corpses that rained down on the frost-coated plants below.

Meanwhile, his scry anchor continued its journey underground, tracing the root system deeper until he reached the end of his range. That left Nym with little choice but to fly over the garden to follow it, and then eventually land once he was outside the garden's reach.

"It's going farther north," he reported. "But I think the real answer is underground."

[Yes, obviously. Do you not see the beetles? Look, they're crawling all over the stem.]

"Yeah, so? They're just bugs."

[Those are scarabs, my naive young half-scendant. Specifically, they're a variety known as blood-burrower scarabs. They're the source of the corruption that's infested the Garden of Winter. Give them another week or two to work and you'll start to see the land physically change. The plants will die, and it'll become a desert.]

"That does sound like a problem for you guys. I'm guessing they're not going to stop at the edge of the garden, are they?"

[No. Infestations like this do not halt on their own. They spread and spread until someone takes action.] The fox's voice turned shrewd. *[You could take action.]*

"I could," Nym agreed, "But that's not our deal, so I won't."

The fox's laughter rang in his head. *[That is fair. Perhaps we might make a new deal though. You expressed interest in breaking the aging curse. You might assist me in clearing out this infestation in exchange for my assistance.]*

Nym thought about it for a second and shook his head. "I've already got a deal with an archmage to break that."

He left unsaid that he wasn't fully confident that Archmage Veran could actually break it, but he would certainly talk to the old man before he agreed to the fox's terms. There was also the option of retrieving all his lost memories once he was able to draw in fifth-layer arcana. He wasn't so desperate yet that the fox had him backed into a corner.

The fox just kept laughing. Eventually it said, *[You've fulfilled our bargain. You are free to do as you wish, and I shall trouble you no more. The students you are protecting are safe from me. Keep the ring. When you change your mind and want to deal, come back to this glacier and use it to contact me.]*

Nym considered the piece of jewelry on his finger with its fox-head emblem. It almost seemed to wink at him, and he shuddered before slipping it off and pocketing it. "Not likely," he muttered, somehow afraid he might be cursing himself just by saying it out loud. But no, he wasn't that superstitious.

It was time to get back to his chaperoning job. Nym flew out of range of the garden and broke the construct holding his lightning aura in place, then followed the trail back south until he found the class huddled more or less into one tight group and moving slowly along.

"How's it going on your end?" he asked as he touched down next to Professor Lakton.

"Slowly, as I'm sure you can see," she said with a sigh. "I'm keeping them all close together, which has been a job in and of itself. Did you get everything taken care of?"

"Kind of, but I think we're going to have to cancel the trip. The garden is infested with a bunch of blood-burrower scarabs."

The professor's face paled, something Nym found particularly impressive given how white it already was. "God protect us. There hasn't been an outbreak in Devros in thirty years. They're usually not seen on this continent."

Nym conjured up an illusion of a few of them crawling along a stem that he'd seen. "They look like this. Does that help?"

"Those are scarabs, yes, though not necessarily blood burrowers. Are you sure of the type? They aren't usually found in cold climates either."

Nym just shrugged. "That's what our uninvited guest called them. It seems risky to walk into that."

"Hmm. Yes. If they are blood burrowers, the students will get sick just from being close by. We'd best take a break and then start back."

"I can start teleporting them back to the base," Nym said. "You go back with the first group to let them in, and I'll get the rest back as soon as I can. This many . . . Maybe half an hour to do them all?"

"I seriously doubt you can teleport twenty-three people in half an hour," Professor Lakton told him.

"Guess we'll find out, unless you want another four hours of walking through the cold and snow, at minimum."

She sighed and nodded. "Very well, let's get started. Class! We're going to have to cancel this trip. I will explain more once we're back on Academy grounds. Gather close please and prepare for teleportation."

CHAPTER FOURTEEN

The entire class was gathered in the lecture hall, which Nym had gone ahead and thrown stone-warming spells onto multiple walls to heat up. Everyone was sick of the cold, everyone was tired, and everyone was annoyed at having spent the whole day freezing and walking only to get nowhere at the end.

"Alright, before I release you all to go gather your possessions and head to the teleportation platform, I thought you'd all like to know what went wrong today. First, a powerful mirror fox infiltrated the class." Professor Lakton shot Nym a look to cut him off when he opened his mouth to speak.

"A mirror fox," she repeated, this time with emphasis, "that was hiding itself and stealing arcana away from you. It was successfully identified, detained, and dealt with without a single person being injured."

Nym could practically hear the fox laughing in the back of his head. She made it sound like Nym had been the one in control, overpowering or outwitting the mystical animal. Nothing could have been further from the truth. The only thing stopping the fox from taking whatever he wanted was his own nature.

"If that were all, it would have been bad enough. We lost several hours of daylight, and you were all left exhausted. Worse, upon arriving at the destination site, it was discovered that it had been overrun with a swarm of blood-burrower scarabs. Now, I know this is not Monstrology, but can anyone tell me why we had to turn back?"

"People who come into contact with the scarabs get sick and die," one of the students said immediately. She hesitated and then added, "Painfully and messily."

"Correct. The infection is dormant at first, so the hosts don't realize right away and spread it to others for the few days they remain healthy. I'm sorry this wasn't discovered until we'd already started our day, but also glad that it was discovered prior to us actually reaching the site."

There was a lot of grumbling from the class, but no one voiced any objections. Up at the lecturer's podium, Professor Lakton looked on wearily. Perhaps seeing that no one was going to start an argument over it, she said, "That is all. We'll have a one-hour break to recover and gather our things, and then everyone is to report to the teleportation platform so we can return to the Academy. You are all dismissed."

They trickled out in a steady line until none were left except for Nym. He didn't need transportation back, and he only had his one pack besides, which he'd never really opened. That book he'd been planning on reading was still buried in the bottom. What he did need was an hour uninterrupted to just rest. Teleporting so many people took all of it out of him.

"Am I interrupting?" a voice asked just as he closed his eyes.

Nym suppressed a sigh but didn't open his eyes back up. "Just tired. What's up, Risa?"

He heard her sit down next to him, but then she didn't say anything. He cracked an eye open to look at her. "What's up?" he asked again.

"Just . . . I wanted to say goodbye, to see if you still want to keep seeing me."

"Of course I do," Nym told her. "I said we'd find time together, didn't I?"

"You did, but . . . You know."

"I don't?" Nym was confused now. Whatever she was trying to say, he was too tired to guess.

"Boys say they'll write. They say they'll find time. But then they don't. Unless they want . . . But then as soon as they get it, they disappear again. I don't want to think you'll be like that too. But you're so far ahead of me, and you've got so much going on, I wouldn't blame you if you forgot about that stupid girl who had a crush on you and you only knew for a few days."

Nym took a breath in and let it out. He took another, and let it out slowly. "Risa, I don't want to be insensitive here. I understand what you're saying. It's just . . . Right now, I am exhausted. I know it's been a long day for all of us, so how about instead of talking, you just scoot a little closer and we can both close our eyes for a few minutes?"

"That sounds good too," she said. Nym put an arm around her, and they enjoyed the warmth still coming off the walls. It was a nice moment, one that ended all too soon.

He helped charge the teleportation platform, of course. The students were all wiped out, and though she put on a strong front, Professor Lakton wasn't doing all that much better. It took them twice as long to get it going compared to when they'd arrived a few days earlier, and Nym pretended not to see the uneasy glances some of the students shot his way.

"Alright, we're all set. Everybody on. Let me do one final roll call. Wouldn't do for someone to get left behind here." The professor called out names off her roster one after another. "Perfect. And we're off."

The world pinched around him, and they were standing in a different room, very similar to the one they'd left. The real difference was that when they opened the door, they were back at the Academy. The students shuffled out, pointedly ignoring Professor Lakton's instructions in a coordinated mutinous effort. Nym didn't have it in him to blame them.

The professor gave it up with an exasperated sigh and waved them off. She tossed Nym a wry glance and shook her head. "Thank you for your help on this trip," she told him. "Really. This has been the worst Glacial Valley field trip I've ever done. Things would have turned out much, much worse without your intervention."

"Yeah, it was very . . . exciting," Nym said. "Do you need me to do anything else? If not, I need to go sleep for at least three days."

"No, go on. You've done more than enough."

"Thanks. See ya around, professor."

"Hmm. Well, we'll see."

Nym gathered up the arcana he needed from the Astral Sea, slowly, and wove his teleport spell together. Never in his life had he hated the archmage's wards more than he did that second, but he was familiar enough with them that it wasn't a real problem, just an annoyance. The spell went off, and he found himself in the foyer of the sanctum.

He trudged to his room, sore beyond belief, and collapsed face-first onto his bed. He was asleep without even kicking off his boots.

Some indeterminate length of time later, Nym finally got upright and dragged himself into a bath. When he was done, he shaved, got dressed in clean clothes, and went looking for Archmage Veran. He found his mentor working in one of his labs, though it wasn't immediately clear what the old man was doing.

"Is this a bad time?" Nym asked from the door.

"Ah, my friend. No, come on in. I'm just whipping up a batch of freezing brain twisters for the staff's upcoming end-of-semester party."

Nym needed a second to process that. "You're making a batch of what now?"

"An alchemically infused dessert that makes you feel like you've been dunked in a vat of ice water for about five seconds."

"Why . . . Why would anyone want that?"

"Well, I confess they're more used as punishments for the professors who lose at various party games and events. Though I do need to renew the nonflammability wards in the main hall before the party starts. Last year, Emdala set the curtains on fire with an ill-advised flame spell trying to warm herself back up."

"Wow, how old are you guys? This sounds wild."

"You're never too old to have fun, young man," the archmage said severely, though there was a twinkle in his eyes. "But I suspect you've come to me with some work, haven't you?"

"Sorry," Nym told him. "I ran into something pretty serious that I'd like to— Oh, your flask is overflowing."

"What?" Archmage Veran spun around so fast the sleeve of his robe swatted a rather delicate-looking measuring device off the table. Nym caught it with a burst of telekinesis and put it back, but the archmage didn't notice. "God's tick-infested taint! That's the fourth time that heater has malfunctioned on me!"

Nym mouthed the words to the curse, then shook his head. That was a good one, one he planned to remember. Surely there'd be an appropriate use for it sooner or later. His train of thought was interrupted by Archmage Veran's wild gesticulations, and he took a cautionary step back. Arcana surged across the table, and four different spells phased into existence whole in the archmage's aura.

That was impressive, not just because there were four of them, but because they'd somehow appeared without needing to be built first. Either they'd been spun out so fast that it simply appeared they'd formed from nothing, or they'd somehow been prebuilt before they were deployed, but Nym didn't know any way in which that would be possible.

Then he noticed the rings on one of Archmage Veran's hands were glowing, and he understood. The spells had been built normally, though probably with great speed and skill, and stored until needed. For all his casual attitude, his mentor was in fact an archmage, and he'd taken appropriate precautions just in case something went wrong.

"Last time I borrow equipment from the school's alchemy lab," Archmage Veran muttered.

"I would think you'd have your own."

"Oh, I did. Most of it was melted to slag when I was dealing with that tear in the veil a few months ago. It just wasn't strong enough to handle the reactions I needed to forge something capable of holding the arcana I needed. I keep meaning to replace it, but there's been so much catching up to do that I haven't had the time. And so I thought I'd just nip over to the lab and borrow a few pieces for the afternoon, but this God-cursed heater has been doing its level best to thwart me all day."

"I . . . I'm sorry. I can leave you alone to focus on this. How about we talk over lunch in an hour or so?"

"No, no, it's fine," Archmage Veran told him. "This batch is ruined now anyway. What was it you wanted to talk to me about?"

"If you're sure," Nym said. "There's a few things. The first is this aging curse. I was wondering how your research into that is coming along."

"Not well, I'm sad to say. I haven't given up, but you should understand that this was a curse wrought by an ascendant. Not just any ascendant either. You. I confess I'm a bit murky on the societal hierarchy of ascendant civilization, such as it is, but from what I understand you were near the top.

"That's not to say that a spell crafted with a stronger layer of arcana can't be broken by someone weaker. It is, as they say, always easier to destroy than it is to create. I'm confident I could break the curse right now, if it came to it. What I am not confident of is how alive you will be when I'm done."

"That does sound like a drawback," Nym allowed. "Realistically, do you think you'll be able to break it in a way that doesn't leave me dead?"

"I don't think it's impossible. I'll continue working on it, but I wouldn't expect it anytime soon. I might have more for you in a week, or a month. You never know. This kind of research can go years completely stalled out, only to make it past a bottleneck and have the whole thing laid out within a week."

"But you don't expect that?" Nym pressed.

"Sadly, no. I did make a deal though, so I will continue the search for answers. Why the sudden impatience?"

"Let me tell you about what happened on that job you sent me on. You see, there was a mirror fox, but not just any mirror fox. This was a mystic-grade animal. Scariest thing I've ever met in my life, and I'm including all that stuff in the mausoleum . . ."

CHAPTER FIFTEEN

Oh, and I guess I need to set up a postal box," Nym added to the end of his explanation. "That has nothing to do with all the other stuff, just a thing I need to take care of and haven't figured out how to do yet."

"Ah, yes, plague-bug infestations and mystical animals possessing stronger magic than me and being reachable by drop box."

Nym's face flushed slightly, and Archmage Veran's expression turned shrewd. "Whom, pray tell, are you expecting a letter from?"

"Not really important here," Nym mumbled. "Forget I mentioned it."

The levity faded from the archmage's face, and he grew serious again. "May I see the ring, please?"

"Oh, I actually left that back at the glacier. I don't think it had any hidden magics on it, but for a creature that powerful, I wasn't willing to risk bringing it into your sanctum without talking to you first. It's sitting on the desk in my suite."

"A sensible precaution. Let me just . . . Ah, there." Arcana formed around Archmage Veran and pulled the ring across space. It fell into his outstretched hand, around which a new cage of magic formed. "Hmm. Interesting. A very elegant design, but not new to me. Yes, I believe your initial assessment was correct. It does exactly what you thought it would and nothing more."

"So do you think this is worth following up on? I'm kind of heavily invested in not dying of old age in the next two decades, and while I'm not saying you won't come up with the solution, I'm not against hedging my bets here," Nym said.

"Quite understandable, my young friend. I won't be offended if you want to make a bargain with this entity, though I will advise as much caution as possible. If it is as powerful as you say it is, sorry, you say *he* is, there's nothing in this world that I know of that can protect you. You will be relying on him to keep his word with no way to hold him to it if he decides not to."

"Nothing beyond the threat of future retaliation from me, which . . . He didn't seem all that concerned about facing an ascendant."

"Then, if you're going to proceed, I may have a few trinkets lying around that would prove useful to you," Archmage Veran said. "Come, let us see if we can improve your chances of success."

Nym followed his mentor down a hallway, only to do a double take at a door that he was sure hadn't existed before. He'd been down the hall many times; it led to the library after all. "This wasn't there yesterday."

"Indeed not. I don't make a habit of just leaving doors lying around when I don't need them."

"I . . . But . . . Okay." Nym let out a defeated sigh and followed Archmage Veran through the new door.

They were inside some sort of trophy room, though it was a strange one. Various pedestals lined the walls, set between cabinets with glass doors. Knickknacks, trinkets, and curios of all shapes and sizes filled the cabinets, while some of the larger and more durable pieces sat on pedestals. Stands with blank busts or hands displayed rings, bracelets, necklaces, amulets, and the like. Plaques were bolted to the walls, or directly to the pedestals, each one with a little gold plate that had text stamped on it.

At the far end of the room, a dozen staffs were held in place on hooks on the wall. Various wands and rods flanked them, and even more of what Nym recognized as mage blades surrounded the wands. The entire wall was filled with what could really only be weapons designed for mages.

"This . . . This is an armory. An archmage's armory," Nym said.

"Indeed it is. I would not recommend trying to find your way in here without me by your side. Some of the most powerful wards ever made by human hands guard this place from would-be thieves. I would not be leading you here if not for the fact that your success in bargaining with this fox creature would discharge one of my own debts to you. In light of that, it seems the least I can do to help prepare you."

"I appreciate that," Nym told him. He'd never much relied on tools to work his magic, mostly because he'd lacked the funds to purchase them and the knowledge to craft them on his own. Considering that it took third-circle magic to make something permanent, very few tools were available to the public. Oh, people had small things that would last for a little while, a few weeks or a limited number of charges, but those inevitably broke or wore out and needed replacement.

He doubted there was much of anything in Archmage Veran's armory that would wear out or break. And if it did, it was probably because it was inconceivably powerful and was designed that way. Some of the things he was looking at were no doubt priceless, possibly one of a kind and created by the archmage himself.

"Now, if you don't mind some advice, I have a few things that I think you'll find helpful for such a task, and there are a few spells you should definitely learn before you return to the far north. You are welcome to browse but let me point out some of the more relevant instruments," Archmage Veran told him.

He opened one of the cabinets, or rather, he caused it to open itself by means of the glass disappearing as it had no actual door. A small broach floated out and hovered in front of Nym. It was shaped like a spiderweb, with the spider itself sitting in the center. Maybe it was a trick of the light, but he could swear he saw the spider twitch.

"This is enchanted to catch bugs of all sizes that might come near you once it's been activated," Archmage Veran told him. "It can't be moved once you've powered it up, but it does cover an impressive range. It should be useful if you encounter a nest of scarabs that you are unable to personally attend to for some reason. It does so by filling an area with webs and making something similar to a golem that tends to them. Actually, many tiny golems. They are quite thorough."

Nym couldn't picture an immediate use for it, since he would no doubt be able to destroy any scarabs that needed destroying with his own magic, but perhaps he might need to leave it somewhere to guard something for him. Either way, it was small enough that it wouldn't hurt anything to take it with him. If he didn't end up using it, that was fine too.

Archmage Veran crossed the room to a pedestal that had a small mirror on it. "This is more for me than you, I'm afraid," he said. "This is an arcana-analysis tool. It is inferior in every way to your sight, but if you use it to take readings and send them back to me, I might be able to advise you on how bad the infestation is and where to find the source. It won't tell you anything directly that you won't be able to see for yourself."

The mirror was about the size of Nym's hand and came with a wooden traveling case to protect it. The inside was lined with a soft material he didn't recognize and already formed to hold the mirror snugly. As Archmage Veran set it inside and closed it up, he added, "This by itself won't be that useful to you. There is a third-circle spell I'll teach you to relay the information back to me. We'll also need to discuss long-range-communication spells, which I know you've been interested in for some time now."

That was true, but there was always something that was a higher priority, and the field itself was complicated. It was tied closely to long-range-scrying spells, since he needed some way to find the recipient of his magical messages, and vast distances were a huge problem that required a lot of ongoing arcana investments in the magic to overcome.

"Moving right along, this may prove valuable to you if for some reason you are unable to teleport to a more accommodating location." Archmage Veran held up a key made of brass and hung from a thin leather cord. "I can't tell you how often I used this in my youth. Ah, it may not . . . smell the freshest. I don't think I ever cleaned it out when I was done."

"Cleaned out . . . the key?" Nym asked. He squinted at it, trying to see what the runes on it were.

"This is a hidden room. I'm afraid I can't demonstrate it here, but if you channel arcana through it properly and turn the key, it will open the door to a space outside of space. Quite useful if you need a safe place to rest, or a quick hiding spot."

Archmage Veran mimed inserting the key into a lock and turned it, but nothing happened. "I'll show you how to power it later. If we used it here, the wards surrounding this room would have a fit."

He passed the key over to Nym and continued on toward the end of the room where the weapons were. Before he got there though, he stopped in front of a pedestal with a glass box on it. Inside was a little golden ball covered in fine runes so tiny that they looked like lines crisscrossing the ball's surface. Archmage Veran considered it for a moment and asked, "How much do you know about scarab infestations?"

"Not much yet. I'd planned on digging through the library for a bestiary with information on them soon. I figured I'd talk to you first because I wasn't going to take the job if you had told me you were close to breaking the curse yourself."

"A fine, logical plan," the archmage agreed. "Alas, I was not able to meet your expectations. There will be plenty more to discuss, but let us talk about the source first, as it relates to this final tool. Scarabs are not naturally occurring animals. They are the result of a curse being unleashed by a human with more power than brains.

"Oftentimes, some brash young grave robber finds a talisman of some sort, usually in a tomb they have no business being in, and quite often hidden amid a dazzling amount of other wealth. They foolishly take the talisman along with the rest of their ill-gotten gains and, in doing so, activate the curse. The talisman begins creating the scarabs, which are most often flesh eaters, who will then kill the grave robber and all their friends. Hopefully, this happens before they escape the tomb itself.

"Normally, this would be the end of it. The scarabs would eventually starve and die, and with the talisman left behind in the tomb, it becomes dormant and waits for the next idiot to touch it. In some cases, however, a particularly foolish mage who thinks he is clever will manage to remove the talisman without activating it, only to accidentally empower it later. The scarabs will then become an infestation with plenty to eat, plenty of space to spread, and a talisman endlessly creating more and more of them."

Archmage Veran held up the orb. "This will contain that curse. At least, it will attempt to. When you find that talisman, activating this orb will split it open, and it will surround the cursed object to seal it. This should stop the infestation from spreading, though it will do nothing to clean up the scarabs that already exist. If the curse is too powerful, well, then we shall have to consider more extreme methods."

He handed the orb over to Nym and said, "Come, you have much to learn about the subject, and we have yet to touch on the worst-case scenario. We shall retire to the library, and I will point you in the direction of the information you'll need."

"There's a worst-case scenario?" Nym asked.

"Yes. It is possible that the talisman has bonded to a host, that the scarabs, rather than consuming the unfortunate fool who found the talisman, are using them as a power source. In that case, they would not only multiply far more rapidly, but the source of the infestation would likely be mobile and far more difficult to find. Given the location of this particular outbreak, I'm not willing to rule out the possibility quite yet."

"Oh," Nym said. He looked down at the stuff he was holding in his hands. "I think I'm going to need to bargain for a better payment."

CHAPTER SIXTEEN

The challenge with all communication-based magic is finding the recipient," Archmage Veran said. "This is by far the biggest arcana investment in even the most basic message spell, and that has a range limited to mere miles and relies heavily on the caster's knowledge of the recipient to direct the search."

He gestured to the fox ring and said, "This circumvents part of that problem by establishing a link not to a person, but to an unchanging item. The spell looks for the ring, and then pushes the communication to whoever is wearing it. Simple, but only effective one way. It cannot, for example, be used to find the fox who gave it to you. I suspect that was purposeful."

"So what is the secret to effective long-range communication then?" Nym asked.

"Simply put? Effective long-range scrying. There's no way of getting around it. Any spell that needs to cover hundreds or thousands of miles to find its intended target is going to be expensive and difficult. For us lowly humans, that means being as efficient as possible in the spell construct, which often means tailoring spells to individual targets.

"For example, I currently have nineteen long-range-communication spells stored in my head, each one keyed to a different person. I have been meaning to create a new one specific to you, but as you know, something else is always coming up."

Nym didn't like that solution. It sounded like an inelegant hack job that only technically accomplished its goal when the parameters were narrowed down to exactly one use case. "What about a pinnacle spell?"

"Better for the scrying portion, complete overkill for the communication part, only really useful if I desperately need to talk to someone who is not one of the aforementioned nineteen people. If you still need my help once your current avatar reaches the fifth layer, I'll show it to you."

"There has got to be a work-around to this," Nym said.

"Oh, there is, but it's so expensive that the king refuses to implement it."

"I . . . What? What would he have to do with . . ." Nym trailed off as he looked at the fox ring. "Some sort of beacon network, right? Set something up every few miles so you can target anyone within a radius of it."

"It has its drawbacks, of course, but if you don't know exactly where someone is, you can toss out a communication spell targeted at a static location, the beacon, and hope they're near it. You might include the reference number for your own beacon so they can communicate back, assuming they have the ability to."

"But then you need infrastructure," Nym realized. "It's not enough to hire a bunch of master mages to build the beacons. They need to be placed; they need staff to maintain the facilities, to guard the beacons against hostile forces, to be recharged as needed."

"And they need safety measures to prevent their abuse. We wouldn't want an invading army taking over our communications network to help them conquer us more efficiently. It all adds up to a massive expenditure of time and money, something I can assure you King Maleotrak is not eager to endorse."

The conversation turned from hypotheticals to creating a concrete communication spell that would link him to the archmage. The parameters for what the scrying portion would look for were locked down tightly: someone of Archmage Veran's height, weight, age, eye color, hair color, and even magical aptitude. There were more than two dozen descriptors all tailored to fit exactly one man. If something were to change about him, even if he put on or lost some weight, it would need to be updated, and beyond that, every few years or so, it would have to be updated anyway.

Archmage Veran created a new copy of the spell using Nym as a profile to demonstrate how it worked. "Normally, I would never bother to go through the effort with someone so young. The spell rarely lasts more than a few months before the target outgrows it, but in this case, I suppose I shall make an exception. Unless something about you changes drastically, it should last for the duration of this job of yours."

Then it was Nym's turn. Archmage Veran couldn't exactly guide him while he constructed his version of the spell, but the theory was simple enough that once he'd watched his mentor do it, it wasn't too terribly difficult to repeat. The tricky part was tweaking the targeting portion, but a few hours of tinkering was enough to brute force it.

So now Nym had a contact–Archmage Veran spell that would work from a thousand miles away. It wasn't good for anyone else, and he wasn't confident he could fill the blanks in for Analia or Bildar without further assistance. For his current purposes though, it worked just fine.

"I'm afraid we're running short on time, and we haven't even really started on the scrying spells you'll need to effectively search the entire northland," Archmage Veran told him.

"I am less worried about that. I think I can just follow the arcana. If I track it far enough, eventually I should discover the source."

"You may be underestimating how far an infestation like this can spread, and how quickly. You could trace the one spot you know about to another, only to find that it goes in six different directions with nothing to tell you which way will take you closer to the origin."

"That's a good point. On the other hand, if I'm going to clean up the entire infestation, I'll need to map it all out anyway, so eventually I'll find the source regardless."

"True, but the sooner you find the talisman that's creating the scarabs, the fewer of them there will be to clean up."

"Also true, but the longer I delay preparing, the more time they have to spread."

"But if you don't prepare well enough, you may not live to exterminate them all."

"Alright, alright. I give!" Nym held up his hands in surrender.

"Excellent. I will clear my schedule tomorrow evening, and we'll continue our preparations. In the meantime, I hate to ask, but I don't suppose you could make a new batch of freezing brain twisters for me? I'm afraid we've rather lost track of time, and I don't have enough hours in my day left to start over now."

"I know next to nothing about alchemy," Nym confessed. "But I do know an accomplished alchemist who owes me a favor or two."

"Perfect. I'll leave the ingredients in the lab for you to take with you. Please place them in the ice chest once they're finished and I'll collect them before the party."

"Uh, how many did you want?"

"As many as can be produced with what I have left," Archmage Veran said.

"I'll see what I can do."

"Perfect. Now then, I must be off. I do have other obligations to attend to."

They said their goodbyes, and Nym walked over to the lab to load up his cargo.

The teleport directly into Cern's workshop was tricky, and even though Nym was confident he could target it precisely enough to stick the landing, he did have some concerns about things like other people being there or surprising an alchemist at work, which could lead to explosions. So, with some regret, he teleported into the sky over Shu-Ain instead, then flew down to the workshop to walk in through the front door. It was locked, but Nym didn't let that stop him.

Cern came storming out of the back room as the door opened, yelling in a rapid stream of the local dialect that he choked off midrant when he saw who it was. "God's blood, kid! Don't just walk in like you own the place. How'd you even get in anyway?"

Nym shrugged. "Magic. Here, got a job for you."

Cern regarded the packaged ingredients suspiciously. "What's this for?"

"Order for Archmage Veran, headmaster of the Academy in Abilanth. He wants as many freezing brain twisters as can be made with this."

"Oh really?" Cern's expression switched from suspicion to greed so fast Nym almost thought he'd imagined the earlier look. "Not terribly difficult to produce, but the ingredients themselves are expensive. That drives the price up. Normally I'd charge four crests for a batch of twenty."

"Well, since the archmage is supplying the ingredients, I think you can forgo the markup. And since he'd asked me to procure them as a favor, and since *you* owe *me* fifty or sixty crests worth of favors, I thought you might just make them for me."

"I . . . Yes. I can do that. Come on then, you can assist me at least."

"Are you sure? I don't know much at all about alchemy."

"Yes, I'll do the complicated stuff, and you'll pour cold-aspected arcana when and where I tell you. Give me twenty minutes to finish up what I've got cooking now. You wait out here."

Then Cern took the package out of Nym's arms, closed the door to the back room in his face, and started rattling around vials and beakers and muttering to himself. Nym just stood there for a minute listening, then shook his head and sent a message to Analia letting her know he was at the workshop.

A few minutes later, he sent another message. It was possible she was out of the city and they just weren't reaching her or that she was sleeping or just otherwise too busy to respond. All things considered though, Nym would feel more comfortable if he knew she was safe. When she didn't respond to the second message, he started scrying.

A regular scry wasn't going to pick her up, but he had some advanced techniques and third-layer arcana available to him now. He started at her apartments and, when those were empty, spread the scry out in a large blanket. Eventually, he came across a distortion in the spell, a person-shaped hole that wasn't giving him the feedback he normally received.

It might not have been Analia. She was hardly the only person in the world who valued their privacy so highly that they repeatedly stitched antiscrying rune sequences onto their clothes. Idly, Nym wondered how much of her money had gone toward the special metal threads needed to keep the runes from burning out every few days.

While he was considering whether or not the person he'd spotted with concealment runes shrouding them was Analia, his scry kept working its way through the city in an ever-expanding radius. It would only go maybe a mile around him before it faded too far to be useful, but that was still a lot of area to go over in just a few minutes. It was a thousand times faster than looking by just flying around.

A second person popped up with a distorted presence, but this one wasn't as well concealed. He recognized Analia immediately. She was standing in a shop of some sort, talking to someone while three other people looked on. Nym couldn't hear what they were saying, but from her posture she looked like she was getting aggressive over something, and they didn't seem to be taking it well.

"I'll be right back," he yelled through the door.

Nym teleported to the roof of the building Analia was in and switched to his anchor-style scrying spell, now enhanced to show arcana too. It slipped down through the ceiling into the room, where he saw she had a spell already prepared to form chunks of hail and fire them off at high speed.

Before he could do anything else, one of the men she was talking to started shouting, and Analia finished the spell in a snap. A chunk of ice tagged the man in the face, which triggered the rest of the men to attack her. A wave of paralysis magic washed out across the room, catching two of them. The last one got a hand on her for a second before her third spell finished.

Pure force, probably the most expensive of the three spells she'd cast, lanced out and caught the man in the gut. His hand was ripped off her shoulder, and he was flung across the room to crash into a pyramid of kegs that had been stacked up against the back wall.

Nym teleported down next to her and said, "Hi. What's going on?"

Analia spun in place, prepared to fire off another spell directly at Nym. When she saw who it was, she scowled and snapped, "Don't do that!"

CHAPTER SEVENTEEN

Nym waited for Analia to explain. Instead, she just glared at him. When he didn't say anything, she said, "I don't need your help with this."

"Didn't say you did. Just wanted to know what's going on."

The glare faltered, and she said, "It's complicated."

"Okay. Are you going to be in any trouble for this?"

"No." She shook her head. "Not with the law or anything. They're criminals, so it's not like they'll go running to the bluehats."

"And . . . what is a bluehat?" Nym asked.

"Local version of the city watch or guard. Look, I'm kind of busy right now. Did you need something?"

"Nothing pressing," Nym said. He noticed one of the men, the one she'd pelted with a giant hailstone, was climbing back to his feet. "You want me to get that for you, or . . . ?"

"No, I've got this," she said. Arcana flowed out of her into a paralysis construct that struck the man. "So why're you in the city? You're a few days early."

"Oh, just doing a favor for someone and needed Cern's help. I've got a job way up north to take care of, so I'm going to be gone for a bit. Hopefully not too long. Depends on how the searching goes. Could be a week. Could be months."

"Oh. I can't . . . It's a really bad time." Analia glanced over at the four men. "Want to help me bust up a local gang of smugglers?"

"You don't need any help. You just told me."

"Don't be a jerk. That was before I knew you were going to be gone for a while. I have to take care of this, so come with me, and we can spend some time together before you go."

"Okay, as long as it's really quick. I have to get back to the workshop to be the arcana battery for Cern in a few minutes."

"I don't know if it'll be that fast. I'll just send him a message and tell him I'm borrowing you."

The spell formed around Analia, but then unraveled before it could finish. "Huh, that's odd," she said.

"Oh, there's antimessaging wards. No wonder you weren't answering me," Nym said. "One second."

He sent a kinetic slash through the wall, destroying one of the runes in the sequence that was lining the room. A few more slashes went out in various spots, mostly randomly. He wasn't worried about explosive feedback in a place like this, and he doubted the runes were booby-trapped. "Try now," he said.

A second message formed, and this one shot out as intended. "Okay, that's done. Let me catch you up on what's going on here," she told him. She gestured to the men. "These four guys are known as the Green Beach Gang. They like to run a route from Shu-Ain across the archipelago and up to the continent."

"Okay, I'm with you so far. I'm guessing you have a problem with them."

"They like to use mules to get the product through the city rather than do it themselves. They can be really aggressive in their recruitment methods, and they absolutely love to target the really, really young kids to do it. I'm talking about kids that are younger than seven."

"I'm familiar with the tactic," Nym said, his face darkening. When he'd been living on the streets in Abilanth, there were a number of the smallest kids who'd done similar work. They were exploited to the extreme, and the job had a high mortality rate, not because they were often caught, but because the types of criminals who used them as mules usually killed them to maintain their operational security.

"So my neighbor has two kids, both in the age range. Both are missing, and these guys are being uncooperative about telling me where they send their mules."

"What's the next step in your plan?" Nym asked.

"Ask them some more questions. Get mean about it if I have to."

"Do you speak the language now? You've only been here a few weeks."

Analia shrugged. "I'm conversant, I guess? Translation spells help bridge the gaps."

"Well, by all means," Nym said with a gesture.

Analia started speaking in halting Byramese, helped by a bridge of arcana linking her to the one she'd pelted with ice. She released him from the paralysis spell while she talked, and when the man pulled himself back to his feet, Nym readied a greater-telekinesis spell just in case he needed to grab the criminal.

He also cast the truth-seeking spell he'd picked up from Analia's brother so long ago, though he wasn't sure if it would work when he didn't understand what was being said. The two chattered back and forth, tempting Nym to cast his own translation spell, but he didn't want to interfere with her connection. She hadn't included him in it, possibly because her second-circle version wasn't strong enough to add extra people.

Truth seeking pinged off something the man said, though Nym wasn't sure what. "What did he just say?" Nym interrupted.

"Hmm? He said he doesn't know where the alchemists who supply them make ocean tears."

"He's lying."

"Is he? That's very interesting." Analia said something else to the man in a much harsher tone, and he paled.

Nym didn't understand the words, but he knew vigorous and frightened denial when he saw it. Whatever the man knew, he knew what was going to happen to him if he told Analia about it. There was of course the obvious intimidation tactic to that: what Analia was going to do to him if he didn't talk. Just the body language alone was enough for him to read that exchange.

It probably helped give her argument weight when she started forming new hailstones in the air, each one the size of her fist and spiked like a sea urchin. They hovered with an application of telekinesis, slowly bobbing up and down in a very deliberate and controlled manner. Nym had to admire the sheer performance of the threat, even if she wouldn't go through with it.

That admiration turned to shock when two of the spiky ice balls shot through the air and struck the man in the chest. The ice had no problem piercing the cloth of his shirt, and he started bleeding immediately. He opened his mouth to scream, and she slipped a gag of air in.

"Huh. That's . . . vicious."

"He deserves it," she said without turning to look away from the man. Two new spiked ice stones formed in the air to replace the ones she'd struck him with. She said something else, and the man whimpered before reluctantly talking.

"Lying that time?" she asked.

"No," Nym said. "That one you hit with a force lance is trying to use magic though. I'll take care of it."

He fired off a few second-circle arcana injections, completely breaking up the spell and causing the man to shriek in surprise and pain. Nym wrapped him in greater telekinesis and brought him over to the other two. "Would it be better to question this guy without the other ones in the room? Might talk more freely without the audience."

"Good idea. Will you hold them in the back room, please?"

"Sure."

Nym lifted all three of them up and floated them out of the main room. He leaned in the doorframe where he could keep an eye on them while still watching the interrogation. Analia didn't have to hit the man again while she was questioning him, but on three different occasions truth seeker pinged, and he raised a finger to signal to her that he was lying.

Finally, she ran out of questions and told Nym, "I think we're done here."

"What are we doing with them?"

"Should kill them. They deserve it. It'll make problems for people I care about if I let them live." She hesitated, then shook her head. "I don't suppose you picked up anything for erasing memories."

"I've been a lot more focused on restoring them," Nym told her dryly.

She let out a quiet little huff of a laugh. "That's fair. No real choice then."

"You could turn them over to the, what did you call them, the bluehats?"

"I might as well just kill them myself. That's likely what'll happen when their boss finds out they talked, even if they're in jail."

"So they need to disappear," Nym said. "Not necessarily killed, but . . . not here."

"Anywhere else you send them, they'll just cause problems there," she said. "They're thieves, slavers, and murderers. They deserve death."

"Up to you. I did see a few smaller islands in the chain that didn't have people on them. We could add four people to the island's population."

"Can you get them there in under five minutes?"

"Ehhhh . . . Maybe ten? I won't be able to teleport them directly there, but I can fly them over."

She considered it for a minute, then gave a short nod. "Okay, let's do that. You'll be using that overland-flight spell?"

"Yeah. Otherwise it'll take me over an hour."

"You do that. I'll go ahead."

Nym wasn't sure that was the best idea, but Analia didn't look like she was in the mood to argue. "Where should I meet you at?"

"They keep the kids in one of two places," she explained. "The first is where they make ocean tears. That's the location this guy didn't want to give up. It's outside the city, on the north coast of the island. That way they don't have to worry about smuggling in the narosin coral they use for it. It's all manufactured in a hidden villa where they keep a stable of kids to smuggle the stuff into Shu-Ain.

"Once the kids have run the first leg, the shipments get split up. Some of it stays local or gets loaded onto small boats to be moved to other nearby islands, but the majority of it goes overseas to other countries where it's far, far more profitable to sell. This is the part where the kids are needed. Despite the lax attitude of the city, they do not joke around about their customs. Ships are rigorously inspected, and ocean tears are very illegal.

"The ocean tears get sealed up, the kids are forced to swallow them, and then they go on the ships to be used as living transport containers. The smugglers will get the tears back out, one way or another, well before they reach the port of destination. Usually the kid doesn't survive the trip."

"Why use kids though?" Nym asked.

Analia shrugged. "Easier to control. Easier to threaten. Disposable. Cheaper than a slave."

Nym turned to look at the man she'd been questioning. "And these guys are part of it?"

"They work as handlers. They kidnap the kids, coerce them into doing the runs, keep an eye on them to make sure they don't lose the product. Unfortunately, killing them wouldn't even be a blip in the operation. It's so big, with so many people doing exactly what this group is."

The more she talked, the quieter and angrier she got. "I don't have time to talk about this anymore," she said. "Moda and Shan could already have their guts full of pellets. They could be getting loaded onto a ship right now. I've got to go."

"Let me drop a heavy paralysis on all of them, blind them too. We'll go together. When we're done, we can come back and deal with them."

She bit her lip but nodded. "Nym, you know I'm going to be killing people today, right?"

"I know. Have you ever killed someone before?"

Analia shook her head. "I don't want to. But for this, to stop it, I will."

"I'll help," he said simply.

"Thank you."

CHAPTER EIGHTEEN

They left the drug runners behind, paralyzed and gagged in the back room. Nym planned to go back for them later, when things weren't so pressing. Analia assured him that she could handle this on her own, but she was still only second circle, despite how strong she'd gotten. He would feel much better about her fighting a cartel if he went with her.

They flew over to the docks and stopped to look around. "It's bigger than I expected," Analia admitted. "The building we're looking for should be in the warehouse district over there. Or . . . maybe the warehouses on the other side?"

"Well, whichever one it is will have a bunch of kids in it, right? And they'll probably be in a cell or something."

"Maybe. It's supposed to be a small one between two big ones, and it has doors on either side. They said it was on Shelsick Street."

"I'm going to start scrying while you look for that," Nym said.

He set one part of his mind to controlling his scry anchor as it swooped around, going through buildings and looking for children. There were a lot of them, to his surprise, but most of them were either outside the buildings or moving around freely. He didn't find anyone trapped in any cages or pens anywhere he looked.

The other part of his mind focused on keeping close to Analia and watching out for danger. He didn't know if she'd alerted the cartel to what she was doing in some way before he'd caught up to her, and he didn't want to get sniped out of the sky by some random spell. His conduits to both the second and third layer were wide-open, and arcana sat in his soul well, ready to be shaped into whatever defense he needed to protect them.

"There, that's the place," she said, pointing down at a squat little building that seemed even smaller because it was surrounded by larger warehouses on all sides. There was a large set of double doors in the front and two separate doors on the side and back. A man was sitting in the alley behind the warehouse, close to the door, but leaned against the opposite wall and holding a jug of liquor in one hand.

He could conceivably have been guarding the door, or he might have just been a drunk. Like so many natives to Shu-Ain, he was wearing very little in the way of clothing, and Nym was confident that he wasn't carrying any weapons. That didn't mean much if he was a mage, and as far as Nym knew, there wasn't any way to tell just by looking.

The interior was divided up into one half a large holding area and one half smaller offices. Nowhere in any of that space was there even a single child, but one of the offices had a trapdoor leading down to a basement. "I think I found what you're looking for, but there's a problem."

There were plenty of pens, big enough for a human child to sit in but not to move around or stand up. They were stacked on top of one another and filled an entire wall, probably forty or fifty of them. They were also empty. The whole warehouse was that way, with only five people in the entire thing.

After describing it to Analia, he said, "Maybe we're too late and the kids have already been stashed on various ships? Or maybe we're too early and they haven't made the initial run in from the coast?"

"We'll check the ships first," Analia said. "If they're on there, we need to rescue them before they set sail."

They flew across the docks in a slow arc, with Nym scrying each ship as they went by. "One child here, doesn't seem to be restrained. Two on this one, also unrestrained. Nothing. Nothing. One. Three here, sitting in a room together. Let me see . . . No, the room's not locked."

Before he could go on, Analia said, "You're talking about this ship here? The three-master with the blue paint on the railing?"

Nym blinked and switched back to his normal sight to confirm. "Yes, that one. They're in the room at the front. The captain's quarters, I think? One of them is going through the desk drawers now, and the other two are tossing something that looks quite expensive back and forth. I don't think they're prisoners."

"We'll keep looking then."

"How would you have done this without me here?" Nym asked.

"Questioned the people in the warehouse and moved forward based on that information."

"That's remarkably cutthroat of you."

"They kidnapped my friend's children," Analia said coldly. "They don't deserve anything better."

Nym pointed to a small ship near the end of the dock. "That one has three adults and seven kids inside of it."

Analia's eyes locked onto it. "*The Mistweaver*. Kind of on the nose for a smuggler's boat, isn't it? Let's go."

They flew over together and landed on the deck, where they were immediately accosted by a native man wearing a pair of pants belted at the waist with a sword strapped to his hip. Nym didn't understand a word of what he said, and there was no time to enact a translation spell. Analia calmly struck him with a force lance and blew him off the side of the ship to splash into the water.

"In the cargo hold?" she asked.

"Yes. There's a ladder over there."

Before they reached it, another man emerged from a cabin and looked around.

"What's this then?" he asked, his accent so thick Nym had to think for a second to understand what he was saying. He wasn't obviously armed, but he was wearing quite a bit of gold jewelry. It was possible there was something magical in there or that he was a mage. Just to be safe, he readied as powerful an arcana injection as possible.

"I seem to have misplaced some children on your ship," Analia said. "I am retrieving them."

"Nah, don't think you are."

Arcana flowed out of the man, but before he could do anything, Nym released his spell into him. The man cried out in pain and collapsed, his whole body spasming and his limbs twisting around. Analia just looked down at him pitilessly for a few seconds, then turned toward the ladder once she seemed sure he wasn't getting back up.

"There's one more adult. She's sitting in the hold with the kids. I'm not sure if she's a handler keeping them controlled or a victim comforting them," Nym said.

"We'll find out soon. This way?" Analia pointed down the hall and, with Nym's nod, flew toward the back of the boat. She stopped at a locked grate leading down into a cargo hold and looked over at him. "Can you get this open, or should I just blast it? I don't want shrapnel hitting them down there if I can avoid it."

"I'll take care of it," he said. A few seconds later, the padlock clicked open, and he pulled it free with telekinesis.

The cargo hold itself was dark, but that was easy enough for practically any mage to fix. A few balls of light popped up, both of them casting the spell simultaneously, and revealed a bench with seven children sitting side by side. All of them had been down in the dark long enough that the sudden light made them cry out and cover their eyes.

A casual observer might not have known they were prisoners. They weren't chained to the floor; there were no shackles around their wrists or ankles or necks. To Nym's eyes though, each of them was affected by magic, some sort of entanglement or holding spell that kept them firmly seated on the bench.

"What do you think you're doing with these children?" Analia asked, her voice low, dangerous.

The woman got in front of them, placed herself between the two intruders and the living cargo she was overseeing. She rattled off something that Nym didn't understand, and this time he got the translation spell up first. He made sure to include himself as well so that he could follow what was going on.

"Why are they being held down here?" he asked.

"Return home to island next mine. Family island wait for them."

That was about as garbled as his previous attempts, but it got the point across. Truth seeker pinged though, and Nym shook his head. "Lie," he said.

"Ocean tears?" Analia asked, though she said it in Byramese.

The woman shook her head vehemently, trying to deny the accusation, but truth seeker warned Nym again. He was impressed with the accuracy of the spell, considering how weak it was. But then, these were very obvious lies, and none of the people they'd questioned had been good at hiding the truth. He would have known she was lying without magical assistance.

Analia swept her aside with a burst of wind and approached the children. Six of them cowered, but one in the middle, a little girl, burst out, "Nala!"

For the first time since he'd found her with those four men, a smile returned to her face. "Hi, Shan. Can you tell me where your brother is?"

Nym spread the translation spell to include the girl, which worked even worse than it had on the adult. The sentence was practically incoherent, but he did get that they'd been separated back at the warehouse after they'd threatened to hurt her brother if she didn't behave.

While they were talking, he started picking apart the spell gluing them to the bench. It came apart easily enough, especially without anyone around to keep pouring more arcana into it. The effect must have been tactile to the kids since as soon as he cut it, every single one of them jumped off the bench and started running around. Nym kept them away from the woman who'd been handling them, but otherwise let them run around the cargo hold.

"Can you teleport this many people at once?" Analia asked after a bit more conversation with the little girl.

"Nine people? Maybe? I could definitely do it in two groups. Where are they going?"

"Back to my home. Or next door, I guess. I need to get Shan back to her mother, and I'm sure she'll keep an eye on the rest of them while we go find Moda."

"I can do Cern's workshop. I'm more familiar with that. I'll send you with a group of three, then follow with the other four."

The children were quickly split up, and Nym enacted the back-to-back teleports. They all landed on the roof, and he quickly flew the group down to ground level. Analia took over shepherding them and said, "I'll be back in a bit. Will you go talk to Cern and tell him I need a batch of poison purge?"

"Oh, to get them to throw up the pellets?"

"Exactly."

"I'm on it," Nym told her. She waved and started herding the kids down the street while Nym went into the shop.

"About time you got back! Get in here. I need your help," Cern yelled from the back room.

"How'd you even know it was me?" Nym asked as he walked in.

"Bunch of people landing on my roof, who else was it going to be?"

Nym laughed and raised his hands in surrender. "You got me. Listen, Analia wants a batch of poison purge for seven kids to get a bunch of ocean-tears pellets out of their stomachs."

Cern whipped around from where he was monitoring a large flask that was just starting to bubble. "She needs what now? What in God's name have you two been up to?"

"Well . . . it's kind of complicated, but I guess some children were kidnapped by this cartel, and she knew a few of them and went to get them back, and now we've got a whole bunch. Oh, and we'll be going back out to find some more because we didn't find both of the kids she was looking for."

Cern just stared at him, slack-jawed.

CHAPTER NINETEEN

Nym expected some complaining at the very least. Cern was a fantastic complainer. But it didn't happen, not this time. He supposed the alchemist probably knew a lot about ocean tears and the kinds of people who were involved because all he really did was direct Nym on what to do in order to keep the project he'd been working on stable, then got started whipping up the medicine.

Analia came into the workshop about half an hour later, by herself now, and walked into the room. Before she could say anything, Cern said, "About five more minutes."

They worked in silence, and when the flask was full, he measured it out into small, thimble-sized portions in thin little vials. "Bring them here for the removal. If the pellet bursts inside them while they're vomiting it up, I might be able to save them. I'll start working on that next. Far better for them to throw it up cleanly though."

"I'll tell Kana. She'll get the kids over here. We're working on figuring out where they live so we can get them back to their families. One of them—at least one of them—won't have a home to go back to. His parents—" Her voice broke, and she took a second to steady herself. "His parents sold him to the cartel for another hit."

Cern's face darkened, but he didn't say anything. He just kept on working. Analia watched for a minute, then said, "I need to go. There's still the villa to raid. Hopefully the rest of the kids are there. Those ones shouldn't be loaded up yet, but we'll see. Nym, are you coming?"

"Yes?" Nym glanced uncertainly over at Cern. "Can I . . . Is this stable if I stop?"

"Hmm? Oh, no. One second." Cern crossed the workshop and fiddled with the setup for a few seconds, then infused one of the beakers with arcana. "There. As soon as all the bubbles disappear in that, you're good. Should only take a minute."

Nym held steady until he got clearance to stop channeling arcana into the mixture. "Thanks," he said. "And, uh, thanks for making these things for me, especially since there's more important stuff going on now."

"Well, they're for an archmage. I figured it would be best not to ruin fifty crests worth of his reagents, you know?"

"Fifty?" Nym's eyes widened. "I didn't realize these were so expensive."

"Oh yes. Really just an absolutely frivolous waste of Academy resources to have them at a faculty party."

"Huh . . . Well, glad I didn't get an education there, I suppose."

Cern snorted. "You didn't get an education anywhere. Not a real one."

"Hey . . ."

"He's right," Analia said with a smile. "You learn random things from random books with no system, no organization, no building a foundation of knowledge. It's remarkable you've been as successful as you have."

"Well, there's no need to be rude about it!"

"Don't pout," Cern said. "It's a lot less cute when you have a mustache growing in."

"I can't believe my friends, who I give so much of myself to, would attack me like this!" Nym said.

"Yes, you're such a martyr," Analia said. "Come on, we've got more kids to save."

The levity evaporated with that statement, and they left shortly thereafter. Nym was under no illusions that they'd reform society in an afternoon, but they would save a few more children, and maybe if they did it right, they might break up a cartel and prevent them from hurting anyone else. But there would probably be a new one moving in to take their place next week.

He supposed it was a good thing that breaking up the cartel wasn't the goal then. Though he did wonder what Analia's long-term plans were. She was turning herself into a target with this, and he didn't think she was strong enough to survive it. Or ruthless enough, though he was starting to change his mind on that.

They flew north out of Shu-Ain and followed the coast east. While they were in the air, Nym put up a bubble of air around them to cut off the wind and asked, "What are you going to do after we get the kids back?"

"Detox and find their families," she said.

"I mean, what are you going to do when these guys hunt you down and try to kill you for interfering with their operation? Cern isn't going to be that much help, and you haven't hit third circle yet."

"I have . . . friends . . . down here, who are invested in stopping stuff like this from happening."

"That makes it sound like you're part of some vigilante group."

Analia didn't say anything.

"Are you part of some vigilante group?" Nym asked.

Her cheeks flushed red, and she mumbled, "We're not vigilantes."

"You've barely been here a few weeks! How are you part of an underground resistance movement fighting drug cartels?"

She mumbled something else, but even with the wind cut off, Nym couldn't hear her. "What was that?"

"My neighbor is part of it," she said again, louder this time.

"The neighbor whose kids got stolen?"

"Yes."

"I wonder why she was targeted," Nym deadpanned. "This is an insanely dangerous thing to get mixed up in. You were supposed to be here to learn alchemy while Cern rebuilds his business."

"And I am doing that! I'm just doing this too."

"Analia."

"You're not my father, Nym. I'm not discussing this with you anymore. Besides, that's the place there, I think."

A set of four houses, one of them large enough that it wouldn't have been out of place at the upper end of a merchant's row, were nestled into the trees right off the coast. "Why don't they just have their ships sail right from here?" he wondered aloud.

"They do, locally. But for the ports that are faraway, it wouldn't be worth it to transport the drug by itself, so they attach themselves to merchant ships carrying legitimate cargo. Also I think they don't want to advertise the location of this place. Not a lot of people even in their own organization know where it is."

"Which begs the question of how that group you put pressure on knew."

"They handle the kids. That includes taking them out here and bringing them back sometimes."

"And because we knew he was lying, he couldn't try to send you into a trap or give you the wrong location."

"Exactly," Analia said. "What is this thing under our feet, by the way?"

"Camouflage screen," Nym told her. "Good for making sure ghouls and wights don't notice you when you're flying overhead. It also works on drug cartels."

"I like it. Is this a second-circle spell?"

"Yes. I can probably get you the book for it if you want."

Analia nodded. "Please. This seems very useful."

"How are you coming along at breaking through to third-layer arcana, by the way?"

"It's been slow progress. We can talk about it later though, after we save those children."

Nym waved a hand down at the villa. "I'm already scrying it. So far I'm seeing a lot of adults, and a lot of alchemy gear, and a lot of herbs, flowers, and other stuff. I don't see any kids yet, but I'm not done looking."

"I need to learn some scrying spells too. This is much easier with you helping."

"I'm glad I was here to help," Nym said. "It's good timing. I'm actually going out on a job of my own that'll take a few weeks."

"Right, you said earlier. What's this one about?" she asked.

Nym explained to her about the fox and the scarabs while he scried the buildings. He told her how Archmage Veran was having trouble finding a solution on his own, and that the job could be the way to break the aging curse.

"So you'd just age normally like the rest of us," she said when he finished. "That'd be nice. You'd only be a few years older than me."

"I agree. I wasn't looking forward to dying of old age in the next decade or two. The sooner I stop it, the better off I'll be. Plus I met someone around my age, and it would be nice to have the time to explore that without looking like I'm dating someone young enough to be my kid."

"You . . . met someone?" Analia asked, a strange expression on her face. "When did that happen?"

"On the last job. She goes to the Academy. I don't know her that well yet, but we're going to spend some more time together."

"Oh. How nice." Analia's voice was faint.

"Hey, are you okay? Want me to take over the flight spell so you can rest?"

"I'm fine," she snapped. "Sorry. I'm glad you found someone you're interested in. We really should focus on what we're doing here though."

"I am," Nym promised. "I've already done those two buildings to the right completely, and I'm working on that one with the walled garden now. I haven't seen anything yet. Do you think the kids might already be in transport?"

"That's possible," Analia said with a frown. "It's going to make them harder to find."

"I'll send out an air golem with perfect vision cast on it," Nym offered.

"You're already holding a flight spell, this camouflage spell, and scrying the villa. Are you sure you have the brain space left to direct a golem on top of everything else?"

"Sure," Nym said. "Once you get to third circle, you can start making improvements to your body. One of those is enhancing your brain's ability to do parallel processing. I've only got two partitions right now, but Archmage Veran told me I can get up to three on the third circle and add a fourth process at archmage level."

"I . . . did not know that. I wonder if . . . you know . . . if that was one of the kinds of things my father tried to do to me."

"Maybe," Nym said. "I know a lot more about the subject now. I guess if we ever got a look at those books again, I could tell you more. From what I remember, some of the stuff was really experimental, and it diverged a lot from what's considered standard body magic for third circle."

"I kind of doubt I'll ever have access to those books again. I'm sure now that Dad's gone home, he's relocated everything to some new hiding spot, not because it'd get him in trouble, but just so nothing happens to it."

Nym sent an air golem out following the foot trail leading away from the villa while he completed his scry on the final building. "I don't think it needs to define who you are," he said. "From what I can tell, I was a psychopath before I lost all my memories. Everyone and everything was transactional and opportunistic. I'm glad I'm not that person anymore. I don't want him to be the benchmark for who I am today."

"I'm glad you're not like that either, even if you are oblivious sometimes," she said.

"I am?" Nym asked.

"Definitely. You're still a good person though."

"Oh. Well, um, thanks. Sorry I missed stuff. What stuff did I miss?"

"It's not important now," Analia said. "Did you find anything yet?"

"Nothing in the villa. The air golem is scouting out the trail. I don't see anyone on— Wait, no, there it is. Four adults, twelve kids in between them. They're a mile that way. I'm not seeing any weapons, so I'm guessing all four are mages. We'll probably be able to handle them without too much trouble."

"Good. Let's go get them back and take them home," Analia said. "And then I think I want to visit this villa again before you go and burn it to the ground."

Nym nodded slowly. "I can help with that, if you're sure. It wouldn't hurt to make sure everyone in there is a willing member though. They could be exploiting adults as well."

"Fine, yes. We'll check that too. But either way, destroying their labs will slow down their operation by a lot."

"I can agree to that," Nym said. "You ready?"

"Let's go."

CHAPTER TWENTY

Ambushing the drug runners wasn't hard. Nym and Analia floated a hundred feet in the air over the group, safely hidden behind his camouflage screen, and hit all four of the adults with paralysis spells. Two of them started casting immediately, so he peppered them with arcana injections. The other two apparently weren't mages, and there was very little they could do to fight back.

Though he hadn't ever seen anyone besides himself push through an arcana injection to keep flinging spells, Nym wasn't about to bank on the idea that they couldn't. These would be desperate men, after all, more than willing to accept a little pain to get in a chump shot when Nym wasn't looking.

So he kept an eye on them while Analia talked with the children. They were tied together with a rope in a single long line, each one with their hands bound and the rope leading off to the next. Nym cut the rope between each child, and Analia untied them the old-fashioned way.

After that, she had some questions for the men, which they were surprisingly steadfast in refusing to answer. They didn't try to lie like the one she'd questioned back in the city. They just glared at her, stone-faced and silent. At least, they did until Nym picked one at random and lifted him a thousand feet into the sky, then let him fall.

He caught the man around the hundred-foot mark and lowered him to the ground itself at a still terrifying, but not dangerous, speed. Part of him felt bad for essentially torturing the guy, but all it took was a glance over at the dozen traumatized children and he got over it. When the man refused to talk, he went for a second ride, and all three of his friends went with him.

He still wouldn't talk, but one of the other guys started blubbering and eagerly spilled his guts, much to the disgust of the other three. Analia asked him some rapid-fire questions, some of which seemed to confuse the man, but in the end she was satisfied with the information.

"We're going to do a lot with this," she told Nym.

"What were you trying to find out?"

"Mostly names and places involved in their organization. We'll hit them and shut them down as fast as we can. This particular cartel is going to lose a lot of money over the next few weeks. We might even shut them down completely."

Nym just shook his head. "This really wasn't what I pictured you doing with your free time."

"I just kind of stumbled onto it, but I don't regret joining."

"Mm-hmm. How illegal is this thing you're doing?"

"No more illegal than what they're doing," she said, jabbing one finger angrily at the drug runners.

"Sure, but that just sounds like everyone gets arrested when the guards notice what's going on. The what did you call them? The bluehats?"

"Only if we get caught," she said grimly. "With you helping, I don't think that'll be an issue."

"Uh, I would not count on that if I were you. I'm helping you specifically this afternoon, but I do have my own work to do."

"Nym, don't you care about what they're doing to these kids? Or what they're doing with this dangerous and addictive drug? The users will stab somebody without a second thought when they start going through withdrawal, anything even for the hint of getting a fix."

Nym shrugged. "I care about you being safe. I would prefer these kids not be mixed up in it. If someone old enough to know better gets hooked on what these guys are selling, that's their problem."

"It's everyone's problem," Analia said.

"Not mine, not really. I'm just making sure it's clear to you that I am here as a favor to you only and that I'm not signing on for your vigilante gang. I don't think you should either, but you'll do what you like."

She glared at him, and Nym stared back, his face blank. He'd never been one to go out of his way trying to right all the wrongs of the world, and he'd thought she'd known that about him. If there was a problem in front of him, sure, Nym would help if he could. What she was doing was on a whole different level, and he was mostly just concerned that she'd get herself killed while he was away.

"I'm not going to have an argument here in the middle of the jungle," she said. "Get these kids back to Shu-Ain for me and I won't bother you anymore. You can go do whatever you want after that."

"Of course I'm going to do that," Nym said, scratching his head. He wasn't sure why she was surprised that he wasn't going to drop everything and rush off to fight an organized crime syndicate. There were too many problems in front of him already to spend months or years trying to help people he didn't even know for no reason other than they needed help.

"I think we're done here then," she told him. "Go on ahead with the kids and I'll join you shortly."

"Why aren't you—"

"I don't want them to see what's going to happen next," she hissed. "Get them out of here while I take care of these guys."

"Are you sure you want to . . ." Nym shot a look at the kids. "You know . . ."

"I don't want to, but I'm going to. I should have done the ones back in the city too instead of letting you talk me out of it."

"That's a bit bloodthirsty."

"It is what it is, Nym. Now please take the children back to Cern's and I will join you in a little bit."

"Hmm . . . Alright. If you're sure." He turned to the children and said, "Who wants to fly all the way back home?"

None of them were eager, but they didn't resist either. Nym lifted them up, and they flew, slowly, back toward the city. He left an air golem behind to keep an eye on Analia, just in case.

Nym didn't mention what Analia did to Cern, or to anybody else. He flew the kids in without any trouble, and she joined him twenty minutes later. If he hadn't watched it happen, he wouldn't have known the men were dead.

"Come on," she told the kids. "We're going to give you some medicine that will get rid of the stuff those bad people made you swallow, and then we're going to find your parents."

He stayed out of the way while she worked. Cern had him finishing up Archmage Veran's orders anyway, so he had plenty to occupy his attention. There was no way he could have done it on his own, but he was able to follow directions, and Cern kept a close eye on the process. It only took an hour to make them. Nym wrapped them in a thermal barrier to keep them frozen, and then he waited for Analia to come back from taking the kids to her friends.

When she did, the first thing she said was, "You're leaving now?"

"Soon," Nym said, tossing a glance over at the boxed-up freezing brain twisters. "I've got a delivery to make."

"And then you're going off on your bug hunt in the uninhabited frozen lands of the north."

Nym could hear the accusation in her tone. She still wanted him to stay and help. "I am. A few weeks or a month is a small price to pay to finally have this aging curse broken."

"That's . . . understandable," she said. "There's a lot of work to be done here, good people who need help. This city isn't really as good a place as it looks. Once you start living here, you see all the awful things, all the time, everywhere. It's hard. I could use your help making it a little bit better when you're done."

Nym didn't really know what to say about that. He had his own things going on and didn't really want to get involved. "I'll think about it," he said. Maybe he'd change his mind, but he didn't see that happening. That wasn't to say he wouldn't help if something landed right in front of him, just that it wasn't really in his nature to go out of his way looking for problems to solve.

"You do that."

"Are you going to be okay?"

"I'm fine," she said.

"Analia."

She stilled and looked at him. "What?"

"I remember the first time I killed someone," Nym said. "He was in the process of trying to murder me, not for anything I'd done, but just because I was in his way. It was . . . easy . . . in the moment. But it was harder later. I lost some sleep thinking about that. Doing it the way you did, doing it cold, against people who couldn't fight back . . . I think that's going to take some time to process."

"Thanks for the unasked-for advice," she said acidly. "Why don't you just get going now?"

"I . . . Yeah. I'll be back in a month or so. Don't get yourself killed and don't let yourself get sucked into this thing. This will drag you under and drown you. The more you kill, the easier it gets to keep justifying it."

"How would you know anyway?"

Nym didn't even know how many people he'd killed. The worst were the soldiers who'd begged him to end it when they'd been caught by geists. Senman was another one that still haunted him, even now. Sometimes he wondered if the wights counted. They'd been people once. Maybe it was possible to reverse that. Surely they deserved to have their lives back. They hadn't asked to be turned into monsters.

Reviving them seemed like something an ascendant could do. He wasn't sure if it made a difference that he hadn't been the one who'd killed them. If he had the power to bring them back, maybe that should weigh on him too that he hadn't. Of course, he didn't have that power, but maybe if he'd been more focused on reaching the fifth layer and recovering all his lost magic, he could have.

Even now, he was putting it off. He knew why. If he could break the aging curse without going to the cube, he might never have to actually recover those memories. Niramyn was a psycho, and Nym didn't want to become him again. Everything he was doing was just a stall to put that off, but he was afraid that someday, something would show up that was too powerful to fight without becoming an Exarch again.

He took a deep breath and shook his head. "I know," he said quietly. "Goodbye, Analia. Don't lose yourself. I'll see you soon."

"Bye," she said. She sounded angry.

Nym picked up the box of freezing brain twisters and constructed the teleportation spell. It felt like there was more to say, but he didn't know what those words were. He suspected she didn't either. Her time in Shu-Ain had changed her and was going to continue changing her. He hoped that when she left, she was still a person he recognized.

The teleport spell caught hold of him and stretched over the box in his arms. Everything went black for a moment, and when the world returned, he was standing in Archmage Veran's sanctum. With another heavy sigh, he trudged to the lab to tuck away the party treats in cold storage. Then he made himself comfortable in the library and continued his preparations for his trip to the northlands.

The longer he sat there, the less it felt like he got anything done. Try as he might, he couldn't keep his mind on the task in front of him. He ended up sitting there, his head in his hands and the open book in front of him forgotten. It was long past dark, and still he sat there in the artificial light of the library, unaware of the hours ticking by.

When the sun rose again, he still hadn't discovered any solutions to his problems.

CHAPTER TWENTY-ONE

T hat's one tricky spell," Nym said.

"I built it myself," Archmage Veran told him. "I don't think I've ever taught it to anyone else."

The spell in question, a long-distance scry, was without a doubt the most complicated spell Nym had ever seen. He'd thought the golem series were bad, but this was so much worse. It was like mashing together teleportation, the detection portion of a communication spell, and various bits and bobs of vision-enhancing magic together into one spell, and then stuffing that inside a framework for a golem spell that had the animating guts ripped out.

In theory, he was projecting his consciousness over hundreds or thousands of miles and forming a sort of spiritual body to see with. Then that spirit anchored the spells for vision and connected back to his mind to let him know what it found and receive directions on how to move. All of that was to say that it was a nightmare to put together fast enough to keep it from failing and required three different intent filters to be held simultaneously since not even his soul well could hold all the arcana needed at once.

The insane arcana input was a limiting factor for most mages; it would require them to work together in a ritualized version of the spell. Since it wasn't designed as a ritual though, it would need to be overhauled if it was going to be used that way. That meant Nym could do it, and obviously Archmage Veran himself could cast the spell, but there were probably only a handful of people in the rest of the world with the capability to channel that much arcana that quickly.

Of course, Nym needed the ability to see arcana through his scrying spell. Now that he finally knew how to make that work, he wasn't going to give it up. That made his version even trickier, but he managed it. Now he had long-range communication, with one person at least, and scrying; he'd advanced his third-circle healing to the point where it could put together anything that might reasonably go wrong with a body; and he was working on his diagnostics spells to actually tell him what was wrong.

Additionally, he'd learned as much as he could about scarabs and curse breaking, studied maps of the northlands, and been loaned a few potent tools by an archmage. He'd also gone out of his way to learn some of the standard versions of heating spells that didn't require constant upkeep. Nym was about as ready as he could possibly be.

Well, that wasn't true. He was still working on breaking into the fifth layer. Boring through the fourth was a slow, tedious process, one that he kept getting bogged down on. The deeper he burrowed, the harder it got to force the conduit through another revolution. He'd been told by his past self to use an arcana-flushed tip to punch straight through, but Nym had nowhere near that kind of willpower.

Instead he was borrowing his mentor's method: a slow bore. Archmage Veran could pierce the fourth layer with about thirty seconds of calm focus. Nym could pierce . . . maybe half of it, with about two hours of work. Then his willpower started to flag and the fourth layer pushed him back out. It was actively fighting against him the entire time he was boring through it, like it was under pressure and wouldn't tolerate an intrusion.

Clearly speed would be key. The harder and faster he pushed, the quicker he'd burrow through it. But Nym just didn't have the mental strength to do it, not yet. Archmage Veran wasn't surprised that he hadn't managed to accomplish it. It was something almost no human achieved, and to expect to have mastered it with barely a few months to work on it was foolish.

"With this, I believe you are as prepared as you can be," Archmage Veran said.

"I think so," Nym agreed. "Good night's sleep, bagful of rations, and I'll head north first thing in the morning."

"A word of unsolicited advice for you. Don't be afraid to retreat if you find yourself in a dangerous situation without a clear plan of action. You have all the tools you need to know what you're walking into and determine how best to handle it."

"That's good advice," Nym said. "Thanks."

"You are quite welcome. Well then, it's quite late, and I think both of us need our rest. Finals start next week, and even though I don't teach any classes directly, it somehow still means quite a bit of extra work for me."

Nym appeared out of nowhere in the open sky above Glacial Valley. He spent a moment orienting himself, then pulled the fox ring out of his pocket and slipped it onto his finger.

[Hello? Can you hear me?] he sent out through the ring.

There was no answer.

[Fox? Are you there?]

Nym waited for a few minutes and tried again. Then he started flying around, shooting out another message every ten miles or so. Eventually, after an hour of looking, he got a response.

[What do you want? I am trying to sleep here!]

The fox appeared in midair in front of him, though Nym immediately recognized him as an illusion. He looked supremely annoyed as he glared at Nym. "Sorry, I didn't mean to wake you. You said to come back if I decided I was willing to clear out the scarab infestation."

[Oh, that? I took care of that two weeks ago.]

"I . . . You . . . Oh. I guess you don't need any help then. I'll just give you this ring back and go?"

[After waking me up, you think I'm just going to let you leave? Oh no, little half-scendant. That's not how this is going to happen at all.]

Arcana rushed out of the illusion and grabbed hold of Nym. He tried to teleport, but the spell fizzled under the fox's magical assault. A moment later, he was in an underground den, if anything that had vaulted ceilings could be called that. The real mystical fox sat in front of him, still looking grumpy as he perched on a gigantic cushion.

Then his sneer faded into a grin, and he laughed. "Gotcha," he said.

Nym, his heart still beating a million times a minute, stood there wide-eyed. "What?"

"I was just messing with you because you interrupted my nap. I still need the scarabs cleaned up. You're going to handle it?"

Nym stared at the fox blankly while his brain tried to catch up. Finally he said, "I thought you were going to try to kill me."

"Please, if I wanted to kill you, there would be no try to it, and you would never know it was coming until it had already happened."

"I'm already regretting this."

"So you don't want me to break that curse on you?"

Nym shrugged. "Can you?"

"Of course I can! I said I could, didn't I?"

"You might be surprised to learn that I didn't necessarily believe every word out of your mouth to be the honest truth."

The fox snickered. "Good. That means you're smarter than you look."

Nym wasn't sure if he was supposed to be offended by that. Before he could figure it out, the fox went on. "Yes, I can. I can even do it without hurting you in any way, shape, or form. You've got a few memory-lock curses on you that I couldn't do unaided without some risk, but the aging curse is simple enough. Any sixth-layer caster could manage it."

"There aren't too many of those just lazing around," Nym said.

"Lucky for you that you met me then," the fox said with a smirk.

"Fine, let's make it official then. I'll eliminate the scarabs and find the cursed talisman that's making them. In return, you will break the curse that is making me age rapidly."

"This I do agree to abide by," the fox spoke, arcana infused into its voice. "This I do so swear to honor. This I am bound and held to."

The words had the feel of a ritual to them. Nym saw a stirring of arcana surround the fox as he spoke, something nebulous that was there one instant, gone the next. He sat upright on his cushion, looking down at Nym, and waited.

"Um. This I do agree to abide by. This I do so swear to honor. This I am bound and held to." Nym repeated.

Again there was a swirling of arcana around him, something more solid this time. He could see the links between him and the fox. It tightened around them and settled into Nym's skin, and he could all of a sudden feel the pact between them. It wasn't something he'd expected, but since he'd had no intentions of not honoring it, it was a nice little bit of insurance.

"Excellent. Now, let me get a good look at you. This will be delicate. Come, have a seat right here."

A chair materialized out of nothing between them. Blinking, Nym sat down in it. Even though he knew it was an illusion, it appeared as solid and real as any other chair he'd ever seen. "How are your illusions so strong?" he asked.

"Perhaps it is not an illusion. Or perhaps it is your mind that is fooled into believing a chair is there, when there is really nothing at all. After all, what is the nature of reality to a being such as myself? It is a malleable thing, easily shaped according to my will and desire. Now, hold still."

"What exactly are you doing?"

The fox rolled his eyes. "What did I just swear I would do?"

"Wait, already?" Nym asked. "I thought you'd wait until I was done."

"Feh. You swore the pact. You would not be able to do that if you did not wholeheartedly plan on honoring your portion of the bargain. For me, this is a simple matter that will only take a few minutes to discharge. Now, be quiet so I can concentrate."

Nym sat there while the fox hopped down from his seat and circled around him. With each lap, the fox grew bigger and the shadows around him shifted more violently. By the ninth lap, he was twice as tall as Nym and the darkness seemed to frame itself around the fox.

"Be unbound by this curse. Let it be cast off, let it fall away. May it be uprooted from your being wholly, and may your spirit be brightened by escaping its shadow."

Each word resonated with arcana, a sort of audible spell construct that Nym didn't fully understand. It enveloped Nym fully, not just in his physical being, but to his soul well and his mind. The sound got louder, and the arcana pulsed through him until he could hear nothing else, feel nothing else.

Then, with a great tearing sensation, the feeling disappeared. With it gone, he felt a void in himself, something hollow that had been ripped away. Nym looked down at himself in wonder. "I feel . . . light. I could practically float away," he said.

"Yes, well, that's to be expected. It was a heavy curse. It tied up much of your body and mind's resources maintaining it. Your magic should be significantly easier without it."

"What does that mean, easier?" Nym opened a conduit to the second layer and pulled in arcana. It rushed in, faster and smoother than ever, and it just kept coming and coming. More poured in, more than he'd ever held. "God, that is amazing."

The fox rolled his eyes. "Go play somewhere else, half-scendant. I am going back to sleep. Come find me when you've completed your half of the pact."

And with that, Nym was back in the sky over Glacial Valley, falling rapidly and laughing all the way. He caught himself on a current of arcana, barely even formed into something like a flight spell, and allowed it to whisk his body away through the air.

CHAPTER TWENTY-TWO

Nym had known that, intellectually, he'd be stronger without the curse. He understood that they worked by setting down roots in the victim's body that drained arcana away whenever any was pulled in, and they were impossible to starve out. They stuffed themselves with massive reservoirs that, if sufficiently drained, would force a conduit to open so they could refill, regardless of how much damage it might do to a victim.

He hadn't known it at the time, but he'd probably come perilously close to having his soul well damaged even further by the curses he suffered from when he hadn't cast any spells for a few months. When he'd been studying up on curses in preparation for this job, he'd been appalled to find out just how much damage a curse could do to a soul well if it forcibly hijacked it to feed itself. None of the healers he'd talked to had ever even mentioned it.

Nym had experienced a version of curse removal when he'd had a geas dissolved, but it hadn't really had a noticeable impact, though at least he now understood exactly why he'd felt a bit lighter with it gone. He'd attributed it to eliminating some stress from his life. He knew better after reading up on curses. It was literally the removal of something weighing down his magic.

He had expected something similar when he finally managed to break the aging curse, but he couldn't have been more wrong. The speed at which arcana flowed through his conduits now, and the amount that he could hold, had both increased dramatically. Nym wasn't sure if the quantity of arcana he could channel without resting had risen to match, but even if it hadn't, he'd still just been handed a massive increase in his explosive power.

It made him wonder exactly how much of his strength was still tied up in the memory curses affecting him. If they were anything like the aging curse, he could actually be twice as powerful as he thought he was. That was kind of scary when he thought about it. He was already far stronger than almost anyone he'd ever met. If he was only half as powerful as an ascendant who hadn't yet reached the fifth layer should be, how unreal would a full ascendant be?

Then he shuddered. If his foxy new friend wasn't afraid of an ascendant, how powerful was he? Why did he even need Nym's help? This should be something he could clear up with a flick of his ear. It didn't matter at this point, really. Nym had already said he would do it, but it was something worth considering for the future.

Nym could have teleported over to the Garden of Winter, but he wanted to push his flight spell and see how fast he could get it going now. After a few minutes, he was happy to say the answer was very, very fast. He felt he'd hit the limits of what the spell could offer him in terms of speed at this point when he shoved so much arcana into it that it had started to break apart under the strain.

The garden was as he remembered, though maybe with another fifteen or twenty feet of expansion at the edges. The miasma of the curse still coated the place, though it shifted about a lot less. The number of pixies that lived there had thinned considerably, probably from both his own attack on the place and from the curse just generally draining them until they had nothing left.

Nym flew to the flower that the cursed arcana originated from and unceremoniously burned it to a crisp. Arcana burst out of it at random, great gushing geysers that shot off in different directions, sometimes even at him. He smoothly deflected it away and let it disperse into the air. It would break down naturally with time now that he'd cut off the source, and he hoped to do the same with the rest of the garden.

The flower was a major hub of cursed arcana, but not the only one. The scarabs themselves were little curse generators, crawling around and infecting everything they touched. Killing them would be the hard part of the task.

With the pixies all dead or dying, it seemed reasonable to assume that the Garden of Winter would soon follow it. That having been said, if he could manage to preserve the area as it was while still killing the infection, he was all for that. Maybe more pixies would show up and carry on with their work, and there'd still be a garden for the next class of Academy students to visit.

When he'd discussed it with Archmage Veran, they'd discussed two spells. The first was a simple bomb. It was a massive ball of arcana, hugely inefficient, that exploded and wiped out all life within the radius of the blast. It had the advantage of only targeting living things, so it wouldn't destroy the land itself, but that didn't differentiate between animal living things and plant living things.

If he used it here, it would completely annihilate the Garden of Winter. Or, well, more realistically, if he used it ten or twelve times, it would cover most of the garden. The radius was only about a hundred feet, after all. Full coverage over such a large area would be an effort in and of itself. It would also be complete overkill.

The second spell was something infinitely more targeted, but also much more taxing and slower. It was one part scrying, one part telekinetic force and would seek out each individual scarab, destroy it, and move on. By Nym's estimates, it would take days, possibly even as long as a week, of just sitting there channeling it before it finished.

That process would be sped up considerably with parallel processing allowing him to run multiple instances of the same spell at a time, but it still promised to be a long and boring campaign. He was hoping there weren't more than four or five hubs to crush and that he could use the bomb spell on the other ones.

Before he sat down and started working on the garden, he sent his scry anchor out to follow the root network back to its source. Following it was the force-crush spell, which killed hundreds and hundreds of scarabs crawling along the roots. Nym followed it straight north for perhaps twenty or so miles and found another infestation that had broken ground.

This one was an empty grotto filled with nothing but scarabs and snow. He dropped three overlapping bombs on the area to clear it out. Each one detonated with explosive force, killing 90 percent of the scarabs aboveground. Nym followed it up with an hour of targeted extermination to make sure he wiped out the survivors before he resumed the hunt.

The plan was to go from node to node until he found the curse. He would perform damage control along the way, but anywhere that took more than an hour or two to clean up would be bypassed for the time being. It was more important to cut the scarabs off at their source so they couldn't keep spreading than it was to clean up each individual location.

Things did not go as planned. Nym found another hub, and another, and another. And each hub he went to had at least two or three connections leading to new hubs. By that evening, he'd given up on doing any sort of cleansing and was grimly mapping out the whole spread of corruption. It was significantly worse than he'd expected.

For one thing, it went hundreds of miles in every direction. How it had gone on unchecked for so long was easy enough to see: nothing with what could be called an advanced civilization lived up in the frozen white north.

That wasn't to say there was nothing alive. He saw plenty of things. He even got excited for a minute when he found a pack of snow wolves, thinking he'd run into his old friends. They weren't the same pack, of course. The odds of that were astronomical. But for a few seconds, he'd hoped.

He also saw a hive of ice worms wrapped up tight around an open pit. They were ironically one of the only areas completely clear of corrupted scarabs. The worms must have attacked them on sight, but the scarabs could apparently fight back and had the whole hive penned in. They were holding their territory but not expanding it.

Somehow, Nym didn't have it in him to feel sorry for them.

There were other things too, lone predators and small packs of prey animals. They were few and far between though, and there wasn't much of anything he'd consider intelligent enough to have a conversation, snow wolves aside. Nym worked through the night, ignoring the cold and darkness to keep mapping out the infestation.

By the time the sun came up, he thought he'd determined more or less how widespread it was. If he assumed the corruption stemmed up from a central point and spread in every direction at the same speed, he'd narrowed his search down to maybe fifty to a hundred square miles. That was still a lot, but far, far better than the alternative.

It would be the work of a lifetime to clear out every little spot with scarabs infesting it by himself. He would need to approach that with a different strategy, but for now he had a goal in sight. He picked a good spot, a mountain with a sharply sloping peak, to use as his teleportation point, spent some time making sure he knew it well enough to come back, and teleported back to the sanctum to get some rest.

"Out working late," Archmage Veran commented when Nym appeared. "Did you find it?"

"Not yet. It's bigger than we expected. A lot bigger."

Nym outlined how far he'd flown looking for the edges of the infestation and his logic in pinpointing where the center might be. Archmage Veran produced a map out of nowhere and laid it out across the table, which he promptly marked up with a grease pencil under Nym's direction. "Incredible," he said. "That may be the biggest infestation in all recorded history. You do know how to find things that will make the history books, don't you?"

"Not on purpose," Nym said with a scowl. "Clearing this out one site at a time isn't a viable strategy, not for one person at least. Got any thoughts on something that can match this kind of scale?"

"I'm afraid I don't, not offhand, but I'll do a bit of research while you rest. This will be a problem for after you've gone after the source of the curse anyway if it turns out they don't die on their own. We have some time to come up with a solution still."

Nym did have time, now that he thought about it. He had probably an extra eighty or ninety years of time now. Actually, that was probably a low estimate. If he managed to break through the fourth layer and learn pinnacle spells, he would likely have even more years. And that wasn't much of an if. It was going to happen, and soon. Now that he was no longer laboring under the aging curse, he was eager to try his hand at forging that conduit again.

That would be a project for later. For now, he needed food and then sleep. And when he woke back up, the hunt would continue. After that was done though, who knew what he'd accomplish? He would certainly need the extra power if he was going to cover thousands of miles of land on a genocidal extermination campaign.

He wondered if his new fox friend had any ideas. Nym made a mental note to ask when he woke up, just before he fell into his bed and passed out.

CHAPTER TWENTY-THREE

Nym floated about fifty feet off the ground and scried deep into the earth. He'd spent the day tracing connections in his target area, going deeper and deeper toward the center, which was apparently far, far underground. That was annoying, if he was being honest. He was sick of having to go underground to resolve problems. It would be nice if just once, some ancient, evil, cursed thing could exist in plain sight.

He wasn't surprised though. It spread primarily through the underground channels that either naturally existed or that the scarabs themselves created, like pipes pumped full of arcana. The difference was that instead of trying to kill him and raise him as an undead, the scarabs just spread a contagion that made anything nearby sicken and die.

Admittedly, that wasn't much of a difference as far as the living people were concerned, but it did make it easier to reduce casualties since the scarabs weren't running anyone down trying to kill them. Though in all fairness, there weren't really any people there, and they would attack someone if they happened to find a person who was uncorrupted.

Nym was sure he'd found the talisman finally. Of course, he'd been sure the last time too, and the time before that. Every time he thought he'd found the center, there'd been another link to the chain. Now though, everything had circled around this one spot.

He just needed to find the talisman, which was something of a problem since it was apparently really, really deep underground. He'd gone down a few hundred feet already and hadn't found the source yet. If he didn't hit it soon, he was going to bump up against the range limit of his scry anchor, which was a problem since nothing else he had could see through solid objects.

Then the worst-case scenario came true: he found the bottom, and the talisman wasn't there. It was just a spot where the paths intersected and tangled up with one another. There was nothing for him to do but kill the scarabs down there and keep looking. He even flew down to stand on the frozen dirt to make sure there was nothing lower, as deep down as he could go.

"It's got to be here," he muttered. "Where else could it be?"

The infestation certainly looked like it had started there, but when he thought about it, that didn't make sense. The talisman would have to have been hundreds of feet underground, and there were no caves or tunnels that he'd found. It could have been buried, but he couldn't think of any reason to bury it so deep, and even if it had been, who'd dug it back up?

Maybe it was just a coincidental intersection that happened to be near the center of the area he'd mapped out. Or maybe he'd mapped it out wrong. Either way, short of actually excavating a quarter-mile-deep mine shaft, he'd checked it as thoroughly as possible. There had to be something he was missing.

Nym flew back up and sat down on a cushion of air surrounded by a thick bubble to block the wind. He pulled out the map he'd been scribbling over to note locations. He knew it wasn't entirely accurate, neither the map itself nor his notations. Whoever had drawn it had made some generous assumptions about the landscape, and no part of it was to scale. Nym had done his best to compensate for those errors, but he was tempted to draw his own map instead.

Being able to stand three miles up in the sky and see fine details on the ground would probably make for a more accurate map than what he had. Adding long-range scrying to that would make it even better. It didn't need to be pretty or finely detailed for his purposes either. It just needed to have everything spaced out properly. The downside of that was that he'd probably have to redo all his work from yesterday.

He pulled out a fresh sheet of paper and started marking it down as best he could while comparing it against the notes he'd put on the old map. It was going to be a long, tedious day.

Three days later, Nym found he had new respect for cartographers. Maps were time-consuming to make, even if he wasn't worried about them being pretty. He'd finally finished recreating the northlands, then spent a few hours copying that over a second time just in case. Only then did he start marking known infestation sites and the paths that connected them together.

Once he saw it all on a map that was accurately sized and scaled, it was obvious what the problem was. He'd been completely off on a center point because the old map had gotten the coast wrong by more than a hundred miles. Nym's surveying painted a picture that pointed toward the water, or more specifically, toward an old ship locked in the ice just off the coast.

Nym flew over the frozen landscape until he reached the ship, then sent a short-range scrying spell down into it. It was half rotted and half frozen, with vast empty holds and a number of corpses entombed in the ice. They had bronzed skin and thick black hair in a way that reminded him of the Byramese, but it wasn't quite the same. He also didn't recognize the ship type from his time on their docks, but he didn't trust his knowledge of ships enough to be able to say if that meant anything.

Wherever they were from, it looked like the ship had been stuck there for years. Ice had grown up over the sides, and the weather had destroyed the sails. A number of holes had formed in the hull, and the only thing that kept it above the water was the fact that it was literally anchored in the ice. He didn't think he could physically get into the interior without resorting to magic to break through all the ice clogging up the place.

Fortunately, he didn't need to in order to scout it out. Unfortunately, there was no talisman in there. He hadn't expected there to be, since there were no scarabs either, but he'd been hoping that his days of mapping things out had pointed him in the right direction. It seemed like he'd missed the mark again, unless . . .

Nym constructed his long-range communication spell and linked it to Archmage Veran. *[Do you have a minute?]*

Nothing came back for about thirty seconds, then he heard the archmage's voice in his head. *[I can spare a few. What do you need?]*

Nym sent an image of the map and the ship through the link and said, *[I traced the center point using a new map that's more accurate. This ship should be it, but there's nothing here. I wanted to get a second opinion on the origin of the corruption, and also, if I'm right, what are the odds that the talisman is still moving around?]*

[One moment.]

While Archmage Veran studied the information he'd sent over, Nym started examining the area around the ship. He sent his scry anchor as deep into the water as he could, just to confirm the talisman hadn't fallen through one of the many, many holes in the ship before they'd all iced over. The ice was a hundred feet thick at least under the ship, a fact which further confirmed to Nym that it had been there for a very long time.

Below that was nothing but darkness, like an endless void stretching out forever, its secrets hidden from even his magic. Nym sent the scry anchor around in an ever-widening circle, trying to find anything besides ice in the water, and when he finally did, it was something so massive that he couldn't even begin to guess what it was. It had skin and muscles. It was alive. That was all he could tell and probably all he needed to know.

[If the bearer of the talisman was still alive, the curse would not have spread like it has. You would be able to trace a line of their movements with smaller offshoots left in their wake. We can safely assume the talisman is not moving. That being said, I agree with your assessment that it should be somewhere in or nearby this ship.]

[It's not, or at least if it is, it's not something my scrying is picking up. There's nothing out here but ice and snow and water that's at least a thousand feet deep, probably much more. I don't even see any arcana here leading to the ship. It's nowhere nearby.]

[It's possible that the curse bearer was still alive when the ship got stuck here and set out on foot. You may find the talisman somewhere within a few miles of your current location, possibly buried under the ice and snow.]

That was going to be a hard search. He'd only covered as much ground as he had by following the corruption pathways, by tracing them back to the center. Supposedly, the scarabs would alter the landscape and kill off anything living there. The problem was that there was nothing living around here to kill! They were just spreading out, taking up more and more landmass and accomplishing nothing.

[Wherever the talisman is, I should be able to find it by following the corrupted arcana trails leading away, right?]

[That is correct.]

[Then this ship is a dead end. There's no sign of corrupted arcana or any scarabs here, let alone the source talisman. Maybe it came to the northlands on this ship and whoever was carrying it disembarked years ago and died elsewhere. But either way, I should still be able to track it back to the source, and I'm not seeing it. Is it possible that something is hiding it? What if at one point in time it was spreading freely, and something else already contained it?]

[In that case, you could clean up the infestation and nothing else would grow to take its place, but the scarabs themselves would have already died off without the talisman to replenish their numbers unless it was removed just recently. If that were the case, you might never find the talisman. It might not even be there anymore.]

Nym thought that over for a minute. It was going to be the work of years to clean everything up, and there were so many already. But if the source had been cut off, they couldn't keep spreading. There wouldn't be any new scarabs to infest new places, and he knew that wasn't correct. He'd seen the proof at the Garden of Winter, where the corruption had continued to push outward from the center.

[I haven't read anything about an infestation like this being able to spread without the source creating more and more scarabs. If the source is sealed up, it couldn't spread, but it still is. So it can't be sealed. It's just . . . hidden, somehow, perhaps some sort of antiscrying ward?]

Archmage Veran didn't answer him immediately. *[I'm sorry, but I'm out of time. It sounds like you've got a few good leads to explore. I trust you'll be able to follow them to a successful conclusion. Have some confidence in yourself to resolve this.]*

And then the connection broke. Nym sat there in the air, somewhat annoyed at how unhelpful his mentor had been. Then again, this was Nym's problem to solve, and it had nothing to do with the archmage. He'd already provided a lot of guidance in the form of new spells, reference material, and even some enchanted tools.

Nym was going to figure it out, but he would be doing the legwork on his own. The situation might not have been what they'd originally expected, but he wasn't going to let that stop him. Now, he just needed to figure out which way to go next.

CHAPTER TWENTY-FOUR

Two weeks of searching and scrying and hunting, two weeks of frustration and annoyance, two weeks of failure. At this point, Nym had run out of possible answers and was revisiting his most basic assumptions, trying to determine where he'd gone wrong. And he was coming up with nothing.

The only thing he had left to conclusively disprove was the idea that there had been a talisman generating the cursed scarabs originally but that someone else had already found it and removed it. Even that idea didn't fit all the facts, specifically that there was still more corrupted arcana flooding the infestation sites, but it didn't seem to be coming from anywhere.

There was one fact that supported the idea: no new infestations had popped up. The ones that already existed were stable and growing, but the overall network wasn't expanding anymore. His most recent theory was that the original talisman had been removed somehow but that the scarabs had found some new source of power that they corrupted and used to fuel their growth.

It seemed impossible to him, and Archmage Veran had confirmed that he'd never heard of anything like that, but Nym had nothing else to explain what he'd found. It also didn't explain the growth patterns, which behaved exactly as they expected if they assumed their initial ideas were correct.

And finally, after two weeks of pounding his head against the proverbial wall, Nym had a new lead. Operating under the idea that the corruption had started to spread near the old ship he'd discovered but was now being powered from a new location, he'd started gathering information about how fast things were growing in an attempt to follow the trail of the most rapidly expanding infestations back to a new source.

All of that led him to a lonely little corner of the world, a great basin of ice easily a mile thick with another four or five miles of open air underneath it. The whole slab of ice sealing it off from the world was probably a hundred miles across, though he hadn't taken the time to measure it accurately. That time had been better spent on making a lot of on-the-fly modifications to scry through that entire shielding ice layer. Since everything he'd put together pointed him to this location, he felt it was time well spent and persevered in his modification attempts.

With that perseverance came, eventually, victory. His scry anchor had lost almost all its flexibility in exchange for greater range, but this new version could just barely make it past the ice. That was all Nym needed though, to be able to scry through the ice so he could teleport down there.

He didn't jump straight there, of course. He flew laps around the ice, scrying from different locations so that he could get a more complete picture of what he was dealing with, then layered up with a thermal barrier, a hyperkinetic barrier, a camouflage screen shaped into a full-body orb, and a net of fresh air, and one part of his mind held a lightning bolt ready to fire.

Only then did he cast teleport to bring him under the ice. He came out of the spell so close that his head nearly bumped against the ceiling and gazed out at the basin. Once, many years ago, it had probably been a deep lake, or maybe it would have been better described as an inland sea. Most of the water was gone now, with only small pockets left here or there.

There was no natural light through over a mile of ice, of course, but there were various spots of glowing lights below him anyway. It wasn't enough to illuminate much of anything to him, instead making him feel like he was looking down at a new, unknown set of stars. Perfect vision didn't need light to see by though, so the darkness hid nothing from him.

Now that he was under the ice, he could see the landscape easily. It was mostly bare rock, or rather lichen-covered rock, as the only plant life growing was that that didn't need any light. There were animals, but they were the kind that sat immobile and waited for something to come by and be snapped up. Some of them were quite large, big enough to swallow him whole at least, but Nym had no intention of getting near them.

The one thing that stood out to him as truly interesting was a thousand-foot-tall slender needle of metal that rose out of the water remaining in the bottom of the basin. To his eyes, it glowed with arcana, practically blazed. It was probably the strongest source of arcana he had ever seen, and he included the likes of Archmage Veran and the mystical fox in that comparison. Whatever it was, it was far, far beyond mortal magic.

That didn't mean it had anything to do with the cursed-scarab infestation sweeping the northlands, but it was damn suspicious. Something was down here, doing something magical, and at a level beyond anything he'd ever experienced. It put Nym into a bit of a quandary. He was approaching something that could be significantly more dangerous than even the tear in the veil had been, and the smart thing to do was to forget he'd ever seen it and leave.

But he had agreed to find the cause of the scarab infestation, and everything he'd been able to find had pointed him in this direction. If this was the source, then he had no choice but to keep exploring. He would do so carefully and perhaps see about convincing the fox to come and help. He would probably know better than Nym what he was looking at anyway.

That seemed like a much better plan to Nym. His decision made, he cast a tele-portation spell to leave. Instead of triggering, it unraveled the moment he finished it.

Nym frowned and stared off into space, mentally reviewing what he'd done wrong. He had never botched a teleport before, not unless something was interfering with it.

It was almost like he was caught inside a teleportation ward, but there couldn't possibly be one big enough to encompass the whole basin. He glanced down at the needle again. Maybe there could be. Something that strong would defy the limits of mortal magic. Perhaps that was how it stayed hidden, by trapping anything that came near.

If he couldn't teleport out, that still didn't mean he was stuck. A mile of ice was a lot, but he could theoretically burrow all the way back to the surface. If he was lucky, he wouldn't need to go that far. He'd just check every few hundred feet to see if he'd escaped the outer bounds of the needle's teleportation-blocking effect.

Except when he tried to break the ice, he found his magic slipping away from it. Elemental water did nothing, but perhaps that was to be expected in the presence of something so powerful. It was mere second-layer arcana, after all. Even his third-circle spells failed though. Heat didn't cause it to melt, and greater telekinesis couldn't even grab onto it, let alone rip chunks out of it. Lightning bolts flashed through the darkness and rebounded away.

As each spell failed one after another, Nym started to grow concerned. Eventually, he ran out of ideas and decided to call for help. He worked the long-range communication spell that connected him to Archmage Veran, only to have it fizzle out after failing to find a target. The spell was successful; it just couldn't figure out where the archmage was.

That shouldn't be possible unless he was dead or had physically changed so much the spell no longer recognized him. He supposed the archmage might have just lost an arm or a leg in the last few hours, but that seemed unlikely. That was probably more interference from the needle's magic. Nym was worried now. It almost felt like the needle was deliberately thwarting his attempts to leave.

That thought gave him pause. As far as he was aware, a sapient magical item was impossible, but he had to throw out all the rules as he knew them at this point. What was impossible for humans could be trivial for ascendants, and this giant metal spike was definitely in the realm of ascendants. Whatever it was doing, whatever it wanted, Nym wasn't strong enough to resist it.

That was happening more and more frequently, that whole running into things that were far beyond him. He'd thought he was past that stage of his new life once he'd reached the third layer and that his progress toward the fifth layer would outpace any new threats. Running into the fox had deflated his ego, and now this thing looked to be even stronger.

He wasn't sure how he knew that; he just did. He could recognize first- or second-layer arcana, even third and fifth layer now, and he knew which was stronger by sight. Fourth was a sort of gray area, in that nobody actually used it, but he supposed he would know it if he saw it in action. The fox had been beyond fifth layer, maybe beyond whatever came after that, given its general contempt for ascendants.

The needle was beyond the fox. It was heat and light and weight all wrapped up in a glowing steel splinter that pierced through the darkness. It was the darkened sky overhead cast down below his feet. It was vast, endless, immeasurable, and unknowable.

It was terrifying.

The more Nym contemplated that needle, the less certain he was that it was even something an ascendant could have created. He couldn't even imagine the kind of power contained in it, perhaps enough to crack the world in half. Whatever being had created it and left it there must have been beyond imagining.

Idly, Nym examined the creatures that lived down in the dark, wondering if there was more to them than he'd initially suspected. Living so close to such incomprehensible power had to have some sort of an impact on them, but no, they were every bit as ordinary as he'd first concluded. They looked like and behaved like bottom-feeders, motionless, conserving energy, waiting for the next meal to get too close.

They were easy enough to dodge. Nym got as far away from the needle as possible, hoping against hope that he would outdistance it. He wasn't surprised when he failed. That thing was strong enough to reach across the planet, and if he got outside of its range, that would only be because it was deliberately limiting itself.

He found no weak points in the ice, and the stone itself was similarly reinforced. The whole basin was sealed off from the world by magic, leaving Nym to wonder how in the world he'd gotten through to begin with. It was possible the barrier was one-way only, freely allowing in anything but letting nothing go.

Having finally exhausted every single idea he could come up with, there was really only one single possibility left: approach the needle and see what it is. If he was lucky, he'd find a way to turn it off. If he was really lucky, he'd confirm that it was somehow powering the corrupted-scarab arcana and end that as well. Realistically, neither of those seemed likely.

He wouldn't find out by floating up near the ice though. Nym flew down through the darkness, his magic giving him sight. He came to a stop a few feet away from the tip of the needle, which was glowing a brilliant, eye-searing pinkish white. And though it was hard to see, there was movement to it. It was alive in some way.

The glow intensified, blinding him, and the last thing he saw was a tendril lashing out to touch him. Then it disappeared completely, and he found himself standing in a room of lustrous, gleaming metal.

A . . . thing stood before him. It looked like a statue of a woman carved from marble but so lifelike that it wouldn't surprise Nym if it started moving. At least, that's what he thought until it turned to look at him. It turned out it was quite surprising indeed.

"Welcome," the statue said in a neutral, pleasant tone. "How may I assist you, Exarch?"

CHAPTER TWENTY-FIVE

Nym's brain stopped working for a second, then started working far too fast. The statue knew who he was, which meant his cover was blown, that he had exactly however many seconds before it reported back to whoever owned the place he was standing in before some ascendant found him. His options were to fight or run. Given everything else he'd found and the absurd levels of magical power on display, he doubted he could so much as scratch the statue.

At the same time, he already knew that running was futile. He hadn't been able to escape prior to being pulled into the needle, or whatever it had done. Maybe if he was lucky, it had transferred him out of the basin and he could flee. Quickly, Nym wove a teleportation spell together, only for it to fizzle out again.

"Are you alright, Exarch?" the statue asked. "Your heart rate has risen tremendously in the last few seconds."

"I . . . I don't know," Nym said. If he couldn't leave, the next best option was to fish for information. "Can you tell me where I am? And how do you know me?"

"Certainly. This is the Region Six Biocreation Research and Production Lab. I was created with the intrinsic knowledge of fourteen ascendants involved with the lab, including you as the highest-ranking member of the team."

"Wait, are you saying this is . . . my lab?"

"You could make that statement with some degree of accuracy, but I suspect some of your colleagues might disagree."

"Oh. And, I'm sorry, not to be rude, but who are you?"

"My name is Naera. I am an artificially constructed research assistant, one of fifty-seven that service this lab."

Nym's eyes widened. "Are . . . Are there any other ascendants here right now?"

"You are the first to visit in the last forty thousand cycles."

He started trying to do the mental math in his head, then gave up and asked, "How long is that?"

Naera gave a prompt, if somewhat depressing answer. "Roughly one hundred and ten years."

"And you've just been keeping this place operational by yourselves all this time?"

"Yes, though without an ascendant around to direct the research, we have accomplished very little beyond maintaining any ongoing projects. Would you like to review the progress on those projects?"

"No, I'm good. Thank you." Nym's mind was working furiously now, trying to figure out the best way to flip this from disaster to opportunity. "So, no one's been here in over a century, and nobody knows I am here right now?"

"That is correct, Exarch."

"Can you make sure none of the other ascendants find out that I'm here?"

"If that is your wish."

"It is," Nym said firmly. It seemed extremely unlikely that any other ascendants would show up, assuming he trusted Naera. He didn't really have much choice about that, considering that he couldn't actually exit on his own yet. Figuring out how to bypass whatever security measures were holding him in the lab needed to be his top priority, but maybe he could get his hands on some ascendant secrets while he was there.

"Very well. Is there anything else I can assist you with today?"

"I would like to look around," Nym said. "Can you walk with me, so I can ask questions as they come up?"

"Of course, Exarch. Assisting you is my primary purpose," Naera said.

That was kind of sad. There were other statues standing around, motionless, watching the seconds turn into days and days into years, just waiting for someone who'd long since ceased caring about their existence to come back and have a use for them again. It made for a melancholy mood as he followed Naera down a hallway.

She started giving Nym a brief explanation for each section of the lab as they walked. "This is a storage area that houses genetic samples when they're not in use being modified or combined," Naera said, pointing at one door. She gestured to another. "And here is where the infusion apparatus is set up."

"The what?" Nym asked.

"The infusion apparatus. It allows the researcher to graft spell patterns to new creatures at a genetic level so that they may be passed down to future offspring."

Nym immediately thought about the snow wolves and their mysterious Creator. It seemed very likely that the first of their species was born right here in this lab. He might even have been the one to make them. "Do you have records of all the species created?" he asked.

"The data archives are this way," Naera said. "Would you like to visit them?"

"Yes."

They changed direction, though Naera kept listing off what each room they passed was used for. Some of them were simple research and experimentation chambers, appropriately warded or otherwise protected to contain the experiments and prevent accidents from damaging the entire lab. Others were a bit more esoteric. He had no idea what a cascading temporal-probability spiral even was, let alone why it needed its own special room to contain it.

The data archives weren't anything like Nym was expecting. He'd pictured books, maybe some maps, some graphs or charts, a lot of desks and stored writing supplies. He was expecting preservation runes sprinkled liberally around the place.

Instead, there was a single pedestal in the center of an otherwise featureless room. It was square cut, about five feet tall, and capped with a floating glass ball two feet wide.

The inside of that ball was a mesmerizing series of lights moving in seemingly random directions. Nym stared at for a minute, just watching the ball, until Naera cleared her throat and said, "Is there a problem, Exarch?"

"I— No, I'm fine. I was just appreciating this." He waved his hand at the glass ball. Then he looked around and said, "How do I get the information out of it?"

Naera blinked and looked down at Nym. "The protocols have not changed. Just form a data conduit to the repository, and it will help you find whatever you're looking for."

Nym wasn't sure what a data conduit was, but he was good at making regular conduits. He reached out mentally, the same way he would if he was trying to connect to another layer of reality, except focused on the glass sphere. Something reached back and grasped at his fumbling attempt. It completed the connection, and Nym found himself somewhere else.

It looked just like that empty white void he'd entered when Niramyn's recorded image had explained what was going on, except that this time, the sphere was floating in front of him. "Hello, Exarch Niramyn. Would you like to link your assistant to this session?" a voice with no apparent source said.

"Yes?"

"Very well."

Naera appeared next to the sphere. She glanced at it briefly, then turned to face Nym. "What are you looking for, Exarch?"

"A species of wolves made within the last three hundred years or so. They would have spell patterns related to reshaping snow and surviving in cold-weather climates."

Dozens of papers appeared in the air and filled Nym's view. There were complex spell constructs, charts measuring population levels over the years, detailed notes about modifications made, and more, all in his face and overwhelming him. Nym split his attention, sending one part of his mind to analyze the data while the other focused on Naera and the sphere.

"We made this then?" he asked.

"Yes. There have been four generations, with approximately forty years between each generation."

"That seems like a long time," Nym said. "Most animals only have a few years between generations, don't they?"

"Naturally occurring ones, yes. Most of the researchers working here decided to err on the side of longer reproductive cycles given the edge their creations would have with intrinsic spell patterns to assist them. There are a few creations that have much faster cycles, and of course there are many animal species we have data on that remain unmodified that reproduce within a year or two of being born."

"You have data on other species too? Interesting. We'll come back to that in a second," Nym said. "These snow wolves, they're supposed to pass the spell patterns down to new generations, right? Why didn't that work?"

"This was an experimental project to see if the spell patterns could grow and become stronger with each successive generation. It was deemed a failure, as the new patterns the offspring exhibited were often defective in some way, with only incidental cases even maintaining a fraction of the parents' abilities."

Nym winced. That lined up pretty well with what he'd been told when he'd talked with the matriarch. "Is there any way to . . . fix them?"

"That depends on what you would like to fix. It would be simplest to create a new species that is functionally identical without all the experimental components."

"No, no. That's no good," Nym said. "I mean I want to help the ones that are already out there."

"That is considerably more difficult but not impossible."

"Not impossible is good. So how do we do it?"

"The method with the highest probability of success would be to modify their temporal presence so that the initial research specimens released into the wild never had the experimental patterns instilled in them. They would need to be modified further as a sort of sleeper condition to avoid cascading temporal anomalies, set to trigger from a pulse signal released from this lab."

Nym understood most of that, he thought. The idea of just reaching back through time and mucking with stuff was a bit over his head though. Unless the lab could do it at his direction and without any direct intervention from him, it probably wasn't a viable solution. There was only one way to find out.

"Do you need me to do anything besides authorize this?" he asked.

"We could technically do it with the remaining arcana stores, though it would drain our reserves to dangerous levels. However, the final pulse may be an issue if you wish to preserve the anonymity of your visit. Even a targeted pulse to the test subjects would still be easily detectable."

"That would be a problem," Nym muttered. He supposed he could maybe have them do it after he left. Or if it was going to be all screwy with time anyway, it didn't much matter when exactly it happened. "Okay, so maybe we'll save that for later."

"Understood. Is there anything else you'd like to review while we're here?"

There was one other thing, now that he thought about it. It had been driven straight out of his mind with everything else going on, but there was an actual reason he was there. He'd traced the scarabs back to this area, kind of. If there was anywhere that could help him figure out exactly what was going on, it was an ascendant research facility.

"Do you have anything on blood-burrower scarabs?" he asked. "There's an outbreak of them right now that I'm trying to get cleared up."

"Yes, of course. We have all the standard data on the species, quite a few historical outbreaks documented, and one ongoing experiment centered around them."

"Oh, good. That should be— I'm sorry, did you say ongoing?"

"I did, yes. Would you like to review the experiment's current status?"

"I think I would."

New papers with new charts and graphs, illustrations, and even some illusionary models of various talismans appeared around him. A number of maps, some of which showed places he recognized and all of which looked to be superbly crafted, showed outbreak zones with color gradients representing time to reflect the speed the infestation had spread.

A separate section, partitioned off from the historical information, showed the ongoing experiment. Perhaps inevitably, the map was of the northlands, and he immediately recognized it. It was remarkably similar to the one he'd spent so many days painstakingly drawing out himself. The infestation he'd been trying to stop for weeks had originated from the ascendant research lab.

CHAPTER TWENTY-SIX

That was too much of a coincidence for it to actually be one, but Nym had a good idea who might be behind it. That fox had to have known about this lab, and probably known that only an ascendant could get in. The infestation wasn't a new one; he could have done something about it years ago if he'd wanted to. Nym wondered if he'd find the talisman that had kicked it all off in the fox's den, assuming that it even existed at all.

He scanned through the notes about the experiment as quickly as possible and confirmed that, yes, the research lab was responsible for supplying the scarabs with the arcana they needed to keep growing and spreading. Of course it was.

"What was the point of this experiment?" he asked, scanning the floating papers in front of him for an answer.

"This was an automated experiment the research lab initiated fifteen hundred cycles ago," Naera said. "Long-range sensors located a new energy source that was spreading an unusual style of arcana across the landscape. Samples were obtained and the arcana spread traced back to its source, here."

She pointed to a map, at a spot along the coast where the old ship Nym had discovered was still locked in ice. "The source was transported to containment here, and the arcana duplicated. The goal was to determine if the parasitic constructs produced by the source would accept the substitute arcana structure and further, to iterate on the construct design and test various alterations. If you'll look over here, you will see a list of various tests performed and their results."

Nym skimmed the list. Some of the ideas were downright bizarre, things like causing the scarabs to grow extra limbs, having them cannibalize one another to build one superscarab, or trying to merge them with plant life to form a symbiotic reproductive cycle.

"Okay, this is great and all, but can we shut the experiment down? These scarabs have kind of taken over around here."

"Certainly. How would you like to proceed?" Naera asked.

"Hmm. Something that kills all the existing scarabs without harming anything else would be ideal. Is that possible?"

"How quickly would you like the scarabs to die off? We have tracked their spread quite closely, but it would still take considerable resources to destroy them all immediately. At best, I am estimating something like ninety percent elimination with the remainder dying off over the next three months without a steady flow of arcana to sustain them."

"Would we still have the resources for the snow-wolf project I have in mind?" Nym asked.

"Not unless you are willing to recharge the arcana batteries."

"Which layers are we using?" Nym was afraid he already knew the answer. There were so many fantastical experiments that defied his knowledge of what was possible with magic that all of them had to be beyond fifth layer.

"There are a total of one hundred seventh-layer batteries and twenty-five eighth-layer batteries powering the experiments. There are five ninth-layer batteries powering the research lab itself, and one twelfth-layer battery, purpose unknown."

"Twelfth?" Nym echoed. Humans had only reached the fifth layer. He couldn't even imagine what kind of magic twelfth-layer arcana was capable of producing. No wonder ascendants were mythical figures, quite literally gods when compared to normal humans.

"Purpose unknown, Exarch," Naera repeated.

"Are there a lot of ascendants at the twelfth layer?"

"I do not know. That was not within the purview of the research lab. You are the only Exarch on staff though, so I believe it is safe to assume the battery exists for your personal use."

"But to do what?" Nym muttered quietly. Then, louder, he added, "How much arcana is still stored in the batteries?"

"The lab is operating at sixty-two percent capacity, with an ongoing drain of approximately half a percent per year under the current ongoing experiment load. Cutting arcana funding for the cursed-scarab experiment would reduce that arcana load by a tiny fraction of a percent. The scarabs would likely die off on their own inside a year. Using resources to wipe out the current population would drain perhaps twenty percent of our total capacity."

"And the snow-wolf project?"

"Thirty percent of our total capacity to launch it, with an ongoing cost of two percent per year over the next ten years to ensure complete coverage of the next generation."

Nym wasn't the best with numbers, and he guessed his former self shared that character flaw. His personal-assistant golem had laid out the costs quite clearly; now he just needed to decide what he wanted to do. Of course, price wasn't the only factor.

"If we send out the kill pulse on the scarabs, who's going to notice it?"

"I would imagine any ascendant currently anchored to the timeline would."

"I . . . don't understand what that means," Nym admitted.

"My knowledge is only cursory, as temporal manipulation is not the focus of this research lab. However, to the best of my understanding, the key difference that separates an ascendant from a human is that an ascendant does not experience subjective linear time. They manipulate it in many ways that mortal species do not. This is achieved through reaching of the sixth layer, what ascendants call Transcendence.

"At any given point in time, some or all ascendants may or may not be present. They may have skipped forward past that point and never experienced it. They may have lost that section of time in battle against another ascendant. Regardless of how it has happened, there are many, many points in time an ascendant may simply not exist in, only to return at a later, or earlier, point."

"What happens if an ascendant wants to go back and redo time he's already experienced?" Nym asked.

Naera shrugged. "My understanding is that it is not possible to live through the same time twice. Most ascendants only appear when they want to, to accomplish a specific purpose, and then leave again. Some ascendants may spend whole stretches of years anchored to time at once. You, for instance, are well-known as an extremely anchored ascendant, a universal constant always present in the world at all times."

"I am? And that's not normal, to be here all the time?"

"The ascendants connected to this research facility appear at random intervals to check up on experiments they are running, refill arcana batteries as needed, and are otherwise often off in their own slices of time where other ascendants are not presently existing."

Nym held up a hand. "Give me a minute to process this."

If he was understanding all of this correctly, ascendants were truly immortal, but in such a way that they skipped back and forth across time, dropping in to do something, only to disappear again when they were done. Where they went, he didn't fully understand. But if they could go into the future and the past, but none of them had caught up with him yet, then that might mean none of them found him, ever.

Or it might mean that he had completely misunderstood what Naera had told him and if he stopped being careful, they'd find him instantly. Or she could be wrong. She had said her knowledge was cursory, so there was probably a lot of important information he was still missing. He needed to be very, very careful here. One mistake could be the end of him if even a single ascendant caught it.

"If I don't want anyone to know this experiment has been halted, the only thing you can do is cut off the arcana flow to it, correct? The scarabs would stop reproducing, and they would slowly die off on their own?"

"That is correct."

"Okay, let's do that."

"Understood. Would you like to begin immediately?" Naera asked.

"Yes."

He'd have to handle the cleanup himself. It would probably be months of work, but as long as they weren't going to keep growing, it would eventually end. Perhaps the fox would agree to letting them die out on their own over a year if he cleaned up specific sites like the Garden of Winter for him. Nym wasn't sure if he'd go for that, but he figured it didn't hurt to ask.

"The experiment's arcana budget has been terminated. No new scarab will be produced with arcana from this point forward. Would you like the source to be placed back in its original location?"

"What? No! No, don't do that. You have it here, right? I'll just take it with me."

"Very well. It will be waiting for you outside the data archives."

"Good, good. One problem taken care of," he said. "I have a few more questions."

"Of course, Exarch," Naera said. "What would you like to discuss next?"

"Let me think for a second. Oh! How do I get out of here? Both the lab and the basin around it, I mean. There seems to be some sort of ward scheme preventing me from teleporting out of the area."

"I believe you are referring to the containment field that prevents the existence of the lab from being spread. It should not be preventing you from leaving unless it is malfunctioning. If you'd like, I can take a new scan of your arcana print and confirm it has been keyed to the spell."

"That sounds like a good idea," Nym said, not that he really thought that. But if it was his only way out, he didn't have much choice. "Let's do that. What if I wanted to bring someone else here who is not an ascendant? How would they leave?"

"That would not be possible without deactivating the containment field. It is difficult to predict what effects that might have, but I do not believe it would be good for the local geographic location."

"Why not?" Nym asked. He pictured those creatures lying in wait in the darkness outside the needle all escaping and wondered what he might accidentally set loose if he was careless.

"The containment field also holds all the ambient arcana the lab has spent locked down for recycling. If the containment field were deactivated, eighth-layer arcana would spill out into the world and would likely devastate everything within a thousand miles."

That was so much worse than what Nym had been picturing. He was really feeling like he was in over his head now, like he was standing in the middle of Cern's alchemy lab, in the dark, trying not to move so he didn't jostle something volatile and blow up half the city. Except it was worse because, while the frozen north was quite vast, a thousand miles was also a long way. Abilanth would probably be caught in that, if nothing else. Technically speaking, it was the nation's capital and destroying it would mean destroying Devros's leadership.

"Okay, so that idea is a bust then. What else is there? Could you provide a list of topics the lab has researched or that exist inside the data archive for me to look over?"

A new sheet of paper, this one several feet long, appeared in the air. Nym started reading through it, looking for anything interesting or relevant. There were a few topics he would like to know about, but when he inquired further, he found that he was still missing a lot of the base knowledge he needed to understand what he was reading.

That reminded him of something though, an experiment someone else had done that he'd stumbled across and read the notes on without any real hope of understanding them. It had technically been a failure anyway, since the person running it hadn't really accomplished his goal. He'd made some progress though. If there was anywhere that had a viable strategy, it was Research Lab Six with a specialty in making and modifying new living creatures.

"I've got a question, but I don't see the relevant topic on this list."

"I will do my best to answer it," Naera assured him.

"Do you know how to make an ascendant?" Nym asked.

CHAPTER TWENTY-SEVEN

Nym stared at Naera silently while he waited for her to put together her answer. It took her a while before she finally started speaking. "I can only present a theory based on reverse engineering the techniques and principles used here."

"That's fine," he told her. "I'd like to hear it."

"Like many of the creatures created by Research Lab Six, an ascendant is, at its core, a human being that has been permanently altered by magic. One could make an argument that it is a separate species, based on the amount of alterations made to it at the most fundamental levels, alterations that it could theoretically pass on to its own offspring."

"And if they weren't passed on, those alterations would have to be made when it's a newborn?" Nym asked.

"Not necessarily, though it would certainly be easier. Older, stronger creatures usually possess a sense of self that can be difficult to alter if they are not cooperative. In the case of the ascendant line though, I believe almost all alterations are made before birth. Certainly a mortal human's mind would break if they had to experience time the same way an ascendant does."

"So what you're saying is that one time, thousands and thousands of years ago, the first ascendants were just humans who altered themselves enough to become something greater?"

"Possibly, or possibly thousands of years that have yet to pass. None of the assistants here at the lab possess the ability to experience time the same way an ascendant does, but my theoretical understanding allows for their future actions to influence what's already in the past."

"But what about humans who reach the sixth layer on their own? Do they become ascendants as well?"

"I am not sure," Naera said after a moment's hesitation. "There is more to an ascendant than reaching the Transcendence layer. Perhaps it would be best to think of them as a half-step or partial ascendant, capable of completing the transformation but not actually having learned how to do so yet."

"Do you think this is an experiment that you could run here?"

"Oh yes, definitely. I can have this up and running within fifty cycles, once we've discussed the goals of the experiment and what methods you'd like to utilize. I would recommend starting out with a sample size of at least one hundred humans to use as test subjects. Depending on the exact goals of the experiment, we may need more to cover a spread of ages."

"You know, maybe we shouldn't run that experiment after all. Yeah, let's just hold off on that one for now."

Naera nodded along. "If that is your wish, Exarch."

"It is," Nym said firmly. The last thing he needed was to be responsible for hundreds of people being abducted and experimented on. Maybe he should just shut this whole lab down if those were the kind of experiments they were running here. There was no telling what kind of alarms that might set off though, which reminded him that he needed to think about leaving soon.

"Okay, the scarab experiment is terminated. You need a new arcana print so I can leave at will. We're not going to do the snow-wolf update until later, and we're not doing the human experimentation at all. That sums it up?"

"Almost. You wanted the original source of the corrupted arcana that produced the scarab. Would you like to take possession of it first or update your arcana print first?"

"Let's do the arcana print first."

"Very well, please step away from the data archive and follow me."

The illusions disappeared as Nym moved away from the center of the room. Naera led him down several halls to a room that contained an enormous padded chair, the back easily six feet tall and wide enough for three Nyms to sit on. As far as he could tell, there was nothing else in the room.

"Please stand here," she said, pointing out a spot directly in front of the chair.

Nym stood facing the chair, waiting for new directions, when a small cube appeared in front of him. It looked identical to the one he had hidden beneath Ciana's cellar, so much so that at first he thought it was the same thing. A glance at Naera showed no surprise on her part about its appearance, so he decided it was far more likely that it was just a standard ascendant design used for multiple purposes.

"Please cast your arcana print into the memory cube," Naera instructed.

Nym had no idea how to do that. After a few silent seconds, she added, "Would you like some help?"

"Please," he said.

"This is the spell used to cast a print." An illusion of a spell diagram appeared in the air along with some notes about an intent filter that represented *self* being used for the arcana. It didn't seem to matter which layer the arcana came from, so Nym just gathered first-layer arcana and quickly built it. He cast the spell into the memory cube, then looked to Naera.

"That's odd," she said. "This does not look anything like your previous print. Sometimes a print can deviate, but I've never seen one outside of tolerance, let alone look so completely different. If I hadn't done the biological scans myself, I would think you are not Exarch Niramyn."

"Oh, that's probably because I'm missing some memories right now," he said. It wasn't even a lie. "I am in disguise."

"I see. Yes, missing memories could explain the drift pattern in this arcana print. Very well, let me update this new print as a subset on your profile."

Nym had no idea what any of that meant, but he hoped she was saying that he'd be able to come and go as he pleased now. It would be nice to pop back in whenever he thought up a new question without having to worry about being trapped. There was still the concern that he'd run into another ascendant here, but if no one had shown up in the last century, they weren't likely to change their habits anytime soon.

Then again, ascendants seemed to have only a passing regard for things like linear time, so Nym could be way off base. There was no reason to assume that one wouldn't come in the future, see that Nym had been here in the past, and then adjust the past so that they were here to meet him. He thought. Maybe. It was very confusing.

"I have completed the update to your profile," Naera told him. "You should be able to leave at any time now."

There were probably a million things he could learn from this place, but he had other priorities. He had a pact to eliminate the scarabs, which reminded him that he still needed to secure the talisman before he left. That could go back to Archmage Veran for safekeeping. He doubted it would be as safe as if he left it here, but then again, when the lab golems had gotten hold of it, they'd started playing with it. He trusted the archmage to keep it contained, but the lab might try to start a new experiment with it in a few years.

"Let me just collect the source of that scarab arcana then, and I think I'm ready to leave," he said.

"Yes, of course. I've sent one of the other assistants to remove it from the specimen vault. If you'll come with me, we will deliver it to you shortly."

A different lab golem met them in the hall, holding a sphere of arcana with an amulet on a gold chain floating in the center of it. The amulet itself was shaped like scarab, the lines of its shell made of diamonds, and the coloring was done with studded rubies. It was probably worth a small fortune just for the gems in it, but Nym could clearly see the curse struggling to break through the containing arcana.

He pulled out the curse capturing orb and handed it to the lab golem. "Please place it in this," he said.

The golem examined the item for a second, then fed it a thin strand of arcana, causing it to explode outward into equally sized pieces. He placed the talisman in the center and retracted his own arcana. The orb snapped back into one solid piece, now with the evil necklace safely tucked away. "An interesting design," he remarked, holding the orb out for Nym to take. "I have saved a copy for future use and will add it to the data archive."

"The orb or the amulet?" Nym asked, bemused.

"The orb," the golem told him. "The amulet was added years ago. We can produce as many as are needed at any time, as long as the batteries retain the necessary arcana."

A shudder worked its way down Nym's spine. Of course they could just make a new one. He'd once again underestimated how powerful the ascendants were, even in a seemingly abandoned lab being run by nothing but sapient golem helpers with almost no initiative. They'd been nothing but courteous to him, but Nym got the distinct impression that not even Archmage Veran could stand up against a single one of them, let alone the whole lab's worth.

"Well then, I think that's all of my business here," Nym said, suddenly eager to leave. "Do I need to do anything special, or can I teleport straight out?"

"It is not impossible to leave directly, but given the divergence of your arcana print, I would recommend exiting through the foyer. The wards there will not stop you. Once you've reappeared outside the lab, you can teleport wherever you please," Naera said.

That was more or less the same set up the archmage's sanctum used. It wasn't impossible to teleport around inside it, but for security reasons, it was heavily restricted. Even reaching the landing platform required a sort of mental key to bypass the wards. It was annoying, but he understood why it worked that way.

He followed Naera back to the entrance. "Thank you for your help," he told the golem.

"You are very welcome, Exarch. Please feel free to return whenever you like."

"I will," Nym said, not at all sure that he'd ever be back. He wanted to return, but there were risks involved that he wasn't prepared to take on. As it was, he'd already spent more time inside the lab than he should have, thanks to his curiosity.

With a thought, he left the lab and disappeared back into the darkness of the basin, lit only by the glowing metal nearby. Nym caught himself before he fell more than a few feet, tucked the orb away into his pack, and flew out into open space. With a final glance around, he took a breath, centered his mind, and teleported to the Garden of Winter.

The scarab infestation there didn't look any different than he remembered, but perhaps the miasma of corrupted arcana was a bit thinner. The true test would be to clear out the remaining scarabs and see what it looked like in the next week or two. Before he did that though, he had some other tasks to take care of. First, he needed to return Archmage Veran's talisman-capturing orb. The last thing the world needed was that floating loose, just waiting for some sort of accident to set it free.

After that, there was a certain fox he needed to talk to. Nym had a lot of suspicions that the fox had known what he was setting Nym up for when he'd sent Nym out on this job, and Nym wasn't too happy to be moving blind. He might not be strong enough to do anything about it now, but he'd just see how strong a mystical fox was once he'd regained ascendant-level abilities.

It wouldn't be much longer now, he was sure. He could practically feel how close he was to breaking through into the fifth layer. Then he'd have some decisions to make, decisions he'd been putting off for too long. Soon.

CHAPTER TWENTY-EIGHT

Fox, do you have a minute?" Nym said to the ring on his finger.

[What now? Don't tell me you're giving up already? I'm not going to help you clean this up. It's your job.]

"No. I found the source and took care of it. The scarabs should die off on their own now even if I don't do a thing to hurry it up."

[Congratulations. I would prefer if you cleaned up the garden at least to preserve it, but I suppose that technically meets the letter of our pact.]

"Yeah, about that. You knew, didn't you? This whole time, you knew where the scarabs were coming from?"

Nym could practically hear the fox grinning that vulpine smirk of his. *[I know many things, but if I knew that, why wouldn't I just take care of it myself?]*

"Oh, I don't know, maybe because you couldn't."

The fox snorted in his head. *[Don't be ridiculous. What could you possibly accomplish that I couldn't do myself?]*

Nym had spent some time thinking about this conversation before he had it. The only thing he absolutely needed to confirm was that the fox considered the pact to be fulfilled, which he did. That meant Nym was off the hook for manually cleaning up the rest of the scarabs, though he thought he would clean up a few spots. There was no time pressure to it now though, meaning he could get back to his attempts at forging a conduit strong enough to bore through the fourth layer.

The other side of the conversation was something he'd debated having. It could come off as antagonistic, but he didn't think the fox would take it that way. He was angling to get a favor out of the beast, something he didn't strictly need help with but that would be a lot easier on him if he could talk the fox into playing along.

"The way I figure it, there is no way you couldn't know about that ascendant research lab. And if you knew about it, then you had to know that's where the scarabs were coming from. But since you didn't fix the problem yourself, you must not be able to get in. Then someone like me comes along, and that must be a once-in-a-lifetime opportunity for you, right?"

[Mmm, I can neither confirm nor deny your speculations.]

"I figured. Anyway, I got in no problem and learned lots of interesting stuff, plus I took care of the corrupted arcana experiment for you. So we're all set there, but . . ."

[But?] The fox sounded interested now. Perfect.

"Like I said, lots of interesting stuff. There's got to be something in there you'd like to know more about," Nym said. "And as it so happens, I need a favor. Maybe you'd be interested in another trade?"

The fox's laughter rolled through Nym's head. "Interesting," his physical voice said from behind Nym. "You've certainly grown bold since our first meeting. Well, you put on a good show of it. I can still smell your fear though."

Nym forced himself not to flinch away from the voice. He turned in the air to face the fox, rolled his eyes, and said, "Couldn't just appear in front of me?"

"It's more fun this way."

"Fun for you maybe."

"That's the only fun that matters."

Nym rolled his eyes and asked, "Are you interested or not?"

"It depends on the favor, and the payment," the fox said.

"I have these friends, they're snow wolves, and there's a problem with their magic that I could fix, but if I do, it puts a target on my back."

Nym laid out what he'd discovered at Research Lab Six, what he was trying to do, and what the problem was. "So that's the real issue. How do I do this without having an ascendant hunting me down afterward? Do you think you could help?"

The fox shook his head. "If it were me doing it, I could hide you, but you'd have to spend the rest of your life stuck by my side hiding in my shadow. It's already too late anyway. Any ascendant who looks will see you were in the lab, regardless of whether you trigger this. The first time one of them has any reason to look, they're going to see that you were there. The best you can hope for now is that none of them exist in the lab anywhere near this point in time."

"Ugh. I hate how you phrase that," Nym said. "Ascendant time stuff is such a pain to talk about."

"This language doesn't have the concepts needed to talk about a being that exists outside of time like they do. Like you will."

"Yeah. Anyway, so . . . Nothing you can do then?"

"Not to protect you from other ascendants, not unless you want to spend every minute of every day sitting next to me. Even if you were willing, I am not. I do not love your company that much."

Nym laughed and shook his head. "No, thanks. Any ideas on how to reverse the biological decay to the snow wolves' magic that don't involve the lab?"

"I appreciate your concern for my little cousins, but this is an issue they'll need to work out on their own," the fox said. He tilted his head, and a small statuette appeared between the two of them. It floated over to Nym, and the fox said, "Take this with you."

Nym examined it carefully but made no move to touch it. It was about nine inches tall and maybe four inches around at the base. The statuette depicted the fox himself, all red fur with dark highlights and glimmering eyes over a vulpine grin. A fine layer of arcana shifted around it, flicking out occasionally like a tail.

"What is it?" he asked, suspicious.

"It is linked to me, and I will hear everything that is said to it, but only if you say my name first. If you find yourself in trouble, hunted by an ascendant, use this to ask for my help."

"I don't know your name," Nym pointed out.

"You're so clever, I'm sure you'd be able to figure it out if you tried. I am something of a legend, after all."

"Or you could just tell me."

The fox snickered. "Where would be the fun in that? Besides, you still distrust me so much that you haven't even touched it yet."

"The more I get to know you, the less I trust you," Nym said, still examining the statuette.

"Good. You're smarter than you look."

"Thanks. I'm so glad you approve."

The statuette appeared to do what the fox claimed, mostly. There were some components to it that deflected attention away from it but that could be overcome with any number of spells or even just raw willpower. There was also a lock-and-key mechanism to it, which prevented it from being used at all if he didn't have a matching piece to slot in.

"Is this bound to the ring?" Nym asked.

"Indeed it is. If you lose this after you activate it, I don't want whatever random person finds it nattering away in my ear."

It was more serious than that, Nym was sure. If someone got their hands on this, it would be a direct link back to the fox. His location could be tracked at the very least, and possibly long-range attacks brought against his mind. "Are you sure you want to trust me with this? You would be . . . vulnerable . . . if this fell into the wrong hands."

The fox snorted. "I do not fear any human magic. I am more concerned about being annoyed than threatened."

"I'm sure. That's why you've gone out of your way to help me here, right? Big softy."

"I will bite you, little half-scendant."

"Rizin?" Nym asked as he studied the activation component of the magic. "I'm not sure if I'm reading this right. That's the audible phrase for using the statuette?"

"And behold, you didn't even have to look it up. I knew you'd figure it out. It was right in front of you, after all."

Nym made no move to pick up the statuette. He was confident it was what the fox said it was, but accepting it came with some implications that he wasn't sure he liked. If he took this with him, he was taking a direct link to Rizin, which could work both ways. It was hard to imagine anyone obfuscating arcana well enough to hide the magic from him, but if there was anything that could do it, it was a mystical fox.

More than that, accepting it meant accepting some obligations in return. Their relationship had been entirely transactional, flavored with just a tinge of extortion at the beginning. The back-and-forth had been very clear up until now. This represented a step into a more ambiguous territory, one Nym was hesitant to venture into.

The fox chuckled. "I'm not trying to marry you here. And this isn't for casual conversation. If your life is genuinely in danger, I'll try to help. Don't count on me saving you. I'm stronger than a lot of ascendants and trickier than the few that can outmuscle me. But even I have limits."

"It's not that I don't appreciate the gesture, but why are you doing this?" Nym asked.

"Do you want the selfish answer? Would it make you feel better to know my base motivations?"

"I just want the truth."

Rizin considered for a second, and then said, "Because you're interesting. I've never seen a broken ascendant before. And because you're very, very different than most ascendants. You're here, dealing with a power that could squash you like a bug, and you're not even doing it for anything you want. You're trying to bargain for a favor for a whole species that you're not a part of. It's fascinating, and I wish to see how everything plays out."

"Like watching a show, huh?"

"Something like that. Say instead that I am invested in the story."

Nym grabbed the statuette and stowed it away in his pack. "Thank you," he said.

"You're quite welcome. What will you do next?"

"Start with the Garden of Winter, maybe hit a few other spots that I can do quick cleanups on and get most of the scarabs. That will limit the damage while time takes care of the rest."

"And then?"

"Visit some friends I haven't seen in a while. Then back to work on myself."

"It sounds like you have it all planned out," the fox said.

"Nah, I just make it up as I go along."

The fox barked out a laugh. "Don't we all."

Nym said his goodbyes, then teleported away. As he'd said, he was going to start with the Garden of Winter. It would be a tedious job, but this one place at least he wanted to clean up. Hopefully without the scarabs infecting everything, the garden would come back to life.

While he set one portion of his mind to work killing scarabs, the other half engaged in long-range scrying. He was looking for something specific, something he hadn't seen when he was at the research lab but he knew was out there somewhere. Perhaps it was farther south, back in Delvros territory.

His scans didn't turn anything up for hours, and eventually even Nym had to give up just from the sheer amount of arcana he'd burned. It was unusual these days, especially after he'd stopped losing so much of it to that aging curse, but after a full day of work, he had to throw in the towel. Wherever Cold Paw and his pack were, Nym still couldn't find them.

Part of him wondered if the worst had happened. The pack's numbers had been devastated from dealing with the ice-worm hive, but last he saw them, they were still limping along. He wasn't going to give up searching, but the longer he looked without finding them, the more concerned he got.

CHAPTER TWENTY-NINE

It took Nym two hours of searching after he teleported to Karu before he finally found the Earth Shapers. They were almost a hundred miles away, literally out in the middle of nowhere, excavating a chunk of forest around a base camp made of familiar-looking buildings. He'd seen their like many times in the military camps and outposts, the quick-and-dirty shelters earth mages put up. They were easy to make and easy to tear down.

He spotted Bildar first, the bearded mage working some sort of magic on the soil to loosen it and eject a tree stump. It was a slow-going spell, with the stump only moving a few inches up a minute. A few other laborers nearby that he didn't recognize were using some sort of specialized cutting spell to process the already felled tree into stacks of timber. It looked vaguely like the cutting spell Nym already knew, except optimized for trimming logs down into planks.

Nym grinned and cast a camouflaging-sphere spell around himself. He drifted down out of the sky, taking his time to ensure there was no wind from his movement. Only when he was a foot away from Bildar and floating in the air right in front of the man did he let the camouflage drop.

"Hi," Nym said.

Bildar regarded him blandly. "Hi, Nym."

Nym's brow furrowed, and he looked around. One of the other workers had jumped when Nym dispelled his camouflage, but Bildar hadn't. "Hmm, I've become too predictable, haven't I?"

"A little bit, yes. Also I knew you were there."

"What? How?"

"Dirt and dust curving across the bottom of your air shell when you came down to get into position."

Nym looked down between his feet. Sure enough, he could see the dust outlining the curve of the hard air. "Damn it. It's too dirty in here."

"Sorry," Bildar told him, not sounding sorry at all. "Might want to take a step back. I've got to pull this stump out. We need to get this whole side cleared this afternoon so the twins can start digging the foundation for the first storage building."

"Oh? What are you guys doing out here, anyway?"

"It's a new town," Bildar said. "Kind of. More of a hunting-and-trapping outpost. The contract is for twenty buildings and fifty miles of road. There's a big company in Karu that wanted the place set up. I guess they think it'll cut operation costs or something. I don't know."

Nym floated up a bit to look around. There definitely wasn't room for even half the supposed buildings, not even if they were all small one- or two-room houses. But then, that's what the deforestation was for. There were six more stumps waiting for Bildar to get to them. "You just need to get these six here pulled out by the end of the day?"

"By the end of the afternoon," Bildar corrected.

"Great," Nym said. He grabbed one with greater telekinesis and ripped it straight up into the air, then a second, then a third. "Where do you want these at?"

The other laborers gawked at Nym while Bildar laughed and shook his head. "I have no idea. There was a team that was hauling them away one by one."

Nym popped the other three stumps out of the ground and left them lying on their sides in the dirt. "Okay, well, they'll figure that out. Come on, let's go get the others."

"And what are we doing?" Bildar asked.

"Lunch. I was thinking the Quarterhouse."

"I haven't had one of their steaks in a year," Bildar said with a happy sigh. "I guess an early lunch break wouldn't go amiss."

"H-hey," one of the other laborers said. "You can't just walk off like that."

"Why?" Bildar made a show of looking around. "Is there a stump somewhere I missed?"

"Well, no, but . . ."

"Then I'll be back in a few hours to start the next project."

The two men exchanged looks, shrugged, and got back to work. Nym could hear them grumbling under their breath the whole time though. "You going to get in trouble for this?" he asked.

"Nah. We're not technically in charge here, but we're a specialist crew, not general labor. The boss doesn't care what we do as long as the work gets done."

"Good. Let me see . . . Ophelia is that way. I bet I could scare her," Nym said.

"You do that. I'll go get the twins."

Nym flew up about ten feet and recast his camouflaging-sphere spell. Then he flew over to where Ophelia was doing some rune work on the framework of what looked like it would be the largest building on the site. She glanced over in his direction, frowned, and stood up.

She took a few steps one way, and then the other, obviously seeing the slight distortion the spell made. When seen from a single angle, it was difficult to notice. Moving made it easier to pick out, more so if Nym was the one moving the camouflage, but there were still small imperfections that could be picked out when the viewer moved if they were paying attention.

"Ah," she said softly. "I thought so."

A ball of mud rose up into the air and shot itself directly at the camouflage shield. Nym let it splatter against it, mostly disappearing against the surface but for the few pieces that bounced off. Nym left the camouflaging shell in place so she'd focus on the distortion, then teleported behind her and said, "Thought what?"

To her credit, Ophelia didn't jump. She did flinch though, and Nym snickered. A second mud ball shot up and splattered across his chest. "Oh, you got me!" he moaned, dramatically throwing his arms out and allowing himself to fall back onto a new air cushion.

"You deserved it." She took a step back and looked him over. "God, you already look another year older. By the time summer comes around, you'll look older than me."

"Nope. Fixed that a few weeks ago. I'll age normally now."

"You did? That's fantastic news. Why did you wait so long to tell us?"

"I had to finish up the work I traded to get the curse broken. Uh . . . I kind of still have more work to do, but I wanted a break. We're going out to lunch."

"Hmm, well, it's a bit early, but I suppose. Where were you thinking?"

"The Quarterhouse."

"Ooooh. Yes, that sounds lovely. Let me just get cleaned up. Did you tell the others yet?"

"Just Bildar," Nym said. "He's going to get Monick and Nomick."

"Let's go find them then," Ophelia said.

"Wait. Before that, I wanted to talk to you."

"Hmm? What's going on, Nym?"

"It's about Analia," Nym said. A sparkle appeared in Ophelia's eyes, and she started to smirk. "She's killing people. I'm concerned."

The smirk vanished. "Tell me everything."

Nym explained about how she'd gotten tangled up with some vigilante group, started fighting drug runners, and was executing the ones she caught now. "I don't really know what to do. It's her business, but . . . I've killed people before. It weighs on you. Even the ones you can justify, the ones where you had no choice, where it was them or you, you lose sleep over them."

"I know," Ophelia said softly. "I know. What do you want to do?"

"Take her away from there before she ends up being the face that haunts someone else's nightmares, or before she gets so used to it that she stops caring. I don't know which one would be worse. Either way, my friend would be gone."

"While I do think one of those fates is markedly worse than the other, I see your point. You know that's not a real solution though, right?"

"I know. It's her life," Nym said. "But . . . What else can we do?"

"It's a hard thing to watch someone you care about do something you don't agree with. This kind of stuff ends friendships and splits up families."

"Yeah, so . . . What do we do?"

"There's not much we can do. She has to live her own life and make her own mistakes. All we can do is be there to support her when she needs it and hope she'll let us."

"It doesn't seem like it's enough."

Ophelia nodded. "I know. But let's look at the alternative. You're an asc— A third-circle mage. You've got plenty of power to spare. Let's say you go over there, teleport Analia out against her will, basically kidnap her, and bring her here. Then what? Do you think she's going to thank you for getting her away from danger without even asking her? Or worse, for doing it after you did ask and she explicitly told you no?"

Nym shook his head. "No, of course not. I wouldn't do that."

"I know, but that's what you're asking me, isn't it, what to do with all this power you have to make her stop doing the things you don't want her to do?"

"No! No. That's not it. I was just hoping you'd know what to say to get her to listen. We kind of fought about it last time we talked. She wanted me to join her whatever group, to start running down people who were part of this cartel, torture them for information, execute them."

"Why'd you say no?" Ophelia asked. "I understand why you're afraid she's in over your head. Honestly, she probably is. She's too young to be doing this stuff, but your situation is different."

Nym shrugged. "Because I'm not a good person, I guess? I don't know. It seems pointless. Sure, I guess I can go in there, kill a bunch of people who maybe deserve it, maybe don't, and deal with everything that comes with that. So what? A few months later, there's a new cartel, new people doing the exact same thing. Do I spend the rest of my life just running around in circles cleaning up all the ugly parts of every human city in the world?"

"It would be an altruistic use of your unique abilities, but I get why it doesn't appeal to you. You're not as bad a person as you seem to think you are though. You've done lots to help people you didn't owe a thing to."

Before Nym could reply, Bildar yelled out from the road, "Hey, you two! Are you ready?"

"To be continued later, I guess," Nym said. "Let me know if you come up with a solution, okay?"

"I'll do some thinking on it," Ophelia promised.

The two of them walked out of the stone framework and joined the other three earth mages. All of them were, well, if not precisely clean, there was no dirt on them at least. Monick lifted a hand in greeting and asked, "How are you doing, Nym?"

"Good!" he said. "I've got news. Big stuff. I can't wait to tell you guys all about it. You're never going to believe what I found."

"Oh yeah? Everything about you is pretty unbelievable, so you'll have to forgive us if we don't act too surprised at the next amazing feat, huh?"

Nym shared a grin with Monick, then looked past the group toward a fat man hustling over their way. "Who's that?"

"That's the guy in charge of this construction project," Bildar said. "I should probably talk to him before we go."

Nym traded sly glances with the twins, and then in unison, all three of them said, "Naaaah."

"Wait, what?" Bildar spun to look at Nym. "Oh no you don't. Don't you da—"

The teleportation spell snagged all four of the Earth Shapers and Nym, pulling them through space and leaving the camp far behind. A moment later, Thrakus popped into view.

"—are," Bildar finished lamely. He heaved an enormous sigh while the rest of the crew laughed. "I'm going to pay for that one later."

CHAPTER THIRTY

Nym knew he needed to check back in with Analia and Cern. If nothing else, Cern should have an assortment of potions, elixirs, tinctures, tonics, salves, and God only knew what else ready, which meant he needed Nym's help transporting it and preparing it to be sold. Analia . . . might not want to talk to him. They hadn't exactly been fighting, but they also hadn't parted ways on friendly terms. If she was still mad, he'd take it as a win. It would mean she wasn't dead.

He busied himself with anything else he could think of. He exchanged letters with Risa and went to visit her, he spent time with the Earth Shapers and helped out occasionally with their projects. He studied in Archmage Veran's library and continued to work on his breakthrough into the fifth layer. And he teleported out to Bloodfin Cove one day to visit Ciana.

She wasn't home when he got there, but he found her easily enough on the bluffs south of town. There was a brace of rabbits nearby, and she was busy resetting a snare line when he caught up to her. Ciana finished up her work, scooped up her dinner, and continued on the loop that would eventually take her home.

Nym dropped out of the air nearby, not really making any effort to hide his approach. Ciana watched him come near, one hand on her hip. "What's wrong with you today?" she asked as soon as he landed.

"Who says there's anything wrong?"

"I do. I haven't seen you in over a month, and for the first time ever, you're not sneaking up on me and scaring me half to death."

"Yeah, well . . . Sorry. I'll scare you twice as hard next time."

"Mmm. Yeah. So, what's wrong?"

Nym shrugged and gestured for her to start walking. He walked next to her and said, "Just having some problems, feeling frustrated about it all. You'd think, all this magic, I'd be able to solve anything, right?"

"Not really. There are plenty of problems that can't be solved with brute force, magical or otherwise."

"Don't I know it."

Ciana pulled a branch up and held it for Nym to walk under. "Thanks," he said. She followed behind him, and they stopped near another snare.

"Damn. Empty."

Nym bit his tongue to keep from offering to set her up somewhere else. He'd already tried that, and she'd declined. It wouldn't be any different if he asked again.

For whatever reason, Ciana didn't want the help. She was . . . maybe not happy with her lot in life, but determined that any changes would be made under her own power, without relying on someone else to fix everything for her.

He could understand that way of thinking, even if he did wish she'd accept just a little more help than she did. Checking crab traps and snares was all well and good, but it wasn't even a fraction of what he could do if she'd let him. Even her cellar had largely gone to waste, if only because there was never so much extra food that she needed it. It was a fine place to store stuff overnight before she took it into town to sell or trade but not much more than that.

"Anyway, you still haven't told me what this problem is," Ciana said when they started walking again.

"I have a friend who's doing something stupid and dangerous. It's her choice, and I can't stop her, but it's frustrating because there's a very real chance she's going to get herself killed."

"Oh." Ciana was silent for a minute. "You don't really need advice then. You already know what I'd say. It's just coming to terms with the fact that you can't tell other people how to live their lives."

"I guess," Nym said. "We had a bit of a fight over it. She wanted me to join up with her group, and I said no. Maybe I should have though, just to help keep her safe?"

"Well," Ciana said slowly. "What exactly is she doing?"

Nym spent the next few minutes describing the state of Shu-Ain's drug trade and what Analia had gotten swept up in, what she'd wanted to drag him into. When he was done, Ciana nodded and said, "I'm not going to tell you if you made the right call or not. There's . . . Well . . . You could consider it a good thing to fight against something like that. You could also say that's not your job and you have every right to live your life without spending it fighting on other people's behalf."

"Sure, but what do I do now?"

"Tough question, kiddo. I wish I had a good answer for you."

"Bah." Nym reached out and shoved Ciana's shoulder. "What kind of older-sister wisdom is that supposed to be?"

Before she could respond, a man appeared on the trail in front of them. Nym's eyes widened, and his mouth went dry. He hurried forward a step and placed himself in front of Ciana. "Who are you?" he demanded.

"Huh. That's strange. You're . . . not here, but you clearly are. How fascinating," the man murmured to himself.

There was no doubt in Nym's mind, none whatsoever, that the man standing in front of him was an ascendant. The magic surrounding him had that same otherworldly quality as the needle-thin metal tower that led to the research lab. The person standing in front of them could obliterate both of them, and probably the whole town of Palmara a few miles away, in an instant, with a single spell, without even trying.

He seemed distracted though, despite having appeared right there on the trail.

Nym reached for his own arcana and started to put together a teleport spell. If he was quick and lucky, he'd get it off before the ascendant realized what was happening. Presumably, the man would be able to see arcana the same as Nym could, so he was banking on distraction and speed to pull it off.

"No, no, please. Stay here for a moment. We need to speak," the man said, absently sending out a single lightning-fast prod of arcana to scramble the delicate teleportation construct. He turned to look at Ciana. "Please wait at your home. I'll have him back to you shortly."

Then she disappeared. There was maybe a flicker of arcana, something so brief and small that if Ciana hadn't vanished, Nym might have thought he'd imagined it. That, more than anything else, scared him. It wasn't enough that the being before him was unfathomably powerful, he was also so fast that Nym couldn't even see the spells he was casting before they went off.

"Now then . . . As I was saying, it's very strange that you seem to be effectively nonexistent to my magic, but I can quite clearly see you with my eyes. If you don't mind, Exarch, I'd like to take a moment to examine this defense. I wouldn't dare remove it; it's no doubt been the key to your extremely effective hiding, but I may be able to assist and bolster it."

"Who are you?" Nym asked again.

"Oh, yes, I'm sorry. You must have used a memory lock to alter yourself enough to avoid detection. My name is Ferro. I am one of your lieutenants."

"Oh . . . I see. Um, what do you want?"

"What? I want to help you, of course."

That was unexpected. From the way the message his former self had sounded, he'd expected any ascendant he met to try to kill him, or capture him, or otherwise wish him some form of harm. "Um, how are you going to do that exactly?"

Ferro looked puzzled for a second. "I'm sure you must need something done that I can assist with. What is currently standing in the way of you recovering your abilities?"

Nym wasn't sure how much to tell the ascendant. For all that he seemed forthcoming and said he wanted to help, it could still be a trap. There could be something he was trying to get, some information he needed, before he turned on Nym. What that might be, Nym couldn't begin to guess.

"Well, let me think for a moment. I don't actually know how to recover my abilities."

"You don't?" Ferro looked confused. "This was a highly unorthodox plan, Exarch. I suppose the speed at which you constructed it and the limited resources available necessitated something with many possible points of failure."

"Uh, yeah. Probably that's what happened, I'm sure."

The ascendant just stared at him expectantly, like he was waiting for Nym to perform a trick. After a moment of awkward silence, Nym said, "I don't think there's much you can do to help me right now. I'm still working on boring through the fourth layer. Then I have to get through the fifth. You know, one step at a time."

"Show me," Ferro said. It wasn't precisely a command, but the arcana churning in the ascendant's soul well was so overpowering that it was impossible not to be at least a little bit intimidated by him.

Nym took a deep breath and forged his conduit. He hadn't really had to consciously think about reaching the third layer with it in months now. That part was automatic, but for the first time in the last thousand attempts, he found himself obsessively going over every minute detail while Ferro watched.

The conduit pierced the membrane of reality and drove through the first layer like it wasn't even there, then shot across the second layer without so much as stuttering when he crashed through the arcana knots studded in that version of reality. At the third layer, it deftly wove through the strange twisting eddies and tides of the Astral Sea as Nym navigated the space between portals.

Then the conduit pierced the membrane separating it from the fourth layer and crashed into the Bulwark. It split the knotted wall of arcana partway before his willpower was no longer strong enough to cut through with brute force. Then Nym twisted the whole conduit and started to bore deeper into the layer, to dig through it.

His will was stretched to snapping, and he hadn't reached the end. He knew he was close, he had to be, but he just couldn't quite make it there. Ferro watched him work, his face impassive, and when he saw that Nym had stalled, he said, "No, not like that. Here, start over."

Nym did as he was instructed, except when he reached the third layer, Ferro somehow redirected his conduit. Nym nearly broke it just from the shock of having someone else able to influence it, but he recovered quickly and let the ascendant nudge him on the way. The pathway he took was entirely different, both shorter and moving with the current, so to speak.

The conduit practically flew through the third layer and, when it crashed into the fourth, it was far stronger than usual. Nym's initial drive split the Bulwark almost as far as he could make it with his boring, and then Ferro did something else to the conduit. Nym felt holes open up in it, but instead of the arcana flooding into his soul well, it surged through the length of the conduit and struck just as the initial momentum from reaching out was dying off.

The fourth layer parted like warm butter before the conduit, and suddenly Nym was past it, burst through the membrane, and the conduit was firmly lodged into the fifth layer of reality. He stood there, shocked, and felt the arcana pour into his soul well. It was nothing like third-layer arcana with its chaotic energy that needed to be tamed before it was useful.

Fifth-layer arcana was something else, something gentle and warm but at the same time enormous. Nym would never be able to control it like he did third-layer arcana. At best, he would guide it along by creating a framework for it to fill. It was just like Archmage Veran had described it.

"Much better," Ferro said. "Now that we've taken care of that, what's next?"

CHAPTER THIRTY-ONE

In a way, Nym almost felt cheated. He'd been working on this for months now, getting lessons from an archmage no less. He'd been so sure he was close, that he had nearly accomplished his goal. And then Ferro had shown up, turned all his progress on its head, and shown him how wrong he'd been about his most basic assumptions.

It had been so easy to do once he'd been shown the right way to do it. The correct path across the third layer moved with the Astral Sea and crossed less than half the distance. The surge of arcana split the Bulwark almost like it wasn't even there. Nym probably wouldn't get it exactly right himself the next time he forged that conduit, but there was no doubt in his mind that he'd get close enough to reach the fifth layer anyway.

Ferro was here to assist Exarch Niramyn. As long as he thought Nym was working toward the goal of regaining his past memories and power, he probably wouldn't be a threat. What Nym wasn't sure of was how the ascendant would react if he found out that Nym wasn't racing headlong to take up his former life again.

"Well, I guess I just keep on practicing until I can reach the next layer," Nym said, scratching his head. "That's the whole idea of being an ascendant, right? To go past the fifth layer, which humans can't do."

"They can, but in order to do it, they have to stop being a human. You helped me cross that chasm a long time ago."

"Oh. I guess that's what I'll start working on next."

"Yes, that's probably a good strategy. Once you've grown strong enough to break the memory-lock curse, you'll have to move quickly to regain your full strength before Myzalik's lackies find you and report back to him."

Nym felt a brief surge of panic at the idea of other ascendants finding him. He doubted he'd be so lucky as to meet a friendly one twice in a row. "Speaking of that, how is it that none of them have found me before now?"

"I've been taking care of the ones who figured out your identity and followed the trail. Almost invariably, they end up coming to this place. I've ambushed six ascendants now and dispersed their temporal anchors. That is of course a temporary solution. The only thing preventing them from sharing this information is their own greed for the reward they would gain for capturing you."

"Then I don't have much time. How strong could I get in so little time though?"

"Your own protections have kept you safe as well, you understand?" Ferro gestured around. "Even now, with you standing in front of me, I can't find you with my magic. I have to use my own eyes to see you. A shroud of arcana would be more than enough to hide you if an ascendant wishing you harm appeared before you."

"Then how did you find me?"

"I did not. I have watched your pet human to ensure her safety, as you appeared quite fond of her before you disappeared from the timeline. I saw her talking to someone, but there was no one there in my scrying, so I came to investigate. And here you are, my master."

Nym didn't know exactly what Ferro meant when he said a shroud of arcana would hide him, but if he understood what the ascendant was saying, then perhaps he had the same kind of magic shielding him that the memory cube did. That appeared as though it were nothing to any scrying he did, and his magic couldn't grip it at all.

But no, Ferro's magic could clearly affect Nym. Then again, it wasn't likely that an ascendant was using something as weak as a second- or third-circle spell. Nym wondered if an arcana shroud was something that was still beyond his capabilities. If not, persuading Ferro to show it to him was at the very top of his priorities list now.

"Can you teach me how to conceal myself from any ascendant that might physically confront me, just in case?"

"Certainly, master. You will need arcana from the Echoing Vastness to complete this spell. Just form a conduit like you did a few minutes ago and I'll guide you through it."

"The what now?" Nym had never heard of that layer.

"The fifth layer. Humans call it . . . something else. Something with religious overtones, I believe."

The process wasn't as smooth, but this time Ferro didn't interrupt. Nym reached the fifth layer and let the arcana fill his soul well. It poured in, more and more, until he was as full as he could possibly be. Ferro watched silently, perhaps measuring Nym's capabilities or perhaps just disappointed that the boy wasn't as strong as a god.

"Good," the ascendant said finally. "That should be enough. Now, let me show you how to properly cast an invisibility spell."

Ferro did the spell once, slowly, while he lectured what each part did and how it connected to the whole. It was complicated, at least on the level of the long-range communications and scrying spells he'd learned, but somehow thicker. It was the arcana he was using as raw material that made the difference, Nym thought.

Just as the spell was completed, Ferro let it fall apart. He gestured for Nym to try, simply saying, "Remember that for this type of arcana, you must build the channels that guide it along. Do not attempt to control its path directly. You are far too weak to do such a thing as you are now. Think of it as heavy, heavy water flowing through the canals you've dug to give it the shape you desire."

That took a few attempts to wrap his head around. Nym was very used to weaving spells, bending and twisting strands of arcana into the shape he desired, and using his intent to imbue the arcana with whatever properties he needed to make it work. Even with third-circle magic, he'd found that once he'd calmed it down, it functioned much the same way. It just took a greater effort of willpower to force it to be still.

Building a framework that would wrap around the arcana and guide it rather than just making the spell out of arcana itself was new, and it was taxing. It took far more effort to make even the simplest patterns than he was used to, but he managed it. If he'd been as limited as he was a month ago before the aging curse was broken, he didn't think he could have done it.

It was probably sloppy and inefficient. He knew his soul well was many, many times bigger than Archmage Veran's, so he could afford to waste far more energy to achieve the same result, but he had no doubt that he was using the same basic technique to define the parameters of the spell. He'd seen his mentor do it, after all.

Nym finished crafting the spell, and everything went white. He reached out a hand and swiped at it, but nothing changed. "Hmm . . . I don't think I did this right," he said. "Everything is just . . . gone, like I'm in a big, endless white void."

"You took too long to finish forming the spell. Go ahead and dismiss it and I'll show you where you went wrong," Ferro's voice came from in front of Nym.

The world returned in all its colorful and shape-filled glory as Nym let the spell collapse. That was an interesting experience in itself, practically staggering him back a step as the arcana fell out of shape. He made a mental note to be more careful with discharging fifth-layer arcana for any future pinnacle spells.

"Alright, watch closely, please. The issue you ran into is a symptom of the two problems you're having. Your will is not strong enough to hold arcana from the Echoing Vastness in shape, and you aren't casting the spell fast enough to fully form it before your will gives out. Because of that, arcana started to spill out of the channels. You see this part here? This is where it bled through and ruined the portion of the spell that allows you to see."

"So I need to reinforce the channels with my will or cast the spell faster but preferably both," Nym said.

"No, of course not. The channels need to be as strong as they need to be to hold the shape until the spell is complete. Any stronger would be wasted effort to achieve the same result. That will take some practice to achieve, of course."

"Oh, of course."

Ferro was kind of an abrupt teacher. It was a sharp contrast to his time with Archmage Veran, who very much liked to tease answers out of Nym with hints and subtle guidance toward logical conclusions. Ferro just kind of plopped the answer down in Nym's lap and left him to figure out what he wanted to do with it.

In some ways, it was refreshing to just have the solution handed to him, but it certainly took some of the challenge out of learning a new spell. He supposed that from Ferro's point of view, he wasn't teaching Nym so much as hastening the return of Exarch Niramyn. Once he regained his old memories and personality, he would already know everything Ferro was telling him, so there was little point in laying down a foundation to build upon.

Nym spent another half an hour practicing the spell under Ferro's guidance until he could cast it without error. He looked at the world around him, fully visible with no blurring or warping like the camouflage spell he'd been using. Then he looked down at his own body, completely invisible to his mundane sight. He could see the crushed leaf under his foot but not the foot itself.

"Amazing. True invisibility," Nym said.

"Yes. This combined with your current . . . extratemporal state . . . should allow you to hide from even an ascendant. It's not foolproof, of course. I would still be able to see you cast a spell just by seeing the arcana form around you, but that's a limit of such a low layer of arcana that you won't be able to get around. And if I absolutely needed to, I could just destroy everything within a few miles of here to make sure I hit you."

"Those are valid points," Nym agreed. "But it's better than nothing."

"Yes, Exarch. What else can I do to assist you?"

Nym considered telling him about the cube but decided against it. Once that secret was out, there was no taking it back, and he didn't know if he trusted Ferro. So far, the ascendant had been nothing but helpful. If that changed, Nym was a dead man. He didn't think he could bluff Ferro like he had the last time someone who knew he was an ascendant wanted something from him. Some measure of the truth was necessary.

"For now, nothing. I have a few memories left to me from my past life that are guiding me along the path I determined was best for myself. If I need your assistance, I will leave a message for you at the mortal's home. You're monitoring it anyway, you said?" At Ferro's nod, Nym continued. "Then you should note the appearance of a simple piece of paper with instructions for you on it easily."

"Yes. That is a good plan, considering the circumstances. Please let me know whenever you need me to do something for you. My skills are at your full disposal."

"Thank you, Ferro. For now, I'm going to finish my visit with the mortal. I will be in contact next time I need you."

"Of course. Then, if that is all, I shall return to my watch. Rest assured, none of your enemies will reach you by following any timeline that leads to this mortal."

Then Ferro was gone, and Nym breathed out a massive sigh of relief. He teleported to Ciana's house immediately. He needed to get her out of there before a godlike being appeared in front of her and obliterated her. That was going to be a fun talk, he knew.

CHAPTER THIRTY-TWO

So you know how you always wanted to take a vacation?" Nym asked.

"No?"

"Well, you did. I definitely heard you say it."

"I don't think I did," Ciana said. "Is this about that guy who showed up, the rude one?"

"Yeah, kind of. Listen, you should . . . not say anything until we leave. Apparently, they can hear everything you say and do, all the time."

"What? That's . . . Why would they even—"

"It's my fault," Nym interrupted her. "My past self gave me protections to help avoid being noticed, but they don't extend to anyone else. So, I'm sorry, but we need to get you out of here as soon as we can. You should just pack up anything you need to take with you, we'll barricade the door, and you can enjoy a nice vacation for a little while, okay?"

"Nym, I'm not going anywhere."

"Ciana, I need you to listen to me. That man who appeared in front of us is the most powerful being you will ever meet. He could obliterate this entire country in seconds if he wanted to. The only reason you're alive right now is because he's been sitting here, watching this house, waiting for me to show up. He told me that he's . . . I don't know . . . not killed, but whatever immortals do to one another, a bunch of other people who showed up looking for me. You. Need. To. Leave."

He wasn't trying to scare her, but it needed to be said. Or maybe he was trying to scare her, not to be mean, but to make her realize how serious the situation was. The only thing he could do to protect her was take her somewhere else and hope that it kept her out of the reach of whatever ascendant showed up next, especially if Ferro couldn't take them out.

"This is ridiculous. Who even are these people?"

She still wasn't scared, not like she should be. Nym took one of his memories and wove it into an illusion. "Look at this," he ordered as he projected the memory of Archmage Veran devastating the forest around the mausoleum. Trees broke apart, and bodies went flying everywhere as explosion after explosion rocked the landscape.

"Do you see this? This was done by an archmage after he spent time preparing the magic. That man we met could do this as easily and quickly as lifting a finger. It wouldn't even be a real effort to him. There is no standing up to them, there is no fighting them. Please, listen to me. Let me protect you the best way I can. Pack up your stuff and I'll take you anywhere you want."

Her eyes were wide as she stared at the pure destruction Archmage Veran had wrought in Nym's memory. He cut the illusion off and grabbed her by the shoulders. "It's going to be okay," he said softly. "We're leaving. I've got some money saved up. We can go anywhere you want, and I'll help you get settled in. I'm sorry, but it's just not safe for you here. Please, go pack up what you need to bring with you."

"Okay," she whispered. Nym watched her walk into the second room of the shack and grab a small sack. She started stuffing it, not that there was much to put in there. Once he was confident that she wouldn't come back out with another argument, he teleported himself into the cellar, tore open the floor, and retrieved the memory cube.

He'd half expected it to trigger another vision, but nothing happened. That was good; he didn't have time to process that right now. Later, when he was safe, he'd channel some fifth-layer arcana into it and see if that triggered something. If not, he'd have to come up with a different plan, but he was pretty sure he was right about what he needed to do.

Once she was packed up, Nym joined Ciana in the main room. "Where do you want to go? There's Thrakus, that place I took you shopping once. Or Abilanth, the capital. It can get cold there, but we can afford some new winter clothes. Uh, a couple small towns here and there. Safe enough for the most part, but occasionally something dangerous does wander by. I have some friends down by the south coast based in Karu I could introduce you to."

He considered Shu-Ain but decided against getting Ciana involved with that whole mess. Cern wouldn't appreciate her being around, she didn't speak the local language, and the last thing she needed was to get tangled up in Analia's problems. Karu wasn't a great fit either, if only because the Earth Shapers weren't actually there right now and Nym didn't know the city well enough to make getting her a place to stay a quick and painless process.

"I don't know, Nym. Wherever you think is best."

Abilanth, maybe. As long as the Feldstals didn't find out about her, she should be safe enough in the middle ring. If it came down to it and there was some sort of emergency, he would work something out with Archmage Veran so that she could talk to him and he could contact Nym to let him know. It was perhaps less safe than Thrakus, but there would at least be someone there she could physically walk over to and who could then notify Nym.

"Here we go," he said. The spell reached out to surround them both, and they disappeared.

Archmage Veran was not in his sanctum. That wasn't particularly unusual. He did have a busy schedule after all, but it was really inconvenient for Nym, who was in full-on panic mode trying to take care of dozens of little details at once. He didn't have time to wait for the archmage to come back, so instead he scribbled a note, left it sitting in the study, grabbed his stash of gold crests, and teleported back to where he'd left Ciana.

After shoving the bag into her hands and giving her brief directions on how to reach the Academy and whom to ask for, he was off again. Hopefully his own protection against ascendant scrying would extend to the teleport spell he'd used on her. Hopefully it worked like he thought it would. Hopefully she wouldn't end up dead because she'd had sympathy for a little boy who'd washed up on a beach near her home.

Hopefully.

One more letter made its way into the postal system, this one addressed to Risa. Nym was vague in it, not outlining the dangers he was facing. Instead, he just told her that he had to go off on a new job and he wasn't sure when he'd be back, that it had been sudden and there was no time for goodbyes.

After dropping that off, Nym teleported to Shu-Ain, right onto the roof of Cern's workshop. He walked in, hoping to find both the alchemist and his apprentice there, but was out of luck. "Cern," he called out. "I need to talk to you real quick."

"I'm busy," Cern called out from the lab.

"Okay, well, some stuff happened, and I need to take care of things. I'll probably be late picking up the next shipment. I'm not sure when I'll actually be back."

There was some cussing and scrambling, and Cern poked his head out of the back room. "How am I supposed to make money if you're not here to transport the goods?"

Nym shrugged. "I don't know what to tell you. This is big. I don't have a choice about this anymore. Do you know where Analia is?"

"No idea," the alchemist said sourly. "She stopped showing up for lessons too. I haven't seen her in a few days. She's . . . probably alright. It's not the first time this has happened."

"Damn," Nym said. "Okay, I'll see if I can find her before I go."

"If you do, tell her she's supposed to be here helping me, not running around like a vigilante."

"Will do," Nym assured Cern.

He got to work scrying, this time sure of what he was looking for. Unfortunately, she was nowhere near the workshop. Or if she was, she had made some changes to her antiscrying rune sequences that were interfering with his ability to find her. Nym doubted that was the case. It was far more likely she just wasn't in that part of the city.

He crafted a message spell and sent it out, asking where she was, but she didn't respond. That might just be because she was still mad at him. Nym debated using a wide-area scry, but he wasn't sure it would pick her up the way the one designed to bypass antiscrying measures could. In the end, it only cost him a bit of arcana and a few minutes of his time, so he gave it a shot.

As expected, nothing came back. Nym cursed his luck but gave up on reaching her. If he really, really needed to, he could find her, but he didn't have the time. He just hoped she was alright, that she was ignoring him because she was busy or upset still and not because she was incapacitated or otherwise in danger.

[The ascendants found me. I met one today. Broke through to the fifth layer. I don't have a choice anymore about whether to take back my old powers. The one I met, if he wanted to, he could have destroyed everyone in a hundred miles with a snap of his fingers. The power they wield is unreal. I'll never be able to match it the way I'm going. I hope you're safe. I hope when it's done, I'm still myself and we'll see each other again.]

He cast the message out into the void, hoping it would reach her. Like the previous message, no response came back. "Please don't be dead," he whispered before teleporting away.

The last step was Karu or, rather, the lumber camp his friends were helping to build. A quick scry showed him that Nomick was the closest, and Nym flew over to him first. "Hey," the earth mage called out when he saw Nym flying his way. "Didn't expect you back so early."

"Yeah, something came up. I ran into an ascendant, and long story short, I need to try to get my old powers back, or they're going to take me out without even blinking. The gap between my magic and theirs is too much right now. I just wanted to say goodbye in case, you know . . . in case things don't go in my favor."

"Hey, hey. Easy there," Nomick said. He pulled Nym into a hug. "Come on, you got this. I believe in you. Let's go talk to everyone else, give you a proper send off. Then you can come back and tell us all about your exciting adventure in a few weeks."

"I don't have time," Nym said. "I really need to get going."

"Five minutes, Nym. You'll regret it if you don't say your farewells. They'll be hurt if you don't stop to talk to them."

He didn't want to. Every second he spent out in the open was another second he was vulnerable to a random ascendant dropping out of the sky and obliterating everything in sight. Nym forced himself to take a breath though. "Okay, but we've got to be quick. I can't even tell you how dangerous this is right now. There just aren't words to describe how powerful a real ascendant is."

He must have gotten through with how urgent it was because Nomick didn't even complain when Nym picked him up and flew him over to collect the other three. Once they were all together, he explained the situation.

"What are you going to do?" Ophelia asked.

"I have an ascendant-crafted thing in my bag," Nym said. "It contains all my lost memories. Everything I was before I became Nym is in there, and that includes all my knowledge about magic. I'm . . . I'm afraid that when I unlock it, I'll stop being Nym again. This was just a small part of my whole life. Exarch Niramyn is immortal, thousands and thousands of years old. How can I change someone like that?"

No one said anything, but Nym could see they'd all reached the inevitable conclusion. "If I don't come back," he said, swallowing once to clear his throat. "If I don't come back, then . . . I'm glad I met all of you. Thank you for everything."

One at a time, he hugged all of them. "I took Ciana to Abilanth," he said. "If you ever end up that way, maybe see if you can find her. I . . . I didn't tell her what I'm about to do. I couldn't."

He forged his conduit, pulled in the arcana, and wove a teleportation spell around him. "Goodbye," he said.

CHAPTER THIRTY-THREE

Nym found himself a nice mountain peak far away from any sort of civilization, settled into a shallow cave on the west side perhaps thirty feet deep, and took the cube out of his bag. It was just as he remembered it, the same as the ones he'd seen in Research Lab Six. But this one was full of his memories, not random information and arcana prints.

He settled down on the ground, made himself comfortable, and set the cube in his lap. Then Nym placed his hands on the sides of it, took a deep breath, and opened up a conduit to the fifth layer. It was a smoother process than his first solo attempt but still rougher than when Ferro had hijacked his conduit and shown him how to do it.

The conduit finished forming, and arcana poured through into his soul well, all heavy and smothering, almost too much to bear as it filled him up. He'd expected that would be enough to trigger the cube, but he'd been wrong. Nym slowly expelled the arcana out, letting it permeate into an aura around him, one that overlapped the cube.

And everything went white.

Exarch Niramyn stood in front of Nym, looking as insufferably smug as ever. "You've reached the threshold between a mortal existence and an ascendant one," Niramyn said. "You'll need to move quickly for this next part. I am going to show you where to find a sanctuary to protect yourself and how to break the spell sealing away all our memories. Once that's done, you'll have moments at best before an ascendant finds you."

Nym didn't bother replying. It was obvious that the memory was another of the noninteractive kind, just a recollection of an illusion his past self had conjured up. Exarch Niramyn gestured, and the endless white around them was replaced by a barren, wind-swept wasteland of cracked and baked earth. The sun burned in the sky, and there was nothing for miles and miles around.

"A place like this is the hardest to teleport to, but of course that's the point. You should have no trouble with it. Feel the environment here, what makes this one specific patch of dirt different from all the rest."

Nym certainly couldn't see a difference. Everywhere he looked, it was all the same. There were no landmarks in sight, no patches of grass or lone twisted trees.

There were no distant mountains off on the horizon, no ridges or ravines. It was just an endless rolling expanse of dead earth being mercilessly scorched under a cloudless sky.

The illusion was so complete that he could feel the heat beating down on him. Unfortunately, there was no arcana here to put up a barrier, nothing to cool him down. He couldn't leave, and he couldn't protect himself. Nym had no choice but to stand there and endure.

"This is a place I chose specifically because of what it lacks. You must define it by what's not there instead of what is. There are no landmarks here, no people, no anything. All of this must be incorporated into your mental image of the place. Take your time, study this illusory world well. Know its every facet."

The earth crumbled and broke apart in a wave, revealing an empty hole beneath it. "Below is the entrance to my sanctuary, our sanctuary. Once you've reached the gates, it will be time to break the curse that seals away your memories," Niramyn said.

At the bottom of the hole was a circle of steel and stone. Nym didn't recognize a single one of the runes etched on its surface, but for the purposes of trying to craft a teleport that took him near it, that was alright. He didn't need every exact detail to be perfect. It went into the mental image he was slowly forming, a welcome anchor to contrast a location that was mostly framed by what it wasn't.

"Stand upon the gate and you will cast this spell to break the curse," Niramyn said.

The spell formed in the air in real time, fifth-layer arcana pouring into forms faster than Nym thought he could do himself, and in a staggering amount. It would push him to the limits to channel that much arcana so quickly, but he thought that he could do it with a soul well full to bursting and at least three conduits feeding more in all at once.

It wasn't too terribly complicated, though it did look to be uniquely suited for this one specific task. That actually helped, since it didn't need a bunch of extra stuff in it that covered other scenarios. Nym couldn't even imagine how complicated a generalized pinnacle curse-breaker spell would be. Though he supposed Niramyn wouldn't consider it a pinnacle spell.

"And though I'm sure this example is more than enough, it is too important to risk you forgetting this spell."

A wave of vertigo washed over Nym, and then he had a memory of him floating in the water while his magic propelled him toward land. It was only a sliver of a memory, barely two seconds long, of him casting six different spells at once. Five of them faded into the background, but the last one was the focus of the memory, of him casting the initial curse that would lock away his memories.

It was the last spell he'd cast before he'd lost consciousness. Nym snapped out of the memory, and suddenly he knew how to cast the curse breaker he'd devised on the spot for this one particular curse. It was an utterly unique spell, cast only once before as a precaution to confirm it would work, destined to be used only once more when it came time to wake himself back up.

"Of course it goes without saying that the cube needs to be brought with you," Niramyn said. "But we'll only have one chance at this. I cannot stress enough that those few seconds between unlocking our memories and entering my sanctuary will be the most perilous of our entire existence. Our enemies will know, and they will react. There will be no time for hesitation. Be sure that you are standing on the gate."

Nym came back to himself and felt a shudder run down his spine. Unlike the previous message, his past self was terse this time, with a lot less ego and a lot more worry barely hidden below the surface. What he was about to do next was something so dangerous an Exarch at the peak of ascendant hierarchy was repeatedly stressing the possibility of catastrophic consequences.

A large part of Nym wanted to abandon the plan. He was sort of safe as long as he didn't break the curse that locked away his memories and personality. He could get Ferro to help him progress, perhaps. It might be smarter to spend twenty or thirty years regaining his power the hard way. But then, if an ascendant who was hostile to him found him even once, or if Ferro decided he was better off without his old master, Nym would be dead.

He knew he was trying to talk himself out of taking this risk, but he couldn't picture another path that was any better. No matter what he did, it was just a matter of time until one of Niramyn's enemies found him. He didn't think they'd care that Nym wasn't that same person anymore. Why take a risk on him coming back when they could just disintegrate him on the spot?

So his only real options were to hope that he could gain the strength to defend himself from ascendant-level threats on his own before those threats materialized or take back the power he used to have and hope he didn't lose himself completely in the process. If it had been just him, he thought he might have risked it. But then he wondered how many of them would be more than willing to go after Ciana. She was already in danger. Was she supposed to spend the rest of her life in hiding, just hoping that a god didn't take notice of her and crush her like a bug?

No, there wasn't really a choice at all.

The teleportation spell was difficult both because he was relying on an illusion of a memory to guide him and because of the nature of the location itself. There were details there but very little to differentiate it from the rest of the barren desert. He held on to the feeling of heat pounding down on him, shaped the thought of his destination with the despondent vista of a never-ending plane devoid of life, and anchored it to the idea of the cool darkness below that earth.

Strangely, the image of the gate wouldn't come back to him. He'd studied it in depth, and even if he couldn't draw the runes from memory, he still knew the general shape, but when he tried to incorporate it into the spell, the image kept slipping away from him. It was probably something to do with them being ascendant runes.

When he thought he'd rebuilt the scene in his head, Nym pulled arcana into his soul well and cast the spell. The cave around him vanished, and when he could see again, he was standing in the middle of the wasteland he'd envisioned. Whether he was in the right spot was still up for debate, but a simple scry would confirm it.

Before that though, he crafted a thermal barrier to protect him from the blistering heat. Perhaps it would have been better to wait a few hours for nightfall, but he didn't know if he had that kind of time. His only ally in all of this was Ferro, and Nym didn't really have much reason to trust him.

His scrying anchor couldn't find the gate into Niramyn's sanctuary, but Nym was experienced enough now to realize when it was skipping over something. He'd run into that effect quite often, and even though it was more subtle here than he'd ever seen and covering a greater area too, he still caught it. With a bit of terrakinesis, he ripped open a hole in the cracked earth and fell down into the darkness.

The gate was just like he'd seen it in the illusion, a round portal perhaps five feet wide. Its frame was steel, with two lines intersecting it through the middle, and the interior filled with some sort of smooth, polished stone. The runes on its surface were barely visible, unlike in his vision. In fact, if he hadn't seen them in full detail, he might not have noticed them at all.

He doubted it would make a difference against an ascendant, but every second he could buy himself was priceless, so he took the time to use terrakinesis again to seal up the hole overhead. That left him in complete darkness, but it didn't matter. He didn't need to see for what would come next.

One at a time, he opened up conduits to the fifth layer. The first one was easy now, but opening a second took an active effort of focused concentration. A third would have been beyond him if not for the mind partition letting him run parallel thought processes. He wouldn't have been able to open all three at once, but he could do one at a time while maintaining the others.

Nym suspected he could do four if he pushed, but he wasn't sure if he'd have any spare willpower leftover to actually shape anything into a spell. If he was right in his calculations though, he wouldn't need a fourth conduit. He just needed to form the framework for the curse breaker.

Unlike the invisibility spell Ferro had taught him, Nym *knew* how to break the memory curse. His past self had made sure of that. It was easy to form the framework and pour the arcana into it. The spell flashed into existence, and the dam gave way. Memories poured into him.

And Nym ceased to exist.

CHAPTER THIRTY-FOUR

Niramyn was forging a conduit to the Transcendence layer even before he opened his eyes and spinning out the wild, thrumming arcana into four separate spells at once. A second passed, and the first spell coalesced into existence. Below him, the gate runes flared to life, primed and ready for the next spell to give them instructions. That spell washed over the runes the instant they activated.

Two seconds had passed now, and he could feel the turbulence in the timeline as an ascendant took notice. The third spell finished, this one designed to sync his current body to the gate's rune matrix and prevent the safety measures from shredding it down to individual cells. Niramyn started two more spells in the first partition of his mind, though they shouldn't be needed.

The third second finished, and the world started to warp around him. That was not his magic, but instead that of another ascendant trying to lock him down in time and space. If that spell finished before he whisked himself away to the safety of his sanctuary, then all would be lost. But he knew that spell, recognized its shape, and knew down to the fraction of a second how long it would take to close around him.

He had time for the fourth of his original spells to trigger, this one aligning his mind to the gate. The new experiences he'd gained in this Nym persona were at odds with his previous existence, but the spell was smart enough to recognize that the core of personality below it was still Niramyn. The gate began to open.

The fourth second passed, and the enemy ascendant's temporal-and-spatial lock snapped closed around the gate with Niramyn still inside it. His fifth spell finished, not that he'd needed it. As expected, the gate held against the attempted trap, but he blew a hole in the arcana matrix and destabilized it anyway. It was best not to let those who were lesser than him think that they had any kind of advantage.

The gate was fully primed now, and Niramyn began to pass through it. Just before he was completely subsumed, he released his final spell, an arcana pulse that wiped away his presence in the timeline. Only those who'd actively witnessed his return would ever know he'd been here, and he'd deal with them later.

Niramyn appeared inside his sanctuary. It would not have been his first choice, but it was the only one he could currently access. This new body hadn't been prepared properly, through no fault of his own. Nym, as he'd called himself, had been a bumbling fool with plenty of energy but no foresight or drive. He hadn't taken proper advantage of the resources at his disposal and instead wasted an inordinate amount of time on his friends, as if those were good for anything.

He would review those memories in depth later, just to see if the Nym persona had actually figured out anything worth knowing, but considering how he'd wasted his time playing instead of working, Niramyn doubted there would be even a single memory that justified the time going through them.

For now, he had many, many preparations to occupy his time. This body was perhaps capable of channeling seventh-layer arcana, but that would be a stretch. Thanks to Myzalik's impossible immortality spell, he'd been regressed haphazardly, with none of the prep work needed for such a delicate procedure. The damage would take weeks to repair.

It was ridiculous. This body still needed to eat! It could actually die without mortal food. Adjusting it to be able to subsist on nothing but arcana was at the top of Niramyn's priority list, followed shortly by restructuring its mind so that its thought processes could continue without a brain limiting it. The fact that Nym had only managed to create one partition the entire time he was in control was disgraceful. He should have reached at least four, even limited to the meat of his body.

Niramyn broke the remaining curses embedded in his mind, one at a time, and in doing so more than tripled his current body's ability to hold arcana. That was good; he didn't have time to go slowly. A sanctuary wasn't impregnable, even if he'd erased his passing into it from history. He'd bought himself time, but there was so much work to do. If he couldn't increase his soul well's size by at least ten times its current maximum in the next week, he didn't deserve to call himself an Exarch.

The sanctuary was nothing but a void of empty space and endless darkness hidden inside the sixth layer of reality. It was impervious to mortal detection, and he'd taken pains when he created it to hide it from other ascendants, but Niramyn knew that time wasn't on his side yet. He began his work.

First, he needed a body that had grown to its full capacity. Nym had foolishly broken the aging curse too early, not that it made much difference. He'd unwittingly done his best to starve it anyway and hadn't aged half as fast as he should have. Niramyn didn't need the curse to modify his age though. He simply cast the spell and fed it pure arcana until he'd reached his peak form, that of a man in his mid- to late twenties.

That doubled his soul well's capacity, which allowed him to start casting some of the heavier spells. First he replaced the troublesome mortal digestive system with one modeled after creatures that survived in the outer layers of reality, the ones that did so on nothing but arcana. He crafted a reservoir to hold the life-sustaining arcana and teleported it into his body, then immediately filled it.

With that completed, Niramyn allowed himself a moment to relax. The amount of arcana he'd stored would keep him alive for several years without food or water, barring injuries that might tax the magic's ability to keep him in peak condition.

Starvation had been his greatest risk inside the sanctuary, where no other physical matter existed.

The next few modifications were going to be riskier. They weren't something someone should just play around with because there were no do-overs. Detaching his mind from his brain could have catastrophic consequences if done incorrectly, and it was best to have someone else on hand to reverse the process if anything went wrong.

Niramyn would, of course, be doing it by himself. He'd already done it a thousand times without issue and had every confidence that the next one wouldn't be the time he screwed it up. At the same time, it wouldn't do to be reckless, so his version of the augmentation included the reversal spells already primed to activate on a timer. If something went wrong, they'd go off automatically and restore him. If everything was successful, he'd manually deactivate them.

It was easier to anchor spells like that in a physical object, but the sanctuary didn't have any matter in it besides him. While he could use his own body as the anchor, that would interfere with his other spells and add an additional layer of complication to an already sensitive and intricate procedure. Unfortunately, he couldn't summon matter from the core layer of reality without breaking the spells that kept the sanctuary hidden.

The solution then was simple. He held up one hand, killed the nerve endings in it, and sliced off four of his fingers. They grew back a moment later, and the arcana reserves in his reservoir dipped lower to accommodate the regeneration. Niramyn anchored his contingency spells to the four fingers and spread them around himself, then started creating the complicated web of magic that would disconnect his mind from his brain.

Normally, the spells would be done sequentially and in two parallel processes. The timing was sensitive, but it was well within his capabilities to channel the arcana at the needed speed. That only worked when done on another person though. Once he started, there would be a point where his mind disconnected from his body but hadn't yet formed the new links of arcana needed to continue controlling it.

These spells he could also prepare ahead of time and set to trigger in order. Essentially, he created them two at a time, in the correct order, at the correct tempo. Each one was set to go off after ten minutes, which was more than enough time to complete the full set. Niramyn gave himself two extra minutes of leeway to prepare his body for the transfer. He would technically be brain-dead for four minutes in the middle of the procedure, and he needed to make sure his body didn't die before he could reconnect to it.

The first two spells activated simultaneously, then the next set, and the next. Two minutes into the procedure, his brain stopped functioning, and four minutes after that, he regained awareness of himself. The final spells forged the new connections to his body, and Niramyn became a creature unbound by flesh once again.

Body and mind powered by nothing but pure, unfiltered arcana now, he was ready to begin the true modifications that differentiated an ascendant from a mortal mage. Permanent pathways had to be blazed through his mind, pathways that would become connections to the deeper layers where true power could be found.

It was no longer enough to be able to cast two spells at once either. Niramyn set one partition to creating new ones, and once those were created, they each repeated the process. Soon, his mind had fractured into twenty-two pieces, each one as capable as the original had been. They were connected through an arcana core lodged in his brain like a tumor, a hive mind directed by his original personality.

The work proceeded significantly faster from that point, though it was still days that bled into weeks before he was fully satisfied. It wasn't perfect by any means. He wasn't an Exarch again yet. But he was out of danger. There were ascendants who might dislodge him from the timeline, force him to lose months or years before reattaching himself, but his existence was no longer in jeopardy.

He couldn't proceed any further without a single resource outside his magic. The ninth layer would be his stopping point, for now. There were other sanctuaries though, ones that were both more secure and better equipped. Getting to them would be a fight. He would need to be both clever and quick.

A rift of light appeared in the darkness, a gaping maw that took a chunk out of the reality around him and ruptured the sanctuary. Niramyn smirked. It had taken exactly as long as he'd expected for them to find a way in, which was more than enough time to reclaim a significant portion of his power. A being appeared in the rift, the physical manifestation of an ascendant, but before he could act, Niramyn trapped it in a cube of paradoxical brilliant darkness.

The ascendant's magic fractured against the paradox's physical form, and Niramyn cast him out of the timeline. With the way clear and his work now finished, he abandoned his sanctuary and willed himself back into existence in the core layer of reality. His power would be less overt here, but so would Myzalik's. The gap between them wouldn't be so hard to bridge, if it came down to it.

Immediately, an ascendant appeared next to him, one he recognized. "Ah, Ferro. Good," he said. "What has happened in my absence?"

"The Ascendant Council has fractured in the wake of Myzalik's attack. Many of those previously loyal to your name have changed their colors, and those that were neutral have fortified their positions or gone into hiding, afraid to be the next to face this new magic. There are thirty-two ascendants unaccounted for, possibly victims of Myzalik."

"And my holdings?"

"In shambles. I saved what I could for you, but the others descended upon them like vultures to cart off what treasures they could steal."

"I see," Niramyn said. "They shall be punished for that. But first, how widespread is this new ascendant-killing spell? Can anyone besides Myzalik use it?"

CHAPTER THIRTY-FIVE

Time didn't have any meaning to Nym anymore. He was aware of it, conceptually, and he remembered experiencing it firsthand but couldn't reconcile those memories with his new state of existence. He was no longer a single point moving forward, but something that sprawled out across the face of eternity, something that dug roots down in a thousand, thousand places and experienced all of it at once.

Nym couldn't wrap his mind around that concept. It was too much, too big. It was only the fact that he had been assimilated into a being that was so much *more* than him that insulated him from the psyche-breaking insanity that was experiencing time all at once. Even that protection was fragile, dubious. It was an unwitting shield of happenstance that could be removed at any time, for any reason or none at all.

Not that he understood that in that particular moment. But he would, in some future moment, and since he would then, he did now. Or something like that. Even then, his understanding was imperfect, and it hurt his head trying to make sense of it. Or it would have, if he still had a body to experience pain.

"Oh, damn it. Damn you, Myzalik. Your stupid spell splintered off a paradoxical existence."

The words echoed across his entire being, but they weren't Nym's. They were a part of the whole, which he supposed in a way made them his as well, even if they hadn't originated from him. And then there was a sensation, the first he'd felt in a subjective eternity, like something had reached down, plunged a hand into his stomach, and grabbed hold of him by his spine. Then it ripped him out of his formless existence and stuffed him back into the world.

Nym blinked against the sudden appearance of light in his eyes. He was sitting on a floor in the middle of a room he'd never seen before. The walls were sheets of solid gold with rich, thick tapestries hung over them, the floor was exquisitely cut marble so polished he could see himself in it, and the furniture was some sort of solid, heavy dark wood.

Directly in front of him was a chair that had been upholstered with cushions dyed a deep purple color, and sitting in that chair was . . . himself. This version was older by maybe a decade, but he had the same dark hair and jawline. Nym saw his own nose in that face, and his own mouth too. The eyes though, they were two frozen chips of ice that flashed through dark colors, reds and blues and greens, and regarded him with coldness and contempt.

"So," the man said. "What to do with you?"

Nym's mind raced, trying to catch up with what was going on. He was no longer part of a gestalt whole, that was for sure. His memories and senses were limited to what his physical body knew and felt, which left him feeling inexplicably empty somehow, like he'd lost a connection to something greater than the sum of its parts. Perhaps he had. But with that feeling of being lesser came the ability to once again fully comprehend his own existence.

"You're him," Nym said. "Or me, in the past."

"And in the future," his adult self said. "Niramyn."

"How are we both existing at the same time?" Nym asked. "This doesn't feel like one of the memory visions you left for me."

"It is not," Niramyn said sourly. "This persona of mine, Nym, should have ceased to exist when I regained all my lost memories."

Nym winced. He'd been afraid of that. It was the expected outcome, honestly. The chances that his not quite two years of existence would hold out against an ascendant were minuscule at best. But there was no other way to protect his friends from becoming casualties of the ascendants once they found him, at least none that he'd ever found.

"What went wrong?" Nym wondered aloud.

"Everything was fine while we existed in the sanctuary. It is removed from the core of reality by so many layers that the paradox was tolerated. I didn't even realize it existed until we returned here, to what mortals consider the real world. I had to form a new body and excise you from my existence just to stabilize myself."

"I don't really understand, but I guess you'd know that already, huh?"

"Indeed. I . . ." Niramyn paused. "I will be honest with you, Nym. I've assimilated your memories into my being. I know every single thought you've ever had, even the ones you thought you'd forgotten later. I know how much those six mortals mean to you. That makes them the six most important mortals in existence because you are me, and that makes them important to me."

Nym's eyebrows shot up. "There shouldn't be any way that my priorities bled over into you any more than if a stranger told you what they cared about."

"Agreed, but what Myzalik did to us, it's unprecedented. Reconstituting the body he stuck us in back to true form caused some complications." Niramyn gestured toward Nym.

"Me? I'm the complication."

"Yes," Niramyn agreed dryly. "I had to resolve the paradox, so I reformed you as a separate entity."

"Isn't that . . . Wouldn't it still be a paradox for both of us to exist at the same time?" Nym asked.

"No."

That was apparently all the answer Nym was going to get. Considering that he'd practically been a comatose mental construct when he was part of Niramyn, unable to comprehend his own existence or understand the passage of time, he supposed it wasn't an unreasonable answer.

"Okay. What happens now?"

"That is the question, isn't it?" Niramyn said, leaning forward. "I'm still establishing the damage that was done while you were screwing around instead of working to bring that pathetic mortal body of ours back to a point where I could hide it away and safely resurrect us. I'm inclined to dispose of you, but it seemed most prudent to give you a chance to fight for your continued existence."

"You want me to . . . argue with you as to why I should get to live?" Nym asked. "Wouldn't you already know any argument I could make?"

"Possibly," Niramyn said. "But I don't think so. Like I said, I know everything you did. I know why you did it. But you didn't make the choices I would have made, almost ever really. Only in a few very tense situations where you believed the stakes were life-and-death did you ever really fall back on me to help you. Even then, you constantly fought back against me. It's clear to me that you exist as a discrete entity, which probably explains why your existence is a paradox."

Nym didn't really see how that explained anything at all, but he knew Niramyn well enough to know that his ascendant persona wasn't fond of teaching. He had no patience for questions, and he expected his commands to be carried out by his underlings whether they understood the purpose or not.

"Let me ask you this," Nym said. "Instead of having to justify why I should be allowed to live, what harm is there in letting me live? Drop me back out anywhere and just let me live my life. You can go back to doing ascendant things and getting revenge and so on. I'll go back to doing my things. We never have to see each other again."

Niramyn started laughing. "No, I won't be doing that. Besides, other ascendants would still come for you. You were a part of me, after all."

"So I'll be bait then. Teach me enough to protect myself for a minute or two, and then let me dangle out in the world. Have Ferro follow me around, and he can take out anyone who tries to get to you through me."

"A better idea," Niramyn acknowledged. "And it would provide me with some minimal benefit, albeit at the expense of effort on my part to prepare you for the role."

The ascendant considered the idea while he watched Nym. "You are . . . weak. Without reaching the Transcendence layer, there is no way you could ever stand against an ascendant, not even for an instant. The first one to find you will destroy you."

"Then I guess they'll have saved you some effort," Nym said.

"Hmm . . . No, we won't be doing that. You will stay here with me for now. I'll have someone see about attempting to raise you to Transcendence. That will be an interesting experiment. You're an alternate version of me, lacking any of the advantages and training I received as a child before I ascended. You have no foundation to build upon and will likely crumble under the pressure long before you approach success."

Nym would much rather just go back to his old life, preferably without the threat of random and instant annihilation looming over him, but he was smart enough to understand that he wasn't being given a choice. Niramyn could kill everyone he'd ever met, probably without ever getting out of his chair. Nym had no choice but to do what he was told.

"And if I do succeed?" he asked quietly.

"Then you will be bait worth dangling. Even if you never reach farther than the sixth layer, that would still be enough to convince some to try to take you, and you would survive the attempt so that I can use you again. Yes, I like this idea."

"What about my friends?"

"What about them?"

"Will they be safe?" Nym asked.

Niramyn shrugged. "Probably. I could harvest their souls and hold them in stasis, if that makes you feel better. You could have them back if you ever reach Transcendence. That might be just the motivator you need."

"No! Leave them alone."

The ascendant laughed and said, "As you wish. It does not matter anyway. Time will not flow for you the same way it does in the mortal world. Whether it takes you ten years or a hundred, you will find that little has changed when you return to them. If you return to them. They will be just as you remember them. It is you who will be different."

"We are in agreement then," Nym said. "I will become an ascendent of my own power, a parallel existence to yours. And then I will be the trap that catches your enemies unawares."

"Well, you will try, at least. When you wake up, your instruction will begin. For now, sleep and accustom yourself to having a physical body again. From here on out, you will succeed or fail only under your own power. You won't have my memories of success to fall back on; I will never give you an answer. You'll work for every excruciating inch of progress. Do you understand?"

"I understand."

Darkness enfolded itself around Nym, darkness that was alive with power. It seeped into him, through his muscles and down to his bones, infecting every bit of his body with arcana like he'd never felt. It was stronger than the fox spirit, stronger than the aura around the research lab. He drowned in it, though he did not need to breathe, and when it cleared, he only knew that he was elsewhere.

Then Nym drifted, alone in his mind while a body that was truly his grew around him. It was only when it was finished that he realized the difference between the form he'd worn when he'd met Niramyn and his true body. The other was an empty shell, a temporary construct that housed his consciousness. This body was real. It was his.

Nym opened his eyes again and found himself in an empty room. This was bare of decorations, just a simple, cold stone floor and unending darkness stretching off in every direction. He climbed to his feet and formed a conduit to the third layer. Perfect vision settled into his eyes, and the darkness was no more.

CHAPTER THIRTY-SIX

Ascendants didn't bother with things like light, Nym supposed. He was in a lavishly decorated bedroom, which included an entire wall of shelves filled with books, an oversize writing desk, the most comfortable-looking chairs he'd ever seen, and a bed big enough to get lost in. There were no windows, but there were orbs hanging from the ceiling in delicate gold wire meshes, so thin as to be nearly invisible.

A door opened in one of the walls, or rather it appeared where there hadn't been one a moment before. Light poured in from outside the room, harsh and sterile white that threw stark shadows across the books and the bed. A human figure appeared in the door, one whose features Nym could only see because of his perfect-vision spell.

"Quite an interesting phenomenon, isn't it?" Ferro asked. "Well, come on then. Get out here and let's get started."

"Started with what?" Nym asked. He approached the door and found himself staring out into empty white space. That seemed to be a theme with ascendants, he was finding. He suspected it was because they weren't meeting in a physical space, and they didn't feel it was worth the effort to impose a background that held no meaning into the mental landscape around him.

Nym joined the ascendant out in the empty void beyond the bedroom, and the door closed behind him. The bedroom disappeared completely, leaving him stranded with Ferro. "Don't worry," the ascendant said when he saw Nym's face. "Your room still exists. You've just stepped through the door into the membrane."

"I don't know what that means," Nym confessed. "I don't even know what we're doing."

"We're teaching you how to become an ascendant, of course. I thought Exarch Niramyn discussed this with you already."

"Oh, he did. He was just vague on the details. When you say membrane . . ." Nym trailed off.

"Yes, the membrane between realities. This one is specifically between the fifth and sixth layer, but they're largely all the same. With no reality to shape their appearances, they can be anything we want them to be, or nothing at all. The only real difference is some of them are empty black space, others are empty white space."

"Why's that?" Nym asked.

"I don't think anyone really knows for sure. If they do, they're not sharing that knowledge with the rest of us. Thousands and thousands of experiments and tests have been done in the in-between spaces, and to the best of my knowledge, no one has ever found a difference."

"Interesting, but I guess that's not what we're supposed to be talking about."

"Not at all," Ferro said. "But it does lead into the actual topic for this lesson. What do you suppose the primary difference between a mortal and an ascendant is?"

"The ability to cast spells using arcana from beyond the fifth layer," Nym said immediately.

"No, not at all. That's more of a by-product. The real difference is that ascendants are connected to their reality echoes on other layers. We are one being."

"What is a reality echo? Wait, are you saying that people exist inside the outer layers of reality?"

"That's exactly what I'm saying," Ferro said. "What did you think the other layers were?"

"I don't know. I've never considered the nature of those layers. They're just where I get arcana to do magic with. Take the essence of a layer that's separate from reality, bring it to reality, magic happens."

Ferro regarded him with a most disdainful sniff. "You have exhibited a profound lack of understanding of the fundamentals of magic. Your knowledge is full of *how it works* without any of the *why it works*."

"In my defense, I'm not even two years old. I haven't had a lot of time to learn or any formal education, and most of my magical education was driven by the need to find tools to solve problems."

"That is a fair excuse," Ferro admitted. "But! It ends now. We have practically unlimited time here, and we shall begin with the basics. Your foundation will be solid by the time I am through with you."

That didn't sound so bad to Nym, actually. He did like learning about magic, and it had always been more a lack of time, resources, and instruction that held him back than any lack of desire or motivation. He just wasn't sure what *practically unlimited time* meant.

"How does time work here in membrane space?" he asked.

"It doesn't work. At all. We're not supposed to be here. It's my magic that's holding us in this space and simulating an illusion of linear time for you. For practical purposes, we could stay here for years, and you would find seconds passed in the core reality."

"Oh. Is that . . . I mean, I'm not technically an ascendant right now. Is that going to hurt me?"

"No," Ferro said. "Not at all. But let's get back on topic here: an ascendant is different than a mortal because we form connections with our echoes in other layers of reality. So, how do we do that?"

"I have no idea," Nym said honestly.

"That will be your first assignment then, figuring that out. It is the stepping stone toward true immortality. For your hint: you'll need fifth-layer arcana to do it, what the mortals call the Infinite Heavens."

"What do ascendants call it?" Nym asked.

"The Echoing Vastness. There's nothing divine about it. It's just really, really big. It's a property of reality there. Everything is stretched out far more than is practical."

Nym considered how he would forge a conduit that just needed to stretch on and on forever. It was no wonder mortals never got past that. There must be some trick to make it work though, something like the tides of the third layer and those strange holes in its reality that connected to one another and allowed mages to reach the far end without their conduits physically traversing the distance.

"I can see what you're thinking," Ferro said. "You can't figure out how a conduit would bridge the distance because you're still thinking like a mortal. You have accepted that you can't make changes to the nature of reality itself, only to your conduit to take advantage of that reality. That is your mistake. Once you've connected yourself to your reality echoes, you won't be limited like that."

"I think I get it," Nym said. "There's a whole set of tools I don't even know exist, let alone the names of them or how to use them. So to start, I need to find the Nym that exists inside the first layer, in that version of existence. And once I do that, I . . . don't know. I connect with him somehow. One step at a time. First, figure out how to even look around another layer. No, first figure out how to send something other than a conduit through the membrane."

"Good thoughts," Ferro said. He pointed over Nym's shoulder to where the doorway had reappeared. "You're going to find a lot of books in that room. Start with the ones bound in blue on the bottom shelves."

"Isn't that room back in reality?" Nym asked. "Time would flow there. Wouldn't it be better to study the books here?"

"No, no. That room is just a partitioned portion of the membrane. It's still far enough removed from the core reality that it is an act of effort to maintain the illusion of linear time there for you. The Exarch himself empowered the arcana batteries that are keeping that sanctuary from collapsing and ejecting you into the world."

Nym peered back through the door. Everything looked just as he remembered it. "I don't suppose you know how to turn the lights on?"

"Just place your hand on that panel there by the door," Ferro said.

Nym found it, pushed his hand against it, and blinked against the warm yellow-gold light that filled the room. "That's convenient."

Ferro shrugged. "You should eventually learn how to do it all with just your mind, but it may take you a bit to figure out how to connect to the room. I'm told it was keyed to you to be able to control it. You may notice that you will not get tired, or thirsty, or feel any of the other biological needs a mortal does here. That is a function of the time dilation inherent to this type of space."

"That's convenient," Nym said. "So . . . just go grab some books and start reading."

"All the supplies you might need should be available to you. You will have one hundred subjective hours of studying before I check up on you. At that point, we'll discuss what you've learned. Any questions?"

"A lot, but let's see what I can figure out on my own first."

"Excellent. Off you go then."

Nym stepped fully into the room, the door closed behind him and disappeared, and he was alone. It was an abrupt change in the mood, but one he welcomed. He really did need some time to steady himself, after all the new information that had been stuffed in his head.

He was concerned that Niramyn was correct, that he would break long before he became an ascendant in truth. There was nothing to do but read, and Nym couldn't imagine stuffing his brain with a hundred hours' worth of knowledge, only to immediately go into a lecture, and then probably be sent back to repeat it.

If that was how ascendants trained their children, it was no wonder he'd been the way he was in his old life. Niramyn was cold and ruthless and viewed everything through a filter of how he could benefit from it, what he could get away with. Those few memories he had left over from Niramyn's childhood were unpleasant in a way he was only starting to fully understand.

It was entirely possible Niramyn's parents had broken his mind, and then put it back together again in a way that suited them. Whatever they'd been trying to build, their techniques and resources were far more advanced than Analia's father had ever dreamed of having access to. In a way, they must have succeeded. If Nym understood ascendant society correctly, Niramyn had been near the very top.

He wasn't going to let them turn him into something like that, but at the same time, he did want to become stronger, and he didn't want to be destroyed just because Niramyn couldn't find a use for him. Nym was playing along, but it was a dangerous game, a fine line between getting what he wanted and being molded into what they wanted him to be.

He suspected the isolation would be the biggest problem. He would have to find a way to stay sane through what would likely be years and years of intense study with only occasional interactions with someone that he could rightfully consider an enemy. He suspected the answers would be found somewhere in the depths of third-circle spells, or perhaps pinnacle spells, in the sections about modifying the human body.

That would come later. For now, he needed to fix his foundation, as Ferro had said, to fill in the many, many gaps in his knowledge of magic and the nature of reality. That at least was a chore he welcomed, especially when he considered the quality of an education he could receive at the hands of an ascendant. No doubt there were a thousand secrets casually hidden in that wall of books that no human had ever been privy to.

Nym would learn them all, one at a time. He wasn't going to break. By the time he was done, he planned on being a true ascendant, one strong enough that Niramyn couldn't just casually toss him aside like a piece of garbage. That was what his past self was trying to mold him into anyway, so that was what he'd become. But he'd do it on his terms, and he'd keep his mind and soul intact.

His face set, Nym reached for the first book.

CHAPTER THIRTY-SEVEN

It was hard to keep track of time, subjective linear or otherwise, while embedded in Niramyn's sanctuary. Nym didn't think his physical body even existed right now; he was just a mind puppeteering an illusion that never needed to sleep, or eat, or go to the bathroom. It was one of the many, many questions he was still trying to answer.

At some point in the early days, he'd conjured up a clock so he could see the hours passing by. It was modeled off some of the clocks he'd seen in Analia's home back when he'd first met her, but that was only an empty outer shell. Its guts were pure magic, not because Nym couldn't make the gears and cogs needed, but because he didn't know what exactly was needed or how to put it together. Magic was simpler, kind of.

He was pretty sure it didn't work right. If he'd been in the core reality, the real world, it would have been fine, but here, he wasn't confident that the parts of the spell construct that actually measured the passage of time were doing it accurately. It didn't seem possible that they could, given that this artificial world lacked any and all of the constants that the spell used as a reference, and his approximations of those constants were just that: approximations.

So he'd dismissed the clock after . . . weeks, maybe? It must have been at least a month. He'd met with Ferro three times so far to discuss what he'd learned, and as boring and stale as those conversations had been, they were the highlight of his existence. Everything else was mindless, dry reading.

There was no arguing that it was important information to know. Nym had learned a thousand things he should have known prior to reaching the third layer, and he was only scratching the surface. All the spells he'd come up with himself, the ones he'd been so proud of for their unique construction that had granted him tools no other mages had, those all seemed childish and shoddy now.

Nym had taken the time to rebuild almost his entire repertoire just as an exercise in the new principles he'd learned from the ascendant texts. Every single one was more arcana efficient and quicker to cast now, though several of them were harder to pull off. The timing was more exacting in exchange for that efficiency, the tolerances tighter. He knew he could manage it easily, and more than that, he was sure most second- and third-circle mages could do the same.

It was getting harder and harder to stay focused now, and he was only halfway through that bottom shelf of blue leather books. And every single one of those books was so densely packed with important information that he couldn't skim even a single paragraph without missing something. A lot of it was familiar to him, but a lot of it also contradicted what he'd already known to be true. To help break up the monotony of reading, he sometimes designed little experiments to test the principles the book was espousing against what he'd already learned.

The books won every single time. No surprise there. Ascendants knew more about magic at its most fundamental levels than mortals did. The really frustrating part was that while all this knowledge was undeniably useful and he was definitely a better mage for having learned it, none of it was what he was actually here for. He needed to find a way to connect with the other versions of himself that existed in the outer layers of reality, to become a singular being.

He wanted to skip ahead from the blue volumes to the red ones on the second shelf, but he couldn't. He'd opened one once, just to see where he was heading, and hadn't been able to make heads or tails of what he was reading. It referenced a few of the foundational principles he was learning now but applied them in new ways he didn't understand or discussed how they reacted to other things he'd never heard of.

Nym had promptly given up and gone back to the books he was supposed to be reading. Even skipping ahead down the line of blue tomes had led to the same problem. He slogged his way through them, one at a time, now on his . . . he'd lost track . . . perhaps seventieth tome. It was probably more than that considering how often he'd had to reread a few of the more obtuse passages.

The door appeared in the wall, prompting Nym to look up with a weary smile. He teleported himself over to it or, rather, used a weaker second-circle version that was only good for a few hundred feet but was near instantaneous. Its primary use was convenience and buying time if he found himself in a situation where he needed to escape something that was far too close. It would have been quite useful in his sparring match against Babkin had he known how to do it.

With everything he'd learned though, he doubted it would be necessary to retreat from Babkin now. Unless the old innkeeper's berserker aura was truly unique in its ability to shed hostile magic, he had plenty of options for penetrating the defense and putting any berserker down with minimal fuss.

He couldn't teleport through the door for some reason he hadn't quite figured out yet. Nym had a few theories, but he thought the answer was simply that tele-portation didn't work for moving between layers of reality, and that the doorway was itself the physical representation of a spell that did allow for that. Figuring out exactly what spell did that was high on his priority list, since he expected it to be instrumental in connecting with his reality echoes.

Ferro was waiting for him in the endless white void, looking the same as always. Nym approached him and started the conversation off. "I wanted to ask: Do you experience the time between our meetings?"

"No," Ferro said. Nym already knew that. All the ascendant's talk about subjective linear time was a pretty big clue. He'd only asked as an opening to the topic to prompt a more thorough explanation.

Ferro didn't oblige him, and after a second, Nym asked, "How do you experience it then?"

"An excellent question, one that I am sure you'll be able to answer yourself eventually."

"Not going to tell me, huh?"

"I'm afraid not."

It had been worth a try, but Nym wasn't surprised. Ferro seemed to always have a good idea of exactly how far Nym had gotten in his studies and which topics he'd covered. He was determined that Nym learn everything in the proper order, with no skipping around. According to the ascendant, Nym's tendency to just research whatever new idea caught his attention was the whole reason his magical foundation was riddled with holes.

"Okay, let me ask a different question then. Why does it matter if arcana pulled from the second layer doesn't resonate properly for the spell? According to Grant's Theorem of Oscillating Resonance, it should self-correct, and the arcana diffusion is so minuscule that it's not even measurable without specialized spells designed to keep track of it."

"Another excellent question. Why do you think it matters?"

"I don't know," Nym said, annoyed. "That's why I'm asking."

Just once, he wished he could find a teacher who didn't do this to him. Every single one of them always wanted to tease him along until he came up with the answer himself. While he recognized some intrinsic value in the process, he'd been teaching himself for hundreds of hours, maybe thousands, using nothing but books. Sometimes he just couldn't figure out an answer and could use some help. He found he missed the Ferro of before whose only goal had been to push Nym past the threshold of reawakening Niramyn.

"Ask a different question," Ferro said.

The refusal to answer was a hint in its own way though. It told Nym that he hadn't advanced far enough to figure out the answer on his own and that it was probably related to the first milestone he was struggling toward: connection to the first-layer reality echo. It wasn't likely to be a direct relation, but something foundational that he'd need to start practicing now so when it was important later, he wouldn't have to relearn it.

It was deeply depressing that these conversations, frustrating as they were, were the high points of his life now. Nym did his best to stifle a sigh and started working his way down his list. If he was lucky, he'd get answers to half of them, though usually those answers were just references to which sections of various books Ferro felt he needed to reread.

Progress was slow, but as the ascendants said, he had all the time in the world, as long as he didn't go crazy first.

* * *

Months later, he hoped, Nym closed the last of the blue volumes and leaned back in his chair. "My brain hurts," he said out loud.

It didn't, really. It couldn't. His suspicion that the physical body he was piloting around wasn't real had become a certainty. He knew how to detect it now and could even replicate it to an extent. His own version didn't include the temporal-dilation effect, but if he wanted to, he could use fifth-layer arcana to trap someone's mind in an illusory world of his own design.

By all mortal measures, he was an archmage in truth now, and a proper one, not just one who'd cheated his way there by looking over someone else's shoulder and copying their homework. Somehow, it didn't seem like enough anymore. That was probably because there was another equally long shelf full of red tomes, and one with green tomes above that, though thankfully that was a significantly smaller collection.

Nym didn't move for hours that turned into days while he internalized the last bits of knowledge he'd stuffed himself full of. Things he'd learned near the beginning that hadn't really clicked all made sense now; things he thought he'd understood the first time around were revisited and hidden layers discovered.

And finally, after however long it had taken, Nym thought he was ready to try to form the bridge between core reality and the first layer. All the answers had been in the texts, once he understood enough to grasp the implications of some of the laws and theories he'd learned. It all fit together in a way that was both frighteningly complex and beautifully elegant.

"Ferro," Nym said. "It's time."

"Are you sure? You have as much time as you need to prepare."

"I'm sure. I know what I need to do now."

Ferro appeared in the room. That was a first; he'd never set foot beyond the threshold before. He gestured toward the second shelf of books and said, "Even if you succeed, you know this is only the beginning?"

"I am aware," Nym said. "And I have thoughts on the next step to take after this one. Before I go too deep though, I want to make sure my initial understanding is correct."

Ferro nodded approvingly. "What is your first step?"

"It's time to go back to reality prime, to the real world. I can't make the connection I need from here. It's too far removed."

"Can't you?"

"No," Nym said firmly. "Not until the chain is complete and each echo is connected to the next."

"What will you do if an ascendant attacks you in the core reality?"

"Hope that you save me."

Ferro laughed at that. "That's fair enough. It wouldn't be wise to expect a child to defeat a seasoned warrior just because he's mastered his first weapon drills. Very well, I will shepherd this attempt. Are you ready to begin?"

Nym went over the spell in his head one last time. Every variable had been accounted for. The formation was perfect. He knew every modification he needed to make to his own physiology before he could attempt the spell, and he knew down to the second how long those would take to complete. He could see the whole chain of events clearly in his mind, each successive step that would lead him toward his ultimate goal.

"I'm ready."

CHAPTER THIRTY-EIGHT

The spell to connect to his reality echo was based at its core upon the idea of the conduit. It was just modified so heavily as to be practically unrecognizable. Nym and Ferro ended up on an isolated island far, far out in the middle of the ocean, a thousand miles or more away from anywhere.

"Wouldn't this make it harder to make the connection if I'm not near where my echo is in his layer?" Nym asked. The books had very clearly listed that as a possible point of failure.

"It would," Ferro agreed. "And when you try to make future connections, that's something to be aware of. However, that first layer is just slightly out of step with the core reality. Chances are good that you and your echo are in pretty close to the same spot, for all the same reasons. Out here, there will be less interference, and if someone comes to snoop around, I'll have plenty of space to handle it."

It felt kind of weird to Nym to think that he could match Archmage Veran spell for spell, even if he didn't have the decades of experience to always know which spell was the best to use, but that he was relying on Ferro to protect him. If he encountered a monstrous ice-worm hive queen now, he could kill it from a mile away with minimal effort. Before, it had been a heroic effort that nearly cost him his life.

And forget human threats like Senman or Valgo. Even that abduction squad from the Collective was a nonissue now. Nym had a whole selection of protective spells he could enact that would keep him safe while he slept, and that was only if he decided he wanted to sleep. It was absurd, but at the same time, it wasn't nearly enough.

"I'm leaving this world behind, aren't I?" he said to himself.

"Yes, you are," Ferro answered anyway. "You may come back to visit, but it will never truly be your home again. You're on the verge of outgrowing it."

Nym didn't like that thought, but at this point he didn't have a choice. He'd willingly opened that cube and brought Niramyn back to life, and now he was going to suffer the consequences, had in fact been suffering for however many months he'd been locked away learning about magic. This was the price he paid for his continued existence, which was better than he'd expected to get.

If it kept his friends safe, it was worth it. He was not going to be the reason they died.

"About time to get started, I guess. It won't get done any faster by hesitating."

The arcana came easily to him now, faster than he'd ever seen his former mentor gather it. He began forging the channels needed to create a framework for the spell, something he didn't expect to need much longer. Even now, his willpower was so strong that he could almost control the arcana with that alone.

Once he'd successfully bonded with his reality echoes, he would be able to push into Transcendence, and everything would change. The rules of magic as he knew them would become obsolete. Well, not all of them, but taking this step would break a lot of the hard limits he was currently laboring under.

Nym realized he was still stalling, even now while he was actively shaping the spell. It wasn't going to be a quick spell, but there was no margin for error, and he couldn't keep dragging his feet. Every part had to be done right, with every parallel process he'd built in his mind fully focused on the task at hand. He was actually building four spells nested inside one another in a kind of knot, and timing was critical to keep them from getting tangled up or breaking down.

There was so much going on that he had to open three more conduits to the fifth layer, but he'd known that would be necessary going in and had already accounted for that. Each one opened smoothly and increased his output as it became necessary. There was so much arcana going into the spell that it was starting to destabilize reality, which was the point. The membrane that held back the Phase Shift layer from the core reality was stressed to the point that it was going to tear.

Unlike the last tear in reality he'd dealt with, this one would be small and temporary. It wasn't leading to a different reality, just an adjacent version of this one. No big deal. It was only the thickest concentration of arcana he'd ever felt in his life forming into a spell not three feet away. If he fumbled it, Ferro was there to act as his safety net.

Except that's when Nym noticed that he wasn't. There was no one else on the island at all, which probably meant there'd been some sort of trouble and he'd been obliged to step in. Nym wondered if he'd resolve it peacefully or if he'd be forced to—

An explosion rippled through reality a hundred miles away. Nym could see it in the air and water, feel it when it washed over him. His spell was safe, but only because he reacted quickly enough to both recognize the attack and to trigger one of his emergency contingencies in the fraction of a second he had before it reached him.

That answered that question then. If he was lucky, that would be the last time that happened before he completed the spell. Nym peered around warily, half expecting fate to punish him for daring to think something like that. When no explosion came, he gave a little mental shrug and turned his full attention back to his work.

And then somehow, suddenly and far too quickly, it was done. The tunnel between realities opened, and Nym stepped through.

Nym and Nym stood face-to-face with each other. Their clothes looked the same. So did their hair. The differences were more subtle than that. It was little things like posture and facial tics, the way one Nym's gaze held steady but the other's eyes occasionally flicked back and forth as they studied each other.

"You're different now," Nym said.

"I know. It was necessary."

"Maybe, but was it for the better?"

"I didn't have another choice. You know what could have happened to our friends."

Nym nodded. "It still could."

"It won't. I'm not going to let it."

"I wish I could believe that," Nym told himself.

"Then help me make sure of it."

Nym considered that. His counterpart from reality prime was markedly stronger than him now. He'd left his reality and grown elsewhere, and Nym's version of the world didn't reflect those changes. He was as weak as always. It wasn't supposed to be like that. His reality was so close to reality prime that they were almost mirrors. Things worked a little differently, sure, but so much had changed that Nym was perhaps the most powerful archmage in his reality while he was barely a pretender to the title.

If he agreed to this, if he fused his core to Nym, they would become a multidimensional being. Nym imagined that this first step was much easier for true ascendants. There was no hesitation there, not with their shared goal. Nym didn't really want to be an ascendant though, and since he didn't want it, neither did Nym.

They needed to connect over something else, and that something was the friends who'd become their new family. Specifically, it was the need to protect them from the threats they'd inherited from their progenitor. But because of what Nym had done, opening that box up and being pulled out of his reality against his own will, he'd left Nym behind. They weren't equals anymore.

"Do you think we can do it together?" Nym asked.

"I don't see why not. You're worried about how unbalanced we are, right?"

"It's a legitimate concern."

"It is," Nym acknowledged. "You know that you'll know everything I know if we become one being, right?"

"It's not that. It's the changes you've made to your mind. We don't feel like we're even the same people now. I don't know if this will work even if we do it."

"I took that into account. It will still work," Nym said.

Nym laughed. "You sound so confident."

"I am."

"Yeah, well, I know how many bad decisions you made that you were confident were right at the time, so I hope you'll forgive me if I don't share that feeling."

"What do you want me to do? Should I lay out the reasons why I think this will work? Would that make you feel better?"

"It might," Nym said.

"We're wasting time. Ferro was fighting another ascendant last I checked. Hopefully he won, but if he didn't, this tunnel needs to close in the next few seconds. Either you're in, or you're not. What's it going to be?"

"You already know the answer."

Nym nodded. He did. If it had been anything other than yes, there wouldn't have been another Nym at the end of the tunnel.

"It'll be a bit different than how it usually goes, I think. I need your help to make the magic work, but I accounted for that. Are you ready?"

"Yes."

Nym and Nym worked together, forming a new spell. One Nym, the prime Nym, took the lead. It should have been a partnership, but that wasn't how it had played out. Instead, Nym was left to fill in the blanks, to make it up as he went along, but even that had been accounted for.

The spell wrapped around the both of them and pulled tight. Nym stumbled forward, caught off guard by the sudden tug. Nym took a smooth step forward, easily moving with the spell's constriction. On the second step, Nym regained his balance and moved under his own power. Nym met him, hand outstretched. Their palms pressed against each other, mirrors that didn't quite reflect what they should.

And then there was only one Nym.

He could feel himself existing in multiple places. It was like being part of Niramyn again, only less overwhelming. There were still two physical bodies, one Nym from each reality, but now they acted in unison. It wasn't symmetrical motion any more than two hands acting together to the will of a single person were symmetrical.

Just like that, the first step toward his ascendance was complete. He would start the process all over again and convince the second-layer version of Nym to join their collective whole, and again, and again, and again. And if he managed all of that, he could become an ascendant for real.

Nym stepped back through the tunnel, leaving the other half of his being inside the first layer. The island he'd been standing on was gone now, and the tunnel opened into empty air. Nym flew up and looked around for Ferro, only to find the ascendant right next to him.

"You won?" Nym asked.

"I did. She should have known better than to challenge me. And you were successful in connecting with your echo, I see."

"Yes." Nym frowned. "It was difficult. Existing inside Niramyn's sanctuary has unbalanced things. I'm not sure if that will make the next time easier or harder."

"Harder for the next one, perhaps. Or it might not matter. It will be a good thing as you get farther out though. Realities there are different in many ways, and your reflections would not have been your equal anyway. At least this way, you'll have the upper hand."

Nym hoped that Ferro was right. There'd been a brief moment when he'd thought he was going to refuse himself, and if that had happened, it could have been the end of his own existence. The other Nym knew that too though. In the end, that had been the deciding factor. They would protect their friends and, in doing so, protect themselves.

CHAPTER THIRTY-NINE

The red books were, if anything, even more dull and tedious than the blue ones had been, but there weren't quite as many of them. More importantly, since they'd fused together, Nym's mental processes were much faster now. Part of his mind was devoted to catching up the portion of him that used to be an echo, but the overall gains more than made up for that. He was reading through them faster now, taking less time to understand and making more connections to other information with each new page he read.

Nym thought about rebuilding the clock now that he understood a bit more about adjacent realities. It might even be accurate this time, but in the end, he decided against it. The passage of time would be marked by his progress through the shelf, however long that took. At least, that was what he intended.

Those plans lasted through about a third of the books. Then Niramyn himself appeared in the center of the room. "Slow," he remarked, eyeing up the bookshelf. "But you've successfully become a multireality entity, so I suppose there is some hope for you."

Nym paused his reading and looked up at his past self. "I wasn't aware that I had any need to rush. I was told I had as much time as I needed to get it right here."

"You have as much time as I allow," Niramyn corrected. "And I will only allow more time if I see a return on the investment of arcana I'm spending keeping this sanctuary from collapsing. Trust me, you wouldn't like that to happen while you're inside. You wouldn't survive being ejected into another layer of reality, not this far from the core world."

He could argue that point, but it wouldn't do anything but anger the ascendant. If Niramyn decided to collapse the sanctuary, Nym would have to open up the tunnel and step down each layer until he got back to the core reality. He could probably do it, as long as nothing interrupted his work. The hardest part would be forging a conduit from the wrong side to get down to the fifth layer, but he thought he could pull that off if he absolutely had to.

It was easy enough to do in the sanctuary, which had little tendrils his own conduits could be threaded through to each layer without him having to manually break through membranes and navigate the layer's natural environment, but outside it, it would be extremely difficult to pass from the sixth layer to the fifth.

So for all practical purposes, Exarch Niramyn was correct that Nym couldn't stand on his own yet. That wouldn't take much longer for him to correct, he thought. He already knew enough to reach his echoes on the second and third layer and was working on figuring out the fourth. It was a unique challenge, in many ways harder than connecting to the fifth-layer reality's echo.

Once they were one being though, he'd be ready to make the jump into the sixth layer, Transcendence. He'd had a peek at the far end of the red-leather-bound shelf. They all discussed that one act, the preparations needed, the dangers to be avoided, when to activate the contingencies he would need to build, and how each piece of his six-dimensional body would need to work together.

It was a daunting task, one he was nowhere near ready to attempt. Once he finished the second shelf, he would establish the connections needed to merge with his other echoes, then return one final time to the sanctuary to learn the intricacies of the final step to ascendance. Then, and only then, would he be useful to Niramyn, and so have his freedom to go back to his life.

It was hard to picture that now. His old life was so . . . limited, always in one place and one time. It was no wonder ascendants were basically mythological figures. They had practically no reason to interact with mere mortals who couldn't even comprehend an immortal existence, let alone relate to it. Even if, no, when, he made it back to the core reality, it would be a hollow victory. His friends were safe, but he didn't think he'd ever talk to them again.

"Why are you still here?" Niramyn asked.

"I . . . What? I'm not finished yet?" Nym gestured at the shelf of red books.

"You should know enough to have bound another two echoes into your being by now. Why haven't you?"

"Last time, we were attacked by another ascendant. I thought it'd be better to know as much as possible to have the highest chance of success and minimize how long it takes to cast the spell."

"Your priorities are wrong. Do not worry about interruptions from other ascendants. You need to advance faster. Connecting to other parts of you will help you do so. Do that first, then come back and continue learning."

Before Nym could reply, he found himself standing on the top of a mountain, one that had a smothering amount of heat coming from it. Niramyn was, of course, nowhere to be found. Nym simultaneously cast a few spells to protect himself from the heat and the fumes he noticed coming up from cracks in the stone. It looks like the mountain was a volcano, and not a dormant one. Pockets of lava dotted its features, and the bowl was a mess of leaking cracks from the pressure building up.

It wasn't where Nym would have chosen to cast the spell to create a tunnel to his second-layer self. Ferro was also nowhere to be found, but Niramyn hadn't said anything about waiting for him, so Nym immediately got to work. As before, he built the tunnel, but this time the other half of his existence modified the spell, extending its target through the first layer to reach the second.

It went off without a hitch, and the tunnel opened. Nym stepped through, only to find that instead of a volcano steadily building pressure, he was in some sort of old monastery. Another version of him sat there in the air, eyes closed. He looked like Nym, but in a way where someone might mistake them for brothers rather than mirror images.

"It will only get worse the farther you go," the seated Nym said without opening his eyes.

"That implies that I will go farther," Nym pointed out. "Does that mean you'll be joining me?"

"I think I will," Nym said. "I don't think I can go much farther on my own."

"It feels like cheating, doesn't it?"

"It does, a little bit. Come on then, let's get it over with."

And just like that, Nym's existence expanded again. He stepped back into the core reality and took a moment to collect himself. So far, he'd been handed the best locations to form a tunnel between realities, but no one was showing up to direct him to the next spot. That wasn't an insurmountable problem, but it was inconvenient. There were spells designed to help, but they could only give a general direction.

Whatever the ascendants were using to figure out where to send him had pinpoint accuracy. Nym couldn't have been any closer to his second-layer echo without actually stepping into the lava. He flew a mile or so away from the volcano, just so he didn't have to deal with the heat and the smell, then started casting the spells that would narrow down which part of the world corresponded with where he needed to end up in the third layer.

Niramyn was no doubt watching to see how he did. Maybe Ferro was too. On some level, Nym recognized that he needed to impress his past self, but it was hard to make himself pretend to care what the ascendant thought of him. He knew he should, considering his fate was in the man's hands, but Nym *did not like* his past self and wanted nothing but to get away from him. It was too bad the only way of doing that was by giving the jerk what he wanted.

Nym was thoroughly annoyed that he was going to give Niramyn anything at all, but that was the deal. He could make the best of it and get to the point where ascendants couldn't push him around, or he could let them snuff him out. If he was lucky, they'd stop at him. That implied threat was the lever they used to move him to their wills.

He'd inherited a stubborn streak and a large measure of independence from his progenitor, no doubt the reasons Niramyn himself was sitting at the top of the heap. Nym would get there too, and then he wouldn't have to play these kinds of games.

He teleported across thousands of miles, casting the interreality scrying spells and following their vague clues to narrow down a radius. The more he looked, the farther away from land he got, until he was floating over the ocean and preparing to go straight down several miles underwater. He layered spells on top of himself, one after another.

First and foremost, he needed to account for the pressure of the water, then he needed to be able to breathe. Sight would also be nice, though not strictly necessary. Freedom of movement was probably more important, though he fully planned on teleporting to the appropriate location. Add to that a few spells to keep him undetected by anything living down there and a few reactive defenses just in case the obscurement magic failed, and he was ready to go.

Nym teleported straight down to the ocean floor. He could see through the water about a thousand feet in every direction, though only in shades of black and white. There were things out there, some small, some not so small, but all of them ignored him. He'd see if that lasted once he started really working his magic.

This being the third time he'd cast the spell, and now with two echoes incorporated into the whole of his being, it was easier than ever to build it. Something rushed through the water as the magic built to a crescendo, only to convulse when a current of lightning coursed through it. The proximity ward reset itself a moment later, and the sea monster retreated.

Nym ignored that and finished the tunnel. He willed himself forward rather than attempt to swim until he passed through the boundary and found himself dry again. Only he could pass through realities with the spell, which thankfully included his clothes. He could fashion himself new ones out of magic, but it was nice to be spared the hassle.

The Astral Sea waited for him on the other side. Unlike the literal ocean he'd stepped out of, it was a void of stars with currents of solar winds drifting through them. His opposite wasn't present and waiting for him, but that was what Nym had expected.

He let himself drift off into the void, guided by his magic, until he fell to the surface of a planet below. Rushing up to meet him, feetfirst, was his reality echo. They were just slightly out of alignment, enough that they'd pass by close enough to touch if nothing interfered. As they reached an equilibrium of height, both slowed down and pulled themselves back to center.

"Was it fun?" Astral Sea Nym asked. His body was more of an outline of a person with no features, but Nym could see fragments of his personality in the being. If nothing else, it had his penchant for mischief, only amplified many times over.

"When I figured out where I needed to form the tunnel, I knew you had something to do with it. You went there deliberately to make me work for it, didn't you?"

"Of course I did. It wouldn't be worth doing otherwise."

"I do like having fun," Nym admitted.

"I know. Me too. This next part is going to be even more fun."

And then they were four.

CHAPTER FORTY

The world was, for all intents and purposes, standing still while Nym did his best to become someone who could survive the incoming storm. He'd completely lost track of how long he'd been trapped inside the box. It could be years for all he knew.

He was going crazy, that was for sure. Having so much going on in his head was causing problems, despite his best efforts. The problem was a simple one: he and his echoes lacked a unified goal, and it was pulling him apart. Incorporating his third-layer echo into his being had done more harm than good. That version of Nym was easily excitable and easily bored.

The parts of him that came from the first-layer echo were close enough to his own personality that he appreciated the occasional alternate point of view. It had the same goals and went about them the same way but saw things just differently enough that it sometimes came up with ideas that Nym wouldn't have.

From his second-layer echo, Nym gained a great deal of patience. That echo was perhaps the easiest one to turn to his current task. It wanted to be stronger, and that was exactly what Nym was doing now. It was content to study the magic laid out in front of him as a path to power.

"But it's so. Damn. Boring," he said. The new echo wasn't incorporating into his being correctly, and he was pretty sure that was because it just couldn't thrive in this environment. He didn't much blame it, to be honest, but the distractions were only going to make it take longer to finish.

It was a weird feeling, being distracted by himself like that. He knew that he was supposed to be reading, to be learning, and he wanted to, but he couldn't make himself do it. And then he weirdly hated himself for not doing what he knew he needed to do, while still making no effort to correct anything about the situation.

The books had plenty of advice about successful integration, but none of it was really applicable to the situation. Ascendants were people driven by the pursuit of power and knowledge, and their echoes reflected that. Consolidating them into one being usually involved broadening goals until all aspects were satisfied and reaching compromises about which goals to pursue first.

In Nym's case, the newest echo's goal was directly contradictory to Nym's. He wanted to get out and go do stuff. He'd loved Nym's life right up until he'd encountered Ferro and decided it was time to stop stalling and accept that if he wanted to protect people, he needed to be strong enough to actually protect them.

Now, that echo was going insane with boredom and threatening to take the entirety of Nym's being with it. He needed to find some way to negotiate with it. Nym quickly cast a spell that created a copy of himself and imbued it with the bulk of the third echo's personality. "Tell me what you need to be satisfied," he said.

"Come on, man. You know. We're the same person. You are just as bored as I am. This is torture. We need to get out and do something."

"I agree. I would love to go somewhere, but that's not the reality in front of us. If we want to get out of here, we need to finish the work first. Niramyn isn't going to let us go on holiday until we're a true ascendant."

"Maybe just a small part could go out and check up on the world. You know, see how people are doing, what's new."

"Nothing's new. We're stuck in a place where time doesn't exist, and we lack the power to scry into the future."

"Okay but hear me out. What if we go check anyway?"

Nym rolled his eyes. "You just want an excuse to go for a walk."

"Yes, damn it! Is that so wrong?"

"Maybe Ferro would be willing to let a piece of us out to look around."

"How would that even work?" the copy asked. "Wouldn't that piece just never come back? It would have to wait until the next time the whole of us leaves to rejoin then."

"It would on its own. Ferro might be able to help with that though."

"Great, let's ask him then. No, we can't. Not until the next time he checks up on us."

"Correct, and he's more likely to agree to the request if we've demonstrated significant progress. So . . . We get back to work, then ask him for a favor later."

"Fine. I'm not happy about this."

"We're not happy, you mean. But the harder we work at this, the sooner it gets done, and the sooner we can go back to having a life."

The copy broke apart into arcana, and Nym was finally, finally, able to sit down and open the book he was supposed to be reading.

"This isn't the core reality," the fragment of Nym said.

"No. It's an in-between space," Ferro explained. "As close as you can get while still remaining hidden outside of time."

"Can I see that reality from here?"

"A . . . cross section of it, if you will. I will help you move your vision forward in time once you've determined where you want to look."

Nym considered that for a second. "This seems like a lot more work than just setting me down in the core reality and coming back to grab me later."

"I cannot do that. It would violate Exarch Niramyn's orders. This, however, is in my power, and it costs me little enough."

It wasn't really what Nym had in mind. He'd wanted to check up on his friends, most of whom the ascendants didn't know about, he thought. Or maybe they did.

They seemed to have an infinite variety of ways to learn things, up to and including looking through the past to watch how events had unfolded, or possibly even living through them. Nym still didn't fully understand how they interacted with the concept of time yet.

Ferro knew about Ciana though. If nothing else, she was already exposed, so it wouldn't hurt to check up on her. Everyone else was probably also in danger, but he wasn't going to confirm their existence on the off chance that he'd be bringing them to an ascendant's attention.

"How does it work?" Nym said.

"Scry as normal but through this point here. It will open up to the core reality and allow your magic to look around."

Nym did as he was instructed and saw the world unfold in his mind. He found Ciana easily enough. She was staying in a three-room house he'd rented for her, though she wasn't home. Once Nym had locked down whom he was looking for, Ferro manipulated his portal, and time started to pass by at an enormous rate. Days went by in minutes, and Nym watched his big sister go through the motions of her day.

She shopped at the market, roamed the streets and explored, and made friends with some of her neighbors. They worked on a little communal garden together, a scraggly thing struggling to thrive in the cold, rocky dirt of Abilanth. She found work as an apprentice leatherworker, not the job Nym would have chosen given the smell, but something she seemed to enjoy nonetheless.

"This isn't a real future, is it?" he asked softly.

"It could be," Ferro said. "If you never come back into her life, this is the next few months. It is the most likely future."

"The most likely future is I'll never see her again?"

"Yes. Once you've been properly prepared, Exarch Niramyn has work for you."

Sometimes, Nym felt like he should have taken his chances with the hostile ascendants that hadn't found him. But no, once Ferro showed up, it was all over. One way or another, he was going to be forced to become Niramyn again. The only way out of that fate would have been if another ascendant interfered and killed Ferro while somehow not finding Nym. It hadn't seemed likely to happen.

"Well, this has been thoroughly depressing," Nym said. "But thank you, Ferro. I appreciate that you went out of your way to help me."

"You're welcome. Let me know when you'd like to go back."

"It's time, I think. This didn't really scratch the itch like I wanted it to."

"You do not wish to check in on your other friends?"

Nym wasn't surprised, but it was another blow to his morale to have it confirmed that Ferro knew about them too. Just in case he was making an erroneous assumption and the ascendant was talking about somebody who wasn't Analia or the Earth Shapers, he said, "No, thank you. I'll see them again when I'm able to travel freely. Or I guess maybe not, all things considered."

Ferro didn't offer him any words of comfort. He merely nodded, cut the arcana to the spell he was powering, and sent the fragment of Nym back to the whole.

"That's just depressing," Nym said.

It was harder to find motivation to keep working, but he could do it. Depression when trapped in a room with nothing but an endless parade of books to occupy his mind was easier to handle than cabin fever.

The primary motivator in his life at this point was spite. Niramyn thought he'd break, and Nym refused to let him be right. He was going to succeed, and he was going to grow to the point where he could tell even an Exarch to go court a swamp hag. In fact, he fully planned to tell both Exarchs that. He was sick of them screwing up his life.

Nym didn't know what he was going to do with himself once he was free of the machinations that had completely derailed it. He just knew that he was going to get out from under Niramyn's thumb somehow. From what he understood about ascendants, they couldn't die, but they still had ways to fight one another.

No doubt he'd learn each and every one of those ways in full detail, seeing as to how he was to be bait to flush out the ascendants stalking through the timeline, searching for Niramyn. Bait worked even better when it could fight back, and if anyone knew how Niramyn thought, it was Nym. He was so arrogant that he couldn't even conceive of anyone having the power to do him harm, even after what Myzalik had done to him.

Nym didn't expect to have any trouble learning how to fight another ascendant, how to get around their immortality and hit them where it hurt. And even if Niramyn and Ferro wouldn't teach him, he knew someone else who wasn't afraid of an ascendant, someone who liked to make deals.

The trick would be getting there unnoticed, but Nym figured he could manage it. While they could literally watch him every second of every day, the whole point was to make him strong enough to survive first contact with an ascendant, and that meant going about his life like a normal person while he waited for one to find him.

That was why the most likely future for his friends was that they'd never see him again, he realized in a flash of insight. He certainly wouldn't go anywhere near them until the threat was gone. They might all die of old age long before that happened.

Damn all ascendants and their internal power struggles. He recognized that he wouldn't exist if not for the two Exarchs, but he didn't care. They were still going to pay. Flush with fresh spiteful vigor, Nym dove back into his work, and all four parts of him were finally in agreement.

CHAPTER FORTY-ONE

Nym was ready to finish recruiting his last two echoes, but Ferro didn't answer when called, and Niramyn wasn't even worth asking. He showed up on his own terms, and he reminded Nym more of the father he'd met in Niramyn's early memories than anything else.

With nothing left to do but wait, Nym started on the top shelf of books. He'd been hoping they'd make more sense once he finished the red set, but he was disappointed to find they were as obtuse as ever. It was so bad that Nym might have thought he was just reading them in the wrong order if he'd been in a normal library. It didn't seem likely that an Exarch's mental fabrication would mix something like that up, but he checked all the other books anyway.

"Nope, that wasn't the problem," he muttered to himself. Something was missing, probably deliberately. He guessed it was some sort of method to control him, to keep him from knowing how to become a true ascendant until they were ready for him. That or there was something special about the fourth- and fifth-layer echoes that he was missing.

Until he could get Ferro to answer though, he was stuck doing nothing but rote memorization on passages he didn't understand and practicing spells he already knew how to cast. It was tedious and frustrating, but he couldn't make himself just turn his brain off and stare at the wall. He supposed there were a few more augmentations he could attempt, but they were dangerous to do without someone around who could help fix anything that went wrong.

He was half-tempted to try them anyway, but that would be crazy. Only an idiot would do something like that, and he suspected he knew exactly where he'd inherited the kind of arrogance a mage needed to think it was a smart idea. Even if it worked, that didn't make it a good idea, and he had essentially unlimited time, so there was no rush.

There were only six green-bound books, and he read them all cover to cover at least a dozen times. It was obvious that they were designed to build on something, but he was missing some vital piece of information, or more likely a whole book's worth. When he did finally get that missing piece though, he hoped it would all snap into place quickly and easily.

And then, without any warning, the sanctuary vanished, and he was standing in the endless white void. A woman he didn't know appeared in front of him, reached out to place one hand on his chest, and *shoved*. Nym had just enough time to get an impression of a tall, slender form with wavy blonde hair before he fell backward through the void, crashed into something, and rebounded off it before he had time to process what was happening.

Outside the sanctuary, he still struggled to break the membrane separating the fifth and sixth layers and so couldn't channel arcana to use any sort of magic to save himself. He went tumbling through chaotic nothingness that was nevertheless full of things he kept bouncing off of. After being tumbled around for a subjective eternity, he broke through something and landed in a world he'd never seen before.

The sky, such as it was, was like some sort of patchwork quilt of different squares of land, except the patches moved around one another in dizzying patterns. Below it, the ground was a reflection of the quilt, an enormous mirror that stretched horizon to horizon. He was heading right for it, and at a dizzying speed. Nym didn't know what would happen if he crashed into it, but he didn't think it would be anything good.

Reflexively, he reached out for arcana to halt his descent. The conduit formed, but then slapped against a membrane he recognized: the one separating the fourth and fifth layers. He was attacking it from the wrong side, which told him he'd somehow been shunted into the fifth layer. He needed to either cast a pinnacle spell to keep him in the air or figure out how to rip through the layers backward to reach at least the third layer.

That thought actually helped center him. Whatever was going on, he had a clear, immediate goal and plenty of tools to help him achieve it. This problem at least was one he'd studied in detail, since he needed to be able to draw arcana from layers besides the one he was in while outside the core reality. It was all theory though, with no real way to practice until now.

Nym broke his first conduit and wove a new one, this one designed to take advantage of the massive weight of fifth-layer arcana and wield it like a hammer to crash through the fourth layer. It slammed down on it, a wide, solid blade of arcana at the tip, and split the membrane in two.

The fourth layer gave way, and Nym's conduit reached the Astral Sea. Greedily, he drank in the arcana needed to perform a flight spell and slowed to a stop. He was still a mile or two from the ground, such as it was. It was hard to gauge altitude without a spell to aid him, and that hadn't been important enough for him to cast one.

Now that he was no longer concerned about splattering across the reflective surface of the ground, Nym's next priority was to make sure he was safe. The other layers of reality could be just as brutal as the core itself, with some threats that were far more dangerous than anything living in the real world.

A series of quick divinations ensured that there was no immediate danger nearby, but that didn't ease Nym's mind. Someone had broken an Exarch's sanctum, and then an ascendant he didn't recognize had appeared and done something to him. Nym wasn't even sure it was magic. Maybe she was friendly, or maybe not. She had pushed him out of a place he was trapped at to a layer that he could conceivably find his own way home from.

That seemed to indicate some degree of helpfulness to Nym, as he doubted it had been an accident. She hadn't stopped to talk to him, not even for a second, but he wasn't sure what conclusion to draw from that. Maybe if he'd known her, he could have said what the reason was, but with nothing to go on, it could be anywhere from she was checking chores off a list to she couldn't communicate for some reason to she didn't have more than an instant of time to work with.

Whatever the reason, he had an opportunity to work without worrying about Ferro looking over his shoulder, unless it was all a trap to see what he'd do if he thought he was free of them. It could be some sort of loyalty test, but fortunately, Nym had the same plan either way. He was going back to the core reality and having a conversation with a certain fox.

If that didn't go well, he wasn't sure what he'd do. He considered paying another visit to the research lab, but that might not be a great idea. Without any frame of reference for what was going on, putting himself in a position where unknown ascendants could find him was a risky move. The lab probably wouldn't have the information he was looking for anyway.

Nym had one other option, but he was going to save that for after his visit. He had enough knowledge now to reach and hopefully absorb his fourth- and fifth-layer echoes into the whole of his being. There wasn't really any downside to doing that; it would only make him stronger and put him in a position where he was ready to take that final step. Of course, if they were as hyper and scatterbrained as his third-layer echo had been, maybe he'd hold off.

He wove together the spell needed to create a tunnel back to the core reality. It was unexpectedly difficult to make complex channels for the arcana to flow through while inside the fifth layer when there was more arcana pushing at the outside of the spell construct too. Nym had to take extra care to keep everything reinforced. No doubt Ferro would have something to say about how long it took him to put the spell together, but since Ferro wasn't here, Nym didn't have to listen to the lecture.

He stepped through and found himself back in reality prime. It took him a second to orient himself and realize that he was upside down, not helped by the fact that all he could see was ocean and sky, and that horizon line was a long way off.

After he righted himself, Nym spent a minute establishing his protections as best he could. He doubted much of anything would be able to get the jump on him, let alone harm him, but every now and then something surprised him. If an ascendant showed up, it wouldn't matter what he did, but against something else that might be into the sixth layer, he thought he had half a chance, at least to run away.

Nym teleported to Archmage Veran's sanctum, did a quick scry to confirm there was no one there, and pilfered the fox ring and statuette from his room. A fortunate side effect of being temporally locked for years, or however long it had been, was that nothing much had changed in the real world. His room was just like he'd left it.

He slipped the ring on, powered the arcana batteries in the fox's eyes, and teleported again to get clear of any wards in the archmage's sanctum that might interfere with the magic. Then he sent out the telepathic call and waited. It didn't take long before Rizin appeared in front of him.

"Oh ho, what's this?!" the fox said with a grin. "I guess I can't call you half-scendant anymore. You're multidimensional now, though . . . perhaps still in progress, yes?"

"Yeah," Nym said. "It's a long story that involves a lot of ascendant shenanigans. Do you, uh, do you have a place where we can talk without worrying about being overheard?"

"Ah, what troubles are you bringing to my den?"

"I thought you weren't afraid of ascendants," Nym shot back.

"Afraid? No. It would be foolish not to respect strength though. Now tell me honestly, will you be bringing a host of powerful foes down on my head?"

"No?" Nym asked as much as said. "I don't think so. Something happened, and I need time to figure out what. Advice would be helpful. I'm kind of sailing in uncharted waters right now."

"Very well," Rizin said after a pause to think. "I can at least hear you out."

The world blurred but didn't quite go black. When it cleared again, Nym was standing next to a giant cushion, many times too big for Rizin's current form. The fox was the biggest Nym had ever seen, easily the size of a wolf, though much sleeker and perhaps more graceful. The cushion he sat on could have doubled as the floor for a house.

The fox grinned at Nym, and the shadows flickered with motion behind him. It reminded Nym of a tail flicking back and forth, except so fast that it was everywhere all at once. He'd seen that before, but at the time, Nym hadn't recognized what it was. Rizin was far more than he appeared to be, obviously, but not just on a magical level. He was hiding even his physical form, presenting a mask in much the same way he'd pretended to be the boy with the yellow jacket when they'd first met.

That was good. Nym needed an ally strong enough to stand up to an ascendant. Hopefully the price for that help wouldn't be too harsh. There was only one way to find out. "You're sure we're safe to speak here?"

"I am."

"Alright, let me try to explain what I know happened, and what I think it means, and we can figure out what to do from there."

CHAPTER FORTY-TWO

It did not take Rizin long to confirm Nym's story. "Looks like they're fighting," he said. "And making a huge mess in the process."

"Who's they?" Nym asked.

"At least two different factions of ascendant society. I guess you could think of Niramyn and Myzalik as lords, and each has weaker ascendants pledged to their service. There are a few other Exarchs with similar deals and one who has a reputation for viciously attacking anything that gets close to him. No vassals for that one."

"And the Niramyn and Myzalik factions are fighting?" Nym asked, trying to even picture what an ascendant fight would look like. He doubted it would just be two groups of mages hurling fire and lightning across the sky at each other.

"Yes, though it might be more accurate to say the Niramyn faction is running away and the Myzalik faction is giving chase. I'm not well-versed in the politics of it, but a lot of people thought Myzalik did the impossible and killed an ascendant. He absorbed a good chunk of manpower with that little move, and I doubt Niramyn welcomed all his former followers back with open arms.

"No, if I were him, I would have moved very cautiously and done my best to keep my return a secret until I'd gathered all my lost strength and very carefully evaluated the political landscape. Someone blundered somewhere and tipped Niramyn's hand early, and Myzalik moved to cut him off before he could grow back into a true threat."

"And since Niramyn was maintaining the sanctuary I was in, when he was attacked, he had to break it or something, which begs the question of whether the woman who showed up and shunted me into the fifth layer was working with him or against him. Maybe she was trying to help me survive, or maybe she was displacing me so he couldn't find me again. But then, why not just kill me?"

"Your existence spans multiple realities now," Rizin said. "Do you understand what that means? Killing this physical body in front of me isn't the end of you, though at your current level, you probably wouldn't be able to rebuild it for a while."

Nym had kind of forgotten that. He knew on an intellectual level that he was multidimensional now, but the idea that he could just shift his consciousness over and have a body in another layer of reality, or even assign one of his eight parallel processes to it while he managed his core-reality body with another one, were still new concepts. Still, since he had no desire to lose his core-reality body, he planned on doing his best not to die.

"What you're saying is I can't assume she was helping me. She might just have not had enough time to thoroughly kill me all the way, so she settled for making Niramyn lose track of me."

"That's a possibility," Rizin said. "What are you going to do?"

"I know how to locate and bond with my next two reality echoes," Nym said. "That seems like a good place to start. That next step is going to be harder. I might need some help."

"Is more power what you really want?" the fox asked. "You didn't strike me as the type."

"If I were just going to be a human and all this ascendant stuff was something I could ignore, no, not really. I'm strong enough now for that. But, well, what are the odds of that happening?"

"What if I told you that I could teach you how to hide yourself even from an ascendant?"

"Can you?" Nym asked.

"Perhaps. Not as you are now, but if you were to bridge that last vital gap and become a true immortal."

"I guess I would ask what it's going to cost me."

"Hmm . . . I do have an idea or two. It would depend on how capable you turn out to be. As you are now, I think any favor I might ask of equal value would be beyond your abilities."

Nym wasn't sure he wanted to owe Rizin another favor anyway. The fox had deliberately kept information from him last time they'd made an agreement, and the stakes were so much higher now. "I think I would need to know what I'm agreeing to before I agree to it. And if it's going to be a long-term partnership, I'm not entering it blindly."

Rizin laughed. It was a strange little yipping sound, almost like hiccups, and completely at odds with his size. "It would take forever to tell you all the details, but very well. What I would like is for you to go back into that little lab and have it start a new experiment. I want a new type of fox bred to my specifications. I will be their progenitor."

"Aren't there already ice foxes with magic?" Nym asked.

"Not an ice fox. Something similar, but . . . different. You may have noticed that I am as much a foreigner in this realm of cold and snow as you are, yes? My coloring isn't suited to the environment. I want a race of my own to take back to the warmer lands."

"And if I go back into the lab and get them to start making that, you'll show me how to hide myself from ascendants?"

"I'll be showing you before you go in, I'm sure. You'll need that knowledge to make sure no one realizes you've been there."

Nym supposed he'd already done one job in there, but things might be different now. The assistant golems might not be so friendly toward him, what with the real Niramyn being back. It would depend on whether or not the Exarch cared enough to visit the lab and correct some errors in judgment the golems had made. He certainly knew about it, since he knew everything Nym had done, which now that he thought about it, his plan to shield his friends from ascendant notice had been a foolish one.

There were probably some long-term ethics to consider about introducing a new race of sapient foxes into the world. They might overtake and wipe out native species, or they might integrate themselves into human civilization. He couldn't see them overthrowing humans as the dominant species on the planet, but then again, Rizin could probably do that more or less by himself. A coalition of every archmage alive might be able to stand up to him, but Nym doubted it.

There were probably other animals with the same level of power the fox had, maybe in hiding or just so far away that humans never crossed their paths. Or they disposed of the unfortunate souls who did. Nym had a few ideas for finding such creatures, but until he'd finished his own ascendance, it was probably a bad move.

"Let's say I agree to this. What exactly am I making?"

"I'll provide you with the specifications, but the short version is one hundred fully sapient fox kits, half male and half female, which would have inborn spells for illusion, darkness, sensory-enhancement, speech, and travel magic. I want them placed on a large uninhabited island I've picked out, some three thousand square miles of space for them to grow in. I'll relocate there myself to ensure their development."

"This isn't some whim you just thought up, is it?" Nym asked.

"No, I've been planning for this ever since I learned about that lab."

Nym wondered how exactly Rizin knew about it. As far as he was aware, that containment field kept it hidden and didn't let anything go. Then again, it did send arcana out into the world for its experiments, and Rizin definitely could have found those. That was more or less how Nym had traced the scarab curse back to its origin, though it still didn't explain how the fox had peeked behind the containment field.

He also wondered why Rizin needed the lab to do it. Perhaps it was just as simple as that the fox's talents didn't run in that direction. Nothing about illusions and tricks painted a picture of crafting a new form of life. Nym wasn't buying that answer though. Unless Rizin was fundamentally different from an ascendant, there was no reason he couldn't branch out and pick up new magic. He almost had to have a firm grounding in anatomical alterations just to make it to the point where his body could handle the levels of magic he played with.

Still, if that was what he wanted, it was at least something Nym could conceive of being able to do. He could probably do it today if it was as simple as giving over the instructions to the golems and having them start it up. The hardest part was probably going to be getting himself to the level where he could recharge the arcana batteries. It was entirely possible that there wouldn't be enough to perform the experiment, given how expensive some of Nym's ideas had been.

"Let's say I agree to this. What exactly are you going to teach me?"

"What do you need right now? Let me see." Rizin hopped off the cushion, a movement that shouldn't have startled Nym, but somehow gave the impression of a monstrously huge creature charging at him. He suppressed a flinch through sheer willpower, but it was close. Despite his new level of power, he was still far below the fox's level.

"You'll need to finish consolidating your reality echoes into your being. You can do that on your own. Then the plunge. The passage. The transition."

Nym snorted. "How poetic."

"It is not something to be mocked. What you're doing right now, you're walking a well-traveled path. You can make mistakes and come back from them. You can turn aside and go back. Once you reach the precipice, the only way forward is to jump. There's no turning back from that. You either learn to fly, or you fall to your death."

"I can already fly."

"Don't be dense. It was obviously a metaphor."

"Terrible metaphor," Nym muttered. "Ow!"

A . . . something vaguely taillike swatted him, though Rizin's tail never moved beyond a twitch. He glared at the fox anyway. Rizin's eyes stared back at him, deadly serious. "This is not a subject to joke about," he said. "This will be the most danger-ous thing you ever attempt, and failure can have catastrophic consequences beyond just your own death."

"Uh, how catastrophic are we talking about?"

"Failure to ascend can leave rents in reality. The mixing of arcana is quite vola-tile. When I say catastrophic, I mean that literally. Disasters worse than any hur-ricane or volcanic eruption. There is only so much that can be done to mitigate it. Failure could mean a loss of life on a scale you can scarcely comprehend."

"Oh . . ."

"We will revisit this when you're ready. I will do what I can to guide you after our pact is formed. For now, you have more tangible, concrete goals. You should not leave my side until you are ready to enter the fourth layer and meet with your echo."

"What about the ascendants still fighting?" Nym asked.

"Not your concern right now. They will not find you while you are under my care, I promise."

"And what do you want in return?"

Rizin rolled his eyes and disappeared. He reformed out of nothing back in his place on top of the giant cushion. "For now, nothing. What you need costs me nothing beyond the space you stand in, space I wasn't using anyway. My den is already well protected from the gaze of those who would call themselves gods."

"And when it's time to open a tunnel to the fourth layer, will I be able to do that from here?"

"Ah, that. No, I think not. I doubt you could muster a fraction of the power needed to step between realities from inside my den. I do not recommend you even try. It could have unpleasant repercussions for you."

"Thanks for the warning," Nym said. Rizin just grinned at him.

CHAPTER FORTY-THREE

Nym didn't even consider trying to force a teleport out of Rizin's den. When he felt he was ready, he simply asked the fox to transport him out. They appeared on the slope of a snow-covered mountain, much to Nym's discomfort. He quickly slapped a warming spell on himself and glared at Rizin.

"One would think you'd be more prepared," the fox said.

"I guess I thought you'd give me a bit of warning."

"That was foolish of you."

Nym rolled his eyes and asked, "Are you here to keep an ascendant from spotting me?"

"I said I would, didn't I?"

"Right, you did." Nym frowned. They hadn't made an official pact yet, but he supposed his position was bad enough that Rizin could afford a little generosity. It made him feel helpless. He didn't like it. "I just thought that would be later on."

"That would be rather pointless, since any ascendant could spot you while you're out here and attack before you could disappear again. I need you alive for now."

"Thanks, I think?"

Nym busied himself casting the spells he needed to locate his echo in the fourth layer. Once he'd narrowed it down, he said, "I need to do some teleporting. Should I bring you with me or would you prefer to move under your own power?"

"I'll follow you," Rizin said. "I'm not sure your spell work is up for moving something like me."

"You think so?" Nym asked. Rizin looked like he couldn't weigh more than a hundred pounds. "I guess the big pillow isn't for show."

"Not at all," the fox agreed.

Nym could spend some time studying the location he wanted to go through his scrying spells, but for the type of work he was doing now, he found it was easier to just line-of-sight teleport a thousand miles or so through the sky. As long as he went high enough, there was practically no risk.

He blipped off toward the horizon several times until he was floating over a desert. Rizin didn't appear next to him, but he got the sense that the fox was hidden nearby anyway. Nym took a minute to switch out his warming spell for a cooling one, then repeated his echo-hunting magics. The next round of teleports sent him south and west over the sea to a new continent. He stopped near the shore over some grasslands that stretched on for a hundred miles and tried again.

"Almost got it," he said aloud, mostly for Rizin's benefit.

The last set of teleports took him back into some mountains, though these ones lacked the snowy white caps that he was more familiar with. Finally, Nym settled down on a wide shelf overlooking a gorge at least a thousand feet wide and twice as deep. "Alright, this is the spot."

"Very well," Rizin's voice came out of nowhere. "I've shrouded this area. You are free to begin."

The spell was a little bit different every time he used it. He had to account both for the layer he was trying to reach and the environment he was casting it from. There were a lot of technical terms that the books spouted off in regard to that particular hurdle, but what it boiled down to was that the farther out he got from reality prime, the more work the magic had to do to make the tunnel.

It wasn't just a distance thing either, it was that it punctured through other layers, and it needed to be solidly anchored to do so. That meant constructing a sort of overlay of the surrounding environment so that the spell could attach itself to the core reality in this specific location and that the location changed every time he cast the spell again.

If everything went well, it would be a lot easier in the future because he would exist on both sides of the tunnel, but for now, the echo was more like a beacon he was aiming for. It made for a lot of prep work, but Nym knew the routine by now, and he finished it up in just a few minutes.

"Alright, time to do it again," he said as the tunnel opened. He stepped through to the other side, where he found a version of himself seated with his back against a tree. Moss, or something resembling it, had grown over his echo's legs and up to his stomach.

The echo didn't take any notice of Nym. In fact, nothing did. He peered around curiously, trying to figure out what was going on. After a moment, he recognized what he was feeling. It was a heaviness in the air, a stillness that smothered the slightest hint of a breeze. There was a quality of absolute silence around him, a quiet winter morning covered in fresh snow.

He caught a flicker of movement out of the corner of his eye and turned to see Rizin looming over him. The fox wasn't small now, not even close. He sat, twenty feet tall at least, with five enormous tails fanned out behind him. Strangely, all of them poked out to the right at various angles, but none on the left. It made Rizin look lopsided, but as Nym peered closer, he got the impression there was in fact something there after all, something that he just couldn't see.

"Oh, um." Nym took a step back. "Yeah, you weren't kidding about being bigger. Kind of lopsided though."

"Am I?" Rizin sounded amused.

"No, probably not."

"You would do well not to forget that."

"Right." Nym's mouth was suddenly very dry.

"Proceed with your task," Rizin said. "Good luck reaching your echo."

Nym wasn't sure why he needed luck, considering the other Nym was right there. He turned to take a step toward it, then stopped. Something weird had just happened. He took another step, then looked around. "Ah, I see."

He was moving, but he wasn't getting any closer to his goal. The more he walked, the farther away his echo appeared to be. That was . . . unfortunate. Not every part of the fourth layer was like this, but the ones that were could be difficult to navigate. He had a spell prepared for that, but it was going to make it all more complicated.

Nym's magic started compressing the space, twisting it around so that everything started to slide closer to him. It was a difficult spell to aim, but he thought he could tighten it down enough that the whole world didn't collapse on him. Once he got it going, he focused on his echo. The rest of the world snapped back into place, and the echo seemed to slide forward, along with the tree he was resting against.

It was a nauseating visual effect, one that Nym countered by focusing on a single point and trying to block out everything else. In this case, he picked the echo's nose. Soon enough, it was close enough to touch. "Hey, are you awake?" he asked.

The echo didn't answer. Being careful not to disrupt the spell, Nym reached out to grab a shoulder and give the echo a shake. "Say something."

"You're not a patient one, are you?" Rizin said.

"I know," Nym said, "But I kind of figured you wanted to be out of here as soon as possible. I don't have hours for this."

"You've got a bit more time still."

Nym huffed, but said, "Fine. The long way then."

Merging with an echo was far, far easier if they agreed to it, but as long as they weren't actively resisting, it was still possible to do. According to the books he'd read, most would-be ascendants found themselves in similar situations, forced to wait for an unknown length of time, possibly minutes, but possibly months, for their echoes to stir.

That was how the fourth layer worked: slowly. Nym didn't have the time for that, so he firmly anchored himself to his echo with magic, then released the spell that compressed physical space. The echo slid backward, taking Nym with him. Once they were both safely returned to their original position, Nym started the next spell.

This one was designed to do something similar to the tunnel spell, except with a person. It did its best to anchor the subject and the target together, to create a metaphysical bridge Nym could traverse to merge the fourth echo into his being. As long as the echo didn't fight back, it would work. The only problem was that it was a slow process normally. Now, even with a hand literally on the echo's shoulder, it might take ten or twelve hours to complete.

There was a way to combine the two spells, to compress that bridge, but doing that and keeping the tunnel open might just be beyond Nym's abilities. If he let the tunnel collapse, well, he wouldn't be stranded, but it would be inconvenient. It might be worth it though if it saved him a few hours. "I'm thinking about letting the tunnel go," he said, turning to look at Rizin.

The fox tilted his head and watched Nym. "Do you think that will be a problem? I don't want to mess up any magic you've got going on."

Rizin started laughing, and Nym realized why. They couldn't hear each other, not with the strangely warped distance and smothering silence of the fourth layer. Shrugging, Nym went back to work. He trusted the fox was canny enough and skilled enough to adapt if he needed to. The tunnel folded up on itself and closed, freeing up a large chunk of Nym's mind to let him cast multiple other spells at once.

It was still a time-consuming process, but he'd been right about it going much faster without him having to exert the effort to hold the tunnel open. Four hours later, the last anchor point locked into place, and Nym activated the merger spell. The echo disappeared, and he felt his awareness of the fourth layer expand.

Rizin stared at him intently, nodded to himself, and then did something Nym didn't catch. A moment later, magic grabbed him by the guts and jerked him forward. He fell through reality and landed back on the mountain where he'd started.

"You'll forgive me, I hope," Rizin said, once more in his small one-tailed fox form. "I really didn't feel like waiting hours more while you fumbled around trying to figure out how to open your gateway back up from the wrong side."

"I know how to do that," Nym said. "It would only have taken a moment."

"And how long would it have taken you to step through?"

"That . . . is a good point."

Nym took a moment to examine himself. His being had expanded again, and honestly, he just felt really, really relaxed. He was at peace now, which he had to admit was a foreign state of being for him. It seemed like he'd struggled and stressed for as long as he could remember, with only brief periods of relief.

This echo of him reminded him of how he'd felt for a few weeks when he'd met the Earth Shapers, when he'd been surrounded by friends and his worries were few and far between. It inspired good memories, but unfortunately, his life hadn't stayed that way.

"One more to go," he said. "I think I'd like to rest for a bit before I tackle that one, if that's okay with you."

Rizin nodded. "You are ready to return to the safety of my den?"

"I don't know how safe it is with you in there, but yes."

Rizin took Nym back in an instant. He was once again sitting on his overlarge cushion, and Nym couldn't help but eyeball it up and compare it to the version of the fox he'd seen in the fourth layer. Even as big as he'd been there, the cushion was still too large for that shape. That was troubling.

It was one thing to know intellectually that Rizin was stronger than him. But the fox kept himself hidden, wrapped in shadows and illusions. Seeing part of that veil stripped away had shocked Nym out of complacency. His new companion was every bit as dangerous as an ascendant; he was just better at hiding it.

Nym tried to convince himself that it was a good thing. If an ascendant did attack, Rizin could fight back. He was only really screwed if Rizin decided to attack him. So far, that hadn't happened. So far. Things did tend to change though. An ally today could be an enemy tomorrow.

He didn't see where he had too many other choices though. No matter what he did, there were risks. Picking the least terrible choice was a hard skill to master. Nym hoped he'd done a good enough job to survive the upcoming storm.

CHAPTER FORTY-FOUR

Nym found it much harder to focus over the next day or two. Every time he repeated this process, he had to incorporate new elements into his being and make terms with them. His first echo had been so close to him that it hadn't really changed much. The second-layer echo had some conflicted desires, but they found common ground before even completing the merger.

The third one had caused problems before he managed to get a handle on that newly exaggerated facet of his personality, but this fourth one was something entirely different. He was just so peaceful and relaxed now that the desire to do anything at all had disappeared. His drive was gone, and without motivation, he had to fall back on sheer discipline and willpower to keep him moving forward.

"If you're going to be this lazy about it, you'll never actually ascend," Rizin said.

Spite helped too.

He knew what Rizin was doing, but it worked, sort of. Integrating new echoes into his being was a process, and normally he'd have time to do that. The books recommended a month for the first two layers, then another month just for the third, and it only took longer from there. By all rights, he should spend the next year finishing the integration of the fourth layer and doing the entire process over again for the fifth.

But Nym didn't have a year, so he was trying to muscle through it on contrariness and grit. It was going about as poorly as he'd expected, but he didn't have a lot of choice. He couldn't just spend the next year of his life sitting next to Rizin to stay hidden. That was a temporary solution at best. He could take his chances and go back out into the world, but that would either put him back under Niramyn's thumb or get him killed by someone from Myzalik's team.

"I'm ready whenever you are," Nym said.

"No, you're not. But you can try if you think you are."

They appeared in the sky above a city that Nym didn't recognize. "Where are we?" he asked, peering down at it with a perfect-vision spell active.

"I don't know."

"Probably best not to linger," he said. "There's no reason to involve whoever lives down there in what I've got going on."

The teleportation spell was unusually difficult in a way he hadn't had a problem with since his very first days of having access to third-circle spells. The arcana didn't want to bend to his will at all. Nym struggled with it for a moment before eventually shaping it into the spell he wanted, and he teleported a few hundred miles east of the city.

"Are you sure you're ready?" Rizin asked.

"No," Nym admitted. "But what choice do I have?"

"The choice not to do something foolish when you haven't prepared yourself for it."

"I would love to put this off. How do you feel about having a houseguest for another two or three months? I promise I don't eat that much."

"Blech. Fine, I see your point."

"No, really," Nym said. "I don't want to do this. I don't think I'm ready. I can think of a dozen ways to help prepare for this, but I need time that I don't have."

"I agree, but to put it bluntly: What's in it for me?" Rizin asked.

"Other than what we've already talked about? We both know there's not much I can do for you."

"That is exactly your problem, Nym. Your needs outweigh your ability to pay for them. I don't envy your position, and I'm not above a spot of charity, but no, I can't and won't be your guardian for years while you prepare yourself to finally ascend."

"I get it," Nym said. And he did, truly. As things stood now, he was only safe while he stood in Rizin's shadow. As soon as he set foot back in the light, people were going to see him again, with no guarantee that it would be the lesser of the two evils that noticed him first. "What would you do in my situation?"

"Do I only have access to your abilities in this hypothetical scenario?"

Nym glared at the fox. "What would be the point otherwise?"

"I'd probably do exactly what you're doing now. You're drowning in the middle of the ocean, and your only option is to keep kicking your legs and hope somebody saves you."

Left unspoken was the implication that Rizin wasn't going to be Nym's savior. He wasn't willing to exert himself more than he already had unless Nym could actually bring some value to the table. He definitely wasn't willing to invest time and resources into keeping Nym's head above water just for the promise of future value.

"So this is me kicking my legs," Nym said.

He could do this. Adding the fourth echo made it harder to focus, to want to do things, but at the same time, it also smoothed over a lot of stress and concern. It didn't really balance out, but he was scrambling for any advantage he could get at this point.

Nym cast the first location spell, then teleported in the direction it indicated. He repeated the process, by now a familiar one, until he'd locked down the proper location for the tunnel. Each time he did it, it got a little easier to force the arcana to do what he wanted. Now it was time to work with fifth-layer arcana though, and that was a whole different skill set.

He struggled through the mental lethargy that dragged on him to form the channels. It was already clear that getting the timing right was going to be a challenge, but Nym was nothing if not disciplined. The last subjective year of his life had forced him to adopt a mindset that pushed him ever forward. He took a breath, allowed himself to feel the weight of tranquility trying to tie himself down, and then pushed himself anyway.

The arcana poured through him, the tunnel formed, and Nym stepped through.

He hadn't been prepared the first time his duplicate from the core reality appeared in his layer. But ever since then, the Nym echo had been watching and waiting. He knew when his opposite started working the magic, and he welcomed it.

The core version was an idiot to try this so soon, but the Nym echo wasn't going to cut him any slack for that. He watched the tunnel form, prepared himself, and waited for his victim to come through. When the core Nym did finally appear, he looked around, confused.

That was when the echo sprang his trap. A massive web spread across the sky, and with it came a reflection on the ground. The echo's magic pulled those two webs toward each other with Nym caught inside. The echo grinned as he watched his opposite struggle.

The grin faded quickly. Nym didn't teleport out of the web like the echo had been expecting. It simply exploded away from him, hurled off and shredded into pieces while Nym floated in the air. The echo's brow furrowed as he watched from his hiding place. He knew there were some temporal shenanigans going on with the core version of himself, but it shouldn't have made that much of a difference.

Apparently, he'd underestimated whatever training core Nym had undergone. Even in an unfamiliar and hostile environment, he'd reacted to the trap almost instantly and cut his way free. The echo wasn't done though. It sent beads of arcana streaking up into the sky, angled to splash into the earth overhead and be mirrored. The connection formed, and the echo laughed. "Got you."

Lightning arced between the beads he'd cast upward and their reflections below. The core Nym was caught in the center of a sudden storm before he could react and struck no less than six times in a second. That had to sting.

Except that when the lights died down, Nym was still floating there, unharmed. There was no way he'd gotten off that stupid little storm-catcher spell that fast, and no way it would have stopped that much lightning anyway. Something was wrong. The fight wasn't supposed to go this way.

Nym felt amazing. Before he'd stepped through the tunnel into the fifth layer, doing anything but sitting there and watching the world go by had been a struggle. Now, it was the exact opposite. He could practically see what was going to happen before it did. Though he was a bit surprised at how violently his echo had attacked him, he wouldn't be the first nascent ascendant to deal with a trial like this.

And all that sluggishness was just gone, or more accurately it had been focused into efficiency. His spells had exactly enough arcana to do what he needed, and they practically leaped out of his soul well. Something about being in the fifth layer had altered how he was connecting to the fourth echo. He couldn't recall reading anything about this when he'd been studying, but he wasn't going to argue with it.

His echo was somewhere nearby, hidden, but not for long. Nym pulled together a pinnacle scrying spell, one that sent his awareness out in a massive omnidirectional pulse. "Got you," he said.

Once upon a time, Nym had sucked with fire magic. Even when he'd gotten sort of good with it, his abilities in that field still lagged far behind everything else. He'd always struggled to get the intent filters needed for second-circle magic right, and once he'd progressed beyond that, the need for sheer destructive firepower had been more than covered with his other spells. Though he supposed an argument could have been made that he should have focused heavily on fire magic when he was helping with that whole undead disaster.

Regardless, he'd finally had the time to correct that deficiency. At Nym's command, fire rained down from the sky, huge swirling spears of superheated air that scorched the entire landscape. They hammered into the mirrored surface below, each one smoothly slipping into the ground like it was made of water. Color bloomed under the mirror until the entire surface was glowing red-hot.

His echo burst out of it in a cloud of shattered glass and shot straight up into the air, lightning dancing across his fingers as he hurled bolt after bolt Nym's way. The lightning curved around the barrier Nym was surrounded by, playing across the surface of it briefly before shooting off into the ground overhead.

"You can't do this," the echo snarled. "You're not stronger than me. You're not!"

"You're going to be a pain, aren't you?" Nym asked calmly.

A cloud of razor-edged ice crystals formed around him and started swirling rapidly. They scraped across the barrier a thousand times in a matter of seconds, but none cut through. His echo switched tactics, going from pure damage to arcana that would blind Nym, or make him sick, or a dozen other effects if they were able to get through.

Nym formed a needle of arcana so thin it was almost invisible. It flicked out and struck the echo midspell, but he deflected it away. "Please, like that would work on me."

Sixteen more needles followed it, and Nym was pleased to see enough of them landed to disrupt the echo's next spell. "So what's the deal?" Nym asked. "I win, you become part of the collective being that is Nym. You win, and . . . what?"

"You become part of my being instead," the echo said.

Nym blinked. "Can you even do that?"

"I can do anything you can do," the echo snapped. "Anything."

"I don't think you can."

"That's because you cheated! You're not supposed to be this strong."

Nym gave his echo a serene smile and said, "Someone told me once that when you're in a fight, if you're not cheating, you're not trying hard enough. We have a deal?"

"Deal," the echo said. Then he smirked and triggered the spell he had been building behind Nym. A massive flash of light eclipsed them both.

CHAPTER FORTY-FIVE

It was a clever spell, one designed to take advantage of the unique terrain of the fifth layer of reality. The light was blinding, and it seared Nym's body, but the true twist was the mirrored surface below them. The light flashed downward, there and gone in an instant, only to reflect back up and bathe the whole area in brilliant, burning heat.

That was nothing outside of Nym's capabilities to handle. He could compensate for being blinded with scrying magic, and the heat wouldn't last long enough to do any real damage through the defensive spells he'd slapped in place the moment his echo had attacked. It would be uncomfortable for a few moments, and then it would be spent. It was only as he started to weave together his first scrying spell that he realized the light was also blocking his ability to see arcana.

Then his echo sprang the second part of his trap. Something struck Nym, something bigger than he was and moving at high speeds. It carried him across the sky and upward into the strange patchwork landscape. Whatever it was his echo had struck him with didn't want to let him stop moving, but he dispersed it with a wave of dispelling arcana. Since he couldn't see what was in it, he couldn't precisely target it to break the spell, so the quick-and-dirty solution was to just hammer it.

By the time Nym broke the spell pushing him upward, gravity was twisting around him strangely. He had to shift the way he was flying to both hold him up and down at the same time just to keep from falling one way or another, at about half strength in each direction. He was just getting a feel for the equilibrium of it when his lateral momentum carried him into a different patchwork square of the sky and everything changed.

Nym shot up instantly, propelled both by his own magic and the suddenly many times stronger reverse gravity. He quickly reconfigured his magic to hold him steady, then strengthened it to start bringing him back down toward the mirrored ground. All the while, he searched for his echo, who had disappeared with the initial burst of light.

Using the strange and unfamiliar laws of the world against Nym was a great strategy. It forced him to split his attention, to handle the threat of the environment itself while fighting against his own echo. Even with all the advantages his time spent in Niramyn's sanctuary granted him, he couldn't really say that he was winning this fight.

In a weird way, he was proud of his echo. He was turning out to be a hell of an opponent, with the echo systematically driving Nym into a corner, forcing him to waste time and resources dealing with obstacles and distractions. Though the echo didn't have the breadth of options Nym did, he was still powerful. Every spell it had thrown at him was a pinnacle spell, and that blinding-light spell had even washed out his ability to see arcana. That was new.

For all of that though, Nym was confident he would win. The echo wasn't throwing anything his way that he couldn't deal with. It felt like he was just using the attacks as a stall while he built up to something big. No doubt, whatever that was, it would take advantage of the physics of the world in an unexpected way.

The win condition was simple then. Nym just had to locate his echo and defeat him before he could pull off whatever he was doing. And with his scrying spells able to see arcana, it was not hard to spot the echo. Or at least, it wasn't hard to spot the echo's arcana, which had popped up in no less than six different places.

"More distractions," Nym said as he sorted through them. One of them was the real one, or possibly none of them were. But if that was the case, then the echo was doing nothing, or he knew some way to hide his arcana that Nym wasn't familiar with. Neither of those seemed likely to him.

He sent his scrying anchors out in various directions to check on the sources of arcana and, as expected, found temporary arcana batteries there inside illusions of himself. That was an odd touch. He and his echo weren't identical, and it would have made more sense for the illusions to match the echo instead.

"Unless they're not distractions," Nym said. "Maybe . . . bait?"

There was no sign of the echo, meaning he was either well and truly hidden, or he did have some way to hide his own arcana use. Nym didn't think that was the case, otherwise the echo would have used such an ability to far greater effect earlier in their match. Being able to read the spells in the echo's aura made it much, much easier to defend against them.

He'd broken three of the illusions when something rippled across the mirror below. Nym looked down and saw what looked like a massive fish swimming inside the ground, heading straight toward one of the illusions. Its jaws practically unhinged, and it took the illusion in one bite. Even though the fish only existed inside the mirror, the illusion it had consumed ceased to exist in reality as well.

Nym understood the trick now. More of the fish were appearing, excitedly darting through mirror space to consume the remaining illusions. Nym was saved more because there were so many that they got in one another's way than because of his own quick reactions. He chained together several defenses with an emphasis on physical alterations that would reflect into the mirror world, then waited inside a bladed sphere of ultradense crystal to see if the mirror fish would be able to batter down the walls of force and earth he'd erected.

A great crash shook the wall when the first fish rammed into it. Its teeth scraped against the wall, but its jaw couldn't open wide enough to take it in one bite. The fish was stymied only for a second before arcana swirled around it and washed out in an explosive blast that sent cracks running through the barriers.

The spell drew more of the fish. If they were anything like the first one, they were going to quickly tear through the defenses he'd put up. So Nym let them gather up around him, let them weaken the wall, and then when it was about to fall and as many as could possibly fit were next to it, he triggered the spiked crystal cocoon. Lances of razor-sharp arcana-infused crystal exploded in every direction through the empty air. And those lances were reflected in the mirrored ground below.

The fish died by the dozens, each one leaking rainbow blood that obscured everything else in the mirror. Nym couldn't even see himself anymore, and he still didn't know where his echo was. His scrying anchors flitted around, searching in every way he could, but the echo was nowhere to be found. He supposed it was possible that the echo had fled when his trap had failed, but that didn't really fit.

The echoes represented parts of his personality, sharpened and magnified by the nature of the reality they hailed from. The fifth-layer echo was proud and violent. He seemed to loathe the idea that he wasn't the original Nym and wanted to prove he was stronger. It seemed silly to Nym, since really, they were all the same being in the end.

So no, he didn't believe for even a moment that his echo had run away. Despite that, there was no sign of him. The only Nyms anywhere around were him and his own reflection a thousand feet below him. Nym glanced down, saw his own feet and his own face looking back up at him and the aura of arcana from his spells surrounding him.

Except now that he looked closely, those weren't the spells he was currently holding on to. He laughed to himself. His echo had once again exploited the world of the fifth layer against him and was hiding in Nym's own reflection. Now that Nym had finally spotted him though, the fight was over.

A combination of teleportation to pull his echo out, greater telekinesis to physically lock him down, and a concentrated shock of crushing psychic force was enough to daze Nym's opponent. He took a moment to slide his own arcana into every single construct the echo still had going and then blasted him with a storm of arcana injections to cripple his soul well's capacity for the next few minutes.

"I think you can agree that I've won," Nym said when the psychic shock wore off.

The echo didn't say anything, but the twisted scowl on his face was enough of a sign to Nym. He started the spell that would bind them together, for the fifth and final time.

Niramyn was frustrated. No matter what he did, it was two steps forward and three steps back. Myzalik had discovered his return far too quickly and was proving remarkably adept at putting obstacles in Niramyn's way. He'd barely finished clawing his way back up to the tenth layer before he'd been discovered.

Someone had betrayed them, someone who thought they stood to gain more in the rival Exarch's service than they did in Niramyn's. He'd been careful about who he'd brought back under his power, both because he'd been wary of this exact scenario and because until he regained access to his full power at the twelfth layer, he was vulnerable to treachery of a more direct sort. The last thing he needed was to find himself pushed out of the timeline for a decade or two, only to come back and find ascendant society fully under Myzalik's control.

His new home lacked the view his palace on Vislarg had boasted, but the arcana-infused wine was still good. He sipped at it idly while he surveyed the rather dreary-looking hall he'd found himself in. It belonged to some petty mortal king of some country or another. Niramyn couldn't remember what the humans called it.

It would do, for now, but it was seriously lacking in amenities. Unfortunately, one of his former vassals had clued Myzalik in to how Niramyn constructed several of his defenses and how best to go about turning them against their owner, so for the time being, this was what he had.

An ascendant appeared nearby and bowed at the waist. "Master," she said. She was tall, thin, had blonde hair. Valicin, he thought her name was.

"What is it?" he snapped. "Good news on our little project, I hope?"

"Of a sort," she said. "I . . . still haven't found him, but his echoes have disappeared from the fourth and fifth layers."

It was nice to know that his offspring, for lack of a better term, was still moving forward. That was one weapon he still had hidden away while it was being honed. Though if they couldn't figure out where the boy had gotten off to, it wouldn't do him much good.

"You need to find him before he begins his ascension. If he transcends the boundary and he's not firmly under my control and sheltered from other ascendants, everything I've invested in him will go to waste. If I lose my investment, I will punish you."

Valicin knew better than to flinch in front of him, but he could see past her blank expression. She was scared. Good. It would motivate her to correct her error in losing him in the first place.

"Is there anything else?" Niramyn asked, idly sipping at his wine again before releasing the goblet to float in the air next to him.

"No, Exarch. I will continue to look for him."

"Do so. Report back to me in a week if you haven't found him by then."

"Yes, Exarch."

Then Valicin was gone. If she hadn't found the missing boy by then, he'd have to attend to it himself. And if he had to do that, she wasn't going to like it.

CHAPTER FORTY-SIX

The secret den of a magical fox that transcended the powers of a mere mortal did not, surprisingly, have a lot to eat. Nym had used magic to stave off the needs of his body, but for the time being, he was still a human. Eventually, he would need food, and that time was drawing close.

"I don't suppose you'd be willing to go on a supply run?" he asked Rizin.

The fox's ear flicked in annoyance, and he cracked an eye open from where he was napping on his enormous cushion. "Humans," he said with disgust. "Fine. Make it quick."

The pair teleported to a small town, one that Nym had never seen before, and a quick scrying spell later, he located a general store to pick up some supplies and an inn to serve a hot meal. Rizin took on the appearance of the boy with the yellow jacket again, and together they sat at a table to wait for their food.

"I didn't think you ate human food," Nym remarked.

"Just because I don't need it doesn't mean I can't eat it. If beings at my level still needed to eat meat, humans would have been hunted to extinction a long, long time ago."

"Charming thought," Nym said. He knew Rizin could hunt with impunity, but it seemed a bit far-fetched to think that he'd need to eat that many people. Then he remembered how big Rizin had appeared in the fourth layer and how big the cushion was. Maybe Nym wasn't giving him enough credit. It was a good thing Rizin actually survived on arcana then.

The server swung by to drop off their meals, enough food easily for five people. They split it roughly evenly, though Rizin definitely favored the meat dishes, and Nym took the entire pot of stew for himself. Neither had a taste for greens when other foods were right in front of them, but Nym was too hungry to leave even a scrap behind. He'd gone at least a week without food, and his magic could only carry him so far.

"How long do you think you'll need to prepare for your ascension?" Rizin asked.

"Hard to say. At least a few more weeks to finish integrating my fourth and fifth echoes." Doing them both at the same time was proving uniquely challenging. He'd gotten lucky in finding an outlet for the sense of lethargy his fourth echo had highlighted in his personality. Channeling that into ruthless efficiency in battle was not something he'd have come up with on his own.

Once the fight was over, it had become a struggle to keep himself moving. He was trying to focus it into parsing his fragmented knowledge of the ascendance process into a semicoherent and useful chunk of information, but it was slow going. Doing that while keeping his highly competitive and volatile fifth echo from overriding his conscious decisions challenged him daily. More than once, he'd caught himself trying to plot out the best way to take out Rizin, a suicidal course of action if he'd ever seen one.

"And after, you will attempt your ascension?"

"I guess," Nym said. "I just . . . I don't know what to do."

"Break through to the sixth layer, of course."

"That's it? Just make a conduit strong enough to reach that far? Why did I spend so much time finding my alternate versions then?"

"If you can't figure out how to leverage that to your advantage, you're going to die when you try to take the final step."

"Thanks, that's helpful."

"Best I can do," he said. "Everyone's ascendance is different. Only way to prepare is to just get better at everything. There's no telling what you'll go through. There's a theory that gets kicked around a lot, that something higher than us exists, that the trials aren't random, that they're deliberately designed to test us."

"Do you believe that?" Nym asked.

"Not at all. I think it's just the nature of the sixth layer to take who you are, twist it, and reflect that back at you. It's just worse the very first time because you've got no experience, and no amount of talking and teaching can prepare you for it."

"Okay, well . . . For the next week or two I'm just going to work on getting myself accustomed to existing in six different realities at the same time, as long as you don't mind me taking up a bit of space."

Rizin made a show of heaving a giant sigh before saying, "I suppose if it's only for a week. Oh, that reminds me though, did you know you've got an ascendant looking for you?"

"Oh? Do you know which one?"

"I'm not exactly on a first-name basis with them, but she matches your description of the one who shoved you into the fifth layer."

"Ah, and do you know which faction she's part of?"

"Not a clue," the fox said cheerily.

"Do you think you could find out?"

"Not likely. Ascendants don't exactly like people spying on them, and they're better than humans at realizing something's lurking around."

Nym snorted. "What kind of fox are you?"

"The kind that survives by keeping his nose out of other godlike beings' business."

Nym thought about that for a second. "Okay, that's fair. But it does still leave me with the problem of not knowing who I can trust."

"That's not your problem. Your problem is that you shouldn't trust anyone."

There was some truth to that. Myzalik's group would kill him out of hand, but Niramyn only kept him around because he wanted to use Nym. If the two factions were already fighting, then the whole plan of being bait to draw out ascendants and ambush them was probably worthless now. Maybe Niramyn would have some other use for him, or maybe he'd be killed.

"You know what I don't get? Why are they even still looking for me at all? Myzalik knows Niramyn is back. They're fighting again. What's the point of hunting me down? It's not like I can make a big difference either way."

"Ascendants aren't so numerous that any of them would be willing to let a single new one that they've already got their hooks into just walk away," Rizin said. "Niramyn will want you because he believes he owns you. Myzalik will kill you because he also believes Niramyn owns you, and he'd rather deny his enemy a new soldier before you have time to grow into a threat."

"No matter what I do, I'm always going to have a target on my back, aren't I?"

"It certainly seems that way."

The plan remained unchanged then. The more Nym learned about these people, the more certain he became that there was no reasoning with them. They expected the world to bend to their whims, and anything that didn't bend would be broken. There were only two ways to survive: avoid their notice or be so strong that they couldn't make him bend. It was too late for the first option. Honestly, it had never been a real option anyway.

"Food's gone," Rizin said, leaning back in his seat. "Anything else you want to do?"

"No." Nym's mouth was set into a grim line. "Time to get back to work."

It wasn't until a month later, when he felt he had fully integrated himself into each layer of reality, that Nym finally started to notice what had changed. When he forged a conduit, he could feel it move through each layer. The part of him that existed in that layer reinforced it, even going so far as to draw arcana directly from that layer without a conduit.

That arcana couldn't come back to Nym without some work, but he did some experimenting and figured out how to forge a sort of internal conduit. It was like storing arcana in his hand, then making a bridge to ferry it over to his soul well for use, except his hand was in another world. Once he got that technique down, it opened up a whole new type of conduit for him to experiment with.

The conduits formed faster. They were stronger, could pull more arcana to him, and were infinitely more flexible. It was easier to form more of them, and he even managed to form a single conduit that pulled arcana from multiple layers at the same time without breaking or mixing them together in his soul well.

"I think I'm ready to try to ascend," Nym said one day. "I . . . probably shouldn't do that here."

"I would appreciate if you didn't. It's noisy the first time."

"Any advice for me?"

The fox cocked his head to the side and thought about it. "When you reach the membrane between the fifth and sixth layers, it's going to feel completely different than anything else. Don't lose your concentration when it reaches back out to you. And, whatever happens after that, try not to let it kill you."

That wasn't all that reassuring, but he supposed Rizin hadn't meant it to be. Nym figured what he was about to do was probably the most dangerous part of the whole ascendant deal. Supposedly they were functionally immortal once they crossed this threshold, so presumably any future missteps would be reversible. This was the universe's last chance to kill him before he stepped past the rules mortals had to play by.

But he had spent months, or hell, years, locked away in a box full of books, learning and practicing spells. He was as powerful as a mortal mage could be, enhanced and augmented by dozens of spells and rituals. His soul well practically filled his entire body now in addition to having five other soul wells connected to it, his conduits resonated through other layers of existence, and he was literally six different versions of himself all mixed together into one being.

"I don't think I can get any more prepared for this than I already am, and I'm sure you're anxious to have your privacy back."

"Something like that," Rizin agreed. "If you survive this, we'll discuss forming a pact."

"I always wondered why you helped me without making the pact first."

"Curiosity, I suppose. I've never seen a mortal attempt to ascend. And you're not a bad sort, as far as mortals go. It's rather like having my very own pet human."

Nym snorted. "It is kind of like that, huh? That's . . . a bit disturbing."

"The comparison is apt, I believe."

"I don't know. I've never had a pet. Never had the time."

Rizin laughed and hopped down from his cushion. "Are you ready?"

"Yeah." Nym eyed the cushion. "What do you do up there all day? You can't possibly be sleeping."

"Maybe, when your brain won't explode from the knowledge, I'll show you. But that's a worry for another day."

The pair of them teleported into the air above the Garden of Winter. "Our last outing together," the fox said. "Is there anywhere in particular you wish to make this attempt?"

Nym thought about that. There were a few places that were relevant to him. The beach where he'd washed ashore was perhaps the place he had the strongest connection to, but too many ascendants had found it. He'd met Analia in Abilanth, though if he was going to consider whole cities, Thrakus, where he'd met the Earth Shapers, had more sentimental value. The potential for collateral damage made them unappealing.

Archmage Veran's sanctum was the closest thing he'd ever had to a long-term home, and the mausoleum where the veil had been torn had probably shaped his life more significantly than anywhere else, at least insofar as it was the source of so many problems he'd been personally involved with. Shu-Ain had never been a home to him, just a place he'd visited his friends at.

The more Nym considered the question, the less he felt any of those places were appropriate. Ascending wasn't about a place where he felt safe or comfortable. It was a step into the unknown, beyond the world, beyond limits. For the last place he'd ever stand on mortal feet, he had a better idea.

Nym teleported to the far north, where the land turned to ice that stretched out for miles and miles over an endless dark sea. He spared the frozen ship below him a glance, then flew north. Finally, he reached the edge where it turned to water. Slowly, he floated down until his feet touched the ice. It gave way under his weight, sinking a few inches and letting frigid, life-stealing water swirl past his shoes.

"Here?" Rizin asked, appearing next to Nym.

"Here."

CHAPTER FORTY-SEVEN

The conduit lanced out past the edge of reality, where it was bolstered by Nym inside the first layer. It leaped ahead, through each consecutive layer, guided by the parts of him that existed there, all the way through the fifth layer until it plunged into that mirrored surface far past the horizon, at the very ends of mortal existence.

The conduit struck that final membrane, and something struck back. Rather than give way to his conduit or firmly rebuff it like other membranes had, this one invaded it. It seeped inside like it was arcana itself, and Nym felt an instinctive urge to recoil. He suppressed that and pushed forward.

The membrane felt cold and slimy, like he was sinking into a pit of mud that seeped into everything. That was strange enough by itself, since no other membrane had ever given any feedback like this, but the fact that it felt alive as it wiggled against him triggered some sort of primitive drive in his brain to break contact. Again, he resisted the urge.

Then he was through. His conduit surged out into an empty space past the membrane, a space with no arcana at all. Nym had only a bare instant to realize that whatever was on the other side of that membrane wasn't a new layer of reality before his conduit started to crumble and break.

Then the membrane shot down the conduit and grabbed Nym by his soul well. It jerked him out of reality and dragged him along the path of his conduit until he crashed into the membrane. So far, nothing was outside of what he'd expected. This was the point where the books got a lot less clear about what was going to happen.

Once he was through the membrane, he needed to survive and reach the sixth layer, but everyone who'd ever managed it had described a different experience. No one had been able to find common threads or any way to predict what kind of challenges the next person to make the attempt would face. He was going in blind.

Nym dove through the membrane and broke out into the other side, where he found nothing waiting except an immense, empty blackness. Pain wracked his body, and he watched in horror as it started to break apart into nothingness. In a matter of moments, his physical form was reduced to dust, or less.

But Nym was more than just his body now. He existed in five other realities, and those parts still housed his consciousness. He wouldn't die from this, but unless he figured out how to cross the endless abyss of darkness beyond the fifth membrane, he would never be able to return to the core reality.

His conduit hung open behind where he used to be, still connected to his insubstantial being. Its ends were frayed and cracked and didn't exist beyond the membrane, but the hole was open. As long as he didn't let it close, he had some sort of presence in the void. He drifted, nothing more than a ghost propelled by desire and intent.

The void pushed back against him, tried to hold him down and tie him in place. Nym fought against it, but it was an insubstantial thing, an opposing effort of will rather than a physical restraint. He didn't even have a body to be trapped now, but his mind couldn't will the nothingness he'd become forward.

So he reached back into his conduit and pulled the part of him that existed in the fifth layer forward. Arcana flooded into the void, and the world appeared around him. It was a small, faded copy of that reality, maybe a thousand feet across, but it was *something* that wasn't darkness and emptiness. His body formed, exactly as the part of him that used to be an echo remembered it.

As soon as the illusory world appeared around him, it started to break. Nym was racing against an invisible clock, and he had at most fifteen or twenty seconds to act. Arcana rushed through his conduit into the bubble of reality he'd formed around him, and every single parallel process in his mind grabbed hold of it to fuel the spells he shaped.

First came the reinforcements, bulwarks against the void that stopped it from encroaching further. Then came the repairs, spell after spell designed to impose his version of reality on the nothingness. Every crack in reality was filled, every rupture and ripple smoothed over. Only once it was stable and holding did Nym allow himself a moment to think instead of just reacting.

He'd built himself a little bubble, a reflection of the fifth layer of reality, but other than the fact that he could wiggle his fingers and toes again, he wasn't sure how it helped him. It didn't help that in this form, he was feeling the full, undiluted personality of his echo. It drove him toward an aggressive course of action, which wasn't necessarily the correct one. It also made him concerned that if he made a similar bubble with his fourth-layer echo in the center, he might become trapped inside his own mind, doing nothing for an eternity.

"Okay, what does this get me?" he asked himself. "Other than an extra thousand feet for my conduit."

If nothing else, it gave him a body to exist in. It wouldn't last long though. Despite everything he'd done, he could feel the void still eating away at the bubble. The spells he'd cast weren't designed to hold something like this back, and he couldn't hold it forever. Even if he could, it didn't accomplish anything. He had to find some way to keep pushing forward, and he had to find some way to escape the void.

There was no going back, if only because there was nothing to go back to. Going forward was the only way out, and that meant that first and foremost, he needed to figure out where he was even going. He couldn't see anything but blackness from his fifth-layer reality bubble, so Nym gathered up as much arcana as he could, and he cast himself out of safety.

The body was left behind, still a part of him but no longer the primary part, and the arcana was drawn onward with him. Once again disembodied, he drifted forward until the pressure of the void pulled him to a stop. Then he expelled the arcana from his soul well and formed a new reality around him. This one was modelled off fourth-layer arcana and was in many ways harder to create.

In reality prime, there was little reason to channel fourth-layer arcana. It was mostly an obstacle and ill-suited for use in the core reality. Here, it was the opposite. The fourth layer was almost extrareal, so dense and thick that the void had trouble eating it. It floated there, a sphere barely large enough for him to exist in, and held back the darkness just by its nature.

Nym manifested inside the sphere, now in the shape of his fourth echo. He smiled softly and peered out into the void. There, so faraway now that it looked like nothing more than a marble, was the replica of the fifth layer he'd created. Nym wasn't sure if he'd just gone much farther than he expected, or if he was drifting on invisible currents, or if it was simply a quirk of traditional three-dimensional space not existing here.

He took some time to just reflect on what he'd learned, on how he'd gotten to this point in his life. There was time for that here. Perhaps there was less than he'd like, but still, some. The void wouldn't crack this sanctuary anytime soon, but as Nym gazed out into it, he saw that his previous sanctuary was not quite so sturdy.

So Nym built a new conduit to it, one that shared the bedrock stability of his own space and stopped the fifth-reality bubble from breaking down. It was a slow process, but one that he worked toward diligently and with great care. By the time he finished, both bubbles were capable of withstanding the ravages of the void.

And then it was time to move on, so once again Nym cast himself out into the darkness. His goal was no closer than ever, but he was determined to try again, as many times as it took. With him was another soul well, this one full of arcana from the Astral Sea.

The void stopped him again, and again he built himself a new shelter. Unlike the fifth-reality's sanctuary, which was huge and aggressively fought the void, or the fourth reality with its unshakable core of strength, this new one was wild. It twitched and spun and broke off tendrils of void that tried to slip in and form new cracks. The void simply couldn't grasp hold of the squirming sliver of reality.

Here, Nym finally caught a glimpse of purpose. He had been throwing himself forward, almost mindlessly, looking for some clue to help guide him. Now he was starting to see the shape of things. His echoes had all been exaggerated reflections of himself, individual pieces of the whole. They were the foundation he would use to rebuild himself, and the new Nym would be strong enough to withstand the void.

No single piece would succeed on its own. Yes, the slice of fourth layer would probably last until the end of time, but it would never do anything. The fifth layer had the drive to overcome obstacles but lacked the direction to find them. And here in this bubble of third-layer arcana, Nym found that insatiable part of himself that was constantly searching for the next horizon, the next new idea.

Once he'd solidified it and connected it to the other two pieces of reality he'd forged, Nym repeated the process again to make a second-layer bubble. That one was easy to understand. It was the same as always: purpose. Second-layer Nym had a reason to exist, people to protect. He tied the other bubbles together and gave them a shove. He told them which way they needed to go. The four of them worked together, each piece contributing.

There was still one piece missing, of course. He had purpose now, combined with the knowledge and drive to go about fulfilling it, and the bedrock certainty that he could endure no matter how hard it got. What was missing was harder to define. That first-layer version was the closest to Nym, the closest to the real world. It lacked the exaggerated personalities of the other echoes.

But Nym built it anyway, out of a sense of symmetry if nothing else. Once he did, it was obvious why it existed. That last little bubble was the key. It led everything else back to Nym, collected it all together, and opened the gate that he hadn't even realized existed.

All five realities merged together, one over top the other over top the next, and then his conduit, that one thin lifeline still holding a piece of him anchored to the core reality, burst through and shattered the void. Nym snapped back to himself, all of himself in every dimension, and pushed through until the conduit burst out of the nothingness and into the sixth layer.

It was a world of paradox, gloriously complex while being reduced to a single, pure point, like being swept up in the mind of a god. All was one, and inside the sixth layer, linear time lost its meaning. It was no wonder ascendants considered themselves immortal. Nym experienced so much of everything all at once, his entire life summed up in an instant, and a thousand-thousand spiraling possibilities in every direction, new instants that might never happen except if he chose to turn to those paths.

Nym could get lost forever in what-ifs and maybe futures. He could see every ripple that would echo out from the part of him that existed in the past if he but willed it to move slightly differently. It was overwhelming, and he knew he had to narrow his focus. Nym picked a new future to follow, one in which he once again walked in a mortal body in the core reality.

Just like that, he blinked, and he was standing at the frozen edge of the world, an endless sea stretched out before him and cold water washing over his feet. Not one single second had passed him by.

CHAPTER FORTY-EIGHT

Everything felt weird now, but Nym couldn't quite figure out exactly how. It obviously had something to do with ascending, but it was indescribable, and he found it annoyingly distracting. "It's like I'm breathing air that's not quite right," he told Rizin, "or, I don't know, like the sun is the wrong color, nothing is the temperature I think it should be, and the corners don't fit together quite right, even for things that don't have corners!"

"That will clear up some after you fully acclimate to your new form of existence and you'll become used to what doesn't go back to how it was before."

"Okay, but why is this happening?"

"Because your body died, Nym. That meat suit you were trapped in is gone. You're nothing but a projection of yourself, cast across multiple realities to walk around and influence this world."

Nym's eyes widened. "I didn't die!"

"Of course you did. No mortal can cross that threshold. It burns them out and reduces them to nothingness. Only the mind and the magic survive the ordeal. And when you reached the other side, you built a new body out of your magic, only it's not quite like the old one."

Nym thought back to the ordeal he'd undergone. He had lost his body at the beginning, but he'd thought he'd rebuilt it using the other parts of his being. Technically, that might count as dying, but the difference seemed largely academic. He was Nym before, and he was Nym now. Why did anything have to be different?

It *was* different though, undeniably so. He was looking at the same world but from a slightly different angle. All the familiar pieces were still there, but they were skewed enough that they didn't feel right. It was very disconcerting, like looking at a bad replica of something he was intimately familiar with and trying to catalog all the things that were wrong with it.

"It's like dipping your finger into a fishbowl," Rizin said suddenly. "Before you were a fish, but now you're this entity that exists outside the water. You can stick a hand in and poke around, but you're too big for this world. All you have here is this avatar, this physical manifestation of yourself that is only a fragment of the whole of your being."

"That's why you just look like a big fox here," Nym realized. "All of you is too much for the world?"

"I could look bigger if I wanted, but what's the point? It would just draw attention." Rizin shifted from fox to human form. "I can look like anything I want. Whatever is convenient is how I appear." He shifted again, this time into a copy of Nym, then into a snow wolf, then back to a fox. "Whatever I want. It's not an illusion, it's just . . . me, altered to my will."

Nym blinked at the copy of himself, then shook his head and laughed. "There's really no reason to even limit myself to being in one place, is there?"

"There are plenty of reasons," Rizin said. "The biggest one for you is that you're still hiding. Speaking of that, you're a real ascendant now, which means it's time to stop living off my charity. Are you ready to make the pact?"

"Yes, let's go over it and make it official."

The pair sat there in Rizin's den for an hour, going over the specifics of what he wanted Nym to make Research Lab Six produce. They talked about everything from fur color to litter size to digestive needs. There were a remarkable number of decisions to make when producing a completely new species, but Rizin had been thinking about this project for a while now.

In exchange for Nym's help, Rizin was going to teach him to use sixth-layer arcana in the core reality. It was a little tricky, since unlike other forms of arcana, it wasn't supposed to exist in mortal realities. That made it less about casting spells and more about enforcing a change in reality through sheer will, with the arcana being burned away to fuel the change.

"In this case, what we're going to do is tell reality that it doesn't know that you exist. You'll be something akin to a ghost, albeit one that can walk and talk. If you want to change something, like if you need a door to be open instead of closed, you don't do it. You just tell reality that the door was always open. Understand?"

"No."

Rizin rolled his eyes. "We'll work on it. Anyway, that's the pact. I'll show you the ropes of being an immortal living in the land of mortals and how to hide your presence from other immortals. In exchange, you'll return to the ascendant research facility and fabricate a new species with me as the template."

"What if I can't get in? Last time, I was Niramyn, just in a younger body. Now we're separate people."

"Then we'll figure out a new way to do it. I don't care how it gets done, just that it does. This seems like the easiest way to me, but if you can't do it, then we'll find a different way forward."

"Alright. I think we have a deal. You will teach me to control the arcana of the sixth layer and how to hide and disguise myself from other ascendants, and I will assist you in creating a new species of magical sapient foxes for you to watch over and guide."

Rizen spoke, his voice resonating with arcana. "This I do agree to abide by. This I do so swear to honor. This I am bound and held to."

"This I do agree to abide by. This I do so swear to honor. This I am bound and held to," Nym echoed, arcana flowing through him as well.

Rizin settled into a sitting position and smirked. "Let's get started."

"Maybe wait until everything stops feeling not quite right with the world first."

"Feh. You'll get over that in time. There's no reason to delay."

"Fine, fine." Nym held his hands up in surrender. "What do we do first?"

It was a good thing Nym's advancement to the sixth layer meant he was able to alter his physical manifestation's physiology to subsist off raw arcana instead of food and water now, and to eliminate the need for sleep. Rizin was a merciless teacher but, in Nym's opinion, not a very good one. He supposed that was an unfair comparison. Rizin's way of doing things was very different than an ascendant's, after all.

Now that he understood the laws of the outer realities better, Nym realized that the sanctuary he'd been studying hadn't just been something Niramyn had dreamed up. Those books were literally his own memories, and as Nym had been born of the Exarch and thought in very similar ways, he couldn't have asked for something more suited for teaching him.

Many of those books on the top shelf still didn't make sense to Nym, but now that he'd passed through the other side and could pick Rizin's brain, some pieces were starting to fall into place. He could still use all his magic, so he didn't feel like the time he'd spent locked away outside of time had been a complete waste, but now that he could reach beyond mortal magic, it felt . . . lacking. His old spells were overly complicated ways to achieve subpar results.

At the same time, a lot of things Rizin taught him weren't present in any of Niramyn's memory books. "Is this because of how you do magic?" Nym asked. "It's different than what ascendants do? Or do you just know things that even Exarchs don't?"

"Don't assume you know even a fraction of what your father does. I'm sure there are very few surprises left for him after existing for so long. Did you know that other ascendants come in and out of the timeline at their leisure? Sometimes they exist in reality prime for years at a time, but most of them only manifest an avatar when they have a reason to, often only for minutes or days as they accomplish whatever task brought them here.

"Niramyn is different. Not counting the year or so after you were born, the Exarch has existed for practically every second of history for as far back as anyone can go."

"Why?" Nym asked. "What's he doing that's so different than any other ascendant?"

"I don't know. I doubt anyone does."

Nym had some of Niramyn's memories, just a few minutes of the Exarch as a child. He couldn't have been an ascendant then, not if he was still learning how to use second- and third-layer arcana. If nothing else, that proved that he'd once been mortal, so there was a time when he didn't exist as Exarch Niramyn.

"Regardless," the fox continued, "I can only teach you the ways I know to alter reality without being detected. It's a delicate art. Now, let's start over."

The lessons continued, some easy and some so twisted that they broke Nym's brain a little bit. They weren't limited to the core reality either. If Nym was going to exist as one entity across multiple layers of reality, he had to learn how to hide himself across all of them at the same time. For the time being, he continued to shelter behind Rizin's magics, but as time went on, the fox started to hint that he'd be withdrawing that protection one layer at a time.

Each layer had to be approached with a different mindset to achieve the same results, which essentially meant Nym had to learn to cast a spell, such as they were, six different ways, and to do so at the same time in each layer of reality. Most spells didn't require that, but the mantle of hidden magic did. It was pointless to obscure his actions in one layer of reality if the goal was to hide from beings that could see in every layer.

One by one, Rizin stopped protecting Nym, until finally he was hiding himself in every layer except one: the sixth. Here he found the rules changed again. In the lower realms, as Rizin called them, what they needed to accomplish could be done through liberal application of the reality-warping arcana of the sixth layer. They didn't cast a spell. Reality had *always* been that way.

Sixth-layer arcana couldn't do that to itself, at least not without some work. It became a game of circular logic, a resonance set up to bounce against itself in such a way that caused it to break itself down so that it never existed in the first place. It was not an easy concept to even wrap his head around, let alone pull off. If Nym wasn't experiencing the reality of the sixth layer firsthand, he never would have been able to accomplish it.

But for all Rizin's faults, he was patient. He pushed Nym to keep improving but never gave up, no matter how long it took for Nym to get the next concept. Sometimes it was easy, but usually it wasn't. The scattered factoids he'd pulled out of the last series of books in Niramyn's memory sanctum were of limited use, but every now and then Rizin taught Nym something that made a piece of information click into place.

By the time they were done, the fox had completed his half of the pact. Nym reached out into reality prime with sixth-layer arcana, and through it he funneled his will. He demanded that he existed in the sky above the island they'd picked out for Rizin's new species instead of inside the fox's lair. Reality accommodated, and Nym floated in the air where he'd envisioned.

It was raining there, but protecting himself from it was as easy as deciding he didn't get wet. The rain slid off him like he was made out of oiled sailcloth. Most importantly, he was there alone. For the first time in over a year of mortal days, Nym stood on his own again.

CHAPTER FORTY-NINE

There were actual spells that used sixth-layer arcana, but Nym only knew one, the hidden-presence spell Rizin had taught him. Anything else was just using the arcana to fiddle with reality. Technically, that was what all arcana did, but there was a big difference between mortal magic and ascendant magic.

Humans used magic by making connections to other layers of reality and bringing back some of the essence of that realm. The farther away from the core reality the essence, arcana, was, the more it was able to influence core reality. The difference was simple: human magic used other layers of reality as catalysts to change their own reality. Ascendant magic affected all layers of reality at the same time.

There were some advantages to using human magic, even now. If all he wanted was to stay flying in the air, it was far simpler and less taxing to simply grab a bit of second-layer arcana and craft a spell that held him up than it would be to evoke Transcendent arcana to tell reality that it was wrong about how gravity affected him. Reality, as it turned out, didn't like being told it was wrong and was continually trying to reassert itself.

It was also far easier to keep himself hidden when using mortal magic. Hidden presence only had to mask him instead of the changes he made through multiple layers of reality that way. For now at least, that was a large part of his motivation. There were times when he needed to bend reality to his will, and there were times when a touch more finesse made everything easier.

Nym had a different sort of problem to deal with. Existing in multiple versions of reality at the same time wasn't new to him by now, but the sixth layer was different. Unlike the inner layers, it didn't mirror the world at all. More importantly, there was a whole ascendant society there. Nym had briefly witnessed it before Rizin's magic fell over him and hid him away.

Now that part of him was sitting, unmoving and isolated, frozen in not-time and waiting for him to acknowledge it while his primary focus returned to the core reality. Someday he'd be strong enough to explore that timeless realm, to see the grand palaces and fantastical landscape each ascendant had carved out of reality through sheer force of will. Today, he had an obligation to meet in the core reality.

He teleported himself to the sheet of ice above the ascendant research lab and waited for Rizin to appear. It only took a few minutes before the fox popped up next to him. "Good," Rizin said. "I had to manually scan the area until I noticed you'd arrived. You're still completely hidden."

"Great," Nym said. "How sure are you that this will work?"

"That you'll be able to freely access the lab? Not at all. That you'll be able to escape the containment field using the magic I taught you? Well, it's always worked for me."

"Using only sixth-layer arcana though?" Nym pressed.

"You worry too much. Fine, let me test it."

Rizin disappeared, and then ten seconds later reappeared. "Yes, using just sixth-layer arcana."

Nym thought he had a perfectly appropriate amount of caution, all things considered. He still hadn't quite forgiven Rizin for setting him up to visit the research lab the first time, but he suspected getting the raw end of that deal had at least a little bit to do with the fox keeping him safe after he'd made his way back to reality prime once the ascendants had started fighting one another.

"Alright, time to see if this works," Nym said.

The lab was just like he remembered it. Some of the research assistants were different, but he recognized at least half of them from his first trip in. Naera was not among them, but within moments of him arriving, he spotted her hustling down the hall in his direction.

"Exarch, welcome back," she said.

Nym didn't physically sigh in relief, but he wanted to. That had been the big risk, not knowing whether he would still have Exarch Niramyn's access. Apparently, the Exarch either hadn't realized Nym would come back or didn't care. Whatever the reason, he was just glad that fulfilling his end of the pact was off to a smooth start.

Considering how much more work his side had been the last time they'd made a pact, Nym felt it was only fair that he got the easier job this time around. Of course, he'd barely gotten started, so it was probably a bad idea to pat himself on the back already.

"Hello, Naera. How have things been going since my last visit?"

"The last of the scarabs from the experiment you terminated died off one hundred fifty-six cycles ago," she reported. "All other experiments are proceeding along expected and desired routes."

"Good, good. Listen, I want to start a new experiment."

"Certainly, Exarch. If you'll come with me, we can get everything set up for that."

Nym followed the assistant golem out of the foyer and down the halls. While they walked, he explained what he was looking to create. She listened intently, and then said, "That should be well within the established purpose of this facility. I believe we could have a viable first generation within a thousand cycles, though we would need to discuss more details first."

That was a relief. All he had to do now was give her the specifications and let them get to work. Just as he was about to speak, she cut him off. "Of course, the lab's arcana batteries will need to be recharged before we can begin working."

"Oh? I thought there was quite a bit left?" Nym asked.

"For maintaining current experiments, yes. For a project of this size, we have insufficient arcana."

"Of course we do," Nym muttered. "Would have been too easy otherwise."

Maybe he could get Rizin to charge the batteries. He could do the seventh- and eighth-layer ones, at least. "Would you need the ninth-layer batteries recharged as well?"

"No, those still have ample power left and, other than producing some sample chambers, would not be needed for this experiment."

"Okay, that's workable then. Hmm . . . What are the protocols for bringing a guest?"

"Unauthorized ascendants are not allowed in the facility," Naera said immediately.

"Right, figured that was going to be the case."

Nym wasn't actually sure it would be a problem. Rizin was going to have to get in to charge the batteries one way or another, and while it certainly would have been easier for him if he could have just escorted the fox through the lab to do the work, he wouldn't be surprised if Rizin refused to even go in through the front door, just on the basis that he didn't want to be seen.

"This place must have some solid automated defenses if they're enough to keep out any ascendant who's not allowed in here," Nym said.

"Very much so, Exarch!"

"What can you tell me about them?"

Naera happily rattled off a bunch of information that Nym understood none of. That was a bit annoying, as he'd thought his days of not having a clue were behind him, but it seemed there was always more to learn, and he was basically starting over at the bottom rung on the immortal side of existence now anyway.

He did his best to remember everything Naera told him, which, thanks to a few enhancements he'd made to his brain, was not that hard to do. "Fascinating," Nym said when she finished explaining how the reality-inversion wards would discharge a resonance breaker into anyone who tried to access the lab via the specimen-teleportation platform if they didn't have a biological-matrix key stored in the data archive.

Hopefully Rizin would know what that meant and how to get past it.

"Right, so I don't have the time to charge the batteries right now, but let's get everything set up so that when I can get them charged, all we need to do is start the experiment," Nym told the golem.

"Of course. I'll just open up a new experiment log here, and we can outline the parameters."

"I've got good news and bad news," Nym said when he appeared in Rizin's den.

"I would prefer you didn't have bad news," the fox said with a yawn.

"Okay, I've got good news and . . . exciting news."

Rizin rolled his eyes and hopped down off his cushion. "Fine, let's hear it."

"So first, you were right, I do still have access. The lab still treats me like I'm Niramyn. I was able to get everything set up for your project, and they're estimating three years before a first generation is produced."

"That long? Hmm. Acceptable, I suppose. And the . . . exciting news?"

"Well, I can't actually start the project. It's set up, but there's a problem. The lab's arcana batteries aren't full enough to run the project, and I can't recharge them myself."

"Ah, I see. You can't, but let me guess: I can?"

"Got it in one," Nym said. "I checked to see if I could bring a guest in, just in case. If it was as easy as just bringing you with me to the batteries, you charging them, and we're all set, then why not?"

"That doesn't sound all that exciting, so I'm guessing the answer was no."

"Correct again. How do you feel about sneaking in?"

Rizin just stared at him.

"Even if I told you that I could explain all the defenses?"

More silence filled the den.

"Look, I can't do it myself. Either you do it, or you're going to be waiting for however long it takes for me to reach the eighth layer."

The fox let out a heavy sigh. "I suppose I should at least hear about the defenses before I say no."

By the time Nym had finished reciting Naera's speech, Rizin had perked up considerably. He had that gleam in his eyes, that one that spoke of mischief. Something in Nym's outline of the defenses had sparked an idea, hopefully one that would actually work.

"I realize that the difficulty of this job was lowered significantly thanks to the fact that the golems are still treating you like you own the place, but really, well done, young ascendant. I think this could actually work. Now, tell me where the batteries are."

Nym thought about that for a second and shook his head. "I do not know. Never thought to ask."

"Just when I was beginning to have hope for you," the fox said sourly.

Then Nym grinned and added, "Nah, I'm just kidding. I know where they are. Here, let me show you a map of the facility I copied from the data archive when I was looking stuff up."

An illusion over ten feet tall and just as wide filled one side of the den, and together the two pored over it. Rizin explained his point of entry and what he needed Nym to do on the inside to distract the golems so that he could get in unseen. They made plans on where to meet up if Rizin couldn't get to the batteries and how Nym could tell that the mission had been completed.

"You know, the funny thing about all of this is that I'm sneaking in to do them a favor," Rizin said.

"Are you? You're only filling the arcana batteries so you can use the lab's equipment for your own purposes. Unless you were going to sneak back in and top them off when you were done?"

"No, probably not."

They both stared at the illusion in silence for a bit, then Nym said, "You think it'll work?"

"Yes. There's a couple sticky spots, but we've got alternative solutions if things don't play out the way we'd like."

"Tomorrow then?"

"Tomorrow," the fox agreed.

CHAPTER FIFTY

The assistant golem regarded Nym steadily. It wasn't one he'd ever spoken with before, but Naera was busy setting everything up to his specifications from the other day. At first, he thought that would be a good thing, since this golem wouldn't know he'd asked all those questions about how the lab's defensive array of spells worked.

As it turned out, the golem did know. All of them knew because they all shared information through some sort of central hub in the data archive. Worse, unlike his personal assistant, this one was considerably more suspicious of him. The golems shared knowledge but had individual personalities. Naera was somewhat naive and trusting, which was an odd character trait for the personal assistant to someone like Exarch Niramyn, but it had worked in Nym's favor the last few times he'd entered the lab.

Whomever this golem worked for, they wanted someone who would question absolutely everything anyone did. Nym spent an idle moment wondering if that included the ascendant who'd made the golem and, if so, how that hadn't driven them insane. He'd only spent three minutes with the assistant and was already considering how best to turn him into a pile of half-melted slag.

"Look, I don't see what's so hard about this. I want to review the lab's specimen-transportation platform and then check on the arcana batteries. Is there some part of this you don't understand?"

"Why do you want to do this?" the golem asked.

"Does it matter? Do I answer to you?"

"No, sir, but the lab protocols . . ."

"I don't care about your protocols. You don't make the decisions around here. I do. If it makes you feel better, you can add a permit to the systems under my name that says I can do what I want."

"Yes . . . Exarch. If you'll follow me."

The golem made no attempt to hide his displeasure at being overruled or at the fact that protocol wasn't being followed. Nym gave silent thanks once again that Niramyn hadn't bothered to come back to the lab and update anything. There was no way he would have been able to bluff his way through if his former self had made even the slightest effort to prevent it.

They came to a room tucked far, far into the back of the lab. It had a triple-wide hallway leading up to double doors made of some sort of metal and completely covered with rune sequences. Nym was surprised to find that he understood most of them, enough so that he knew they were designed both to contain whatever was inside and to prevent the teleportation locks on the rest of the lab from functioning inside the room.

Once he got inside, he found a similar set of runes on the far wall, and it didn't take much examination for him to revise his opinion of their function. The ones on the door were actually to set a boundary on how far the teleportation lock was suppressed. The wall runes did the actual suppression.

The room was otherwise empty except for a thirty-foot-wide circle inscribed in the center of the floor. It was perfectly round, and its perimeter was composed of a long-form rune sequence with eight gaps spaced equally along its length. Nym had never seen one like it, but he'd read enough to know its purpose. The gaps weren't actually empty, but instead linked to other layers of reality. If he were to visit the fifth-layer version of Research Lab Six, he'd find at least one of those gaps filled in, more likely parts of every gap.

It created a mazelike effect that intruders would have to navigate, jumping between layers to work their way through one step at a time. Of course, there would be a single spot somewhere in there that could be opened when someone inside the lab with the appropriate key needed to use the room. When not in use, that opening would be sealed back closed, and the labyrinth defense would leave would-be intruders trapped in a continuous loop of layer hopping as they tried to navigate a maze with no exit.

They would, at least, if they didn't have the backdoor key Nym had given to Rizin. He made a bit of a show of examining the rune sequences, which were legitimately interesting, so it wasn't that much of an act. "Ah, this part right here," he said, pointing to a section that functioned to automatically redirect any summoning done with the circle to the center. "What did we use to calibrate this?"

The assistant golem peered over at the section Nym was pointing to. "I believe that was completed by the chief of research using a temporal arc array based on the locked position of the Fourth Cataclysm in relation to the End Time's floating variable."

"Ah, that makes sense."

It didn't, not really. The only part he understood was that the point where the timeline terminated was referred to as the End Time, and its exact temporal position was constantly in flux as fresh alterations were introduced and timelines splintered, were reconciled, and merged back together. He was just hoping his question wasn't so stupid that the assistant would be even more on his guard.

[Look less baffled,] Rizin said in his head. *[Also, I'm here now. The defenses are formidable but not enough to stop me.]*

[I'd hope not. I gave you the key to the door.]

[It wasn't really as easy as you seem to think.]

"Exarch? Will there be anything else here?"

"No, thank you. I just need to charge the arcana batteries for my new experiment, and I'll be done."

They left together, Nym following along behind the golem and Rizin presumably trailing both of them invisibly. He didn't look around to try to spot the fox, didn't even use any magic to do it. Rizin was both too good for any spell Nym had at his disposal to work, and it would just draw unnecessary attention to the fact that there was something worth looking for.

When they reached the arcana-storage room, Nym held the door open and looked around. It was an interesting setup, just a long hallway with dozens and dozens of thick pillars lining the walls. They were some sort of glass framed in what looked like brass with intricate lines connected to the tops and bottoms in some bizarre pattern he'd never seen before.

Each pillar was connected to the one before and after it, and the two closest to the door had their own connection that flowed across the wall above the door. At the far end of the hall was another door, presumably leading to even more batteries. Then again, that wouldn't be a very convenient setup.

"Is this all the batteries?" he asked.

"No, just the one hundred seventh-layer block. The eighth layer is in the next room over. The ninth- and twelfth-layer batteries are stored in a separate location. Would you like to head there now?"

"Not yet," Nym said. "These need to be charged up first. Thank you for your help. That will be all."

"I . . . You would like me to leave now?" the golem asked.

"Yes. I don't need an audience for this. It's just necessary, if boring, work. You may return to whatever you were working on."

"I see. Then, if you need further assistance, please don't hesitate to ask any of the assistants."

"Thanks, I will if I need help."

Then Nym turned away from the assistant, hoping the golem would take the hint and just leave already. Only once the door closed behind him did he let out the breath he'd been holding and look around for Rizin. *[You made it in alright?]*

[Of course I did. Don't insult me.]

[Sorry. So what do you think? Can we get these topped off quickly?]

[Define quickly. This might take a few days just for this room, depending how drained they are.]

Nym glanced around again at the pillars. *[Ah. That's . . . bad? I thought it'd be quicker.]*

[Hopefully it won't be that long. We'll see. The ones at the front at least are mostly full. Just stay by the door and keep anyone from coming in.]

Nym settled in place and waited. There wasn't anything he could do to speed things up but keep Rizin from being interrupted. If everything went well, it would be a long and boring process. Hopefully that would be the case because, if things went sideways, he wasn't sure how he was going to get back out of the lab.

But he was sure it would all be fine.

Things were not fine.

That stupid assistant golem had come back three times already, Rizin was barely halfway done, and now Naera was here and refusing to leave. Nym stood in the doorway, blocking her from walking into the battery chamber, but it looked like she was about ready to physically shove him out of the way.

"Naera, please, just go back to work. I'm fine. I promise. I don't need you to do anything for me but finish setting up the new experiment so it can start as soon as the batteries are recharged."

"Exarch, I couldn't leave you unattended while you're here. I've delegated the work to a few other golems."

"I really don't need the company right now," Nym said. "I've got a lot on my mind, and I don't want the distractions while I work."

"It won't be a problem, Exarch, really. I will wait by the door. You won't even know I'm there unless you need me for something."

Nym pinched the bridge of his nose in one hand, took a deep breath, and said, "Thank you. That is not necessary. Please return to your work preparing the experiment. I want it to start as soon as possible. That will be all, Naera."

Then he closed the door in her face, groaned, and took a few steps into the room. "She didn't leave," he muttered. He hadn't checked, but he knew he was right.

[She did not, no.]

[How many hours do you need to finish this room?]

[Six or seven.]

There was no way he was keeping the golems out of the battery room for that long. [I only see two options. You keep charging the batteries without me and we hope nobody notices, or we don't charge them all the way. If we have to keep stopping to get rid of nosy assistants every twenty minutes, we'll never get this done.]

[Barricade the door,] the fox suggested.

Nym had considered that, but he was worried using mortal magic might tip them off. When he'd first visited under his truthful identity, that hadn't been an issue. Now he was pretending to be Niramyn, and Niramyn had the ability to work on arcana batteries of the seventh and eighth layers. Using mortal magic would be suspicious, and a few of the assistants were already looking at him too closely.

[I have some concerns about getting into an actual spell duel with these guys. I know they're only golems, but they're golems made by ascendants, and I'm not really that confident that I can win. They can use arcana from these batteries, right? So that means they're equivalent to at least a ninth-circle ascendant?]

Rizin snorted out a laugh. [Caution is fine, but temper it with wisdom. The golems *here do not cast any spells. They are not able to. They merely administer to the devices and artifacts entrusted to them.]*

[But how would they do that if they can't use arcana to activate the devices?] Nym asked. *[Are you saying that all the equipment here could be used by literally anybody with a finger to push a button?]*

[Provided they knew which buttons to push, yes. Everything would function until the batteries ran dry.]

Nym would have said that was impossible. He'd never heard of any magic item that could be activated by someone without at least the ability to handle arcana, even if they didn't actively supply it themselves. Even with all the things he'd studied after Niramyn had returned, nothing had hinted at that being a possibility.

He still had a lot to learn about being an ascendant.

"So just a barrier across the door then. I can do that."

CHAPTER FIFTY-ONE

There were no less than a dozen assistant golems waiting for Nym when he finally opened the door. "Exarch! You're alright," Naera said, stepping forward from the crowd.

"Of course I'm alright. Why wouldn't I be? Didn't I ask you to go finish preparing the fox experiment?"

"Yes, Exarch. Everything is all set up and ready, as soon as the batteries are fully charged."

Nym made a show of looking around. "And you needed twelve other golems with you to tell me that?"

"Ah, no, about that. Baracia wanted to be notified the instant you were finished. Every time she asked and you weren't done, she sent another golem to watch the door."

That explained why nine of them were already reorganizing themselves into a line and heading down the hall, but he didn't know who Baracia was. He gave it even odds that it was another ascendant or the golem in charge of organizing all the other ones. There was only one way to find out though.

"Who is Baracia, again?"

"She heads up the research for all plant-based experiments," Naera said.

That didn't answer his question, though he was leaning more toward the idea that she was an ascendant. If so, the fact that she was interested in him was extremely bad news. He assumed every ascendant who had access to the facility was in some way loyal to Exarch Niramyn, but that had also been prior to the whole . . . everything . . . that had resulted in the creation of Nym.

[Incoming.]

The world pulsed and shivered around him as something pushed through reality, shoving it aside and taking its place. A woman stood next to him, had always been standing next to him now that she'd dictated that reality. She was tall, well over six feet, with pale skin and glowing midnight blue hair that fell halfway down her back. Her eyes, soft, gleaming silver, trained over to Nym, and she let out a soft little, "Ah. I had wondered."

"Baracia?" Nym asked, trying to sound more confident than he felt. She was at least into the eighth layer, based on the crushing presence of the arcana he felt around her. Unless Rizin jumped in to save him, Nym was completely at the woman's mercy. He swore right then and there that if he ever found out that one of the golems reached out to summon her, he would dismantle them.

"That is correct," she said. "You do not have the capability to recharge these arcana batteries. Whatever scheme you're up to, I won't let it disrupt the lab."

"That was not my goal."

"A new ascendant, hmm, and a hidden one at that. Someone has been playing games they should not be playing. Tell me, what *is* your goal?"

"At this moment? Get as many of these batteries charged as possible. I'm open to suggestions after that."

"Fascinating" was all she said.

After a long moment's awkward silence, he asked, "Is there something I can help you with?"

"Perhaps, but not right now. I just came to see who was mucking around with my lab."

"I wouldn't call it that," Nym said.

"No? You've canceled an ongoing experiment on a whim and are setting up another one. Neither jeopardizes any of my experiments, so I'm not inclined to complain. You are lucky that Joarsin is not here. He would not be happy that you removed that mortal talisman from the vault, even if the lab can manufacture another in an instant."

"Lucky me," Nym said. "If you don't need anything then, I have some more work to do."

"You do not," Baracia said firmly. "But when your associate is finished, please make sure he leaves the lab without damaging anything."

"I— Yes, of course. If there's nothing else?"

Her eyes lingered on him for an uncomfortably long time before she said, "For now. I will call on you again soon."

"I'll be expecting you then," Nym said. If he was lucky, the hidden-presence spell would protect him from that particular future. As far as he could tell, it was still working. Baracia had only found him because of those nosy golems, or perhaps some sort of internal alarm he'd missed. If that was the case, either Naera had lied to him, or she hadn't known about it herself.

"Mmm. I doubt it. Spend your time in this reality wisely. You don't yet realize how limited it is and how foolishly you are squandering it."

Then reality flexed again, and the strange woman was gone. Nym wanted to heave a huge sigh of relief, but Naera and three other golems were still loitering in the hall with him. He turned a baleful glare on them and asked, "Did you need something else?"

"No, Exarch," Naera answered for them. "The four of us are the team working on your new experiment. Everything is ready to go. We are just waiting on the arcana to be placed in the batteries and your word to start."

"Can you tell that the batteries are ready to go from where you have the experiment set up?" Nym asked.

"Yes, of course."

"Then I would like you to go wait there. As soon as the batteries are full enough, start the experiment."

The four golems all bowed in unison and walked off. Nym glowered at their backs, then scrubbed a hand across his face. He'd thought things were going well until he'd opened that door. Now he had an extremely creepy ascendant interested in him, one who was very, very aware of what he'd been up to in the lab. Thankfully, she didn't seem to care.

[Well, this has been a disaster,] he said to Rizin.

[It could have been much worse. I've already started on the next set of batteries. Fortunately, there are only a fraction of the first room's, and they are in relatively better shape. This should not take more than six to eight hours.]

Nym thought he heard a touch of weariness in the fox's mental voice, which wasn't surprising, considering how much magical heavy lifting he'd been doing. He let himself into the second battery room, cast a new barrier spell just in case the golems got annoying about what he was doing in there again, and settled down to wait.

[Do you know anything about that ascendant?] he asked.

[I'm not familiar with ascendant culture other than that they have two large hubs. One is in the sixth layer and, as I understand it, is considered something of a slum. Ascendants who are unable to take the next step and stall out at your current level forever exist in this hub. Those who manage to reach at least the eighth layer have another hub there. Of course, those who ascend even higher have their own private sanctuaries, which they place wherever they please.]

[All of that,] Nym mused. There was so much he didn't know about them still. *[And yet you're still sitting here on reality prime.]*

[One part of me is, yes. It is important to my goals.]

That was fair. Rizin obviously wanted company. Maybe there weren't too many mystic foxes in the universe, and he was hoping some of this new race would rise to the occasion, that they would become the fox equivalent of an ascendant. That was as good a reason as any to spend a lot of time in the mortal world.

[I wonder what she wants? She was annoyingly vague.]

[Whatever it is, it will no doubt be good for her and unlikely good for anyone else. Be careful about letting her use you.]

[I don't plan on letting her find me again. The only reason she ran into me was because of where we are. Once this program is running, we shouldn't have to set foot in here again.]

[A shame,] Rizin mused. *[There are many fascinating things here. Also, you wished to help the snow wolves, did you not?]*

[I did, but I suppose I could do that now. The primary factor holding me back was

the need for secrecy. I've already been discovered, so I might as well take care of that before we leave. In fact, I think I'll go do that right now.]

Nym sent a scrying spell out through the lab to locate Naera, then followed it to her location. Though he couldn't teleport, there was nothing stopping him from skimming across the floor at high speeds. "Naera, I forgot to tell you. Once you're done with all of this, please implement the procedure we discussed for fixing the snow wolves as well."

She glanced up from some sort of illusory display she was studying and looked toward the doorway Nym was standing in. "Of course, Exarch. We should have more than enough arcana left over to do that as well. We would need an additional arcana infusion in another three thousand cycles when reserves begin to dip dangerously low in this case."

"That's fine."

Baracia or some other ascendant could do the next one. Nym didn't have a lot of plans for returning to the lab once they left. Idly, he wondered what would happen to the containment field and all the weird monsters living inside it if the batteries died completely. Maybe they'd scatter into the frozen wastelands of the north and die of exposure or starvation. He doubted many of them would adapt well to a world that was both considerably warmer than their current environment and blindingly bright.

"Thank you, Naera."

Nym zipped back across Research Lab Six to the battery chamber and crossed his barrier. It was designed to let him through and no one else, though it wouldn't stand up to someone with Rizin's power. Even a mortal archmage could probably cross it if they were clever or patient enough to figure out the key. It definitely stopped nosy golems though, and that was the important part.

[All set on the snow-wolf project. The golems want another recharge in a decade or so, but I'm sure some other ascendant will come along and take care of the next top-up.]

[One can only hope. My own project should be long since completed by then, and it shall no longer be my problem.]

They didn't talk much after that. Nym spent his time getting a feel for the arcana that filled the room. It was something heavy, something that pressed down on the room despite being contained in the batteries, or perhaps for that brief moment of Rizin channeling the arcana into the batteries. It was an uncomfortable sensation, like being deep underwater.

The pressure didn't ease up, but in time he grew more used to it. It wasn't a physical sensation, and he wondered what effect it would have on his magic if he tried to use something weaker than fifth-layer arcana. It was possible the effect would warp the delicate construct of the spell itself if he cast it in the room.

[There! It's done.]

Nym blinked and stood up. Within seconds, the crushing feeling had all but disappeared. Of Rizin himself, there was no sign. But they both knew the plan.

He would slip back out through the specimen-teleportation platform, Nym would nudge the piece he'd loosened back into place, and then he'd leave through the foyer.

He skimmed down the halls again, desiring nothing so much as leaving quickly before some assistant golem found him and started trying to keep him around. Or worse, Baracia changed her mind and found him again before he could get out. He was a lot more confident in his ability to hide once his actual physical location wasn't known.

Part of him wondered if he was overconfident. She'd known there was something else with him, though that could have been a logical deduction on her part. Nym couldn't refill the batteries, so something else must have been doing it. He made a mental note to ask Rizin if he'd been spotted by the ascendant once they were both clear of the lab.

[I'm through,] the fox said in his mind once he reached the specimen-teleportation room. Nym relocked the part of the rune sequence he'd left open for the fox to slip through, then made his own exit. Nobody tried to stop him, including Baracia. Just like that, he'd done his part for the pact.

CHAPTER FIFTY-TWO

Nym stood there, awkwardly waiting for Rizin to say something. The fox didn't oblige him, having chosen instead to lay on his oversize cushion and pretend to be napping. "I guess . . . we're done then?" Nym asked. "Go our separate ways?"

"Indeed," Rizin said, his eyes still closed. "You know how to get ahold of me if you need something."

"What if you need something?" Nym asked. "The hidden-presence spell will keep you from finding me."

"It does not block messages if you know the recipient," Rizin explained. "How else would you be able to contact me?"

"Ah, that's true. So we could still communicate if we needed to."

"We could, and we may need to in a few years if the lab doesn't meet our expectations. For now, our business is concluded. Do not take offense, but you have lived with me for long enough. It's time for you to leave the nest and fly free."

Nym felt like he should probably be offended, but the truth of it was that he was just as sick of spending all his waking time with the fox. He didn't have any definite plans for where he was going or what he was going to do next, but he thought he might carve out his own little sanctuary somewhere. Then he would have a place in the core reality where he could let his defenses down, at least a little bit.

"Well, see you around then."

Nym left the den under his own power using sixth-layer arcana to tell reality that he was somewhere else. It bypassed any and all wards, at least wards made of fifth-layer or below arcana, but he knew that if Rizin had truly wanted to contest his version of reality, he'd have lost. Nym considered it a partial victory, but a victory nonetheless.

With physical distance irrelevant to him and environmental factors basically a nonissue, Nym decided his own sanctuary would be modeled off something similar to the one Exarch Niramyn had guided him to. He needed a place so bland and devoid of identifying features that even someone who'd been there wouldn't ever be able to find it again.

There were a few options to explore. He could, and probably would, carve out extradimensional space to form the sanctum, enough so that the only part of it that actually existed was the doorway. It would take a lot of extra work to stabilize the space and make it habitable, but he had the time and knowledge. At this point, his resources were infinite. He could literally channel sixth-layer arcana and will gold crests into existence if for some reason he needed money, but that would only happen if he wanted to give some to someone else.

Nym supposed he probably should refill Ciana's purse, if nothing else. He had plucked her from her home, after all. Though with Niramyn's return made public in the world of ascendants, he didn't think there would be anyone else coming to look for her. She could probably return to her home if she wanted. Nym would have to take some precautions, but he thought he might be able to reach out to her if he was careful.

It would no doubt be an interesting conversation, but that was a project for another day. He had a sanctuary to build first, and he hadn't even picked out the location for the gate that would lead to it. His first instinct was to copy Niramyn's use of the desert, but there were other options as well. Innumerable mountain caves could serve as his entryway, or even a gate deep under the ocean. He supposed it would even be possible to anchor it in the sky and render it invisible.

The most important thing, in his mind, was that he didn't want to have to worry about anything stumbling across the gate. Natural defenses would help with that, but he could also scribe rune sequences across its surface to repel the curious. Really, unless he was trying to defend against other beings who'd reached the sixth layer, he could put the gate wherever he wanted.

In a fit of sentimentality, he briefly considered placing it at the bottom of Bloodfin Cove. Nothing but the sharks was likely to ever find it there, but he immediately changed his mind. He had too much history, and it would be stupid to be discovered just because someone stumbled across it while they were searching through his timeline. No, it was far better to place the gate somewhere that he had no connection to.

Nym teleported himself to the southern sea, only a few hundred miles away from Shu-Ain, and scried until he found a small, windswept island that jutted up from the water perhaps a hundred feet. There were no trees, just bare rocks haphazardly piled up. Nym selected a pile of particularly flat boulders resting against one another in something of a chair-shaped heap. It was well over thirty feet tall, and he dubbed it the Giant's Throne.

That was sufficiently memorable to allow for easy teleportation, but the whole island was far, far away from civilization of any kind, and there was no reason to ever come to this island at the moment. It would do for his first sanctuary, even if it wasn't quite as bland as he'd been looking for.

He was reminded briefly of his days working with the Earth Shapers to dig and build, but other than the fact that he'd have a place to live when he finished, there really wasn't anything in common between the earth magics he'd employed long ago and what he was using today.

Nym wove pinnacle spells modeled after Archmage Veran's own sanctum, then infused the whole creation with a heavy dose of sixth-layer arcana to make it extra-real and so heavy that reality couldn't support it. Gently, he guided its shape as it collapsed through reality, and he caught the pieces to be rewoven together into his sanctum. Other parts of him echoed the process across each of the layers, expanding on his new pocket dimension and stabilizing it.

Once he was done, there appeared to be a large stone chamber carved from the interior of the rock, which was of course impossible. The rock was at best ten feet thick and perhaps thirty feet wide, and the chamber stretched back hundreds of feet and was five times wider than the stone it was anchored to. All that was left was to stabilize his creation, to anchor it across multiple layers of existence so that it wouldn't close up when reality tried to exert itself back to its original shape.

With the space itself secured, Nym turned his efforts to defense. Over the next hour, he traced a few thousand runes around the stone, even going so far as to layer sequences on top of one another in order to keep them tight around the gate. That was an art in and of itself, one he was happy to finally have a practical use for.

When he was done, the Giant's Throne looked exactly as it had before he'd arrived. Anyone unable to see arcana would never be able to tell there was anything at all there. For Nym, it was still a blazing portal, but once he passed through and the gate became passive again, it would be far less noticeable.

Nym spent the rest of the evening inside his new sanctum, humming to himself while he conjured up walls to partition the space and furniture to fill the new rooms. He modelled it off Archmage Veran's sanctum, though without the alchemy lab. That had never been Nym's passion, even if he'd spent months and months learning the fundamentals of it. It all sounded so terribly tedious to him, an art that required an immense amount of patience and whose primary value was that it imparted power to others.

Nym could replicate just about anything a potion or elixir could do with his own magic, and he had no need of the money alchemy could bring in. So he left out the lab and replaced it with a kitchen. Unlike alchemy, he was extremely interested in tasty food, and since his recent education had spent precisely zero pages on the discipline, he thought it would be a good distraction when he needed to relax.

Of course, he didn't need to actually eat the food anymore. Like every other ascendant, he could survive on nothing but pure arcana, but eating was fun. Food tasted good, at least when it was cooked by someone else, but that was something he could learn too. Maybe someday he'd even be able to share a meal again, if any of his friends were still alive by the time he sorted out the whole ascendant mess.

He could exist outside of time, so now that he thought of it, there was no reason that shouldn't be possible. He just needed to not waste all the time he had left here in the core reality before they died. It was the only place where the hours and days wasted mattered, just like Baracia had told him.

Suddenly, he felt foolish for spending so much time building a sanctum he didn't need. That was only slightly mitigated by the fact that one day he might need a bolt-hole, so he could reframe it from frivolous waste to wise precaution. That made him feel a bit better about it, but his adventures in interior decorating were unnecessary.

With a heavy sigh, Nym filled the rest of the rooms with utilitarian beds, desks, chairs, tables, armoires, and shelves. They weren't pretty, but they were solid and sturdy. That was enough. Maybe he'd spend some of his unlimited time outside the core reality refining his designs, then come back and replace it all one day.

Nym was starting to see why the ascendants preferred plain white or black voids for their backdrops. It was kind of sad though to have the ability to conjure up literally anything and to be so concerned about every wasted second that they couldn't be bothered to make even the simplest setting.

Now that his sanctuary was fully functional, if not as aesthetically pleasing as he'd hoped, Nym was ready to move on to his next task. He wanted to check on his friends, resupply Ciana with some gold if she needed it, and otherwise confirm that everything was still proceeding smoothly. He'd even designed the sanctum's wards with that thought in mind and created a scrying room where he could see out into the world by opening a sort of peephole.

There were a lot of possible designs, though for some reason everyone seemed to use reflective surfaces. Mirrors and pools were common recommendations, or crystal balls if the user didn't mind being that close to them. Nym went in a different direction. Rather than use a medium that created a physical image, he'd inscribed a simple circle into the stone. When he stood in it, it allowed him to scry out and receive the divination directly into his mind.

He supposed for a mortal mage, that might have been overwhelming. For him, each scry kept a single one of his parallel processes mildly busy. He found his friends, one after another, and confirmed all were healthy and alive. The Earth Shapers were prospering, and Ciana seemed to have settled into her new life. Analia was by far the worst off of them all, and Nym cursed his past self for not being able to see what was so blindingly obvious now.

She'd been geased, strongly and against her will. It was not hard to come up with a guess as to who'd done it. Breaking it wouldn't be difficult, but it would be hard on her and should be performed with some amount of delicacy. He moved his visit to her up on his timetable. Ciana would last without a bag of gold for another few days. Analia was already close to breaking from the strain.

Naturally, as soon as he broke the scry, he found a sealed letter floating in the air directly in front of him. His new sanctuary hadn't lasted even an hour before someone had penetrated its defenses.

CHAPTER FIFTY-THREE

That was the problem with peepholes. It was impossible to look out without making himself vulnerable to others looking in. Whoever had sent him the letter was likely an ascendant, which meant it was probably set to appear at the first opportunity. If he'd waited a week to scry, it would have appeared then instead.

Other than the spell holding it aloft, there was nothing magical about it. With some trepidation, Nym snatched it out of the air and started reading.

To our newest ascendant,

First, allow me to apologize for intruding. Rest assured that I have no information about where or when you are or what defenses you've employed to protect yourself. The spell merely finds the earliest point in your personal timeline where the letter would be able to reach you and delivers it.

Hopefully, that assuages any concerns you might have about this show-ing up unannounced in your life. If we hadn't met in person at Research Lab Six, I would not even have been able to send this letter. For a new ascendant, your skills at obfuscation are remarkable. I am curious where you picked them up.

It is obvious from your appearance, if nothing else, that you have ties to Exarch Niramyn, perhaps some descendent of his that he took a special interest in. Fear not, I shall not pry. It is also obvious that you are try-ing to remain apart from the recent struggles plaguing our society, which I can wholeheartedly support. The squabbles between Exarchs Niramyn and Myzalik have cost us many irreplaceable treasures, and it is the will of the Ascendant Council that they be ended as soon as possible.

To that end, I would like to invite you to review some public records of Council business that you may not have had access to, given your penchant for remaining apart from our society. I shall detail a location for you to retrieve them if you have an interest. I highly recommend you do so, as it will help update you on the politics of it all so that you can find a place for yourself.

Further, several of my colleagues and I would like to meet with you as a new ascendant and do what we can to help steer you away from being embroiled in this conflict. While I recognize that you may be justifiably skittish, given your apparent connection to one of the factions, I can assure you that I am requesting this meeting as a representative of the Council itself, what you might consider a third neutral faction that desires nothing more than the end to wholesale conflict between the two Exarchs.

Please, feel free to take any and all precautions you deem appropriate when reviewing the provided records and deciding if you would like to discuss these issues further.

Ascendant Council Senior Research Lead,
Baracia

Listed below that was a long code of reference words and symbols favored by mortal cartographers that gave Nym a broad idea of where to find the promised records. If they were tagged with any kind of arcana signal, it would be easy enough to pick them up, but he decided to hold off on that.

Before he did anything else, he spent some time layering even more defenses across his scrying room, to the point where it felt like a ridiculous amount of over-kill and it actually became a hassle to even scry out. He wasn't sure if it would be enough, but it was absolutely everything he could stack up to fortify that weak point in his sanctum.

The fact that he needed to suppress four active defenses and use six different keyed spells to so much as look out his front door was more than a little annoying, but he wanted *nothing* getting in that way again. Despite the reassurances the letter offered, he was considering relocating the entire sanctum as an additional defense, or at least setting up a second one and abandoning his current home. It could collapse on its own from lack of maintenance.

As far as good news went, at least the part of him that existed in the sixth layer was still whole and undetected. He'd stayed far, far away from anything that might interest an ascendant, had in fact done very little exploration at all. He supposed he'd been given a good opportunity to leave the core reality behind and explore beyond the mortal layers, but only if he trusted Baracia.

On the one hand, she hadn't done anything to hinder him once she'd determined that his own projects weren't going to disrupt or endanger hers. On the other, just because she hadn't done anything there didn't guarantee she was extending a sincere offer of friendship and collaboration to him. He wasn't particularly interested in getting dragged into politics, and her letter sounded like exactly that.

There was the one part though, where she mentioned ending the conflict. That part was of immense interest to Nym, since Niramyn and Myzalik's spat was the reason he had to live under a constant hidden-presence spell, that he wasn't free to see his mortal friends and might not be before they died of old age, and why he'd spent hours fortifying a sanctuary that he was not at all confident would protect him from even the weakest ascendant should anyone find its physical location.

Even without that location, Baracia could have just as easily sent some sort of hostile magic through instead of a simple piece of paper. The fact that she hadn't only proved that she thought he was more valuable as a resource to exploit than an enemy to be dispatched. He shook that thought away. It was still hard for him to remember that he wasn't vulnerable the way a human mage was anymore. Destroying his physical body would be a nuisance but not the end of him. He could always rebuild it, given enough time and the right magic.

Physical destruction wasn't the game now, which meant that assuming goodwill just because she hadn't tried to attack him was not a good idea. At the same time, assuming every single person he met was going to try to use him or kill him was a pretty awful way to live. He was going to have to take risks eventually, unless he wanted to spend a literal eternity as a hermit who actively avoided contact with anyone and everyone.

Since Nym did not want that to be his future, he needed to decide how and when he was going to participate in ascendant society. This gave him an option and, perhaps more importantly, information. Rizin knew a bit about what was going on as well, though he'd never admitted how exactly he'd obtained that knowledge.

There were a few reasonable precautions he could take, the first of which was not retrieving the records himself. Magic could find them and grab them, and then take them to a new location of his choice, where he would determine the best way to access them without exposing himself to potential traps. With a great deal of annoyance, he went through the lengthy process of opening up his scrying peephole and consulted his memory for the cartographer's notes at the bottom of the letter, which he'd destroyed as soon as he'd finished reading it.

Considering where they'd met, it was not surprising to Nym that Baracia chose a place in the frozen northlands to store the information. He quickly located a memory cube lodged in the ice on the side of a mountain, not so far from the troll tribe that had tried to bury him and a bunch of Academy students in an avalanche. The cube was sufficiently well shielded that the trolls hadn't noticed it, and Nym teleported it a thousand miles away to a stretch of forest he'd flown over a few times.

While he was locating it, another part of his mind constructed a copy of his body and sent him out into the world. His copy armed himself with as many protections, shields, wards, and barriers as he could and approached the cube. He was fully disconnected from the original and operating on a limited life of about a week before he ran out of arcana and broke down.

His only purpose was to absorb the contents of the cube and determine if it was safe for the original Nym to let them into his mind, or to act as a decoy if anyone showed up to try to do anything to him after he took possession of the knowledge. The copy absorbed the cube's contents after a cursory examination, then waited to see if anyone would go wrong.

After three days with no noticeable side effects, and having had plenty of time to review everything the cube had contained, the copy returned to the sanctum. Nym absorbed him back into the whole of his being and began reviewing the new knowledge.

Mostly it was boring meetings where people he didn't know discussed events and places he'd never heard of. The big thing Nym took away from it was that the council members were equal parts terrified and enraged that Myzalik had figured out a way to permanently remove an immortal from all timelines. Promises and favors were a huge part of how their society functioned, always with the implicit understanding that an ascendant might sit on a favor for a thousand years of mortal time before calling it in, but that the person who owed them that favor would still be around.

So they were losing political capital, not to mention fully a fifth of all known ascendants had disappeared. That had caused a massive split where ascendants who were afraid they'd be targeted next tried to ingratiate themselves to Myzalik to protect themselves or flocked to Niramyn's side to fight back. The neutral faction was still numerous enough to hold some sway over things, but it was far, far too late to stop the fight now.

Myzalik needed to go. Everyone on the Ascendant Council agreed about that. His new form of magic was too dangerous to be allowed to exist. What they couldn't agree on was the best way to do it. Imprisoning an ascendant was next to impossible, though with the Exarch apparently killing them now, they might need to redefine what was and wasn't possible.

For the moment, the council members wanted to undermine Myzalik's position by pulling back all the ascendants who'd joined him out of fear, and they also wanted to curb Niramyn's influence before he returned to his original strength. He wasn't technically an Exarch anymore, but everyone knew it was a matter of time and resources before he corrected that. Ideally, they'd pull most of the weaker ascendants out of both camps, find some way to contain Myzalik, and prevent Niramyn from regaining his position as the most powerful of the five current Exarchs.

Nym could get behind the goals, since getting rid of Niramyn and Myzalik would make his life immeasurably easier, but none of them seemed to have a clue how to go about doing that. If they couldn't figure it out, he wasn't sure how he could help. He was the least experienced ascendant there was. It had been impossible to keep track, but he figured that he was subjectively somewhere between five and ten years old now. Pitting him against ascendants that had subjective life spans measuring in centuries or more was a fool's errand.

So either Baracia knew something he didn't, or she was making some assumptions about him that were completely wrong. He supposed the simplest explanation was that she wasn't expecting him to help the Ascendant Council stop either Exarch, but just that they wanted to make sure he wasn't going to start helping them. That was a legitimate concern because, if Niramyn ever got ahold of Nym again, he would likely be forced to cooperate with whatever scheme the Exarch had cooked up.

Nym wondered what measures the Ascendant Council could take to prevent something like that happening. It might just be worth it to talk to them and find out.

CHAPTER FIFTY-FOUR

Since he'd had the time anyway while he waited for his copy to absorb the information Baracia had sent him and confirm it wasn't trapped in some way, Nym went ahead and set up four more sanctuaries in random locations. He also delivered a pouch of money to Ciana, mostly shields with a few crests, that would keep her for another year or two. He included a letter with it letting her know he was still alive and dealing with stuff but didn't go into specifics.

It was very possible that she could return to her old home now, but until he knew for sure, he wasn't going to take that risk. Any ascendant working for Myzalik might still come snooping around there and find her. Hopefully if she wasn't physically there, they wouldn't be inclined to chase her down. Sometimes that seemed like a thin hope, but he didn't have the ability to obscure his timeline and prevent people from finding out about the beach.

The only other piece of business he felt he really needed to address in the core reality was Analia's geas, but that wasn't something he could take care of without visiting her in person, so to speak. He could send out a copy to break it if he wanted, but his hidden-presence spell would keep anyone from following him, even if they were watching the timeline for his activities. What it might not protect him from was anyone who was watching Analia to see if he made contact.

Sometimes being an ascendant sucked. Their politics were awful, and no matter how strong he got, it seemed like he couldn't ever overpower his problems. It would barely take a few minutes out of his day to find her, remove the geas, and get her somewhere safe to recover, but he hesitated to do it. He could keep himself safe, but if anyone found her and decided she was a target to get at him, he wasn't strong enough to do anything about it. It would put him in a position where he was forced to rely on someone else to solve his problems, again.

The other option was to let her keep going while under the effects of the geas, which was definitely bad for her. The longer it was left on her, the worse it was going to be when it broke. He supposed he could transport her to one of his new sanctuaries and work on her there. She'd be as protected as he was that way. Leaving would be another matter, but she'd need time to recover anyway, weeks at least, possibly longer.

Nym wasn't sure what the best course of action was. The geas needed to be broken, but he didn't necessarily have time to take care of her afterward, and if he was the one who did it, it brought some risk on them both. On the other hand, the only mortal person he knew and trusted who could break a geas was Archmage Veran.

The archmage was already connected to Niramyn in some way, though Nym had never gotten the details on that. He suspected the ascendant had helped him reach the fifth layer, possibly as a move in one of his weird games. If so, either Archmage Veran didn't know or didn't care. Nym wanted to say that set a precedent for assisting mortals, but the truth of the matter was he wasn't an Exarch. Other ascendants that wouldn't dare to touch a mortal Niramyn had helped wouldn't think twice about killing one that a measly sixth-layer ascendant was fond of.

So no, as much as he wanted to help Analia, he couldn't find a way to do it that didn't leave both of them open to an unacceptable amount of risk. For the time being, the best thing he could do was stay far, far away from his mortal friends. The only solution he had at the moment was to spirit her away to one of his sanctuaries, break the geas, and then keep her safe inside what would become her prison for an indeterminable length of time. She could end up dying there, never able to see the outside world again.

Living her life under the burden of that geas would still be better than having no life at all.

Reluctantly, Nym set aside the idea of helping Analia. Once he learned more about where he fit into everything and had a better idea, he'd revisit it. Hopefully it would be safe to make contact with her then. In the meantime, he needed to consider how best to approach Baracia, or even if that was the right way to go about it.

Thanks in part to the memories she'd given him, Nym had the names of at least three other council members he could approach, although he didn't see much to recommend one over the other. He was sure there were differences, but whatever personal agendas they had weren't part of the memories he'd been given to review. All of them were opposed to the Myzalik-Niramyn conflict, and all of them agreed that Myzalik needed to be controlled or restrained in some way.

He suspected the memories had been carefully curated to present a specific impression. If he wanted to know whom he could trust and whom he couldn't, he was going to have to find out for himself. Every last ascendant had some sort of personal agenda, some sort of goal they were working toward that didn't necessarily include Nym's well-being.

No matter which way he moved, it was going to be a risk. The only way to stay safe was to never move at all, and who wanted an eternity of that? He might as well just die now if that's all he was good for. He had all the information he was going to get. It was time to make a decision.

Ascendants had a strange relationship with the core reality. They dipped in and out of it at will, aging while they were there and existing eternally otherwise. When

Nym decided to exist on the sixth layer, he stopped existing in reality prime. His physical body just vanished, pulled across the layers of reality to rejoin that part of him that existed outside time.

They called those parts anchors, and they devoted a considerable amount of their efforts to making more and more of them. A single one was all it took to tether him to immortality, but the more of them they made, the easier it was to pull themselves back and forth through time. If Nym understood the concept properly, he would be limited in his ability to bounce around through the timeline until he established new anchors.

For now at least, he could freely move around the sixth layer of reality. Much like how he exercised its power in the core world, navigating the sixth layer was an act of willpower. Nym existed in an endless nothingness when he arrived, and he wanted to exist somewhere else. He pitted his willpower against reality and over-wrote it. Reality conformed to his belief that he was not in a null space, but instead in a receiving hall in a very, very fancy home.

He was no stranger to extravagance now. The Feldstal manor had been just the start, and Archmage Veran's private sanctum was as luxurious as anywhere. But Nym had scried thousands and thousands of miles, and that included more than a few castles, mansions, and palaces. He'd seen the insides to some pretty amazing places, but none of them compared to the home Baracia had built for herself.

Gold was everywhere. It edged windows that peaked out at fantastical scenery, it framed doorways, and it crawled across marble pillars in imitation of living vines. That gold was in fact alive and growing wild up trellises in the patch of garden that circled around a great crystalline fountain in the center of the foyer. The fountain was ringed with gemstone flowers, cut so delicately that they appeared alive. Perhaps they were. It certainly wouldn't have surprised Nym.

Statues lined the walls, interspersed with the pillars, and a rich carpet made of some sort of material Nym didn't recognize led deeper into Baracia's home. Artwork decorated the walls, a hundred pictures that were so vividly rendered, Nym could actually see into them. The frames were much like windows, with views that changed when he took a step forward.

That was just the landing room, a place that visitors were redirected to when they arrived. When Nym attempted to will himself into existence inside the palace, he met a contesting force that pushed him to a specific room. He thought he could have overcome it with effort, but it seemed rude when the opposing will wasn't try-ing to harm him. It was rather like being chided to enter by the front door instead of climbing in through the nearest open window.

A . . . thing appeared. Nym wasn't sure how to describe it. It was almost like an animated arcana construct, except he couldn't see any arcana in it. Whatever it was, it had no corporeal body, but then again, Nym was in the sixth layer now. Bodies were optional.

"Hello," he said.

"Greetings, initiate." The words weren't spoken out loud, so much as just willed into existence. Nym knew he had heard them without ever actually having to hear them. "The mistress bids me invite you to her study, where she'll join you shortly."

"Of course. You'll lead the way?"

"I shall transport you there directly, if you are ready."

In the mortal world, he might have objected to placing himself in such a vulnerable position without even knowing how to get back out. Here, it made very little difference. If he wanted to leave and Baracia didn't want to let him, it would be a contest of wills. He'd already decided to trust her enough to meet with her, so doing it in a different room changed nothing.

"Very well," he told the manifestation.

Nym was sitting inside a brightly lit room, in a chair that was sinfully comfortable. A cup of tea still steamed on the table next to him. Across from him was a second chair, currently empty. On the far side of the room, framed by the floor-to-ceiling windows that overlooked a vast city of towering ivory spires poking out of clouds, was a desk so large Nym could have used it as a bed.

It was disorientating to feel reality change around him so rapidly, to have to rebuff its attempts to rewrite his personal history so that he believed this new version had always been true. Baracia must have realized that he would struggle with it, else she would have been seated across from him already.

He hoped it was a coincidence of timing rather than her predicting him that well, but either way, as soon as he'd finished acclimating to the change in reality, she was sitting in her chair, a cup of tea held in her hands. She looked much as he remembered, though her outfit had changed to a black dress accented in silver with a considerable amount of jewelry to match.

"Nym," she said, perhaps a touch more warmly than she'd spoken during their first meeting. "How nice to see you. Did you get a chance to review the memory cube I sent you?"

"I did, thank you," he said. "It was . . . enlightening. Of course, for every question it answered, it raised a dozen more."

She laughed softly. "Such is the way of knowledge. The more you learn, the more certain you become that you know very little after all."

"So I've learned."

"Well then, I have set aside some time for this meeting. Let's get to know each other better, yes? And we'll see if we can't get you up to speed."

"Yeah," Nym said. "That sounds like a good idea."

CHAPTER FIFTY-FIVE

Once the pleasantries were done, Nym and Baracia dove right into the meat of the conversation. "How much do you know about what's happening in our society, about the fight between two of our Exarchs?" the councilor asked.

"More than I want to, less than I should," Nym said dryly.

"Then you are aware of the Ascendant Council's major concern."

"That Myzalik is somehow killing ascendants, which should be impossible."

"Exactly. We can't ignore a threat like this," Baracia said. "He needs to be stopped."

"So you're siding with Niramyn?" Nym asked, afraid he already knew the answer. The memories he'd been given for review had only given him bits and pieces, mostly names and faces of those he assumed were important ascendants. The politics of it all were well hidden.

"Not exactly. It's complicated."

"Doesn't seem complicated," Nym said. "You want to stop Myzalik. Niramyn wants the same thing. Cooperate and stop him."

"The council as a whole can't," Baracia said. "There are too many old alliances and favors owed on both sides. So while many of us wish, individually, to stop Myzalik, we are unable to move as one group. This is complicated by the fact that not only is Myzalik owed favors by prominent council members, he has a large following who are also calling in their favors as well. It's forced the council to a standstill."

"Let me see if I've got this straight. You all agree you want to stop this guy because he could be killing you next, but no one is willing to do it because of prior obligations to his faction. So your plan is to just let him do whatever he wants and hope that the people who don't owe him a favor will take care of him for you."

"That's . . . not necessarily wrong, but it misses a great deal of nuance."

Nym resisted the urge to roll his eyes. He left unsaid that it was likely anyone who could take a swing at Myzalik probably wasn't willing to try, just in case they missed and found themselves suddenly mortal. If he had to guess, he'd say the only reason Niramyn was fighting back was that he had no choice. Myzalik was coming after him, had already tried once. Maybe when they fought next time, Nym could get a little brother out of it.

"There are a few ascendants who joined Niramyn when he returned, and they are calling in their favors as well," Baracia said. "It's a delicate situation, with favors and counterfavors being traded and used to check one another. The politics of it is a bit of a nightmare. That's why it was so interesting to encounter you, a fresh ascendant, barely even at initiate rank, who is owed no favors and owes none. You could do anything you wanted, and there would be no political backlash."

"I suppose you have some ideas about what I should want to do," Nym said.

"I wouldn't want to tie us together by suggesting you do any favors for me," she said. "But if you were to let me know what goals you have, I could advise on a possible course to meet those goals. As long as I don't actually help you, there'd be no obligation on either end. It would just be idle chatter."

Nym's lips pressed into a thin line as he considered what Baracia was proposing. It was a frustrating, roundabout, stupid, pointless fiction designed to let her off on a technicality, to maintain the polite facade that she was politically neutral just like the rest of the council. He didn't want to get dragged into a convoluted mess like that, and it might just be better to just thank Baracia for her time and get out of there.

Of course, if he did that, he might as well go straight back into hiding. He could fling himself off into some far corner of nothingness, work on his magic in peace, and abandon society completely. There were probably many ascendants out there doing exactly that. But the thought of being alone, doing nothing but working on his magic, never talking to anyone or experiencing anything else . . . Nym couldn't do it again, not forever. He'd already spent subjective years being trapped and alone, and Rizin hadn't been spectacular company either.

He wanted to live his life, not just keep it. So he was going to play the game, at least a little bit. "I guess the first thing I need to figure out is if anyone in Myzalik's camp is still trying to find me," Nym said. "I can't really make too many plans moving forward until I know who's looking for me."

No doubt Niramyn would like to get Nym back under his control. Both sides were potentially hostile to him, though he supposed not deadly, not anymore. What exactly ascendants did when they fought was still a bit of a mystery. It was something to do with their anchors, he knew. For beings who were supposed to be immortal, they placed a lot of value on time.

"Hmm . . . I do know some things about that, but I don't think I can tell you without you incurring a favor. And if you owed me a favor, you'd end up tied to me instead of being a free agent."

Nym's eye twitched. She knew what he wanted to know but wouldn't tell him because politics. He needed to come at it from a different direction, ask more oblique questions, he supposed. Maybe he wouldn't get that specific answer, but he might piece it together from other information if he was clever enough.

"So, what's common knowledge about Myzalik and his crew?" Nym asked. "What does everybody know? What's the latest gossip?"

"Ah. I see. Well then, have you heard what Karacho has been up to lately?"

"I haven't," Nym said. He also didn't know who Karacho was.

"The way I heard it, he didn't actually want to join Myzalik's faction, but he owed a whole bunch of favors to Enkati, and she called them all in to get him to help. He's been all over the eighth-layer hub, asking questions and running people down."

Nym smiled and nodded. He had no idea who either of those people were or what lurking around the eighth layer meant. "Sounds like an annoying job, but at least he'll have fulfilled a bunch of obligations when he's done."

"That's true. I don't think anyone expected him to worm his way out from under Enkati. She's not known for letting people go once she gets her hooks into them."

That was good to know. He made a mental note to never ask Enkati for a favor, if he ever met her. Presumably, what with the society being only a few hundred people and them all living forever, he'd meet everyone eventually. That must get awkward when there were long-standing grudges involved.

However, it wasn't relevant to him right now, not unless the eighth-layer hub was in some way connected to mortal people in the core reality. Since that didn't seem likely to be the case, he wasn't sure why Baracia was talking about it. His best guess was that it was going to be something that was relevant later.

"Has he just been hanging around the hub or chasing people down in other layers too?"

"I heard he's got Abdun chasing down the lower-layer stuff for him, but he's extremely annoyed because Abdun went and got his anchors severed in a wide chunk of mortal time, and that's right where the ascendants who are playing around in the core world are at."

"Oh yeah? There been a lot of ascendants in that situation? Anchorless, I mean."

"Better to say loose anchors," Baracia corrected him. "They just need to be reattached somewhere new. And yes, it seems there's a stretch of about a decade or so in real time where ascendants are descending to the core reality to fight. The young ones can be so hotheaded, present company excluded of course."

"Oh, uh, no offense taken, I think. So ascendants are fighting, and the losers are getting booted out of the core reality for a time-out." Nym had to wonder if it was really that much of a game to them. They couldn't die, so they just bickered, except that the amount of destruction they could cause was on the scale of warring demigods. He hadn't seen anything like that though. "When are they fighting?"

Baracia rattled off some numbers that Nym didn't really understand. He knew ascendants measured time from specific events rather than linearly, but he didn't have the frames of reference needed to translate that into something that made sense to him. "What, uh, what would that be on the Latorsikan calendar?"

"Hmm . . . Let me think," Baracia said. "1216 through 1225 is the range I believe they're fighting over."

Nym blinked at that. It was only a year into the future from what he considered to be present day. If the ascendants were fighting spell duels like he pictured, that could lead to a cataclysm that wiped out huge chunks of life on the planet. His friends could end up dead just as collateral damage, without any ascendant ever knowing about them at all.

"Oh, don't worry," Baracia said, noting the look on his face. "The council holds them responsible for anything they break. The winners have to fix the landscape, revive anyone who dies, and so on. It encourages the fighters to limit themselves to reasonable levels, barely worse than mortals."

That wasn't all that reassuring. Nym could still vividly remember Archmage Veran raining destruction down across miles of woodland on the undead in there, or when he'd attempted to obliterate the corpse root and it had taken multiple mages working together just to protect themselves against the area effects of a spell that wasn't even aimed at them. Two or three ascendants unleashing pinnacle spells would flatten an entire region in no time.

He supposed it was better than unraveling reality. At least the damage would be mostly reversible, but the idea of dozens of ascendants brawling at archmage levels over a decade-long time span was more than a little unnerving. He'd foolishly assumed the ascendants would limit their fights to the outer layers, but it made a certain kind of sense that they'd fight in a place where victory actually had meaning: the place where time mattered. Suddenly, Nym found himself a lot more interested in getting some more details.

Baracia was more than happy to chat about who'd fought where, and who the winner was. Nym listened attentively and took down names and tactics whenever he could get them. After all, there was every chance he might end up fighting some of those same ascendants one day, and having a good idea of their tactics and tricks could only help him.

Nym lost track of time while they talked. The teapot never got any emptier, and there was no day-and-night cycle to be seen through the windows. Without the need for sleep or other bodily functions to remind him, it was hard to care about passing hours. It couldn't have been more than a day though. They'd covered a broad range of topics, but it hadn't been that long.

Maybe it was two days. He frowned. Technically, it didn't matter, but it bothered him that he couldn't keep track when he was on the sixth layer. He needed to do something about that. Perhaps there was some sort of spell to keep track of subjective linear time, even when they were in a reality where time didn't exist.

"Nym, is there a problem?" Baracia asked. "You've gone quiet on me."

"Oh, sorry. I was just wondering how long we've been having tea. It's taking me a bit to wrap my head around the idea of unlimited time."

"I understand. All of this takes some adjusting. No matter how well you prepare, a mortal can't really understand a timeless existence. We've tried explaining it to them. It doesn't work. It's something you have to experience for yourself. As to your question though, subjectively speaking, it's been fifty-six days."

"What? No, that . . . that's not right."

"I can assure you it is."

If that was the case . . . how had they talked for that long? And if he'd spent close to two months just casually chatting, how long had he really been trapped in Niramyn's study?

CHAPTER FIFTY-SIX

No, it's impossible," Nym said. "There's no way."

He could buy that he'd lost track of time, that maybe he'd been there for a day instead of twelve hours, but almost two months was stretching it past breaking. Even just a week was stretching it. If Baracia wasn't lying to him, then he was missing something about how time worked in the outer layers.

"I assure you, I am able to keep track quite easily," Baracia said.

"But . . . No. It's just . . . How could it possibly be that long?"

"Ah, I think I understand. Let me assure you first that if this room were located in the core reality, the sun would have risen and set on us fifty-six times. This is an objective fact. But." Baracia raised a finger. "Out here in the sixth layer, linear time is optional. You are thinking of our conversation as something that happened for so long that weeks passed, but that isn't the case. Time is a mental construct, and I've simply collected all the time you spent processing this new information into one solid chunk."

"So, you're saying that every random thought I've had about all of this, and every thought I'm going to have in the future, has already happened?"

"Or is currently happening, if it makes you feel better to think of it that way. Truly, I'm surprised the conversation is so short. I put aside years to work this out with you."

"Oh, I think I get it!" Nym hoped he was right, at least. "It's not the same as sitting in a room for months like it would be for mortals. It's past time, future time, and present time all mixed together, pulled into one piece instead of scattered as individual moments."

"Ehhh, no, not really. Your whole idea hinges on the assumption that there are past and future times, which isn't correct. Only beings who can experience single instants of time in a fixed order think like that. Think of it like this instead."

An illusion of a thick line appeared in the air between them, with a small dot in the middle. The dot disappeared, and a new one that was the exact same size appeared right next to where the old one had been. That dot disappeared, and another one replaced it just slightly farther over, giving the illusion that it was slowly moving forward. This continued until the dot reached the end of the line, a process that only took a few seconds.

"This is how mortals experience time. Well, human mortals. There's some case-specific stuff I'm not going to get into, since it's not relevant. There is a timeline, this thick line here, and they move through it sequentially," Baracia explained. "And this is how immortals like you and I experience time."

Instead of a dot, a small, thin line appeared in the middle of the thick line that represented time. Then a dot appeared a few inches away, and the thin line stretched to reach it. More dots appeared, sometimes in front or behind the line, sometimes off to the side. Each time, the line grew until it was longer and thicker.

"Each of these dots is an anchor you'll create. The more of them you have, the more parts of the timeline you're touching. Your presence in time is very small right now, only a few objective linear months from when you established your first anchor to when you left the core reality. That's time you've already used. You can't go back into reality at those points ever again. When you establish new anchors, you'll have access to new times, and you won't have to burn up all the time between when you left reality and when you return to it."

"But that's in the mortal layers," Nym said, his mind working furiously to follow the logic. "So out here, in this space where time isn't linear, those fifty-six days' worth of time could be scattered all over, little slivers and pinpricks pulled from anywhere and stuck together into one big blob."

"That is theoretically possible but not very efficient. You'll notice in this illusion that the timeline is thicker than your experience of it, even as an ascendant. Those are other possible iterations of existence, alternate versions where events played out differently. We can take from them as well."

"Then, that means that even though I can't go back to the time I already experienced in the core reality, I could go see alternate versions of it?"

"You could, if you were strong enough. I wouldn't recommend setting anchors sideways just yet. Focus on extending them through one iteration of reality before you explore parallel paths. Going sideways is more of a goal for ascendants who reach the Crushing Void anyway."

"That being the seventh layer?" Nym asked.

"Yes, followed by the Heart of the Stars, Labyrinth, Illusory Mirror, Edge of Reality, and finally, exclusive to Exarchs: Hungering Chasms."

"I see. It seems like I have a long way to go before I push up against the boundaries of the collective knowledge of the ascendants."

"Don't we all," Baracia murmured.

"Right, well . . . It was nice chatting, but I should probably get some work done."

"Oh, you have a project in mind?"

Nym stared at her blankly. He had no clue what he was going to do next, other than trying to decipher some more of the green-leather-book knowledge locked in his brain that he still didn't understand.

"If you've got free time, I have an acquaintance who's looking for someone to do some work for him. I recommend approaching him and trading a favor or two.

If you don't already know how, learning to build new anchors and place them is an essential skill, and you have so much free time available that I'm sure you'll be able to come to some sort of agreement. Would you like me to arrange an introduction?"

"Sure. That sounds good."

"Very well, next time you return to the core reality, I'll have another letter set to find you at the earliest possible moment."

"Thanks," Nym said.

Nym spent a lot of time just floating out in the void, thinking about what Baracia had told him and trying to wrap his head around the fact that he'd spent enough time talking to her to fill close to two months. It still didn't seem possible to him. Even with her explanation, it felt like he was missing something.

Eventually, he gave up and turned instead to building himself something to exist in. That was mostly an effort of will, but the techniques and mental constructs he'd used to create spells served him well here. The same kinds of skills went into creating rooms. The hidden-presence spell was woven into them, modified to shield a place instead of a person, and the whole thing ended up looking similar to his first core-reality sanctuary.

It was a bit smaller, since he doubted he'd ever need anything like a guest room. None of his mortal friends were likely to ascend, not even if he helped them along. Perhaps Analia might be able to do it, but she'd be racing against time to try to modify herself enough to be able to handle the amount of arcana needed just to step between layers. It was far more likely she'd die of old age first.

Perhaps if he grew strong enough, he could set up a place like where Niramyn had stuck him to give her more time. Of course, he should talk to her first and find out if she even wanted to do something like that. It was a lot of work, and he wasn't at all sure it was worth it. He certainly would have been happier to remain mortal if he could have ensured that the ascendants would have left him alone.

Once he considered the idea, he wondered if Niramyn had done something similar with Archmage Veran. He'd gotten the sense that the ascendant had helped the mortal, if only as part of one of their games they played against one another. It had worked out well for Nym though, perhaps suspiciously so. Had the Exarch known he'd one day need a mortal's help and groomed him for it?

That didn't seem likely, since if he'd known that, he'd have known enough not to let Myzalik zap him with the spell that had turned him into Nym. Obviously Niramyn didn't know that, so . . . Nym wasn't sure exactly how existing across a spectrum of time instead of a single point translated to living in the core reality. Time was undoubtedly linear there.

Nym spent time, or didn't spend it, whatever the case may be, teasing out bits of pieces of knowledge from his brain and connecting them to other things he'd recently learned. It was a slow process, but it wasn't like he had somewhere to be or something to do. Idly, he wondered how ascendants measured progress. There were so many things that didn't seem like they should work; like, if time didn't exist, how did they measure change?

Nym could say that a number of years back, he'd been unable to use fifth-layer arcana, and six months before that, unable to use third. There were still more layers to reach ahead of him, so it stood to reason that they had some way to measure how fast someone progressed.

There was a lot more to that puzzle, but he felt like he was missing too many pieces to figure it out, and maybe some of the pieces he had were from a different puzzle. He wasn't sure yet, but it was giving him a killer headache. Until he had a bit more to go on, that was going to be a subject to pick at some other time.

He'd spent an inordinate amount of time chatting about random things with Baracia, common knowledge to gossip and rumors, nothing that was immediately actionable by itself, but it painted a picture of a tangled web and really drove home exactly how ascendant society functioned. They only had two things they valued: knowledge and time in the core reality. Nym was severely lacking in the first category, but he was the richest ascendant of all in the second.

Not all time was equal either. When ascendants wanted to experiment with something that required them to be on reality prime, they tended to spend time during portions of history where people didn't yet exist, at least not in any form of civilized society. There was less cleanup if things went wrong, and since there was less going on, the time being wasted likely wouldn't see any other use.

That wasn't an option for Nym, not yet. He'd need to form four or five anchors at absolute minimum to stretch that far back from his current anchor, the point in time where he'd ascended. Using time around that anchor seemed like a bad idea, if only because that's when his friends were still alive and also because it seemed like a decade-long slice coming up was being used as the arena for the newest scuffle. No doubt that would put a premium on those years for any ascendants who were interested in the outcome.

Since one possible outcome was an Exarch who could kill the unkillable taking control of everything, Nym assumed that every ascendant had an interest. So then, if he wanted to do anything in the core reality while preserving his own personal time around his one and only anchor, the solution was obvious. He needed to make a new anchor.

He might be able to puzzle that out on his own, but it would be easier if there was someone to show him. That would incur a favor and would be one step toward being entangled in ascendant politics. As long as he was careful though, that might not be a bad thing. It opened up the possibility of other ascendants owing him favors, and that might be just what he needed to keep himself safe from two Exarchs who had more interest in him than was healthy.

Nym just needed to go back to core reality for a minute to get his letter from Baracia, and he'd be on his way.

CHAPTER FIFTY-SEVEN

The ascendant Nym was meeting was named Hozim. Baracia had arranged the meeting, and Nym waited with her for the new ascendant to show up. "Anything I should know about him?" Nym asked.

"He is easygoing and loves to teach. Truthfully, there probably isn't anyone better to show you how to make new anchors and cast them through time. For the advanced stuff, you'll need to seek out other ascendants or make your own path, but you're still decades away from that point. Hozim will teach you the basics, and the favors he'll trade you for are nothing too onerous."

Given Nym's track record with instruction, he gave it a coin toss whether he'd appreciate Hozim's style of teaching. It was somewhat depressing to think that his best instructor to date had been a shelf full of books tailored from Niramyn's own memories. Things had been so well laid out, and followed his own thought processes so closely, that it was rare to have a question that the early books couldn't answer.

Of course, that had all vanished on the final shelf, but Nym suspected that was on purpose. Or maybe he'd just diverged from his past life's way of thinking enough that once he was past the basics, they were no longer in sync. If so, that was fine with Nym. He didn't particularly like Niramyn and wouldn't shed any tears if Myzalik did manage to kill him for real next time.

"He's here," Baracia said.

A man who looked like he was in his early thirties appeared in the doorway. He was dressed in strange clothes, some kind of pants and a coat made from materials Nym didn't recognize. There were patches on the elbows of his coat, and he was wearing a vest underneath, one that only buttoned up about halfway. A strip of cloth made of some other material hung down from his neck and was tucked into the vest.

"Ah, yes, I get that a lot," the man said with a chuckle when he saw Nym blinking at his outfit. "My eccentric fashion sense. Trust me, it's quite the popular look in one of the possible alternate timelines I favor."

"Yeah . . . I'm sure. Hozim, I presume?"

"The one and only."

"I'm Nym, but I guess you probably already knew that."

"Indeed, I did, young man. A fresh ascendant, and so young too. I'm not sure we've ever had one younger," Hozim said. "Quite the accomplishment."

"There were some extenuating circumstances," Nym said. "But thank you."

"And he's modest too! Where'd you find this one, Baracia?" Hozim's chuckle turned into a full laugh, and he added, "Stand and be proud. You are an immortal now, one of the few, one of the elite."

Nym glanced over at Baracia, who just rolled her eyes and sighed. "Hozim is, well, you can see for yourself. But I promise he's a good person."

"I am boisterous and grating on the nerves," Hozim said, leaning forward and giving Nym a conspiratorial wink. "But come, come, let's make ourselves comfortable, then discuss some business. I have dozens of little tasks to do that are perfect for a new ascendant, and you no doubt have many questions that I can provide answers to."

Baracia led the two of them into her study, only this time the desk was missing, there was an extra thirty feet of length to the interior of the room, and an enormous table dominated the space near the windows. Three chairs were situated around it, and the other two ascendants popped across the room with magic to appear in their chairs. Nym exerted a flicker of will and blipped over to the third chair between them.

"Oh ho! Excellent. You're already able to manifest your will in opposition to Baracia's home. That will save us from some tedious exercises, though it wouldn't hurt to learn them anyway," Hozim said. "One can't ever really be too prepared, after all."

"Perhaps later," Nym deflected. "Priorities and all of that."

"Of course, of course. Baracia, might you be planning on serving those delicious little cakes? You know those are half the reason I come to your events."

"I would be happy to," she said. A dozen little plates, each with its own yellow-frosted cake a few inches wide and studded with a chunked strawberry scattered across its top, appeared on the table. "Please, help yourself."

Nym manifested a fork, floated the nearest cake over to him, and took a bite. His eyebrows shot up in surprise, and he examined the cake more closely. A subtle flow of arcana trickled from the cake as he chewed it, technically poisoning him since it wasn't being directed into his soul well, but so weak that it wasn't any real effort to cleanse it. He didn't doubt that it could be much stronger, though he suspected he would have been able to tell before he tasted it if it was.

"Interesting cake," Nym said. He took another bite and chewed slowly, wondering if it could be served to humans. It was probably safe, as long as they were forewarned, but he'd be the first to admit that his idea of how much arcana a human could safely process outside of their soul well was a bit skewed.

Hozim was working on this third before Nym finished his first and set his fork down. It disappeared almost as soon as it touched the table, his will no longer actively working against Baracia's home to maintain its shape. "Thank you," he told her. "I might try to steal the recipe from you to make it myself, assuming there is one."

"Ah, hrmm. I suppose it was based off something I had once before I ascended.

I couldn't honestly tell you what it was made of, or even if these are an accurate recollection of the taste. I conjured them from my memories of eating one as a child, you see."

"And an excellent conjuring it was!" Hozim cut in. He stacked the plates together and set them aside. "Now then, to the heart of the matter. You need to learn how to create new anchors and how to place them in different spots in the timeline. I can teach you that. In exchange, I'll have you perform some small tasks for me in the core reality during specific times that I've already used. How does that sound?"

"Depending on the tasks and when they need to happen, it sounds like an excellent arrangement."

"Well let's talk about that. I'm going to assume that you're still using a mortal calendar as a frame of reference?"

"Yeah," Nym admitted. "I haven't quite figured out how ascendants measure that kind of stuff yet."

"We break timelines down by catastrophic events that have a tendency to occur regardless of which timeline you end up mucking around in. It's a lot easier to record time from that volcanic eruption that sank a prosperous island nation or the meteorite swarm that decimated a sizable portion of a continent, since those tend to always happen in every timeline, regardless of what the humans are doing."

"That makes sense," Nym said. "I'm used to the Latorsikan calendar, but there are probably timelines where it doesn't exist at all, or where it does but has a different starting point. My 1215 might be another timeline's 1225."

"Exactly, yes. Of course, there are a lot of years to cover, and nobody wants to get up into the hundreds of thousands of years, so we just generally agreed on specific events that we call the Third Cataclysm or the Ninth Cataclysm."

Nym supposed for a group of people whose existence never ended, it would eventually be necessary to remove the variables inherent by mortal timekeeping methods. No doubt both of the other people in this room could name a dozen or more civilizations that had kept their own calendars, and that wasn't even getting into alternate versions of those civilizations.

"Let me see now . . . 1215 of the Latorsikan calendar." Hozim tapped his chin with his finger. "Oh! I know. I have just the project going on in that time frame. There's a group of mages I gathered a few hundred years earlier who were studying how to become ascendants, and they kind of died out about fifty years earlier than when you're from. I'll show you how to make an anchor, and you go back and kick-start them to get things going again. Maybe this time they'll get lucky and make some progress."

"So . . . You want me to give some magic lessons to some humans half a century before the point in time I ascended?"

"Indeed. No need to lay it all out for them, just cut away some of the wrong ideas that are choking the Collective out, get them pointed in the right direction, and send them on their way."

Nym froze. "I'm sorry, did you say the Collective?"

"Hmm, yes. It seemed overly dramatic to me, but that is what they called themselves."

He couldn't help it; he started laughing. "So if I don't do this, they cease to exist decades before I meet them. That might be worth it."

"Well, no, not exactly," Hozim said. "The primary timeline likes to remain the same. It finds ways to correct itself. We generally try to help it along if we're able, though sometimes an alternate timeline is desired, and in those cases, we exert a massive amount of influence to shift the timeline. If you don't do it and no other ascendants exert any pressure on the primary timeline, someone else will step in, or they'll figure something out on their own. Or a different organization will take their place and accomplish many of the same things."

"Seems like if it's going to happen either way, there's not a lot of reason to go help it along," Nym pointed out.

"In the long term, no, it's not necessary to interfere unless you are trying to alter something big in the primary timeline. However, let's just say that assisting could result in the Collective getting back on its feet earlier, which might result in different leadership, and that could perhaps allow me to tweak another ascendant's nose that I got my candidate into a leadership position over his."

Of course that was the reason. There were very few explanations for ascendants going to the core reality at all, though perhaps encouraging mortals to try to grow in magic and possibly ascend themselves might be a good one. Nym wasn't actually sure if the current group of ascendants wanted to increase their number or not. It was just as likely that they didn't care for competition, but he supposed it might get lonely or boring after a few millennia of not having new people to talk to. So far, none of the ascendants he'd spoken with seemed particularly concerned about him joining their ranks, so he decided it was probably a good thing if more people managed it.

"I did not have great experiences with the Collective when I was a mortal," Nym said. "What would happen if someone else took over?"

Hozim shrugged. "Excellent question, and I'm sure we can find an alternate timeline to explore where that's exactly what happened. But in reality prime, if you don't help the Collective, someone else will. You'll find that a few decades is more than long enough for the timeline to course correct. Most alterations we make are by necessity minor and not long reaching."

"Alright, I guess if it's not going to change my own interactions with them either way, it wouldn't hurt anything."

Hozim flashed him a wide grin, and said, "That's your side of the exchange settled then. Let's talk about mine. You'll need to know how to make anchors, so I'll teach you that and help you place your first one. We'll place it before your current anchor, and you can use it to help me out. Come, come, let's get started. Oh, wait, Baracia, dear, might I take one of these cakes with me?"

CHAPTER FIFTY-EIGHT

The Abilanth of fifty years ago looked a lot like the version Nym was familiar with. There were some superficial changes, sure, but the street layout was the same, and the walls limited the sprawling growth a city like Thrakus would undergo. The Academy still sat right where it always did, though the mage guildhall was in a different location. The spot Nym remembered it being was currently occupied by a rune scribing business. It was the same building, so he assumed at some point in time, ownership would change hands.

That had practically nothing to do with why he was in 1165's version of Abilanth, so other than noting the change and that he was unlikely to find Analia's great-grandfather there, Nym ignored it. He floated above the city and studied it intently through his scrying spell, starting with the Feldstal manor. There were plenty of people there, and the interior looked far, far different than the future version he'd visited, but unfortunately, the man he was looking for wasn't home.

The hidden lab in their library was there, but it didn't look like anyone had used it in years. It was possible the current generation didn't even know about it. There were a lot of books in there he didn't recognize, five or six times as many as had existed when Nym had found it. He sent a copy of himself down to investigate what those other books were while he continued looking for the current Lord Feldstal.

Even after ascending, it turned out that finding someone was difficult. Limited as he was to the use of mortal magic with only a few sixth-layer spells to his name, Nym didn't expect to find Lord Feldstal quickly. If he'd been at home, maybe it would have been a different story, but that wasn't the case. He'd just have to wait for the man to return home and visit his library so that Nym could reveal the secret lab to him. If Hozim was correct in his predictions, that would be all it took to renew the interest in the Collective's mission. The mortals would take that discovery and run with it.

Finding the right moment to reveal the lab to Lord Feldstal was the trick of the job. It needed to be a time when he was alone in the library, and a nobleman was rarely ever alone at any time. Nym supposed a bodyguard or two wouldn't necessarily be an issue, though he would prefer to not be responsible for any extreme measures being taken to ensure the proper secrecy Lord Feldstal would demand.

The actual Collective as he knew it wouldn't come into existence for another generation, but by tipping off this Lord Feldstal to the existence of the lab and all the workings his own ancestors had left behind, Nym was laying the groundwork for him to carry on that research, to recruit others, and to secure funding.

The books hidden inside that lab were a pale shadow of the knowledge the Collective would have one day, but they set the stage for what was to come. Nym's copy made a few annotations, crossing out certain branches that led the wrong way, and completely removed no less than four books that focused on necromantic workings designed to empower enslaved spirits chained to their own moldering corpses as a sort of protowight.

That knowledge would exist elsewhere someday too, but it wouldn't be in the hands of the Collective. He destroyed the books and teleported the ashes fifty miles straight up, where they were scattered beyond recovery. Then, once he'd tweaked the knowledge contained in the Feldstal lab, Nym started skimming forward in time. Lord Feldstal returned to his manor that evening but never entered the library.

He went through his daily routine while Nym watched, waiting for his chance. Finally, after moving forward three weeks, Lord Feldstal visited his library one evening. He had a single guard with him, but the man stayed a respectful distance away, near the doors, and left Lord Feldstal to his reading.

The positioning wasn't ideal, with the nobleman about a hundred feet away from the entrance to the lab, but Nym thought he could get Lord Feldstal's attention. The hidden door in this time period was actually on mechanical hinges, and Nym figured that inducing a few failures in the mechanism would cause the door portion of it to fall forward. That ought to make a loud thump, and if it didn't, Nym would simulate it.

His magic threaded its way through the room and rent steel, causing a loud squealing sound to fill the air. Lord Feldstal looked up immediately but didn't seem to know where the noise was coming from. So Nym broke the other one. Now the nobleman was on his feet and approaching the bookshelf, though he still hadn't figured out exactly what he was hearing.

It looked like the shelf was balanced well enough on its own that even without the mechanism to move it in place, it would still hold up. That ran counter to Nym's goals, so he used greater telekinesis to shift it slightly, just enough that it would be obvious there was something behind it. He made sure to grab the shelf from the top so that it would groan under its own weight when he moved it.

"What in God's name is that?" Lord Feldstal muttered to himself. He cast a quick glance around the library, then moved closer to examine the shelf.

Nym waited to make sure Feldstal was going to actually open it up and look around inside before he stepped out of reality prime and back to where Hozim waited for him. "All set?" he asked the senior ascendant.

"Looks like it. Everything is happening as it should now. Incidentally, did you know they never fixed the hinges you broke?"

"Yeah, I remember moving the shelf the hard way when I found it in my time."

"It looks like that doesn't change either. Well then, congratulations on your first successful favor! I have plenty of other projects in times I've already been, if you're interested in learning some new tricks. Perhaps you'd like to learn how to reverse the age on your mortal form? That one is all but mandatory for any ascendant who's going to spend time in the core reality. The years pile up quicker than you could imagine."

"That would be useful," Nym said, though he thought he could figure that one out himself. The fragmented knowledge floating in his head had actually touched on the reversal of aging, though it mostly went over some of the dangers of improperly performing the spell. It wasn't a simple time reversal, but a delicate procedure designed to restore the body to youth while at the same time preserving all the enhancements and modifications the ascendant had performed on themselves.

Still, if it was a choice between having an experienced ascendant guide him through the process or hacking something together through trial and error, that wasn't a hard decision to make. While he was at it, he also wanted to learn how to scry across layers. It would be nice to be able to pinpoint exactly what he was looking for before dropping into reality prime.

The two continued to hash out deals as Nym worked on generating new anchors and spreading them out. At this point, he just needed to invest arcana and effort into it, something he could easily do while he spoke with Hozim. They were placed at the older ascendant's instruction so that Nym could get access to time periods Hozim wanted work done in, but he showed Nym how to move them around later if he needed to.

Their talk was interspersed with a few other jobs at different time points, sometimes simple things like spooking superstitious people into taking the left path instead of the right to keep them from meeting a grisly end, other times requiring Nym to actually spend days or even weeks helping someone, or setting up an area with precious resources that might not be discovered for years or even decades.

Once, he even went into what he considered the future, only about fifty years or so. That was by far the most bizarre job he undertook, and he had to firmly resist the urge to peek in on his friends, just to see what they looked like when they were all old. If he'd found out any of them had died, he was sure he'd end up devoting time and energy to finding out how and preventing it. It was better to let things play out naturally than to have an ascendant interfering in their lives.

That was a sad realization for him, knowing that he might briefly visit them occasionally, if he ever cleared up his issues with other ascendants trying to find him, but that he wouldn't be part of their lives again. He simply couldn't afford to waste the years directly around his ascension on socializing, not when it was so hotly contested by the factions being championed by Niramyn and Myzalik.

While Nym worked at making new anchors, Hozim explained the exact mechanics of the age-reversal spell and guided him through shaping it. It was more or less what Nym had expected, but it was nice to have a few potential flaws pointed out without having to discover them the hard way. By the time they were done with their meeting, Nym had spent a year of his time in reality prime. Those weeks were scattered quite liberally around a span of about three centuries, a range that was only going to keep expanding.

"I think that's about everything for now," Hozim said. "This has been a very profitable arrangement for me, and I hope you feel the same."

"I do," Nym said, which was mostly true. He probably could have figured out everything Hozim had shown him on his own without spending a year of time, but it had been nice to have the company and the instruction.

"Then I'll leave you to practice, for now, but if you'd like to learn a few new spells, I'll show you where to find me."

Hozim launched into a lengthy explanation about navigating the sixth layer's hub, which was achieved through a few artificial reference points the ascendants had set up that marked common meeting locations, and also through personal invitations to individual abodes. "Here, let me give you the waypoint for my own home," the ascendant said, after explaining how to set up the personal reference points. "This is similar in a way to knocking on a door. It lets me know that you're trying to visit me."

Then the strangely dressed ascendant disappeared. Nym took a moment to orient himself and teleported back to his own sanctuary. After visiting Baracia's again, he had a few ideas for how he wanted to update it, and his magical defenses could use some work. Right now, the only thing that was keeping it safe was the persistent hidden-presence spell he'd tied to it. Anybody who stumbled across it accidentally would be able to breach the defenses with ease.

Additionally, if Nym was going to be hosting other ascendants eventually, he felt an upgrade in decor was in order. Baracia's home, as outrageously expensive and flamboyant as it was, wasn't an outlier. Even the common areas that ascendants shared were some sort of opulent dream that the richest kings and queens back in the core reality could scarcely imagine.

Humming to himself as he worked, Nym started redecorating. Rooms got shuffled around, new ones added, and sizes altered. He borrowed some design philosophies from other areas he'd seen, and though it was nowhere as outrageous, his sanctuary was much more refined by the time he was done.

"Maybe I'll get the hang of this ascendant thing after all," he said, hands on his hips while he surveyed his work. If these were the people he was going to be spending eternity with, it would help to learn their culture.

CHAPTER FIFTY-NINE

As his control over Transcendent arcana grew, Nym became more comfortable with using it to do actual magic. In many ways, it reminded him of the early days when he was still exploring first- and second-circle mortal magic. It wasn't the spells themselves, of course. Those were hideously complex compared to anything he'd cast back when his existence had been limited to a single body in the core reality. But the feeling of always discovering something new, that there was more just around the corner, that was alive again in him.

Hozim was a great help at first, but eventually he started running out of tasks for Nym. "I'm sorry," he said during one of their meetings. "But you just don't have the anchor spread to do anything else on my agenda."

"I understand," Nym said. "Time for me to venture out into the world and do things on my own."

"I didn't say I couldn't still help you," Hozim protested. "You'd just have to owe me a favor at a later date."

"What kind of favor are you talking about?" Nym asked warily.

"The same kinds of things you do for me now. I just don't know what those favors would be yet."

"That doesn't sound too terrible. You do seem to have a lot of little things."

"Oh, most of those aren't for me," Hozim explained with a laugh. "Almost everything I've had you do has been on behalf of other ascendants that I owed favors to. Thanks to you, I've caught up an enormous amount of debt I owed to several dozen other people. If you'd like, I could introduce you to some of them, and you can try to strike up some deals directly. It's entirely possible they owe favors that you could solve as well."

Nym wasn't sure how exactly that helped him stay out of the politics of it all like Baracia wanted, but he trusted her to be more invested in that than he was. "I'll consider it," he said. "In the meantime, there is one more spell I'd like to learn."

"What's that? I think we've covered all the big ones already."

"I . . . don't know how to do it, or what it's even called, but when I was mortal, I was under a spell that scrubbed me from the timeline. Or maybe just made me invisible? Ascendants couldn't see me when they looked through it. One of them described it as if people were talking to themselves when I had a conversation with them, or that objects I interacted with just disappeared while I was using them, only to reappear later in a new location when I was done."

Hozim shook his head. "That one might be a bit beyond me. It sounds like something powerful, maybe even Exarch-level strong. I could show you a spell that blanks out the timeline around an event so that anyone scrying it wouldn't be able to casually see what happened, but they would know it had been interfered with."

"That might be a good start. I have some business with a few mortals in reality prime that I don't need other ascendants snooping around on."

"Oh, really now? That sounds fascinating. Care to tell me about it?"

"No," Nym said flatly. "I'm only telling you this much to make sure the spell you have in mind will work for what I need."

"It definitely won't do what you were describing earlier, but if you ever do figure out how that effect happens, please consider coming back here to talk to me about it. That's a spell I wouldn't mind trading a favor or two to learn. In the meantime, there's an ascendant I could introduce you to. Her name is Pyoka. She might be able to teach you the spell you're looking for."

"Is she part of the neutral council faction?" Nym asked.

"Yes, indeed. I take it you're determined to take no sides."

"That's the plan."

"Indeed. Hmm. I would have thought you'd be on Niramyn's side, all things considered. It's not too far off the council's own position, and you have . . . Well, you know."

"I have what?" Nym asked. He did know, but he wanted Hozim to say it.

"You're connected to Niramyn somehow." Hozim gestured toward Nym's face. "You look just like him, though the body is a bit younger than he prefers. Add another ten or fifteen years and you could be twins."

That sounded like something that would be more of a hindrance than a help. Posing as Niramyn had been useful for his work in Research Lab Six, but he wasn't going to fool an ascendant the same way he did the golems of the lab. There was something unique about every ascendant he'd met, some intangible feeling that he couldn't quite describe.

"Perhaps I should rebuild this body," he mused aloud. "Advertising a connection to a politically divisive ascendant who's in the middle of a war doesn't do me any favors."

"Easy enough to do," Hozim said.

"I'll do that first then. You'll introduce me to Pyoka?"

"I will," the ascendant promised.

That was one good thing he'd discovered about their economic system of trading favors. None of them considered an introduction a favor, if only because it was incredibly difficult to even find another ascendant if one didn't already know where they were. A few of them advertised openly with their own beacons to follow, but that was by far the exception to the rule.

Either way, neither Baracia nor Hozim seemed to consider it some sort of obligation or debt he owed them when they made introductions. Nym figured it was either because it was the cornerstone of their economy, or because it didn't involve spending time on reality prime or any sort of secret knowledge. Whatever the case, he was happy to take advantage of it.

Before that though, he needed a new face.

Pyoka wasn't exactly what Nym was expecting from an ascendant. For one thing, she wasn't human. Maybe she'd been at one time, but now she just looked like some sort of four-dimensional geometric pattern that shifted and folded in on itself endlessly. Nym wasn't even sure how *she* applied in this case, but if that was what Pyoka wanted, he wasn't going to argue with her about it.

She also served as a stark reminder that changing the thickness of their nose or hair color was the very least an ascendant who wanted to hide their identity could do. Pyoka's current physical form was so disturbing that it actually hurt his eyes to look at her. It was an effort of will to look directly at her, though that was helped perhaps by a background just as disturbing.

Like the ascendant herself, the whole thing was infinitely complex geometric designs all moving in some sort of coordinated dance that he didn't understand the rules to. Nothing was ever in the same place twice, and if there was some sort of pattern, it was far beyond him to figure it out.

If Hozim was to be believed, she specialized in scrying and divinations, more so than the average ascendant, at least. If they could come to an agreement, Nym was hoping to get a better handle on the mechanics of reading timelines without having to actually go to those times and to learn how to hide his own tracks from other ascendants attempting to chase him down.

The copy Nym sent to meet the strange ascendant looked nothing like him, which he probably should have been doing from the start, but he both hadn't thought to and hadn't known how. It didn't take much to figure out how to alter the physical construct he manifested to interact with the constructs the other ascendants used. It seemed like using something that resembled the mortal bodies they'd once had was a popular choice, but Nym couldn't be sure. He didn't know what any of them had looked like when they were mortal.

Perhaps most importantly, Pyoka wasn't involved with the Niramyn or the Myzalik factions and was well-known among the community for her discretion when it came to interactions with other ascendants. She was about as close to perfect as Nym could reasonably hope for, except for one particular detail.

"I have no need for your assistance at the moment," she spoke in a weirdly flat tone.

"There's nothing at all?"

"I am happy to bank a favor for future use," Pyoka said. "It would not need to be a large one, as the skills you are seeking to master require little in the way of instruction on my part. The concepts are not difficult; it is the execution that requires effort."

"I don't think so," Nym said. "I am not big on owing open-ended favors, especially with everything going on right now. If you do decide you need help with something, please let me know."

"Ah. Wise, perhaps. I have seen several new ascendants drive themselves so deeply into debt that they become virtual slaves to those who are more powerful. But be careful not to be too cautious, lest you find yourself never advancing at all. There is much collective ground we have trodden and very little need to make all those discoveries all over again."

Nym didn't need advice about being careful whom he worked with or what favors he traded away. That was the big reason he didn't want to be owing anyone anything undefined. If they couldn't work out an agreement in the moment, then that was that. He had essentially unlimited time, kind of, and if that meant figuring it out himself to avoid being in debt, that was how he'd do it. Maybe when the whole feud was over, he'd change his mind.

"Well, if that's that, then I guess I'll leave you to your work." If he had to look at the ever-shifting landscape any longer, something in his brain was going to break.

"Farewell, young ascendant. If you should happen to change your mind, feel free to reach out to me again."

"Thank you, I will."

"Dead end, huh?" Hozim asked. "Hmm, Pyoka would be my first pick for teaching you what you're interested in, but she's not the only one. I can think of a few other ascendants who have similar interests, especially in Myzalik's faction. You're sure you don't—"

"Absolutely not," Nym cut in. "I don't want anything to do with anyone on either side of that."

Hozim snorted. "That's basically impossible. The only ascendants who don't have a connection in some way are the ones who won't participate in our society at all. They just sit out there, locked away in their own private fortresses, slowly amassing power and refusing to speak to the rest of us. There's nothing to be learned there. Best to just leave them alone."

Considering they had all of eternity to accomplish whatever their goals were, Nym could see the advantages, but he shuddered to think of the kind of mind that could handle an existence that never included another person. Maybe they'd crafted servants to keep them company, like their own private little kingdoms. It still sounded like a nightmare to him though.

"There is one person," Hozim began. He grimaced and shook his head. "He's neutral, aggressively so. Strong. Smart. Kind of demanding though. Not to put too fine of a point on it, he's not a pleasant man. It won't cost you anything to talk to him, but as picky as you are, I would be surprised if you managed to work out any sort of deal."

"I guess it couldn't hurt," Nym said. "I'm used to dealing with unpleasant people."

"Not like this guy. I promise you, he's one of a kind."

CHAPTER SIXTY

"Τ his place looks familiar," Nym said.

They stood in front of a large four-story manor house. It was impressive, he supposed, but he'd seen far more spectacular—not to mention physics defying—abodes in his short time as an immortal. But there was something about this particular building that tickled his brain. He just couldn't quite put his finger on what it was.

Hozim glanced over at him and shrugged. "One of his many eccentricities. Eriam has always been a strange one, almost hostile toward other ascendants. He can be quite rude, but he's also fair. There's a lot of speculation as to why he's even here and not locked away where no one would ever find him."

The two went in, and Nym lost a step when he saw the interior.

"Something wrong?" Hozim asked.

"Er, no. It's . . . It's fine." The place had the exact same layout as the Feldstal manor in Abilanth. The decorations were different, but even there, Nym saw a lot of similarities. Some of the pieces were straight out of his memories. "Does it always look like this?"

"The manor? Yes, it's a bit dumpy by ascendant standards, isn't it?"

That was true enough. The vistas some of the ascendants had constructed were beyond beautiful, more majestic than anything the inner layers could offer. Sometimes they were just as disturbing as they were beautiful, but each and every one was something special.

This place was . . . just a place, a typical mortal home for a typical mortal noble. It was unique only in how common it was. Nym idly smiled to himself when he remembered how awed he'd been at the Feldstals' home when he'd first seen it. Now here it was, replicated in shape and form, and his initial thoughts were of how dingy and boring it was compared to what he'd become used to.

The two of them walked down the halls, unable to teleport inside the manor. That was an unusual choice as well, but perhaps Eriam simply wanted to make the mighty ascendants who came to his door feel mortal again. Perhaps that was why he was so disliked. Being made to feel powerless would certainly rub any of the ascendants he'd met the wrong way.

"To the library?" Nym asked softly, more to himself than Hozim. He'd walked those halls enough times to know which rooms were in the direction they were heading. And besides, what better place to meet with an ascendant?

"How'd you know?" Hozim asked. "Been here before?"

"No. It's just very familiar to me."

They entered the library, and Nym's eyes immediately went to his favorite table. He'd spent a lot of hours with Analia there, figuring out and teaching each other the basics of magic. Sitting there, leaning back in one of the huge padded chairs that Nym had used himself, was a man who looked very much like Bardin Feldstal. He looked up as they entered and traded a nod with Hozim.

"I think you can take it from here," Hozim told Nym. "I'll just be on my way."

"Yeah. Thanks for the help," Nym said absently. His eyes were locked on Eriam's face. It was so familiar, but there were differences. The man came from the Feldstal line though, Nym was sure. Perhaps that was the real reason the Feldstals were so intertwined with the Collective. They had an ancestor who'd ascended hundreds or thousands of years before Nym's time.

It couldn't be thousands of years though, not with the manor looking the way it did. Eriam had to be within a few generations of Analia and Bardin. Nym wasn't sure if that was a good thing or not though. Considering how things had gone with Analia's father and brother, he'd had more bad encounters with various members of her family than good ones. Analia herself was an outlier.

"Well, well," Eriam murmured as Nym approached.

"Well?"

"You don't look like I expected you to."

"Oh? What were you expecting?"

"Someone ten years younger, darker hair, finer facial features, less muscle. You've already started disguising yourself."

"That's creepy," Nym said. "Do we know each other?"

Eriam tilted his head and studied him. "Time works strangely out here. New ascendants rarely appear, and we've never quite figured out what determines the order we show up. The only thing we're sure of is that it has nothing to do with the chronological order that we ascend from the core reality."

"I . . . see."

"No, you don't."

"I suppose not," Nym agreed. "Did you want to try making sense, maybe?"

The ascendant threw his head back and laughed. "You haven't changed at all." Then he sobered and added, "There's only so much I can tell you, you know? You made me promise."

"Did I? I don't think we've met."

"Not yet, from your point of view. But you were already an ascendant when I was born. I'm sure you know where I came from. I met you back when I was still a mortal."

Considering that Nym could exist in whatever time he wanted, that didn't mean much to him, but he suspected Eriam had been born sometime after Nym's mortal adventures. Nym just hadn't met him yet in his own personal timeline.

"You said you didn't want me to ruin the surprise," Eriam said. "I remember you were quite insistent about that, that life wasn't as fun if you already knew how it was going to happen."

"I'm not really sure what you're talking about," Nym said.

"Oh, come on, you're just being intentionally dense."

"Maybe I'm not interested in trying to tease it out of you."

"Spoilsport," Eriam said. "Fine. You helped me when I was a mortal, set me in the right direction for my own ascendance. You told me about this meeting we would have one day, made me promise not to tell you certain things and made me promise to be sure to tell you others."

"Sometimes I hate this time-travel stuff," Nym muttered. "Gives me a headache."

"That was actually something you were quite specific that I clear up for you. You've got a problem with trying to reconcile this reality with the concept of time. You need to stop thinking of this as a place where time doesn't exist and start thinking of it as a separate time. You have two clocks. One is your time in the core reality, only for you it's not a straight line. You can jump in and out wherever you want. Your body is mortal, and accumulated time spent there will age you into nothingness.

"You already know how to fix that, I believe. It's important to keep your mortal avatar in good condition. Let too much age build up and it starts causing problems and takes more effort to fix. But you don't need me to tell you about this. This is the part you've more or less wrapped your head around. It's outer-layer time that you're struggling with."

"So what's the big secret?" Nym asked, leaning forward on the table.

"That it's not as timeless as you think. This is where the second clock comes into play. When you're not spending time in reality prime, you're here. Your time here progresses linearly, much like you were used to in your mortal life, except that it pauses while you're not here, then resumes when you come back. The other important thing to understand is that it's not synced to reality prime. Two ascendants can ascend within moments of each other, but one could exist in the outer layers for centuries before the other comes into being. An ascendant who won't ascend for a thousand years after you did could exist here for hundreds of years before you do."

"And you have no idea why it works that way?" Nym asked.

Eriam shrugged. "You know how everyone's ascendance is personal? Nobody's is quite the same. It's just a part of that. Even after millions of years of cumulative knowledge and experience, no one knows. Or, if someone does, they're not sharing. But I doubt it, personally."

Nym flopped down into the chair opposite Eriam. "How long have you been waiting to tell me that?" he asked.

"I don't keep track of years. They're meaningless here. Hundreds at least. Maybe more."

"Oh. Heh. And you can't tell me anything about when we first met?"

"Nope," Eriam smirked. "Sorry, your orders."

"Damn you, past or future me."

A book whipped off the shelf and landed in front of Nym. It scooted forward until it was practically in his lap. "What's this?"

"The spell you came here for."

Nym looked down at the book, then carefully slid it back into the center of the table. "What do you want for it? You'll forgive me if I'm not interested in owing you any favors."

"No, it's not like that. This is me repaying you. After all these years, I'm finally settling the debt I've been carrying."

"Something I'll do in my personal timeline's future but your timeline's past?"

"Makes your head hurt, right? I'll be glad to wipe the slate clean on this."

"Are you going to tell me what it is?" Nym asked.

"Look at me." Eriam's voice was suddenly a lot sterner. He'd been relaxed throughout the conversation, not really at all like Hozim had described him, but that was gone now. "You know where I come from. I've told you enough to guess *when* I come from. Take the book. Master the spell. And go do exactly what you're planning on doing already. And take my thanks for helping. I wouldn't exist without you."

Nym's breath caught. He wanted the spell to go help Analia. Eriam was obviously part of the family but from sometime in Nym's future. "Huh," he said, connecting the dots. "That's interesting."

"Isn't it?"

"Yeah. So . . . I guess I'll see you around."

"One way or another. Though, maybe not me as an immortal ascendant. You know, I don't really like what they're doing here. It reminds me too much of the politics nobles play. I guess it's better, since it doesn't usually lead to the deaths of other mortals. But still, now that you've arrived and I've discharged my last debt, I think I might disappear for a while."

"Where will you go?"

"I don't know." Eriam smiled. "Anywhere I want, I suppose. Any time I want. We all hoard those precious seconds on reality prime, but what worth are they if we only use them to check one another in our games? Are any of us really living a life worth living here? I wonder sometimes. Maybe you had the right idea."

"What idea is that?" Nym asked.

"Ah, but that would be telling, now wouldn't it?"

Nym gave Eriam a sour glare. "You just remember that I'll get you back for this when I meet you next time."

Eriam snorted. "I'm not afraid of you. You're a big softy. Now, off you go. You've got magic to learn and people to save. And I've got a domain to pack away and new adventures to have. What's the point of being an immortal demigod if you don't do anything?"

"Right? All these guys do is sit here contemplating the mysteries of the universe or whatever. Do any of them ever have fun?"

"No," Eriam said seriously. "They don't. Ever. It's so boring. Why do you think I hate it here?"

"But you stayed for centuries, waiting for me?"

"Someone taught me to take my debts seriously, back when I was young."

"Good lesson, that."

"It was," Eriam agreed.

"I think, in the future, once I've lived the part you remember, I would like to get together again."

"I'd like that too."

"I guess we'll see each other then," Nym said. "Not sure how, but I'll figure it out."

"Bring Cold Paw with you. I've missed him."

That brought Nym up short. Then he laughed and said, "Yeah, I'll see what I can do. A snow-wolf ascendant though? You think it's possible?"

"I think . . . I think that I believe in you."

CHAPTER SIXTY-ONE

The spell wasn't quite as good as the one he'd been under after he'd touched Niramyn's memory cube, but it did have the advantage of being usable by Nym. An ascendant might notice a presence in the mortal timeline if they knew where to look, but they wouldn't be able to tell who was there or what exactly they'd done. At least, that was the theory.

In practice, there were counterspells and divinations that might pierce the obfuscation, but it gave Nym enough assurances that he could finally right a problem he'd been wanting to address for a long time.

That was why he stood in the air, completely invisible, and looked down on the city of Shu-Ain. Somewhere below him was a young woman, by his count now fifteen years old and still laboring under a nasty set of geasa he'd detected subjective years ago. Today was the day those broke and she started healing.

Nym recognized now what had happened to Analia, what had driven her to join up with that vigilante group and fight. He wished he'd known back when he still could have fixed it instead of leaving her to suffer for years, but he couldn't take the risk of leading an ascendant to her.

It was dark now, well after midnight on a cool summer night. Analia wasn't asleep though. She was lying in her bed, tossing and turning, her mind fighting against the geasa that drove her. Even as Nym watched, she threw the blankets off and started pacing around her room. He guessed that wasn't an unusual behavior for her, given that the women she was sharing the room with didn't so much as roll over in their own beds.

She looked different now, her hair cut short and her eyes sunk into her skull. Gone was the sparkle that had once danced in their depths, replaced instead by dark bags hanging under them. Her lips were turned down into a permanent frown. Her body had a nervous tension to it, an almost feral energy that demanded she do something, anything.

One of the other women sat up and turned to her. "Can't sleep again?"

"No," Analia said shortly. "Too much on my mind."

"It's going to be a long day tomorrow. You need to rest."

"When I can. I'll go outside. Sorry to wake you."

The woman shrugged and went back to bed. Analia strode down the hall and out into a garden joined to the barracks she was staying in. Guards nodded to her as she went by but otherwise ignored her. She paced around the garden for several minutes, just doing laps around the outer wall.

There was a tree in the center, a nice tall thing that would be excellent for shade on a hot, lazy summer day. There was even a bench underneath it, flanked on either side by raised flower beds. Still invisible, Nym teleported himself down to sit on it and watched Analia go by. For the last hour, he'd been studying how the geasa were driving her behavior, what they were designed to do and how she'd managed to channel those demands into something constructive instead.

It was messy and dangerous and had driven her to near madness. For all his power, Nym wasn't sure if removing them would save her mind or break it. He didn't feel there was much of a choice though, not if she was going to live another year. Leaving them in place would destroy her.

He let the invisibility drop as she was walking by and said, "Hi."

Arcana flowed through her, instantly snapping into place to burst forth and bathe him in a wave of fire. Nym casually picked it apart with a few well-placed threads of his own arcana, and the flames sputtered out. "Wow, you're jumpy, aren't you?"

"Who— Nym?! You're alive!"

"So far," he said. "Been a rough . . . Well, I've lost track. Time works differently on the other side. Twenty years, maybe?"

"You're alive," she said again, her voice softer. "What happened to you?"

"I ascended," Nym said. "Didn't have a choice. The ascendants finally found me. I tried to find you to say goodbye, but . . ."

"Yeah. Cern was not happy with you, you know? You messed his whole scheme up. He actually moved back home about a year ago, went into business with that merchant family you connected him with."

"I'll make it up to him someday," Nym said. He flicked his fingers and gold coins flew through the air in every direction. A second gesture sent them all back into nothingness. "I'm sure he'll forgive me. But that's not why I'm here."

"So why are you here?"

"For you. I know what your father did to you, Analia."

Her legs went weak and went out from beneath her. A cushion of air caught her before she could collapse to the ground, and her chest jerked in a ragged sob. "I'm sorry," she choked out. "I tried to fight it. I didn't want to betray you, but I couldn't stop myself. I wasn't strong enough."

"It's okay. I know it wasn't your fault. I'm sorry I didn't see it back then. I should have. I would have, if I hadn't been so stupid."

"It was better once you were gone. I couldn't betray you then. You weren't there, so there was nothing to tell him. But the geasa kept pushing me to move, to do something, to hunt you down and find you, to stick to you so that I could tell him everything you said and did."

"Yeah, I figured it out later, why you were so pushy about me joining your group, why you were even here in the first place. It was an outlet for the urges, a way for you to cope. But it's getting worse now."

"I'm not going to last much longer," she said. "We've got a big job tomorrow, probably my last one."

"Because you're quitting?" Nym asked quietly. He already knew that wasn't the answer.

Analia looked away and didn't say anything.

"Because you're going to throw your life away for the cause," he said.

"I can't hold it back anymore."

Eriam had been right. Nym had done him a big favor, inadvertently. If his suspicions were right, without Nym interfering now, Eriam wasn't going to exist in the future. He just hadn't realized he'd been cutting it so close. It was kind of scary to think how little time he had before Analia died. He'd wasted so much of it just hiding away.

"I can break the geasa," Nym said.

Her head snapped up to look at him. He could practically see her thoughts on her face. The backlash from it would likely kill her, and if it didn't, it would still break her mind. It was too late to save her. She opened her mouth, but before she could speak, Nym cut her off.

"I am an ascendant, a real one now. You have some idea of what that means, right? It's . . . It's power like you can't even imagine. I don't even need to cast spells anymore if I don't want to. I can just push my will on reality and force it to obey. I can break the geasa and make you whole, if you trust me to do it."

"I . . . What about my friends here? They're relying on me. I can't just abandon them."

"No one is asking you to," Nym said. "I can leave a copy of you here to fulfill your obligations. If you want to step back in afterward, that's your choice. If you'd prefer them to think you died doing whatever it is you're doing, that can be arranged too."

Analia didn't say anything for a long time, and Nym let her think. He was putting a lot on her and not giving her a lot of time to process it. She needed to make choices in the next few hours that would determine whether she lived or died and, if she lived, what kind of life she wanted to lead. Anyone would need more than a few minutes to wrestle with that.

"I need to know that my friends will be alright if I'm not there," she said.

Nym created a copy of himself, only shaped to look exactly like Analia. "This is a part of me," he said. "He, or she I suppose, knows everything I know. I'll take the knowledge she needs to do whatever you're supposed to do tomorrow right out of your mind, and she'll do it. But she'll have all the power of an ascendant behind her. Not to be mean, but she'll be many, many times more effective than you could hope to be."

"You can do that?" Analia asked.

"For all practical purposes, here, in this world, I can do anything I want. Unless another ascendant shows up to oppose my will, I am basically a god."

That wasn't quite true, but it was close enough for the purposes of this discussion. He was still fallible, could still be surprised. If he got careless, it was possible for someone to kill his mortal avatar. That would only be an inconvenience. It wasn't like he couldn't make a new one, though the time he'd lose rebuilding it would be annoying. If it came down to it, he'd pick some dead time where nothing interesting was happening to grow a new avatar.

"This is insane," she said. "I . . . I don't want to die, but I can't live like this. I don't want my friends to die either. And there's all the people we'll save if we pull this off. There's a lot going on. If I'm not here to help, and . . . Can she really do this?"

"She can. I can. I will, if you trust me. I'm not going to force this on you, Analia. It has to be your choice."

"Maybe it would be easier if it wasn't."

"Maybe, but that's not how it works. I'm not that kind of person."

"Yeah, I know. You were always all about freedom. It's good to see that hasn't changed."

Analia sat down on the bench next to Nym and leaned her head on his shoulder. "I missed you, you know? I didn't know if you were dead or if you'd just abandoned me. The things the geas made me do to you, I don't think anyone would be surprised if you didn't want to see me again. Even now, it's telling me to latch on to you, forcing me to. It's going berserk because I'm not supposed to reveal it to you, ever, or to anyone else who doesn't already know about it. But you do know, so I can talk to you, but I'm not allowed to, and it's going around in circles."

"I'm sorry."

Now that he knew how, he could see the strands of magic wrapped around her mind, anchored in her spirit, and fed by her soul well. They were ugly, knotted things tangled so tightly around her that they were choking her to death. It was a slow death, full of pain and misery, and she was at the brink. He could still pull her back, but only if she would let him.

Eriam existed, and if Nym was right about his guesses, Analia would choose to live. Nym desperately hoped he was right. If she died from the geasa, he would kill her father. If she survived, he might still do it anyway. Jaspar Feldstal was an awful, sadistic person who in every way deserved death. The only thing that would spare him was Analia's decision not to kill him, but she couldn't make that decision unless she lived through the geasa.

They sat there together for hours, neither saying anything, until the sun started to brighten the sky. Finally, Nym shifted and said, "I'm sorry, but it's time to make a decision."

"Yeah. Can't put it off any longer. You promise everyone will be safe?"

"I promise."

She took a deep breath and nodded. "I want to live. Please help me."

CHAPTER SIXTY-TWO

In many ways, it would have been kinder to let Analia proceed with her suicidal combat plan. The amount of pain breaking the multiple geasa her father had laid on her was going to inflict was indescribable, and as much as he wanted to shield her from it, not even Nym had that kind of power. It was going to hurt, both physically and mentally.

Before they got to that, Nym needed to mold his copy to take her place. He took her back to one of his sanctums and opened a scrying window for her to see through. Together, they watched the copy, linked to Nym and Nym linked to Analia, take point on an assault against some sort of fortified manor a hundred miles outside the city.

There was a whole contingent of aerial mages leading the first strike, every one of them specialized in causing destruction. Under the fake Analia's direction, they rained fire and ice from the sky. Men and women swarmed out of the manor and returned fire, filling the air with brilliant flashes of light, hurricane-strength winds, and shimmering lances of solid ice. Earthen shields rose from the ground as whole groups of mages worked in concert to pull them up in seconds.

Analia's job was to break defenses and kill important enemy targets. She'd specialized in that over the last few years, and her repertoire was full of spells that focused on pinpoint accuracy and bypassing or outright ignoring defenses. When that wasn't possible, she had a full set of ward-countering spells, including one particularly nasty piece of work that was designed to overload the targeted ward with arcana and cause it to explode.

"This spell would work better if you could cast it from a distance," Nym said when Analia's copy used it to bust apart a thermal ward that was preventing the fire from spreading across the manor's roof. The copy had broken it apart, but the backlash caught her in the explosion, forcing her to drain her own strength defending from the explosion she'd set off.

"We couldn't ever figure out how to do it from more than ten feet away. The farther the magic has to travel, the weaker it gets. How is it that no one is noticing that's not me? Some of those spells you've used aren't even spells I know."

"I'm sure several of them have taken note, but the copy is channeling a spell that deflects attention away from her. Look there. See how that one mage is sniping at anyone flying? He hasn't even tried to take a shot at your copy."

"Oh, yeah." Analia peered into the scrying illusion he was projecting for her.

"She should look more tired. That much magic would wipe me out, not even counting the stuff you're doing to keep anyone from looking too closely at me."

"It won't be an issue. Your copy is actually casting five or six spells no one can see for each flashy explosion or ice spear anyway. A lot of enemy mages have found spells going wide at the last second. By my count, at least fourteen people on your team are only alive because of your interference, and that's not even considering how many enemy mages you've killed."

Analia didn't even bat an eye at the death toll. Once, it would have been a monumental decision she wrestled with, trying to find another way. Now, she accepted it, maybe even reveled in it. Killing wasn't a last resort for her; it was a preferred solution. Nym expected that mindset to cause her a lot of grief over the next day. He'd held off on breaking her mind until the battle was over so that she could witness what happened.

With her copy taking point, the casualties to her side were nonexistent, but the enemy mages were completely decimated. Within a few minutes, they'd been routed and abandoned their defense of the manor. Many of them flew off into the wilderness, and groups of three mages peeled off to chase them down.

"That seems like a bad strategy," Nym remarked. "You're losing three units for every one of theirs."

"It's not about battle tactics. Every one of them is a slaver. We don't want them surviving to regroup later and start up again in a new location. This is the fourth time we've crushed this cartel, and every time they break apart and the majority of them survive."

"Hmm."

Nym teleported the fleeing mages one at a time, always sending them backward into the arms of their pursuers. After the initial surprise, Analia's team captured or executed the fleeing mages there, then returned to the battle. She gave him a questioning glance.

"What?" he asked.

"How will they explain that?"

"I don't know. I'm not that worried about it. My only concern here is you and the fact that you're practically vibrating in place. You want to be out there, fighting for your life and dying for a worthy cause."

She didn't answer.

"I think that's enough of this," Nym said. "Your friends are safe. The battle is won. I've even disabled the teleportation platform the cartel was trying to use to evacuate. Your copy will make sure nothing goes wrong. It's time to focus on healing you."

"How bad will it be?" she asked, fear in her voice.

"Bad, but I won't let you die. You're going to need time to recover, days at least, probably weeks. And then you'll have a lot of mental scars that you'll carry with you for the rest of your life. Things are never going to be like they were before."

"I know. I'm scared, but . . . I trust you."

Nym pulled her into a hug and said, "It's okay to be scared. I'm sorry this happened to you. I'm sorry I didn't see it before it got this bad."

"It's not your fault. It's . . . I couldn't believe he would do that to me, at first. Who would do something like this to a stranger, let alone to their own child?"

"When you're better, you can decide what you want to do about that. There's no hurry. Now, come on, let's get you comfortable, and then I'm going to put you to sleep. When you wake back up, the hard part will be over."

A bed appeared for Analia. Once she was lying down and comfortable, Nym dismissed the scrying illusion and cast a spell to put her to sleep. Her eyes closed immediately, and Nym got to work. The bed disappeared, leaving her on a cushion of air that took up just enough space to hold her and also served to keep her from moving around. Hopefully the illusion of normalcy gave her some comfort in her last few moments of consciousness.

There were three geasa tied to Analia, all tangled around one another. The first was simple enough. It demanded that she stay as close to Nym as possible and that, when she wasn't near him, she attempted to correct that. It had driven her practically insane, and she'd fought that compulsion by developing violent habits that drove her to exhaustion, then forced her to start moving again as soon as she could.

The second geas was tied closely to the first, and it called for her to tell her father everything she learned about Nym. This one was subtler and in some ways easier to resist. It didn't force her to seek Jaspar Feldstal out, but she did need to make some attempt to communicate with him. She'd been sending regular letters every month saying that Nym was gone once he'd disappeared as a way to deal with the compulsion. The geas didn't exactly punish her for not having new information, but it was a burr in her brain, a constant agitating force that twinged every time she sent another letter saying the same thing. It must have been a maddening distraction.

The third geas was both the easiest and the hardest to deal with. It was a simple command not to tell anyone that she was under a geas, to actively hide and protect that secret. As long as no one suspected anything, the geas didn't do anything but compel her not to tell anyone. That was easy enough to comply with but also a sort of soft torture, being trapped inside her own head and not able to ask for help when she'd desperately wanted to.

Even if Nym had figured it out years ago, he didn't think she would have been able to tell him the truth. Only someone who *knew* about the geas was allowed to talk to her about it, which Lord Feldstal had no doubt meant to be only himself. Nym could have confronted her with suspicions, and she would have been forced to deny them. By coming to her not as her friend, but as an ascendant, a being of godlike proportions, and telling her that he knew, not guessed but knew, she'd accepted it.

The first two geasa were wound tightly around each other, each reinforcing the other and strangling her free will. The final geas wrapped it all up into a neat little package that protected itself. He would need to break that one first, but before he did, her soul well needed to be shielded against the backlash. Snapping the connection would flood her with all the arcana it had leached out of her and leave her vulnerable to more damage as the other two geasa continued to function.

Analia had never reached the third layer and started the process of converting her body into a soul well. Coincidentally, that helped protect against arcana poisoning, up to a point, and it would have helped here too. He couldn't do it for her, or rather wouldn't. Instead, he opened up a conduit between the two of them and built an artificial partition around where the three geasa connected. Any backlash would pass through her and into him, where he would deal with the damage.

Then would come the hard part: holding Analia together through the physical pain that would come with reversing the damage the geasa had done to her brain. If there was any point where she might die just from the shock, it was there. Ironically, the other two geasa would help at this point, but there would be scars. When he removed the final geas, things would be at their worst.

And then they'd find out how much was left of Analia beneath the layer of compulsions that had taken over her life and how much could be rebuilt. Nym was confident he could heal the physical damage the geasa had done to her mind, but the rest would take time and effort and care.

He'd spent a great deal of time thinking about this procedure, how best to perform it with a focus on her survival and limiting the damage to her mind. He could fix her brain, could even fix any damage to the soul well with a bit of time. It was her way of thinking, her personality, that he wasn't sure about.

She would live through the breaking of the geasa. Whether she would still be Analia was still in question. There were going to be changes, and all he could do was give her the time and care she needed to reconcile those. Hopefully that would be enough.

Heart heavy with worry, Nym started the delicate process of detaching the first geas from her soul well and unraveling it from around her mind. It had put down deep roots, but one at a time, he gently pried them loose. His patient whimpered in her sleep and tried to thrash, but the cocoon of air held her still and safe. His magic rejuvenated her body even as it worked on her mind.

And slowly, one painful spot at a time, he broke her free from the spells tormenting her.

CHAPTER SIXTY-THREE

Analia stayed in Nym's sanctuary for a week. When he'd finished his work and allowed her to wake up, she was as physically healthy as she'd ever been, more so than when he'd started even. Analia had run her body into the ground repeatedly for years and done very little to protect it. Nym's magic had repaired a lot of damage.

Her mind was another story. She spent a lot of her time staring at a wall, so much so that Nym created little scrying portals that opened up over breathtaking landscapes all over the world for her to see. He didn't know if it helped, but she seemed to appreciate it.

She also spent a lot of time silently crying. Tears ran down her face, unheeded, to drip off her chin. For that, the only thing he could do was sit next to her in silence and hold her hand. He gave her that time, as much as he could, and did his best to be a comforting presence.

That wasn't to say Nym did nothing while he sat there. With Analia's copy leading the way to victory over the cartel they'd been fighting, her vigilante mages did some celebrating of their own, and Nym took that time to start distancing her from the friends she'd made. Maybe she would want to return to that life when she was better, and if so, Nym wanted to leave her a way back to it.

But he hoped she would choose something besides endless violence and being exposed to some of the worst behaviors humanity had to offer. That kind of life took its toll on people who weren't cursed with magic driving their behaviors and impulses. He didn't think it was a good place for her to recover for however many months or years it took.

On the second day, Analia started eating again. Nym took that as a good sign, but he didn't push. One part of him stayed with her while other copies of him went out and handled other matters. He found and confirmed the Earth Shapers were alive and well, checked up on Ciana and left her another purse of gold with plans to stop in and actually speak to her later, and finally, after many, many days of searching, found the snow-wolf pack he'd met in his travels. Nym promptly added a visit to Cold Paw to his agenda.

It wasn't until the third day that she finally spoke. It was just a simple question. "Where is this?" she asked, her voice a cracked and dry whisper.

The scry panned across a lush tropical island with a brilliant lagoon in it. It was only a mile or so across, somewhere deep in the ocean thousands of miles west of

Shu-Ain. Nym had discovered it randomly while searching for places to build his first sanctum but dismissed it due to the amount of wildlife living there.

"Somewhere in the west ocean," he said. "I doubt any human has ever set foot on it."

"It's beautiful," she said.

"Do you want to visit?"

Her lips curled up slightly, but she shook her head. "It's enough just to see it."

"Okay. If you change your mind, we can go."

Her hand tightened on his. "Thank you."

The old Nym might have chafed at sitting still and doing nothing for so long, but he'd learned a great deal of patience in the years he'd been gone. Perhaps it was the merging of his fourth-layer echo that had really solidified it as part of who he was, but regardless of how it happened, he was happy to wait with her for as long as it took.

By the end of the week, she was walking around and talking to him. They discussed some of the places he'd shown her, and he caught her up on what the vigilantes had been doing and how he'd extracted her from their group by saying she had to take care of some personal business.

"You can go back to them if you want," he said.

"But you think I shouldn't."

"No. Not right away at least. You're recovering from an almost fatal curse. I don't think there are more than five or six mortals in the world who could have kept you from dying. You need to take it easy, to take some time for yourself."

"Nym, don't take this the wrong way. You are crazy talented in so many ways, but you are terrible at what you're trying to do right now. Thank you for helping me. I will never be able to express how grateful I am for that. But I'm ready to take control of my life again. I need to take control."

"And you're going to do that by going back to fighting for it?"

Analia shook her head. "No. It's good work, and it should be done. But . . . I think I need to step back and let someone else do it. If I do keep helping them, I'll have to do some other kind of work, something that's not fighting. Maybe some information gathering. But I need to do something else first."

"Do you know what?" Nym asked.

"Not yet."

"And . . . your father?"

Raw, naked hatred flashed across her face. "I'll take care of him myself."

"Alright." Nym paused and thought about it. "How can I help? I'll take you anywhere you want to go and give you enough money to live for a year. If you want some wards or rune sequences to keep anyone from finding you, I can do that too. Do . . . Do you want me to show you how to forge a conduit to the third layer?"

"Can you do that?" Analia asked, surprised.

"Yes, if you want me to. If you would rather do it on your own, that's fine too."

Nym still remembered Ferro taking control of his conduit and threading it through the Astral Sea. It hadn't been so much an unpleasant experience as somewhat violating, and it had stolen what should have been a moment of triumph, the reward for all his hard work snatched away at the last second. He wouldn't force that on her.

"I'll think about that. I'm not against the idea, but I have to figure out what I want to do first."

"Should I give you some privacy?"

"Please."

For the rest of that day, Nym left her to her own devices while he finished extracting the copy he'd shaped like Analia from the camp. There were a few good-byes and well-wishes, and once she was free of them, the copy simply returned to him. It had been a lot of extra work to keep this one going, since it was only semi-autonomous. Being connected to Analia had required a degree of direct control he was glad his normal copies didn't need.

While she took some time to herself, Nym made a new copy and sent it out to visit some old friends.

Not only were all four Earth Shapers alive and prospering, but it looked like they'd added a fifth member to their crew. Nym didn't recognize the woman, but it was easy to tell she was working with them on a permanent basis. They'd finally gotten back to that job of building the border keep they were talking about when he'd first met them, and they'd done well enough for themselves down south that they'd acquired three wagons. The woman's name was Kazie, and it seemed like she and Nomick were together, just based on the brief time he'd spent studying them when he'd found them with his scrying.

Conjured food was fine in a pinch, but it didn't satisfy quite the same way real food did, so Nym made a quick detour before he showed up at dinnertime. The five earth mages were sitting at an outdoor table near a mess hall that had been set up for the construction crews, eating and discussing work. Nym appeared at the end of the table, sitting on a chair that hadn't been there before, with a small basket of desserts on the table in front of him.

"Ack!" Monick, who was closest to him, cried out. The earth mage threw himself backward and toppled out of his chair.

"Hi," Nym said. "How's it going, guys?"

"Nym! You're . . . You're alive," Bildar said. He eyed up the basket. "Damn, it's good to see you again. And it looks like nothing's changed."

"Some things have, but some things were worth keeping the same." Nym patted the basket and scooted it closer to the center of the table.

"Amen to that!" Nomick said, scooping it up. "Oooh, only one custard. Well, good thing I got to it fir— Hey! Give that back!"

Bildar swiped the basket, located the custard, and claimed it. "Welcome back, Nym," he said with a grin as he took a bite.

"Oh, honestly, boys," Ophelia said. "Is no one even going to ask how Nym's doing?"

"He's doing fine," Bildar said around a mouthful of custard. "Look at him. If he wasn't fine, he'd say. You're fine, right?"

"Mostly," Nym said. "Still a lot going on, a lot to do, but I had something pressing to take care of. It was kind of time sensitive."

"Um, I don't mean to cut in here, but should I leave?" Kazie asked. "Give you some time to catch up with your friend."

"No, no. That's not necessary," Nym told her. "I'm Nym. Nice to meet you. You're Kazie. You've been with the Earth Shapers for about four months now, mostly because of Nomick."

"I . . . Yes. How do you know that?"

"Magic!"

"Nym, it's not that we're not happy to see you, but what are you doing here?"

Nym's smile slipped off his face, and he sighed. "I should have come earlier, but I had to figure out how to make sure no one would find out I'd slipped away. You would not believe the ways those people have of keeping tabs on you. I didn't want to lead anyone your way. But then I couldn't delay any longer, not without letting Analia die."

The mood dropped around the table, with everyone sobering up, though Kazie looked confused. "What happened to her?" Bildar asked.

"I figured out what was wrong with her. That father of hers put a geas on her. Three of them, actually. For years, she's been fighting them."

"Oh God, that's . . . What kind of person . . ."

Nym glanced over at Ophelia. "Yeah, it was a mess. But that's why . . . All the everything, you know? The arguments. The fighting she was doing. He wanted her spying on me at all times and reporting back to him, and no one was supposed to ever know about the geasa. I broke them, but that's a lot of damage to recover from. She's barely spoken for the last week."

"You should bring her here," Bildar said immediately. "She can stay with us. It'll do her good to be around friends who love her. We'll take care of her."

"I will offer her that option, but it will be her decision. I just wanted to talk to you first. You guys are like family to me, and hey, I even got a new sister-in-law, but the level of care she's going to need isn't something you just dump on someone without any warning. And I can't stick around forever. There's still . . . everything . . . It's not dealt with, and the longer I stay here, the more likely it is someone figures it out just by accident."

"Bring her here," Ophelia said, her voice firm. "Even if it's just for an afternoon visit. She doesn't have to stay, but we'd like to see her too."

Back in Nym's sanctuary, the copy he'd left there knocked on the door of the bedroom he'd given Analia. "I'm talking to the Earth Shapers right now," he said. "They'd like to see you. Do you feel up to visiting them?"

"I'll come. One moment."

Analia opened the door, and Nym offered his hand. The instant she took it, she appeared next to his body sitting at the table. The sudden change in light caused her to squint, and when she looked around and saw her friends, she started crying.

"Hi, guys," she said. That was all she got out before she was buried in hugs.

CHAPTER SIXTY-FOUR

Nym sat at the table with Kazie while Analia fended off the Earth Shapers' combined affection. "So, do you like this kind of work?" he asked.

"It's alright. I don't have the passion for it that Nomick does, but I'm capable, and it lets me contribute. How about you?"

"I did it for a little while, but earth magic was never my specialty. Sort of the opposite, actually. I started as an air mage."

"Oh yeah? My first element was water."

"That's a good one too. Lots of utility out on the coast."

"That's where I was when I met Nomick. That smooth talker charmed me right out of my job, and I don't even think he was trying to."

"Heh. Good for him though. You seem like a nice person."

"I like to think so." Kazie leaned forward. "I hope you won't think me too rude for asking this, but who are you? Obviously you know Nomick and the others, but they've never said a word about you."

"Smart of them. I am . . . How to put this . . . There are some people who are interested in me, in knowing where I am and what I'm doing, and who my friends are. Not mentioning me is a good way for them to not get caught up in my problems."

It was clear Kazie didn't really believe him, and he didn't blame her. He didn't look like much, just an eighteen-year-old kid with a basketful of sugary treats who'd popped up out of nowhere. That didn't stop her from saying, "If it's that dangerous to be around you, if your mere presence puts everyone around you at risk, then tell me this. Why are you here?"

"Because I need their help," Nym said simply. "Because she needs their help. Because I'm insensitive and oblivious and didn't realize what had happened until it was far, far too late. I've done everything I can to help her, but what she needs now is friends and family, people she trusts."

He was using *family* loosely there, since he wouldn't trust her brother with her care, and he was still actively considering murdering her father. Idly, he wondered if Hozim would be upset about him disrupting the Collective again, and so soon after he'd gone out of his way to get them back on the right track with Analia's grandfather.

"So you'd risk their lives because you need something from them," Kazie said. "I can't imagine why they're excited to see you. Do they not know?"

"They know. I don't think they understand the full extent of the risk, but . . . they know. I spent years trying to figure out a safe way to contact them. At this point, I've got so much magic hiding me that unless someone who knows me by sight happens to walk by, I'm safe. No divination or scrying should be able to track me."

"You're sure of that?"

"As sure as I can be," he said.

Kazie leaned back and crossed her arms. "No offense, but if you bring half as much trouble with you as you seem to think, maybe it's best to keep this visit short and not come back."

That stung but mostly because Nym knew it was true. According to everything he knew, he should be safe. But there were so many ascendants, all stronger than him, and he couldn't honestly say he knew what they were capable of. Eriam's assurances that he had the spell he needed was the basis for Nym's confidence, but then, that only really extended as far as helping Analia.

It might be best to cut short his little vacation. As much as he still wanted to visit Ciana and Cold Paw, it could be better for them if he didn't. He'd considered tracking Risa down, though he had to admit that in that case, their relationship had been far too new to withstand him disappearing for years. That conversation would be more of an apology than an attempt to rekindle anything.

"You might be right," he said. "I won't be staying long, either way. Excuse me, would you?"

Without waiting for an answer, Nym teleported the fifteen feet or so over to where his friends were sitting in a circle on the grass. "Hey, guys, I need to go soon. It was really good seeing you all again, but the longer I stay here, the more of a risk it is for you all. Analia, I'm sorry for pushing this decision on you, but I need to know if you're going to stay here or go somewhere else."

"Stay," Ophelia said immediately. "You should be with us right now."

"Stay," the others echoed, one after another.

Analia looked around the circle and huffed out a laugh. "I think I'm staying," she said.

"Alright. Let me just help ease that transition."

Gold crests appeared out of thin air and piled up into a neat stack twenty high in front of Analia. Next to them was an earring made out of obsidian with veins of white gold in it. On the other side of the gold was a small hair pin, jade with ivory filigree. Nym pointed to the gold and said, "That should be more than enough to live off of for a little bit." His finger moved to the earring, and he added, "As an emergency defense, if you channel arcana into this, it will teleport you to a location you've set ahead of time. It's vulnerable to teleportation wards, and it can't bring anyone else with you."

Her eyes wide, Analia picked the earring up and fastened it to her ear. Then she held up the hair pin and gave him a questioning look. "Only once, this will protect your mind from being ensnared by a geas," he explained. "I hope you are never in a situation where you need it. But I wanted you to have some peace of mind to know that you have a defense."

He was already stretching the limits of mortal magic in making those trinkets for her. If he made them any stronger, it would be like handing her a sign for other ascendants to see, a bright, shining sign that would draw their attention. He could perhaps make one more small thing, but anything else he could do that was small enough not to be noticed was also magic that was well within her capabilities to do on her own.

Instead, he conjured up a small book, barely bigger than his hand and only twenty pages long. He held it out to her. "If you ever decide you need some help reaching the third layer, give this a read."

Monick let out a low whistle. "I didn't know you were bringing party favors."

Nym considered that for a second and shrugged. A few small things wouldn't be all that noticeable, and it was only a minor effort of will to force the trinkets into reality. With a thought, a diamond-tipped etcher appeared in front of Ophelia. "Enchanted to carve into any surface, and I do mean any surface. I trust you won't misuse it on anything that's still alive."

For Monick, he created an automatic mortar and pestle. Some materials used by alchemists were notoriously difficult to break down and could take hours upon hours of work. "Watch your fingers when you use this," Nym warned. "It will grind up anything without you having to do any of the work. Anything. Even stone or steel."

Bildar received a simple leather bag, but its inside held five times as much space as it should. "I couldn't even tell you how much this is worth if you decide to sell it but be careful who you let know about it."

And for Nomick, a pair of rings made of braided gold and silver, with a carbuncle set into one and a sapphire into the other. "Messaging rings," Nym said. "For you and your special friend. They've got a range of about twenty miles, which I would not advertise if I was you, since it takes a pinnacle spell to duplicate that."

"You don't have to do this. These are too much," Ophelia said, only to be shushed by Bildar and Monick. Nomick just sat there, stunned, and stared at the matched rings.

"It's fine," Nym assured them. "Not to brag, but I'm kind of a magical power-house now. My only real concern is that these are valuable, too valuable for anyone who's not at least a third-circle mage. Be discreet with them, please. It would break my heart to find out any of you came to a bad end because someone decided they wanted the gifts I gave you."

"We'll be careful," Ophelia promised. "Uh, when you say this can write on anything . . ."

"Stone. Wood. Gems. Metal. Flesh. Anything."

Ophelia paled when he said *flesh*, and she nodded. "I'll be responsible with it."

As much as he wanted to stay longer, Nym needed to go. The core reality wasn't his world anymore. His body wasn't even real. It was just a construction of arcana that walked and talked and aged, a sad little meat puppet that held a fraction of his existence because that was all it could stand to take before it burst.

These connections, these people, they were important to the old Nym. But now, as he watched them with their jaws hanging open as he casually handed out trinkets that took him mere seconds to conjure up, he could only feel out of place. He'd understood that there was a difference between him and the humans who had been his friends, but this really drove it home.

They couldn't understand his existence, not unless they ascended themselves. None of them but Analia had even the slightest chance. And that gap was only going to grow wider. He was going to return to the outer layers, and years would go by, decades even. Maybe he'd return to this moment someday, maybe not.

It was another reason to make him hesitate to see Ciana. He didn't want to feel that disconnected from her, even if it was true. His visit to the Earth Shapers drove that point home. He didn't belong here anymore. Helping Analia had been something he'd thought about for years, and now that he'd done his part, it was up to her to heal with the people who were like her.

And it was up to him to return to where he'd come from, to people who could understand even the smallest fraction of what he was now. Trying to talk to them about magic was like holding a conversation with toddlers. They could understand the words, but they didn't get the meaning behind them.

"It's time," he said sadly. "It was good to see you all again. I don't know if I'll ever be back."

"Why not?"

Nym stopped and looked over at Analia. "Why not?" he repeated. He wasn't even sure how to begin explaining everything to her.

"So you're a full ascendant now, so what? Does that mean you can't have friends? Just because we can't do the things you can do doesn't mean we don't enjoy your company. It doesn't mean you can't enjoy ours."

"I . . . Maybe. There's more to it than that. It's . . . I can't really live here anymore. The world is too small for me. I can visit, sometimes."

"So visit then. Don't disappear forever."

Nym smiled. "Okay. I'll do my best. I really do need to go now. Goodbye, everyone."

Nym pulled back from reality prime and let his being snap back into place in the sixth layer. It had been good to take care of that piece of business, good to see some of his friends again. He wanted to see the rest of them, but there was more work to do.

He was worried that there would always be more work to do, that it would never end. What kind of existence would eternity be if he never took time for anything but work?

CHAPTER SIXTY-FIVE

From what Nym understood, advancing to the next layer after ascending wasn't a simple matter of finding a fun new way to manipulate a conduit so that it was stronger or more flexible. What exactly he did need to do was still up for debate. That was the kind of information no one seemed to want to trade for. Perhaps they didn't want company on whatever layer they'd gotten stuck on or didn't want to see anyone surpass them.

He knew he couldn't dodge Niramyn forever, but he'd hoped that when he was finally forced to see his progenitor again, he'd be a bit closer in power. That didn't seem likely to happen, not unless he became a hermit for hundreds or thousands of years. If he'd thought he could do it without going insane, he would have seriously considered it. The ascendants could fight among themselves, kill one another off or whatever, and he'd just let it pass him by.

That would be nice.

"Someone is asking around about you," Hozim told him.

"Me? Why?" Nym asked, as if he didn't already know the answer. There weren't that many possibilities.

"She didn't say."

"Well, who is she?"

"Her name is Valicin. She's one of Niramyn's group."

Nym had no idea who that was. Unless . . . "Tall, skinny? Kind of a lot of blonde hair? Like it's a dominant feature?"

"That's her," Hozim confirmed.

"Huh. Yeah, I don't want to talk to her."

"That's bad news for you because she is quite aggressive about finding you."

At least he knew now who'd knocked him back down to the inner layers after Niramyn's sanctuary had vanished. If he had to pick between the two factions, he figured he was marginally safer on Niramyn's side, but only marginally. Nym had no interest whatsoever in working for his father, wasn't even really all that sure that he wouldn't be killed out of hand if they happened to cross paths.

Or maybe not killed, but whatever ascendants did to each other. He was still trying to figure out exactly how that worked, other than that it involved cutting anchors loose and limiting their access to the core reality. Nym wasn't entirely sure if this was a permanent thing that cost them time, or if they could repair it and get those lost days or months back. That was another one of those topics that it was hard to get a straight answer on.

If he could have found Eriam again, Nym would have taken his questions there. He was sure the man would be far more helpful than anyone else he'd talked to. Unfortunately, Eriam had been dead serious about being sick of ascendants and disappearing once he'd discharged his final obligation. Nobody knew where Eriam was; nobody knew how to contact him.

"How aggressive?" Nym asked.

"Uh, very. Very. She offered to forgive quite a bit of my own debt if I could help her find you. Practically all of it, really."

"And you of course turned her down."

"Wellllll . . ."

"Oh, you bastard."

Right on cue, he felt a ripple in reality, and the woman, Valicin, appeared next to Hozim. "Nym, there you are. Perfect. You have no idea how hard I've been trying to find you."

"And yet I assume you know exactly how hard I've been trying to avoid being found. So with that said . . ." Nym tried to vanish, only to find reality resisting his will. He remained firmly anchored in the lecture hall Hozim had conjured up for the meeting.

"Sorry, but we need to have a talk."

"I really don't have anything to say to you."

"That is unfortunate because you're not leaving," Valicin said.

Nym could try to fight his way out, but even if Hozim stood aside, he doubted he was going to beat another ascendant when he barely had a handful of spells at his disposal and she'd already proven her will was stronger than his. He could play along and try to fish for information, but he suspected all she was doing was fetching him for her master.

Or he could activate his escape tactic, which had its own drawbacks. It would be better to find a way to outfight or outrun her, or to escape the range of whatever she was locking him down with. He pushed against it again, trying to figure out if there was a weakness he could exploit. Maybe if he got her distracted, she'd slip up. Relying on an opponent to make a mistake as his only strategy wasn't great, but he didn't think he was going to escape otherwise.

"What do you want?" he asked.

"I want you to come with me."

Nym glanced over at Hozim, who at least had the decency to look embarrassed. "Nothing to say to that?"

"Sorry, Nym. This is between you and her. My job was only to let her know where and when the next meeting was. And with that, I no longer owe anything, so I'll bid you both farewell."

Hozim disappeared without another word, leaving Nym alone with his would-be kidnapper. He looked her over and said, "You're the woman who showed up when I was stranded between layers."

"At our master's orders, I assure you. I have no interest in you personally."

"I wouldn't say *our* master or that it makes me feel any better than you're just doing your job. What does *your* master want? This whole situation is well past the point where I could be of any use to him."

He at least got the pleasure of watching Valicin's face twist into a ferocious scowl, and she said in a tight, clipped tone, "It is not my place to question him. It is only my place to execute his will. Now, you will be coming with me."

"I don't think that I will," Nym said. "I don't think you can make me."

Everything around him locked down all at once. He couldn't see, or hear, or smell. Reality vanished, for all intents and purposes, and he found himself in a void with no arcana at all. He took a few seconds to confirm he was well and truly trapped, then nodded to himself.

He hadn't expected her to make a mistake that he could exploit, and she hadn't. She'd overpowered him quite easily, and he was thoroughly stuck. There really was only one thing left to do if he wanted to avoid a face-to-face with Niramyn.

The copy stopped concentrating on holding himself together, and he was quickly reduced to a mass of raw, featureless arcana. His last thought before he returned to nothingness was that he hoped the real Nym had gotten enough from the scry link to know what had happened to him.

"Not good. Kind of expected it to happen, but still, not good."

Nym had known Niramyn's minion was looking for him prior to his meeting, had in fact known prior to his last six meetings, and had been sending out copies for everything. His paranoia had been fully vindicated, and even though he'd missed the end of the conversation once Valicin started acting directly against his copy to prevent escape or summoning help, he could guess what she'd had to say easily enough.

That was going to complicate things if Niramyn and his crew knew that he had fully ascended. He'd suspected they'd known, perhaps had always known, but now he was certain. In a way, he'd gotten lucky meeting Baracia when he did. He didn't think she would have hesitated to turn on him for the right price either, but Niramyn hadn't been offering it back then.

His introduction to ascendant society could have gone much worse, but he'd have to be far, far more careful about his interactions with other ascendants in the future. The ongoing war between Niramyn and Myzalik had claimed even more ascendants, but the fear of utter annihilation had spurred more of the neutral ascendants to join Niramyn's side.

From what he'd heard, his progenitor had almost regained all his lost power now too. No doubt as soon as Niramyn was back to full strength, the fighting would change from skirmishes in the dark to all-out bloody warfare. If Nym got lucky, everyone who was involved would kill one another, leaving him and the rest of the ascendants who wanted nothing to do with the fight alone.

On the off chance that he wasn't that lucky, he needed to prepare himself to survive the coming storm.

Niramyn was in an excellent mood. It had been a long, rough road, but he'd made it back to pinnacle in record time. It had taken him a thousand years to reach the twelfth layer the first time, not that there was anyone around who remembered that now, at least not in this seed. If he diverged far enough from the primary timeline, he might find one or two of the eldest ascendants had survived there, but they knew their place: hiding far, far away from him.

Things were going well. Myzalik killed a few of his disposable pawns using that strange new magic of his, and for every one lost, a dozen more ran to his side to support him against the devil who was upsetting the status quo. No one wanted to lose eternity, and he was the rallying point of resistance to that fate.

Now, if he could just figure out how Myzalik did it, things would be perfect. No one could ever know that he knew that spell though, lest he become the new devil to be expunged from their ranks. He needed someone else to handle that part for him, someone who could be conveniently disposed of afterward.

Once that last little piece fell into place, he could end this farce of a war. Even better, he could finally remove that thorn in his side that he'd long since given up on. Myzalik's mastery of time magic had made it impossible to dispatch the other Exarch. Every time Niramyn tried, his rival just came back. For centuries now, he'd had to content himself with opposing every plan he could, of gloating at each and every victory.

That last gloat would be glorious, and he was so close, he could taste it.

An ascendant appeared in his receiving hall, the one he'd sent to reacquire the by-product after she'd fumbled his rescue and lost him in the inner layers of reality, of all places. Seeing as how she still didn't have the boy, he could only assume she'd failed. Again.

"My master," she said as he allowed her to pass through the receiving hall and directly into his presence.

"You don't seem to have succeeded in the task I set you to," he said.

She flinched, though his tone had been mild. "No, Exarch. I managed to track him to an associate, but he sent a mere copy of himself to the meeting. I was able to partially trace a scry link back to the source, but it cut before I got all the way. I . . . know that it's possible to trace the link after it's been severed, but it is beyond my ability."

"So you came running back to get help covering your own inadequacies," Niramyn said, his voice flat.

"Yes, master."

He considered punishing Valicin for her failure, but in truth, she'd made the right call. It was more important that the boy was recovered than that she be the one to do it. She'd found a lead, capitalized on it, and once she'd realized she would need help to follow it to its source, she'd promptly returned to request that help.

There was hope for her yet, if only she'd get over that stubborn insistence that she could push through the Heart of the Stars using nothing but a conduit shell. It didn't work that way, but she seemed to have run out of ideas. Perhaps he'd reward her with a hint or two once she returned with the boy.

"Very well. I'll send Ferro to you, and you will show him the connection so that he can retrieve the boy."

"Thank you, Exarch."

Niramyn waved her off with a flick of his fingers and went back to contemplating the secrets of Myzalik's new immortal-killing spell. He understood what it did, of course he did! He'd experienced it firsthand, and as far as he knew, he was the only one to survive it. But the specifics of how it did that were still a mystery, one he meant to solve.

CHAPTER SIXTY-SIX

Nym promptly abandoned the sanctuary he'd constructed for himself. He also abandoned the front he'd built, a sort of decoy sanctuary that he gave out as the place to go in order to see him. The copy that manned that returned to him, as well as all his other copies. Nym washed his hands of everything he'd begun to build in ascendant society and disappeared deep into the empty void that was the sixth layer.

Empty wasn't really the right word for it. There was plenty of arcana there, but it wasn't a physical thing, and it was still hard to adjust to the idea of looping arcana currents replacing an actual landscape. Considering how many ascendants wove their portions of the shared reality into grand vistas or improbably luxurious palaces, Nym thought that was probably a common sentiment.

There was nothing to gather up or store away in either location. In the sixth layer, matter was more a manifestation of will than something that existed on its own. Anything he wanted to reproduce, he could. Anything he took with him might be a liability in the end. Besides, he'd built his own sanctuary from nothing once already. He could do it again.

"But still," he said to himself, "here I am, running away from my problems again. Some things never change."

Then again, fleeing from problems that could crush him without any noticeable effort was always a winning strategy for him. He was hard-pressed to think of a time it had backfired on him but could easily think of a few instances where being stubborn and sticking around had caused him problems.

"Oh, right, the abduction squad. Couldn't outrun that one."

But then again, he couldn't have defeated them either, so running had still been the best option. He just hadn't been prepared enough, and they'd gotten the drop on him, which he'd learned from and was taking appropriate actions right now, before new enemies tracked him down.

Hidden presence was going at all times, and anything he did in the inner layers got an obscure-timeline spell thrown on it, not that he'd done much there since he'd visited his mortal friends. Idly, he wondered how that was coming along. He could scry out their futures if he wanted; the years were well within the range of his own temporal anchors, but he had some security concerns about the scry being traced back to him from the other end.

Truthfully, it probably hadn't been a good move to save Analia, from a selfish perspective. He'd left himself vulnerable to retaliation, but abandoning his base of operations and scrubbing any lingering trace of his presence should solve that issue.

Both his decoy sanctuary and his true one collapsed into nothingness, the process sped up not just by withdrawing his will from the construct, but by actively working to assist the natural entropy of the sixth layer that tried to return everything to arcana. Once they were both gone, Nym willed himself away to random locations several times. It cost him little enough to do, and it would help slow down anyone who might be following after him if they had to figure out each destination he willed himself to in order to follow the chain.

After a few hours of random travel, he settled on an unremarkable location and began constructing his new home. By necessity, he started small so that he could rebuild his defenses as quickly as possible. The sanctuary was little more than a bare box fortified with every ward, obfuscation, and active defense he could think to layer on it.

In the interest of keeping it as secure as possible, it had no scrying port and no exit. He literally sealed himself inside it, in essence creating his own tomb. Safely ensconced in a shell formed of his own magic, Nym finally allowed himself a chance to relax. If anything approached, his magic would tell him, but as long as hidden presence held, it should be impossible for anything to detect him. Theoretically, the only way to find his sanctum was to physically bump into it while traveling through null space.

Nym wasn't content to rely on invisibility and nothing but an early warning that something had crossed his wards to protect him. As soon as he'd recovered, he set to work creating something new. The main problem with wards was that other than the part actively scanning for a trigger, they were dormant. That was great under normal circumstances, when mages were trying to save arcana. A ward running at full strength would run itself dry so often that it was almost useless. A ward that only came to life when it was needed could last for years without maintenance.

But he wanted to see through his wards, and scrying out from his sanctum introduced a vulnerability he was not willing to deal with. If he could make the wards themselves function as a sort of local-area scry, he figured he could get sensory feedback on anything that came close enough. That way, he didn't need to worry about someone sneaking something over the ward line that he hadn't thought to include in the trigger conditions.

That meant they were going to take considerably more arcana than standard wards to keep powered, since they would never go dormant. Nym didn't love that idea, but considering he wasn't planning on moving anytime in the near future, he would be there to provide a constant source of arcana. He didn't need to sleep, or eat, or use the facilities, so there would never be a time he had to step away and risk something sneaking up on him.

The other problem was something that was unique to ascendants. He could see wards that were currently active, which meant that every other ascendant could see them too. If his wards were always on, it would defeat the purpose of hiding. Any ascendant that happened to come by would immediately see that the wards existed and naturally assume that since there was no reason to ward empty space, that there must be something in the middle of those wards.

Nym spent a few days tinkering with the ward scheme before he figured out a solution. It was a hybrid of hidden presence and an upscaled version of camouflage mixed together into the rune sequences that formed the wards. Functionally, they were still visible, but with hidden presence keeping ascendants from noticing them from afar and camouflage blending them into the eddies and swirls of background arcana, he thought he'd achieved his goal.

The problem then became arcana intensity. Powering normal wards was trivially easy. Powering his special always-on wards was difficult but manageable. Powering the new hybrid wards that also had to run two other active effects was just too much. The arcana draw was more than he could channel, which meant he could only get a few hours at most from them before he needed to rest.

It wasn't an ideal solution, but Nym managed to come up with something he felt was workable. By his reasoning, the sixth layer wasn't like the core reality. It was a vast empty space, nothing but arcana suffusing it. If he didn't want to be bothered by anybody, then a ward with a trigger of literally anything that came by would be sufficient to give him early warning, as long as it was far enough out and, more importantly, he made it prophetic.

That was a whole new headache to work out the details on, since he wasn't all that great at scrying on inner-layer timelines yet, and the outer layer was a whole different beast, but he thought he had it right. Unfortunately, without anyone showing up to actually trigger the wards, it was hard to test them.

If he'd done it right, and he was reasonably certain he had, the prophetic ward would trigger when something was going to enter its radius but hadn't yet. That would send feedback to let him know he had incoming guests, and the ward itself would collapse and vanish before anyone arrived. There should be no risk of anyone finding him via his wards that way.

At that point, he could activate his limited-use invisible scrying ward to get a more accurate assessment of just who exactly had shown up and decide if he needed to relocate again. He had a strong suspicion that he would be running for it if anyone managed to find the box he'd sealed himself in. It was a tough shell, too strong for a mortal to crack, but there were no mortals in the sixth layer.

In the meantime, his new stronghold gave him a place to practice and improve his magic in relative peace. There were still a lot of sixth-layer skills to pick up, but he decided to focus his efforts into figuring out how to breach the reality membrane and reach the seventh. Being able to travel to a deeper outer layer was a far, far better escape plan than anything he could construct now. If he was lucky, anybody who was looking for him wouldn't even realize they were in the wrong reality.

Nym spent the next month working on the problem. In some ways, he thought it was easier to reach the seventh layer than it was the fifth, at least from his position. Once he'd stepped across the chasm, he'd formed a new existence in the sixth layer, which meant it was a single step over to the next one. Simple.

Except it wasn't, not at all. He could feel a membrane that encircled the reality he was currently stuck in, but conduits worked differently in the outer layers. Every trick he knew, every rule he thought should apply, was worthless. The membrane was solid. It had no wiggle, no give. It didn't flex when he prodded it. If he had to compare it to something else, he would have said it was like boring through the fourth layer, except a thousand times more difficult.

Brute force obviously wasn't the answer. He was never going to puncture that membrane, and it would take decades to dig his way through it. He supposed he had the time, but there had to be a better way. Or maybe there wasn't, and every ascendant had their own channel they'd dug open. If that was the case, it was no wonder they were so secretive about it. Of course, if that was the case, that meant that once it was opened, they would have to maintain that connection forever. It would be a constant fight to keep the membrane from closing again.

His contemplations into that mystery were interrupted by his prophetic ward. Two beings would appear very soon, and he could only hope that they wouldn't find him. The ward collapsed and was washed away even as Nym realized this fact, and he hurried to deploy the invisible scrying ward in its place.

He wasn't entirely surprised to see Valicin, though he wasn't pleased. He hadn't been expecting her to give up, but he also thought he'd covered his trail well enough after his copy had met her to get away. She'd found him anyway, or rather, he assumed the other ascendant with her had. Ferro looked exactly the same as Nym remembered him, and he remained one of the most powerful ascendants Nym had ever met.

He was a lot less confident about escaping Ferro than he would have been if it had only been Valicin. Nym waited with bated breath while the two looked around. If he had any luck at all, they would assume they'd lost his trail and backtrack to try again, giving him enough time to flee and get ahead of them.

That didn't happen. Instead, a third ascendant appeared. Nym didn't recognize this one, though from the sudden stiffening he saw in Ferro and Valicin, they did. Curious, he focused on them and tried to pick up the conversation.

"Exarch," Ferro said, his voice almost but not quite steady.

"Exarch," Valicin echoed, her own voice quavering.

"Well, well, what is this? Two of Niramyn's stooges, out in the middle of nowhere, with nowhere to run and no way to fight back. How lucky for me."

CHAPTER SIXTY-SEVEN

There were only a handful of ascendants at the twelfth layer, powerful enough to be called Exarchs. Of those, there were only two who would be actively hostile toward Ferro and Valicin. One of them had a blanket hatred toward everyone and would attack anyone who got too close to him on sight. But his attitude and the locations he frequented were well-known, well-documented, and thoroughly avoided by anybody with a lick of sense. Even Nym, who'd been an ascendant for a bare handful of years, knew that much.

The other one was Myzalik. Nym hadn't ever met the man, but he'd gotten descriptions, and unless someone else was imitating an Exarch, it looked like he'd come calling.

Except, he hadn't. Not really. Myzalik wasn't there for Nym. He might not even know Nym was there. He was confronting two of Niramyn's followers, and given his status as the only known ascendant killer, Nym did not think this meeting was going to end well for them.

"You know why I'm here?" Myzalik asked.

"To weaken my master's support. You know, of course, that your actions are having the opposite effect," Ferro said.

"You think so?"

"It is fact. For every ascendant you consign to oblivion, ten more join Exarch Niramyn's cause to stop you."

"Indeed." Myzalik flashed his teeth at Ferro. It reminded Nym of the shark that used to follow him around every time he went to the cove. "That's good. None of you can stop me, and I would like to remove anyone who thinks to try in one swoop. When I'm done purging this society of anyone who would oppose me, I'll be free to rebuild it to my designs."

"A madman's ambition," Ferro scoffed.

Myzalik ignored him and said to Valicin, "Do you have anything to say on the subject?"

She was considerably less confident than Ferro, and Nym noticed the casual arrogance she'd displayed when she'd overpowered his copy was absent as well. He supposed she was a bit of a bully, full of swagger when facing someone weaker than her. Though he didn't blame her for cowering in front of Myzalik. Nym was practically sweating from his hiding spot, metaphorically speaking. He didn't actually do that anymore.

"Nothing?" Myzalik prodded. "Come on now, you must have some sort of opinion on the matter." Valicin jerked her head back and forth, just once. Myzalik snorted and said, "Well, you're smart enough to know when to keep your opinions to yourself at least. However, I know you're working for the idiot, which makes you an idiot too. I already beat him once. I'm going to do it again, only this time he won't slip the trap at the last instant."

"What do you want?" Ferro asked flatly, shifting to put himself between Myzalik and Valicin.

"Well it's obvious, isn't it? I'm cutting away Niramyn's support."

Nym could see the exact moment they both tried to flee. They knew it was futile, but they also knew they had no chance of victory. As expected, it didn't work. Myzalik blocked the arcana from forming around them, trapped them in place. For their sakes, Nym hoped the two ascendants were copy bodies, but he suspected if that was the case, Myzalik would know.

Ferro must have agreed because his body became insubstantial, and arcana burst forth from him in a burning aurora that stretched out for miles. Nym had never seen an ascendant fully cut loose, and he knew Ferro was at least two steps away from Exarch level. If his own magic poured off from him in such large quantities that it could blanket mortal cities, how much worse was Myzalik's?

The arcana aura washed over the Exarch but failed to touch him. Like smoke billowing against a glass window, it roiled around him, but Myzalik was safe inside whatever defenses he'd devised. And then, so abruptly that Nym almost missed it, his own aura extended out in a smooth, straight plane that bisected the ferocious power Ferro was emitting cleanly.

"You can't have believed that would do anything," Myzalik said dryly.

"No, it was just to distract you, to force you to focus on me."

"Why, did you think your friend was going to get away?"

Nym blinked and looked around, trying to figure out where Valicin had gone. Wherever she was, she was out of the range of his scrying ward, but Myzalik just lifted a hand and plucked something out of the air, something that wasn't there, except that all of a sudden Valicin *was* there, her arm caught in Myzalik's grasp.

"Just a little temporal stutter when she tried to flee," the Exarch explained. "You've made your valiant attempt to escape, tried to sacrifice yourself for it, really. It got you nowhere. Your choices are simple at this point: surrender or perish."

Gravity didn't exist in the sixth layer. Something like that required land and sky, sea and stars, and the endless void had none of those things. Ascendants made their own gravity when they constructed their palaces and fortresses. Or when they tried to crush their opponents with it, as Ferro's next attack demonstrated.

Exarch Myzalik's whole body seemed to fold up on itself, reduced in an instant to a pinprick of color as Ferro's spell crushed him. Valicin jerked herself clear of the effect, though she lost her arm in the process. An instant later, the pinprick flowed back out into the Exarch's human form again. He smirked and shook his head. "Perish it is."

Arcana surged out of Myzalik and slammed into Valicin. Her body locked into place, her expression frozen, and Nym had the strangest feeling that she'd stopped existing. All that was left was the illusion of a person, a sort of placeholder in space and time of what she had been. Myzalik treated her like a distraction, something to shoo away so he could work in peace.

New arcana poured into existence around Myzalik, dark and hungry and infinitely deep. It jumped from the Exarch to his victim but served to do nothing but establish a framework. Ferro was locked in it, his expression pained, his body unable to struggle. "I had to develop this adaption to make it work from the other direction," Myzalik said. "The original spell was designed with your master in mind, of course. But as we all know, he is *always* in reality prime." He stopped and snorted. "Almost always.

"Other ascendants aren't, but of course if just hiding out here in the outer layers was all it took to defend against me, then the spell wouldn't be worth knowing. Fortunately, that was easily remedied, easily for me, I mean. You're not a hidden Exarch, are you? No. Don't bother trying to answer."

A new spell bloomed inside the framework, one that looked remarkably similar to the age-reversal spell Nym had learned when he'd first arrived. As he watched it grow, he realized the similarities were surface level only. Many of the pieces were familiar, sometimes even identical, but the arrangement, the order of composition, the emphasis given to them, all different. The connections were wrong too, sometimes backward, other times unlike any part of the spell he knew.

Nym didn't understand even half of what he was seeing, but one of the great things about being an ascendant was having utterly perfect memory. The spell Myzalik was casting was a combination of at least twenty-two other spells, and that wasn't even including the framework made of what Nym could only assume was twelfth-layer arcana. He didn't understand it, but he could replicate it. Much like speaking a foreign word phonetically, Nym could reproduce individual pieces, and the ones he didn't know how to make, he at least knew what they'd look like when they were completed.

The spell took minutes to cast, but then it was ready, held in place and checked by Myzalik's will. "Do you see?" he asked, laughing again. "So simple, right? How did none of us ever figure this out? I couldn't believe it when I put the pieces together."

Then he unleashed the spell, directly into Ferro. The framework caught it, sped it through the ascendant's entire essence, and stretched it down to the core reality. Ferro melted away, his body broken apart into raw arcana as the connections he'd formed were severed. Nym wasn't about to scry other layers of reality to see what was happening there, not with Myzalik so close. But he could guess.

He was witnessing the death of an immortal.

The ending was anticlimactic. The spell collapsed on itself in the space where Ferro used to be and disappeared. There was nothing there, had never been anything there. Ferro didn't exist because the mortal who'd forged an existence that spanned multiple realities didn't exist, had in fact never existed in reality prime's timeline.

As far as any ascendant was concerned, he was dead. With that completed, Myzalik turned to Valicin and unfroze her. She jerked forward, then blinked and looked around. "What did you do?" she asked quietly. "Killed him?"

"Yes. He fought to the end to give you time to run. Obviously, he was not successful. So now I'll offer you the same choice. Surrender or perish."

"What does surrender mean to you?"

"Servitude. But life. It's really no different than your current life. You'll just be trading one master for another. Of course, I'll have to be a bit stricter than your old one, if only to ensure your new loyalties don't waver."

Valicin looked around again, like she expected Ferro to pop up any moment and tell her that it was all a joke. When he didn't, her shoulders sloped down, and she nodded. "I will serve."

"I knew you were more sensible than that stodgy old man. Come then, I have much work to do on you, and you have many, many secrets to whisper into my ear."

The two of them disappeared, and Nym held his breath. He was almost expecting Myzalik to come back, to laugh at the foolish little ascendant who thought to hide from a god. But nothing happened. Myzalik didn't return. Eventually, Nym ran out of arcana for the scrying ward, and he was left alone in his invisible box.

He spent a long time just thinking about what he'd witnessed. Two ascendants had been sent to hunt him down but had been intercepted. One had been killed, the other subverted. That could theoretically mean that no one knew where he was now, that no one was following his trail. Just to be safe, he would need to relocate again, as soon as he was sure it was safe to do so. He didn't plan on setting one foot outside the box until he knew Myzalik hadn't left any sort of trap behind.

But then, when he ran out of other things to think about and plans to make, his mind turned back to the immortal-killing spell. If he discounted the framework, which was clearly beyond his ability to mimic, everything else had been simple sixth-layer arcana. The spell forms were eerily familiar. He could learn to weave those together. With enough practice, he could cast that spell too.

That then was the reason that nobody ever saw Myzalik do it. There were probably dozens of ascendants who could duplicate that spell with practically no effort, if only they knew how. He had to kill anyone who saw it, or else he was risking his greatest weapon getting into the hands of his enemies.

That was valuable knowledge. If Nym could figure out how to leverage that, he might just have a way out of this mess once and for all. He would need to keep it quiet though. If anyone learned that he had the god-killer spell, he'd be the next target, and he wasn't nearly as well defended as Myzalik. It would be easy for someone to capture him and take the spell from his mind.

Secrecy was the key. Secrecy and opportunity. He just needed to be patient. As soon as he figured out how to put the puzzle together, all he would need was the right set of circumstances.

CHAPTER SIXTY-EIGHT

Nym didn't trust any of the other ascendants at this point. Niramyn would no doubt send new hunters after him, and if Myzalik ever learned that someone had witnessed his god-killer spell, Nym was sure he would immediately jump to the top of the priority list there. Even supposedly neutral ascendants like Hozim were willing to sell him out for the right price.

Maybe if he knew any of them better, he might have considered it. They might be fair in their dealings with him, but they also had no loyalty to him, and Nym couldn't think of a good way to know whom he could trust and whom he couldn't. Even the ones who didn't owe any favors to Niramyn could be bought. No one was going out of their way to side with the new ascendant who had nothing to offer but time.

Time and a spell that had the potential to radically alter everything, but since he wasn't going to tell anyone about that, it didn't count. He'd given it further consideration, tried to find a way to make it work for him instead of against him, but no matter how he looked at it, knowing that spell made him a target. The only way he didn't . . . well, not die, but get imprisoned or something, was if nobody found out he knew it. Or if he spread it around so quickly that everyone knew it, but that came with a whole host of drawbacks he wasn't prepared to consider.

That left the option of him becoming a hermit, at least temporarily. If other people could figure this stuff out though, he could too. He even had an advantage in that he'd seen the spell being cast. There were still pieces he didn't understand, but he had an unlimited amount of time to work on that.

The new sanctum had to be abandoned, of course. Ferro and Valicin had gotten way too close, but at least he'd proven his prophetic and scrying wards worked. It was actually a bit surprising that they'd worked so well, given that he knew they weren't actually invisible. They faded into the background arcana of the sixth layer, but surely a powerful and clever ascendant could spot them anyway.

Except that they hadn't. Whether that was blind luck or a truly ingenious piece of spell crafting on his part, Nym didn't know. He suspected the answer was more mundane than that. Ferro hadn't had time to see them, or maybe even had seen them, but Myzalik's interference had focused the ascendants firmly on one another. Simply put, they were too busy to look.

Nym took every precaution he could think of, including trying his hand at seeing into the future. It was a lot harder in the outer layers where time worked differently, and he had no anchors spread across it. He couldn't manage more than a few seconds, which wasn't ideal but would do for his purposes. Once he'd finished preparations, he scanned those few precious seconds to confirm he wouldn't be interrupted, then willed himself away.

More than a hundred jumps through random locations later, Nym started building his new sanctuary. It was almost exactly the same as the old one, except bigger. He needed some room to do research and practice in, after all. That made it slightly more exposed, but the real defense had always been the fact that it was hidden well away from the hub of ascendant activity in the layer. If, however, many dozens or even hundreds of ascendants could hermit out in the void, he could do it too.

In all fairness, they probably had fewer people looking for them, but Nym was still confident in his preparations. They weren't impregnable, but they were the best he could do. He'd taken every precaution he could think of, and now there was nothing left but to do the work.

Nym split himself into four teams of two, each part in charge of working out a different piece of the spell. Every now and then, they'd all merge back into one being to consolidate what they'd figured out and see if one team had come up with something that would help another one. Then they'd split back apart and repeat the cycle. In that way, Nym felt his progress was sped up significantly.

It had another side effect, one that he hadn't anticipated but that he was happy to exploit. For some reason he didn't yet understand, having all the copies of himself in close proximity working together seemed to be, for lack of a better term, cracking the membrane between layers. He had no clue why that was happening, but it was.

So Nym did what any good researcher would do. He split off two more copies to investigate that. That, of course, made the cracks worse. Presumably, that was a good thing. If he could break through into the seventh layer, he'd be that much more likely to survive.

He did have one final concern with the whole project. He wasn't an Exarch, and twenty-two spells at one time was above his limit. He could do fourteen, no problem. If they were simple spells, he could reasonably expect to double that. But the god-killer spell was anything but simple, and he needed a parallel process devoted to each and every spell in order to cast them all at the same time.

That meant he needed to start digging into new modifications to his physical form, which meant more experimentation. Sadly, the brain was the most dangerous place to work on. It wasn't that he was in any physical danger of dying if he messed up, but if he scrambled his brain too hard, he would have to obliterate his avatar and start a new one from scratch.

There was some leeway though, so he pushed to his limits and spun out one final pair to start messing with that. His little sanctum was quite crowded at that point, but none of the Nyms seemed to mind. They worked together in harmony, shared knowledge with one another, and got just a little bit stronger with each passing hour.

"We think we've figured out the membrane crack," Nym said to the group. They weren't due for a merger to redistribute information for another week, but the membrane project was the one they had the highest hopes for in terms of an immediate jump in power. The parallel-processing team had practically stalled out while they waited for it.

"It's a bit early, but if you're sure, it's worth coming back together to share that knowledge," another Nym said.

"No! No. That's the opposite of what we need. We know it's being caused by so many of us in close proximity, right? Remember when you guys were trying to hook pieces of the spell together and passing it back and forth the other day? Well, the cracks got . . . deeper, I guess is the best way to put it. The spells are putting pressure on it. The more we have going at once, the harder it is for the membrane to hold against them."

"We knew it had to be something we were doing. It's not really that surprising that it's the magic. That's all we're doing here. But what are we supposed to do, just make more magic until the membrane gives completely?"

"No, you're not listening. It's not that we're all doing magic, it's the magic being shared and passed back and forth."

"Why would that make a difference?" one of the Nyms asked. "It's the same amount of arcana either way."

"Must be the motion of it," another Nym said.

"Maybe the positioning is relevant."

"Our theory," the researcher Nym said, interrupting the speculation, "is that because we're all one Nym manifesting in multiple bodies, when we start working together, drawing arcana into group projects, it's acting as a sort of pseudoconduit that's connecting two parts of ourself."

"It couldn't really be that simple though, could it?"

Nym shrugged. "Why not? Have we met a single ascendant who's stuck at the sixth layer?"

"No, but we haven't met all that many."

"Let's say we're wrong," Nym said. "What's the worst-case scenario? A couple of copies break apart?"

"It could disrupt all the spells hiding us and lead Niramyn or Myzalik straight to this location. That would be far worse than having to remake a few copies."

"Maybe we could do it without the original here," one of the Nym's said.

"I don't think that would work. Without the original as the focal point, even if we manage to break through, I don't think we'll be able to access the other side."

The arguments went on for another hour before everyone agreed that it was better to reconcile all the information, make a decision, and then reform the copies. It generally took Nym some time to get everything sorted out once he pulled himself together, but he still considered it a net win if he got eleven times as much work done but had to take a day to figure it all out once every few weeks.

Once he was done, he was pretty sure he had a method to fully break through the membrane. What he wasn't sure of was what was on the other side or how to prepare for that. Personal experience told him that every layer was different, but all he had to go on was that the ascendants called the seventh layer the Crushing Void.

How something could be both an empty void and crush at the same time was beyond Nym. He assumed it was some colorful language rather than an accurate description, but for all he knew, it could be literal. With that thought in mind, he set about building himself a sort of arcana-pressurized cage, something that he could shelter in while he explored. It had pinprick holes in it, designed to let only a little bit of arcana in at a time so that he could study it in relative safety.

If he was lucky, it wouldn't even be necessary. Nym intended to use a planar scry on the seventh layer before he fully entered it, and it was possible all his preparations were a waste of time. Every one of his copies agreed that it was better to be safe though, so he built the box anyway. Once that was done, his copies got into position and started passing arcana back and forth around him in the pattern they'd deemed to have the biggest impact.

The membrane cracked, then started to split, and finally the barest hint of a fissure tore open between the layers. Nym had a moment to peer curiously into it before something black and heavy blasted out and slammed him into the ceiling. The arcana pattern was immediately disrupted, and the fissure sealed itself closed.

"Ow," Nym said as he willed himself back down. "So, that could have gone better. Ideas on what went wrong?"

"I don't think we did anything wrong," one of the copies said. "We just didn't make adequate preparations for defenses against the new environment. It's obviously not like this one."

"That was raw arcana that struck you too, so I think it's safe to say that being fully immersed in it is going to require considerable willpower and defensive capabilities."

The various Nyms continued to toss theories back and forth, argue over spells, and refine the cage Nym had built. He hadn't even gotten a chance to use it, but they all agreed that it felt inadequate, knowing that even the slightest opening between layers caused arcana to erupt like that.

Further testing was necessary, but Nym had proven to himself that he could break through the membrane. He supposed that technically made him a seventh-layer ascendant, but until he figured out how to safely tap into the arcana and control it, he planned to hold off introducing himself that way.

Still, it wouldn't be much longer.

CHAPTER SIXTY-NINE

The cage didn't work. Despite everything he'd done to reinforce it, it seemed to lack the weight needed to withstand the arcana. As soon as the first fissure opened, the cage got blasted around every bit as easily as Nym himself. It wasn't a physical weight either. It didn't matter how dense the cage was, every iteration met with the same result. Some attempts had actually ruptured it completely, forcing Nym to build a new one from nothing.

He was about to try a different tactic. Instead of a physical object he'd created and weighed down with arcana, he was going to form a sort of bubble around himself, a perfect sphere packed as densely as he could make it with sixth-layer arcana. Even if it wasn't as strong as seventh layer, he was hoping the quantity would counteract that.

The Nyms gathered into formation and opened the rift. The inky-black arcana surged out, struck the bubble, and . . . sheared right through it, once again tossing Nym into the ceiling of his sanctum before it cut out.

"That didn't work," Nym grumbled, climbing back to his feet after he fell. "Thoughts?"

"Still not dense enough," several Nyms said immediately.

"Yes, obviously. Thoughts on why?"

There were a lot of thoughts, but none of them were original or new, and eventually the Nyms all broke back apart to their individual roles. The god-killer spell was coming along, at least so far as to say he'd identified five distinct parts that he had no idea how to recreate. The rest of it was doable, though not fast enough to make it actually work without somehow increasing the number of parallel processes his mind could run.

Those projects were all in the works though, each one slowly advancing into what he hoped would eventually become a unified and coherent whole. The problem was that the whole hermit thing was a lot harder than he'd expected it to be. He'd figured that after his stint in Niramyn's library, he could handle it. Inarguably, he'd spent far more time there.

As it turned out, making constant progress helped a lot. The knowledge had been there; all he needed to do was absorb it. Now, it was endless days that turned into weeks and then into months of research, of trying and failing and trying again in an endless cycle. There were no breaks to talk to somebody besides himself. He didn't leave to attend to some task or other.

Nym was starting to crack. He could feel it. If something didn't change soon, his mind was going to break. The idea that there were somehow hundreds of ascendants floating out in the void, slowly chipping away at advancing to the next layer, always advancing, never doing anything else, was so unreal to him now that he didn't know how he'd ever not found it laughable.

There had to be some way to insulate his mind from the isolation, some spell that he just didn't know about that altered how he thought or felt. He was half-tempted to put a Nym copy on researching that, but he was already approaching his limits.

It was dangerous, but he had to get out of the box he'd stuffed himself into. He needed to see something, hear other people's voices. It would probably be fine, just for a little while. Hidden presence had always worked for him before. As long as someone didn't directly stumble across him, he had no reason to believe it would fail him now.

For the first time in he didn't know how long, Nym stepped outside of his sanctuary.

"I will admit, I am surprised to see you again," Rizin said.

"Would you believe that I'm just checking in?"

"No."

"How about that I haven't spoken to another living being in what I am sure is at least six months and I'm slowly losing my mind?"

"That one I believe."

Nym paced back and forth in front of the fox's massive cushion. "How do you do it? You've been here for years, decades maybe. How do you handle the solitude?"

"Perhaps it's just that I enjoy it," Rizin said. "Or, perhaps, it is that I am not trapped here. I can leave whenever I want, and I frequently do. I am not so isolated as you seem to think, and the thought of walking among the mortals in various disguises does not disturb me in the slightest. It is in my nature to deceive, after all."

"Is that what I should do? Just take a vacation every few weeks?" Nym asked.

"You seem agitated."

Nym forced himself to stop pacing and took a deep breath. "I am. I just . . . Sometimes I don't think I can do this. Nothing I do ever feels like it's enough."

"That is probably because you have set yourself against forces that are inconceivably powerful, even for an immortal. It is a fool's errand, and you will never find peace until you give it up."

"That's your advice?" Nym demanded. "Just give up and let them do whatever they want? Take whatever they decide to dish out because they're stronger?"

"Do you have a choice? You may one day be strong enough to dictate your own terms, but today is not that day."

Nym thought about telling Rizin about the god-killer spell. If there was anyone who was good at plotting and scheming, it was the mystic fox. But no, Nym didn't trust him *that* much. He didn't trust anyone that much.

"Well let me ask you this," Nym said. "I've been trying to break into the seventh layer, and I am so close, but every time I manage to get through the membrane, the arcana is uncontrollable."

He described his process to Rizin, who listened with sleepy indifference. When he was done, the fox said, "If you think you need more arcana density, why are you splitting yourself into a dozen separate bodies?"

"Because . . . I can't split open the membrane without them?"

"Hmm. Seems like that's your problem then."

"Maybe, yeah. Thanks. I'll see if I can figure it out from that direction."

"Then if that's all?"

"Actually, no. Want to get a bite to eat?" Nym asked.

Rizin cracked open an eye to look at him. "You don't need to eat anymore."

"I still like to though. Plus, like you said, you go out whenever you want."

"Is this just an excuse to try to interrogate me for advice on your various problems?"

"No," Nym said. "It's also an excuse to socialize, which I think I need more."

"Fine." Rizin rolled his eyes, then climbed to his feet and disappeared. A girl in her early twenties appeared in his place and hopped down from the cushion. "Where to?"

"That's . . . uh, that's what you're going out as today?"

"Is that a problem?"

"Nope. Not at all."

The girl looked suspiciously like Risa though. Maybe it was a coincidence. Probably not. Rizin did like to mess with him.

"How long have you been living in the outer layers?" Rizin asked while he tore into a rack of ribs. It was a bit disconcerting to see him do it in a petite woman's body, and judging by the looks they were receiving, Nym wasn't the only one to think so.

"I don't even know anymore. I've been all over the timeline here too. Maybe ten years since our pact?"

Nym wondered if he should take better care to keep track of time, but it seemed largely pointless in a society where nobody ever got older and everyone did whatever they wanted at their own pace. It was only ever in the core reality that they showed any sense of urgency. Their stupid games were the only things they cared about besides gaining more personal power. Sometimes he wondered if ascendants actually served any purpose at all.

"Ten years with almost no contact? No wonder you're going stir-crazy."

"Well, maybe less. And I did talk to some ascendants at first, but then they tried to sell me out and I had to go into hiding."

"Are you sure you want to live among them at all then? There's no reason you couldn't stay here."

"If I thought it was safe for me, I'd consider it. But I tried to visit some of my old friends, and it just felt weird. It was like I was playing with little kids."

"So what?" Rizin asked.

Nym titled his head. "What do you mean?"

"So what if it was like playing with little kids? Is it a bad thing to be stronger than them? Does that make them somehow less than they were before because your power has outgrown theirs?"

"No, but it's hard to relate to them now."

"No, it's not. Not if you let yourself. You will have plenty of centuries to be a prim and proper immortal who is above it all. Let yourself be who you want to be now."

It was a good thought, but with the looming threat of two Exarchs hanging over his head, he couldn't see himself ever truly able to relax. Of course, if everything worked like he hoped, maybe that wouldn't be a forever threat. He could live a life, almost a vacation of sorts and, when it was time to pass on, return to being an immortal instead.

If there was ever a span of years to do that, it was the ones he'd been born into, so to speak. Eriam had even implied Nym had been around in some way when Eriam was still mortal, which he took to mean sometime in the near future. It was comforting, in a way, to know that he had a future to look forward to.

That comfort was tempered by the fact that ascendants spent a lot of their energy manipulating the primary timeline, trying to weave threads of alternate times into it in order to meet their own agendas. He'd even done it himself dozens of times on behalf of Hozim. Though that did raise the question of if a timeline was alterable to make it so someone who would have ascended never did, could Nym in theory stop an ascendant from existing?

Evidence strongly suggested the answer was no. The primary timeline would tolerate small changes easily enough, but something like erasing an ascendant was not a small change. That could be big enough to shift everything over to a new primary. If Myzalik never existed, then Nym wouldn't exist. Presumably, that meant that those dozens of ascendants he'd executed would continue to exist, and making those kinds of changes to beings operating on that scale would quickly lead to a cascading chain of events that could overwrite the primary.

But then, if it wasn't possible, if the timeline was self-correcting, then how exactly did Myzalik's god-killer work? Nym had all the pieces, but he didn't understand what they did. Perhaps it was time to take a closer look at the reverse-aging spell and figure out exactly how it did what it did, instead of just taking it for granted.

"You okay over there?" Rizin asked, snapping him out of his thoughts.

"Yeah, why?"

"You stopped eating and have been staring off into space for a few minutes now. I stole half your food off your plate, and you didn't even notice."

"Wait, what?" Nym glanced down and saw that, indeed, his plate was mostly empty now.

"I'm a predator and a thief. Come on now. If you're not going to pay attention, why would you expect any other outcome?"

Nym just sighed and put his fork down. "Listen, I've got an important question. You know how ascendants keep their mortal avatars young, right?"

"Right."

"I can do the spell, but I want to dig into exactly how it works, not just how to do it. I think it could be important."

"That's easy enough," Rizin said. "I could explain it all right now. But what's in it for me?"

Nym did not like that glint in his eyes, not at all.

CHAPTER SEVENTY

I don't understand," Nym said.

"You don't need to understand to do it."

"But—"

"Are you willing or not?"

"I mean, sure, it's not a big deal. I just don't get why."

Rizin just stared at Nym, his lips pursed and reminding him disturbingly of Risa's. Nym wanted to say something, but that would be an open invitation for the fox to double down on teasing him. It definitely wasn't a coincidence that his appearance was so close to that of a person Nym had had some form of intimacy with, however slight it had ended up being.

"Fine. Whatever. I'll do it. Now spill. How does the age-reversal spell work?"

"To start, I want to say that my knowledge is theoretical. I don't need this spell since I don't age. If you tried to reverse my age by a thousand years, I'd just look exactly like I do now. Of course, I can't jump around the timeline like ascendants can, so . . . trade-offs."

"You can't?" Nym asked, surprised. He'd just assumed anything he could do Rizin could do too. Probably better actually.

"No. My existence is tied very firmly to this body. I can act in different layers, but I can't pull myself completely out of this one." Rizin gave him a flat look. "This is not information to be shared, of course.

"Ascendants can dip out of the timeline in the inner layers by shifting themselves completely to the sixth layer, or farther. It doesn't make a lot of difference exactly which outer layer you end up on, just that it puts you outside of time here."

"What does this have to do with age reversal?" Nym asked.

"With the spell itself? Not much. I'm just explaining to you why it works on ascendants but not on other beings. You can fully withdraw from the inner layers. I'll assume at this point that you know about alternate timelines."

"Yeah. When changes are made to the primary, it can cause the timeline to fork until the change can be reconciled. If enough changes happen in a short period or a single huge change occurs, it can cause the timeline to deviate completely into an alternate line. It's like a sort of sideways reality. I have not experienced them myself; I was told it would take me a few more layers before I got to that point."

"Exactly, yes. But just because you, Nym the ascendant sitting here eating lunch with me, can't go to the alternate timelines doesn't mean you can't interact with them. And that's what the age-reversal spell does."

"It . . . sends me to an alternate timeline? That doesn't seem right."

"No." Rizin rolled his eyes. "It takes a version of you from an alternate timeline, a version that's younger, and uses it as a model to rebuild your avatar in this timeline. If your mortal avatar were to die, you would need to do something similar to rebuild it, unless you no longer wanted to be Nym. You could build a new body completely from nothing instead of using an alternate version of you as your baseline."

"But what if that alternate version of you is wrong in some way? I wouldn't want a copy of myself that was missing all the changes I've made to my body."

"Exactly! That's why it reaches through multiple timelines and sort of compiles matching traits to what you've got going for you now and just puts it all into a younger body. It's extremely delicate. You want a safe place and an abundant amount of free time before you use this spell."

"I used it once to turn back my age by a few years when I was learning how to do it," Nym said with a frown. "It didn't take that long."

"You're a new ascendant. You said yourself it's barely been a decade to you personally, and I imagine most of that time was spent in the outer layers. There hasn't been a lot to diverge, and you weren't going back very far. The spell probably had lots of samples to choose from, with very little need to take pieces from different possibilities and merge them into one.

"Now imagine you're a thousand years old, into the tenth or eleventh layer, with so many enhancements and alterations to your physical form that it would take years to rebuild them all. And it's all balanced just right. How long do you think it would take the spell to find everything exactly the way you have it right now? How long would it take for it to put that all together into something that looks like you, only with fewer wrinkles and a fuller head of hair?"

Rizin had a point. Even now, Nym had tinkered with his physiology and his soul well enough that he would have a month or more of work to repeat all the spell work if he focused every moment on nothing else. The more things he changed, the harder it would become to find an alternate-timeline version of himself that matched those changes. Once the spell had to tap into multiple sources and merge them together to get what he was looking for, it would get cumbersome.

"And we can't just take our own version of ourselves from the past because then we lose all the progress we've made. We could redo it, possibly faster, but why remake it when we can steal it from realities that never existed instead?"

"There you go. So, that's the theory behind age-reversal magic. You can't cast the spell on anyone besides yourself, and mortals can't cast it at all. Besides lacking access to sixth-layer arcana, they would kill themselves in the process. Only an immortal can use this magic, and even then, only one like an ascendant who can survive wholly without a body in the inner layers."

"I see. I have questions about some specifics," Nym said.

Rizin groaned. "You are really asking the wrong person."

"It's fine if you can't answer them, but if you can, I want to know."

"Fine, but then you go run that errand for me."

"Okay, so there's a part of the spell that looks like this, but what if . . .'"

Eventually, Nym had picked Rizin's brain of everything relevant he could get. Or maybe Rizin had just gotten sick of the questions. Either way, the conversation had ended, the meal was over, they'd released the spells preventing anyone from over-hearing what they were saying or really even remembering that they were there, and they'd gone their separate ways.

It wasn't hard for Nym to make the jump backward, but Rizin's den had a completely different set of defenses, and he hadn't been invited through them back then. Getting inside took a bit of effort, so much so that it ended up costing him close to a week of time before he finally worked his way through and appeared in front of the fox.

Rizin of three hundred years ago was a lot scarier than the Rizin he knew, though Nym was willing to bet that it was mostly a matter of perspective. His Rizin was a lot more friendly than the past version, probably because Nym hadn't barged into his den in their original meeting. Also, past Rizin seemed to be . . . bigger and growing.

"How did you get in here, ascendant?"

"Well it wasn't easy," Nym groused. "Knowing where the place was helped, but it still took me a few days to get through all the wards and misdirects."

Rizin, now sized to the point where he was twice Nym's height, leaned down from his cushion. "There is little point to a secret den if someone finds it. Now I need to either find a new one or take care of you. After you explain how exactly you knew where it was, I'll decide what to do."

Nym rolled his eyes and said, "You sent me back here from the future of this timeline to give you a message, although I'm pretty sure now that the message was just an excuse to hassle me."

"Unlikely," Rizin said. "I'm not friends with any ascendants."

"Who knows what the future will bring," Nym said dryly. "Oh wait, I do. And you wanted your past self to know too."

The fox gave Nym that same glare he'd grown so used to, and he smirked a little. "I guess some things don't change, no matter how many years go by."

"Ugh. Fine, let's say that I believe you. What is this message?"

"Keeping in mind that I have no idea what this means and you're a jackass who refused to tell me, my job is to tell you that the juniper shines in the spring of the lonely mountain."

Rizin stared at him blankly, as though waiting for Nym to continue. When he didn't, the fox heaved a sigh of disgust. "Whatever that means. Now, you're going to tell me how you got in here."

"Hey," Nym said suddenly. "Are you missing a tail?"

"What? No!"

"Are you sure? I feel like you had one more in the time I come from."

"Just because I can't kill you doesn't mean I can't make you wish you were dead," Rizin threatened.

"Oooh, scary. You know, you almost never go full size around me. Why is that, do you think?"

Rizin snapped at him, but Nym teleported twenty feet back and avoided the gnashing teeth. He cocked an eyebrow at the fox, who was poised to leap forward.

"Definitely missing a tail. I could swear you had nine."

"Maybe I'll grow another one, just to spite you."

Nym shrugged. "Doesn't matter to me. I'm just saying, the Rizin I know can use eighth-layer arcana, and you can't. So, that's something to look forward to in the future. And you'll have a whole new ward setup. And you'll have a spell I call 'hidden presence' that prevents ascendants from finding you with magic. So, you know, if you don't have that figured out already, something to work on."

"Are you telling me that you know fox magic?"

"Just the one spell," Nym said. He wove an illusion of the spell construct in the air for Rizin to see. "This one. You teach it to me."

"Impossible," Rizin said. "I'd never . . . What's so special about you?"

"You'll see when you meet me again, I guess. I wouldn't want to ruin the surprise."

"Wait, what are you—"

Before he could finish, Nym vanished from the den.

Rizin of the past sat there, thoroughly confused. Somehow, he'd befriended an ascendant, of all things. Or at least, he trusted one enough to let him into his den in the future and even teach him fox magic. That would probably prove to be exciting. No doubt having access to ascendant resources would open many new avenues for him to explore.

But first, he needed to redo his warding scheme. That annoying immortal had somehow managed to slip all the way through without disturbing anything, a feat Rizin would have said was impossible. He started poking at it, looking for the weakness he hadn't known existed, and idly wondered what that message from his future self meant.

Knowing himself as well as he did, he suspected it was probably gibberish meant to waste his time. But what if it wasn't? What if it was important in some way? He might not understand it now, but it could be relevant anytime in the next few centuries. Was it an opportunity he'd left slip by and was determined to correct? If it didn't happen in the near future, then why send an ascendant so far back to deliver it?

Damn himself anyway. Now he'd have to hang on to that phrase for possibly centuries, looking for whatever situation he was warning himself about, assuming it even existed. It was a lot more fun playing tricks on others than on himself.

CHAPTER SEVENTY-ONE

That little vacation had done wonders for Nym's mental health, but now he was back in the box. Rizin had given him some valuable hints, and Nym was determined to milk them for all they were worth. First, he was planning to resume his attempts to crack the membrane to the seventh layer and withstand the arcana that blasted out of it.

Rizin said the problem was his own personal density was being spread too thin by splitting himself a dozen or so different ways but hadn't given him an answer on how to breach the membrane without doing that. Passing arcana back and forth as the different copies of himself worked in conjunction was how he'd amassed enough weight to crack the membrane in the first place.

Nym started by trying to create a sort of relay station that functioned as a stand-in for his copy. After all, it wasn't that they were capable of making independent decisions that was necessary. It was just the ability to pass arcana around. If he could push the arcana into the relay and make it send it to another one, and another, and another, it would functionally be the same.

That didn't work. It took him a little while to realize the problem, but eventually he hit on the idea to include himself in the middle of the relay chain so he could examine the arcana as it bounced around and found that it degraded with each pass, both in density and in the speed at which it moved. Nym tried to patch that up but couldn't ever achieve the perfect efficiency his copies had managed.

When that experiment failed, he went back to using copies, only fewer of them. His hope was that he could find a balance between maintaining the needed density and having enough copies to pass the arcana around so that they could break the membrane. There didn't seem to be a happy medium though, since the lowest number of Nyms it took to break through was six, and dividing his density six ways was just as bad as dividing it eleven.

Finally, he hit on a solution. Instead of multiple Nyms or relay points passing arcana around, he built a sort of conduit that started and ended at himself. That idea took several iterations of refinement before he got it to start cracking the membrane, and it wasn't until the conduit basically enveloped him completely that the membrane split open.

Arcana shot out, rolled across the conduit, and was blasted aside. Before Nym could process this, he fell into the crack and passed from the sixth layer into the seventh. It immediately sealed up behind him, and he found himself in a world of darkness. That wasn't much of a change, really. The sixth layer was an empty white void, and the seventh was a black one.

The real difference was the amount of pressure he could feel against his conduit. It came at him from every direction now, like when he was deep underwater, except he didn't have any spells to mitigate that. It came down to sheer grit and willpower to hold his conduit in place. Nym could feel the strain already, but it wasn't so bad that he couldn't continue.

Like the sixth layer, he couldn't really feel much of anything there. It was just a vast, empty nothingness. At least, the area he was in was. No matter how far he moved, nothing changed. That wasn't really a problem though. Nym wasn't there to sightsee. He was there to learn to harness a stronger form of arcana. It was all around him, pressing against his conduit, so he decided to just let a bit in.

Instantly, his soul well was flooded, and he had to scramble to try to close the conduit back up before he gave himself arcana poisoning. Nym wasn't even sure how that would work, all things considered, but he had no doubt it would be unpleasant.

The arcana had so much force behind it that he couldn't get the conduit to close again. The only thing he could do was cut it completely before his soul well overflowed, but the conduit was also the only thing holding the pressure back. Nym took a half second to consider his options, then cut the conduit. He could always rebuild it if he needed to, but recovering from seventh-layer arcana poisoning was sure to be complicated and painful.

As soon as the conduit broke apart, the arcana pressed on him directly. It squeezed him and pushed, and within seconds, Nym found himself flung back into the sixth layer. He flew backward across the empty white background he'd become accustomed to until he could arrest his momentum. Then he teleported himself back to where he knew his box to be. It was funny, from the outside, even he couldn't see it.

But he'd built it and designed its defenses himself. He knew how to slip past them. Soon enough, he was safely ensconced in his sanctum again, his soul well still full of seventh-layer arcana. He had plans for that, but he was going to need a lot more, and a more reliable way of harvesting it.

"Experiment number fourteen," Nym said. "Here we go."

The conduit wrapped around him to create the weight needed, but was also spread out like a web, hopefully anchoring him to the layer of reality he was currently in. If all went according to plan, he'd dip a single piece into the rift and have arcana on tap.

The membrane split open, and Nym fell into it. His supposedly anchoring conduit tendrils came in right behind him. "Damn it," he muttered as he fell back into the inky blackness and the membrane sealed itself closed behind him.

*   *   *

"Number twenty-six," Nym said.

This time he had split himself in two, and they were running a conduit that connected them. The idea was that by having one Nym on either side, he could hold the membrane open. The cracks started to form, and Nym fell into it, as planned.

Then, with only one Nym left on the other side or, really, half a Nym as far as the membrane was concerned, it snapped closed again, severing the conduit, flooding him with arcana for a brief moment before he could break it off from his soul well, and then spitting him back out into the sixth layer.

"That didn't work," the other Nym said.

"So it would seem."

"How many attempts have we made now?" Nym asked.

"I lost track. Don't make me count them all up."

"Any new ideas?"

"Nothing we've tried has worked. Go ask Rizin for help?"

"Do you think he would?"

Nym shrugged. "Maybe, if he wants something right now."

"We do already have a way to stay in the seventh layer," Nym said. "It was the first thing we tried, the conduit cocoon."

"Yes, but when we tried to pull in arcana, the conduit broke."

"I think the structure was too fragile for the environment."

Nym considered that for a second. "Let's say we're right. We could alter the shape. Remember when we did the bubble thing when we were still trying to force the density requirement?"

That was a possibility. It would certainly be a lot easier to stabilize the conduit if it was one large piece, but without the movement of the arcana, Nym wasn't sure it would actually split open the membrane. "Oh, what if we do a double conduit?"

"One in the bubble shape and another that spins the arcana? You could discard the other one as soon as you're through, then keep the bubble and reinforce it as needed."

"Exactly. Should we try it?"

"I don't see why not."

Nym sat in the darkness of the seventh layer and considered how best to harvest arcana from it. He could reliably reach it now, but getting an appropriate amount of arcana through his bubble conduit without drawing in too much was still a problem. He wasn't overly worried about that though, since it appeared to just be a simple problem of fine control.

With some practice, he thought he'd get better. What he really needed now was time to grow accustomed to existing in the seventh layer. It was a constant drain to withstand the pressure, and no matter how many different ways he tried to be clever about it, it really just came down to a simple question. Was he strong enough to hold against the pressure?

The answer to that was also simple. Yes, he was, for a while. Eventually he'd get tired and weaken, would lose focus, and then he'd be spit back out. But every time he went back in, he lasted longer. He was to the point where he was no longer worried about being ejected if his concentration slipped, though not to the point where he could just exist indefinitely.

His new idea for obtaining arcana was to expand the bubble into layers, to make a second conduit that would grow over top the one he was using to protect himself. Then, when that was fully sealed with a layer of arcana sandwiched between the two conduits, he'd simply break down the inner layer. Then he'd have a measured and contained amount of arcana to play with.

That worked alright, as far as things went, but it was also slow. It would be time-consuming to get a usable amount, and it made it impossible for him to work any kind of magic that required more arcana than what he could hold in his soul well. Since he knew it was quite possible to cast seventh-layer spells by continuously channeling arcana, he had to be doing something wrong.

Once again, his mind came back to the idea that he simply wasn't strong enough and that the only solution was to spend more time there, to train himself to withstand the pressure. His only other idea was that there were probably a few new modifications he could make, small ones that relied on seventh-layer arcana and could be done without massive amounts of it.

Those might help, but they wouldn't solve the issue for him. Still, it gave him something to play with while he sat there and waited for the pressure to mount to the point where it became unbearable. Or, more realistically, he was waiting for the pressure to remain exactly the same and his own reserves to weaken.

Perhaps he'd work on adding new parallel processes to his mind. He was still short by a few if he wanted to be able to cast the god-killer spell, and this was an opportunity to take a step toward fixing that. That would be a good use of his time and resources.

"I knew it," Nym said, laughing to himself.

It really had been the simple, obvious solution. Time and effort spent to grow stronger, to grow accustomed to the reality of the seventh layer, that was all he really needed. The conduit was hardened around him now, projected from his soul well like a second skin. When he needed arcana, he weakened it just a bit and let a trickle absorb into him. When he had enough, he flexed the conduit back to its full strength. The more he needed, and the faster he needed it, the more he just relaxed that conduit-shaped muscle.

If there was ever a point in this whole experiment where he could say that he honestly felt like he'd advanced to the seventh layer, it was right now. He still couldn't stay there indefinitely, but he could control the arcana he took from it completely. That opened up plenty of new ways for him to improve, possibly even enough to cast the god-killer spell. Soon, he'd be able to move onto the next part: spying and waiting for the right moment to strike.

CHAPTER SEVENTY-TWO

The modifications went well. They weren't terribly dangerous, but mistakes could have unacceptable delays, so Nym was glad to have performed them all properly in the first attempt. More accurately, he was glad to have not made any irreversible mistakes. It took him more time than he wanted, but when he was done, everything worked right, and he was one step closer to being able to handle each part of the god-killer spell simultaneously.

There was less progress on the front of actually casting the spell, but he was still advancing steadily toward the goal. Of the framework that Myzalik had used, Nym had no hopes whatsoever that he could replicate that, but since Niramyn always maintained a presence in the core reality, Nym hoped that meant the inevitable confrontation would also take place there.

That was where Nym ran into his first real problem. He'd deliberately isolated himself, which was great for working in peace, but it made it very, very difficult to know what was going on with the rest of the ascendants. If he didn't know what they were doing, it was hard to find the opportunity to strike. He'd done some scrying, but that was risky, and he'd strictly limited the amount of spying he did. It didn't matter if he had the perfect opportunity tomorrow since he couldn't actually use the god-killer spell yet.

Still, it was prudent to start laying out the foundations of his plan now, so Nym reluctantly broke his ban on speaking with other ascendants. Eriam would have been his preferred contact, as Nym felt the most connection with him and bore some goodwill toward the ascendant. Unfortunately, he was still gone, or at least had hidden himself away well enough that his location wasn't freely available.

Working on the theory that members high up in the Ascendant Council would be less likely to sell him out to either of the warring factions, Nym decided to approach Baracia again. Of the few ascendants he'd worked with, she'd been the most vocally outspoken against the fighting. That wasn't to say that she didn't want to get rid of Myzalik, just that she didn't support Niramyn.

She was also something of a public figure and made no effort to hide her home. There were a few other ascendants who operated in a similar manner, but Nym didn't know them personally, and he wasn't willing to take the risk of speaking to someone with unknown alliances.

He was barely willing to risk talking to Baracia and took every precaution to protect himself. He sent in a copy, of course, but only after he created a brand-new sanctum in a random location for his copy to use as a base. The copy then willed himself around a few dozen times to make the trail as hard to follow as possible, then finally sent a request for a meeting as a letter he willed into existence and sent her way.

The copy was, by necessity, vulnerable to attack, but rather than keep an active scry link, Nym just waited for his double to return. He didn't want to take a chance with someone tracing the scry back to him, and if his copy didn't return to the decoy sanctum in the expected time frame, Nym would take that for an answer.

And then something went right. The copy did show back up, whole and unharmed. Nym met with him, still somewhat uneasy about the idea of being ambushed but with no better ideas to secure himself than what he'd already done.

"You met with her?" he asked his copy.

"Everything went smoothly. She was more than happy to gossip, as she calls it, and apologized for introducing us to Hozim."

"That's good. What did we learn?"

"The ascendants are still fighting in that block of time right after we ascended, but there's a bit of a hitch. I'm not sure if they've been blocked from it or already used that time, but it seems like neither Exarch has taken to the field, so to speak. They're both sitting back in the outer layers and letting their minions duke it out."

"Why? What's the point?"

"For Niramyn, who knows? For Myzalik . . ."

There was no real explanation required there. Myzalik could kill ascendants just as easily in the outer layer as he could in the core reality, and since ascendants only had to exist in the outer layer, he didn't actually need to go to the core reality. On the other hand, it was markedly easier to find another person in reality prime than it was in the sixth layer.

There was nothing to say that rumor was fact though. Just because no one was talking about spotting him in reality prime didn't mean Myzalik never went there. He could step in, kill an immortal, and be gone again in minutes, with no one else the wiser. Or maybe he couldn't. Maybe he'd used all the time in those years already.

Maybe it didn't actually matter. Now that he thought of it, it wasn't really relevant when he killed Myzalik, just that he did. He could just pick a different time when the Exarch was in reality prime and attack him then. That actually might be better. He could find out exactly what had happened and plan around that. It would give him time to figure out exactly what defenses the Exarch had and how to breach them.

More likely, Nym would find out that he couldn't get close, at least not if he picked some time when Myzalik was safe in his own fortress. There had to be times when he wasn't though, when he clashed with Niramyn. From what Nym understood of their whole history, they'd been at each other's throats for millennia.

Thank God for timeline splits and corrections because he couldn't even begin to trace the waves of changes killing Myzalik like that would cause. It might even be enough to cause a deviation of the prime timeline, but if so, Nym was happy to leap into that alternate future. What he was really concerned about was that the timeline itself would resist the change, and he would be working against fate, for lack of a better term.

On the other hand, Myzalik had killed a few dozen of the supposedly immortal ascendants already, so it couldn't have been that much of an issue. Whatever impact it had made, it wasn't enough to split the timeline that hard. That was good news, since it meant he likely wasn't working against the inertia of history.

"Did you want to hear about the rest of the meeting, or are we done?" the other Nym asked.

"Hmm? Oh, sorry. I had an idea for how to target Myzalik and got distracted."

"Targeting him during one of his past confrontations with Niramyn, right? I had the exact same thought as soon as I found out he wasn't participating in the current block of years' conflict."

"Pretty much. I take it you asked Baracia for information about that."

"I did, yes. I got a list of more forty encounters they've had in the core reality, but there are only three that take place inside our current range. One of them actually caused our birth."

"We'll have to confirm and see if we can find out more details. I think I'd feel a bit more comfortable if we chose a different one, just on the off chance that we wipe ourselves out of existence by interrupting that one."

"Agreed."

"I don't suppose Eriam has shown his face, has he?"

"No such luck," the other Nym said.

"Too much to hope for, I guess."

"Valicin is out on the front lines, fighting for Myzalik now. There was lots of chatter about her switching sides, and more than a few have correctly speculated why she did it."

Nym shrugged. "Is anyone from Myzalik's side looking for us? I imagine she probably told him everything she knows."

"If they are, they're keeping it quiet. Then again, Niramyn's side is also keeping it quiet, and we know he's still looking for us. Maybe we got lucky and dropped down far enough on his priorities that he didn't assign anyone new to take Valicin's spot, especially after he lost Ferro."

"We'll still have to be cautious, but I think we can start trying to look into those three incidents of the two Exarchs fighting and figure out which ones suit us best."

"Maybe, but those are probably the two worst people we could possibly spy on. There's some real risk of getting caught, and if Niramyn is the one who does it, then we're likely to immediately jump back to the top of his priorities."

"I know. I wish we could just trust him not to screw us over, but there's no other ascendant I know better than him, and he absolutely would sacrifice us to Myzalik if he thought it meant getting a clear shot at him."

"Same reason we can't trust him with the god-killer spell," the other Nym said.

"Yeah. How long did the meeting with Baracia end up being?"

"I don't know. A month or so I think. She keeps track of things in a weird way. I don't really understand it."

"Is that the highlights then? I don't want to be going through this and find out something important we forgot to talk about next week after we've already started making plans."

"Pretty much everything important. Baracia recommended a few of the stronger neutral ascendants we could try to work with. One of them is actually part of the senior membership of the council. He might be a good bet. Goes by Abarach. I'm pretty leery about any of the other ones, and it seemed more important to get started on figuring out the plan of attack than to take on additional work or get in favor debt with some ascendants we've never met."

"No reason we can't do both," Nym muttered, not that he disagreed.

The two Nyms merged back together soon after that. Nym broke down his decoy sanctum, willed himself away a few dozen times, and eventually arrived back at his original sanctum. It was, as far as he could tell, still undisturbed.

Scrying into the past in the core reality wasn't terribly difficult, but scrying on an ascendant's business was a bit trickier. For one thing, if he wasn't careful, they might realize someone was looking at them, and for another, he was hardly the only person to employ various blocking spells. Nym had a sinking feeling that he was about to embark on developing a whole new skill set just to be able to get a clear look at the potential battlefields he could use for his plan.

The problem with learning things now was that there were no more libraries to raid. His only options were to figure it out on his own, which took a lot of time and effort, or to talk someone else into teaching him. Most ascendants were very willing to teach, especially because Nym was still learning some pretty basic stuff, despite his recent breakthrough to the seventh layer. That had practically been an accident anyway.

But they weren't willing to teach for free, and a lot of them wanted open-ended favors to be specified at a later date. Nym was leery of committing himself to doing something without knowing exactly what it was, and it didn't help that his pool of ascendants to draw knowledge from was sharply limited by the ongoing feud between two Exarchs and their followers. Even the neutral ascendants kept getting dragged into it in various ways.

Maybe that senior councilor would be able to help out, if Nym could figure out a way to get the information he wanted without giving away exactly why he needed it. It could be tricky, but if the Ascendant Council was truly committed to ending the fight and, more importantly, ending Myzalik, it might be worth exploring.

CHAPTER SEVENTY-THREE

Abarach's home was unique in how boring and pedestrian it was. It was big, sure, but it was plain, with almost nothing in the way of ornamentation or even furniture. The windows were featureless squares of glass that illuminated the rooms, but there wasn't actually any sort of landscape beyond them.

Nym met the Ascendant Councilor in the entry hall of his home and was promptly invited to a sitting room that lacked any actual chairs. Abarach simply perched on empty air, so Nym did the same. A pot of tea appeared in the space between them, and Abarach asked, "Would you like some?"

"Yes, thank you."

Why was it always tea? It was fine to drink, Nym supposed, but he was kind of disappointed that no one ever came up with anything better to serve. He resolved right then and there that as soon as he had time, he was going to find a new drink to replace tea as the traditional polite refreshment to offer.

Abarach himself was every bit as plain as his home. He was a tall man with short gray hair and a set of fine wrinkles around his eyes and mouth. Truthfully, the only distinguishing feature he possessed was how old he looked. Every other ascendant had appeared as a youthful person in their twenties or early thirties, or else hadn't looked human at all.

After the tea was served, Abarach settled back and asked, "What brings you to visit? I'm afraid I don't know much about our newest ascendant."

Leaving the teacup floating next to him untouched, Nym said, "I was hoping to get some insight into a spell I'm working on. I think I'm almost done, but there are a few pieces that aren't quite working like I want them to."

"I don't really do that," Abarach said with a frown. "Surely there are other ascendants who could help."

"Probably, but it's an issue of trust," Nym said. "The last ascendant who was supposed to be working with me sold me out to someone in Niramyn's faction who then tried to abduct me."

"Ah, yes. Hozim. You understand that we are not a government and do not have any sort of system in place for punishing other ascendants?" At Nym's nod, Abarach continued, "But I do understand why you would come to someone with a seat directly on the council after that little debacle. Unfortunately, the fact remains that I have little interest in instructing on the basics, and I very much doubt you could afford my help even if I did."

"Ah, it's not really . . . a basic problem, I don't think. Let me just impose on a few minutes of your time to show you what I'm trying to do, and you can decide if it's something worth discussing."

Abarach took a sip of his tea and, with a sigh, said, "Very well. Go on then."

Nym immediately brought up an illusion that showed the spell construct he was trying to form but only the part he was currently working on. "This is what I'm trying to make," he said, "and it seems to be stable on its own. However, I can't connect it to the rest of the spell without an arcana surge coming through and blowing out this spot here."

"What kind of linkage system are you using?"

"I started with Voth's Inversal Theorems. That's what the base spell used, but it failed completely in this modified version, so I tried the Mindarian Method, the Jubei Stasis Coupler, the Grinkle Linkage, even the old standard array port. Every time, the arcana hits this bend and destroys the whole thing. I'm thinking that the linkage system might not even be the real problem."

"Hmm. Interesting. Alright, you've got my attention. This is fascinating stuff. Can you show me more of the spell?"

"Not really," Nym said. "I understand why that might make it harder to figure out the problem, but I'm not able to reveal the rest of it. I was hoping more for advice about some other angles to approach the issue."

"How very mysterious of you, but I understand. We are all of us jealous guards of our secrets, as they say."

"Yeah. I wish I could just show you the whole thing. I'm sure you'd be able to tell me what's wrong in an instant, but those are the constraints I'm laboring under."

Abarach watched the illusion for a minute while he sipped his tea. When the cup was empty, it disappeared, and he crafted his own illusion. "Do you have a spot that looks something like this?"

"I . . . Yes," Nym said. "But that shouldn't . . ."

"No, not on its own, but there's an interesting effect you may not be aware of. It's called the Hemodan Ripple, and it occurs when you cross-connect an auxiliary supply of arcana through two or more modular spell frames."

Nym knew what the Hemodan Ripple was, and he knew that wasn't what was going wrong here. There was only one solution for it: use a higher layer of arcana. But his memory was perfect, and he *knew* that Myzalik had done the whole thing with sixth-layer arcana, except for the framework.

Could the framework itself somehow be stabilizing the spell and preventing the ripple from forming? "Would it be possible to block the reaction that forms the ripple using a framework of stronger arcana rather than directly replacing the affected portion of the spell construct?"

"Theoretically? I suppose so, but that would be an incredibly roundabout and inefficient way of doing it."

"What if the spell wasn't cast in an outer layer? If I did it using only the sixth-layer arcana I brought with me to reality prime, that would mitigate the ripple's damage since there wouldn't be any ambient arcana to resonate with."

"Ah," Abarach said. "Clever of you. Yes, that would do it."

Nym groaned and dismissed the image. That was it then. He couldn't even put the spell together to practice it unless he went to the core reality. Hiding something that complicated was not going to be easy. For the sake of appearances, he said out loud, "I'm going to have to rethink this whole thing then. There's no way to make this work as it is."

"Nym, this spell you're making, you know you're not the only one trying to figure out how Exarch Myzalik did it, right? For someone claiming to want to remain neutral, this is not the direction you want to be moving in."

Nym froze for a fraction of a second, then shook his head. "I want no part of this conflict. I'm just trying to get out of it alive."

"Then I would advise you to abandon this line of research, keep your head down, and wait it out. Exarch Myzalik has made quite a few enemies, all of whom are more dangerous than you."

"Right, I understand. Thank you for the advice, sir."

"Do not trouble yourself over a debt. Consider it a repayment for Hozim's actions. They reflect poorly on the Council as a whole, and I hope you won't hold it against us. Of course, this is the only freebie you'll be getting from me."

"Of course," Nym said. "That's very generous of you."

"Yes, I'm sure. If that's all, you should enjoy your tea and be on your way."

"Oh, yes, I'm sorry. I'm sure you're very busy."

"Endlessly," Abarach said dryly. "For a group of supposedly independent immortals, we can be remarkably stubborn about needing our disputes to be resolved by the Council."

"I won't take up any more of your time then," Nym said.

He said his goodbyes and left.

All the pieces fit together now. Nym just needed to return to the core reality to test the spell out. That was a bit of a problem because he wasn't sure it could actually work on anyone but an ascendant, which meant that his only viable test subject was himself. At the same time, there was no way he was going to take a spell he'd never even successfully cast and attempt to use it on the Exarch who'd created it.

That was why he was standing in one of his hidden sanctuaries in front of a giant glass cage full of butterflies. He'd done his best to block out absolutely everyone from being able to penetrate his defenses by any means. If he was right, the wards would block every sort of scrying and divination, thanks largely to hidden presence's influence. Hiding the arcana was trickier, but he'd set up a few experimental spells for that. Hopefully they'd be enough to hide what was undoubtedly the most massive and complicated spell he'd ever tried.

Nym picked one of the butterflies, a pretty thing with purple-and-black wings, and started the spell. He'd cast each individual component thousands of times, or his copies had at least, and he'd taken the time to really assimilate all their knowledge and experience into himself, however painstaking it had been. He knew he could do this spell.

The spell disagreed and promptly fell apart.

Undaunted, Nym started again. It took all his ability to simultaneously cast all the parts of it needed and bring them into a unified whole, and just like his first attempt, he failed to complete it. That was fine; he hadn't expected it to be easy.

Twelve hours later, he had his first success. The spell didn't work, but it also hadn't collapsed while he was building it. He reviewed his work and compared it to that pristine memory of Myzalik casting it, then nodded to himself. He'd suspected he had made a mistake, and once he took the time to analyze things, he'd confirmed it.

The next attempt went better, though he was finding it difficult to keep everything organized. Crafting each individual portion of the spell separately and then slotting them together was necessary for something this size, but it did add an extra layer of difficulty he wasn't accustomed to dealing with.

More than that, he was getting tired. Physically, he was fine, but he'd channeled a massive amount of arcana throughout the day. With a weary sigh, Nym retreated to the sixth layer to rest and recover. He hadn't expected the spell to be easy, but considering how much time he'd spent working on individual pieces and that he had perfect recall to see over and over how Myzalik had cast it in real time, he was surprised that he was having this much difficulty.

The only bright side was that as a stress test for his experimental arcana-hiding wards, things were going fantastic. Nobody had so much as glanced in his direction, as far as all his divinations could tell. Admittedly, they weren't the best he could create, but he'd sacrificed being able to detect people in the name of staying better hidden.

When he was ready, he went back and started over again. It took him a bit to get back into the right mindset, but soon enough he was chipping away at the problem. Three more times during that session, he managed to complete the whole spell without any part collapsing, though none of those attempts resulted in him being able to successfully cast it.

On the third round of training, things got easier. All his practice linking them together and holding them at the same time finally paid off, and Nym grinned fiercely as he looked into the cage. There, hanging from a branch directly in front of him, was a tiny little cocoon. It existed for a fraction of a second, then a caterpillar fell from the branch. It shrunk away into nothingness before touching the ground.

It was the result of his age-reversal spell, which in the case of the butterfly had actually forced it back into its metamorphic stage and beyond. He was almost surprised that it worked, considering it had been created for ascendants, but he supposed Myzalik had built the spell with a superb amount of flexibility in mind. It was designed by an Exarch, after all.

Or maybe it was just the nature of the spell. It was designed to break things, and there was no delicacy needed there. The god-killer rewound the target's personal time to the point before they became immortal, to the point before they even existed if it ran long enough.

One minor success was far from enough practice. Nym started again from the beginning.

CHAPTER SEVENTY-FOUR

Of his three possible ambush points, Nym most wanted the one that took place a hundred years in the future from what he considered to be present day to be the one that worked. He was fully aware that which time he struck during in the core reality would have made no difference on when Myzalik's existence unraveled in the outer layers, but Nym was far from an expert on temporal manipulation. It just seemed less risky to him that way.

He'd learned as much as he could about all three of the events prior to witnessing them personally, mostly because there was every chance that he could be detected when he went there in person. That was why he didn't go. Instead, he sent a copy to the weeks preceding the actual confrontation, and then another to the days following it.

Two other pairs went to examine the other possible ambush sites, and the real Nym waited in his sanctuary, impatient and nervous and a bit twitchy. A part of him kept expecting an Exarch to knock down the walls at any moment. Surely, they must have noticed him, must have caught one of his copies, or all of them, and squeezed every bit of information out of them.

That didn't happen, of course, but the copies took their time coming back. That was a bit of an issue for Nym, since if they didn't return, and with no scry link, he wouldn't get their memories, but he would still have spent precious time in the core reality scouting. If things took a turn for the worse, he wouldn't be able to visit those days again, and he'd have nothing to show for it.

He'd weighed that risk against the risk of going in person and decided that he could always continue to extend his anchor out and look for new opportunities, even if it would be harder since his target was now aware of Nym. But if he got caught scouting out the battlefield, that was likely it for him.

So he waited, and he worried.

Past Nym stood in a little town about a hundred and fifty years earlier than he'd encountered it in his mortal life. At the time, Thrakus was barely more than a crossroads town with a well-established farmers market. Its central position brought in traders, merchants, and tinkerers by wagon, and many a caravan left with significantly less diversity in its loads, having swapped their cargo for grains, crops, and meat.

Somehow, it still smelled just as bad despite being less than a hundredth of its future size. Nym really didn't get that one, since it wasn't a market day, and there were precisely zero farm animals in sight. The smell just lingered in the air anyway. It should have been impossible. The only reasonable explanation was that the land was under some sort of manure-based curse.

He was sure that he was correct, despite having no evidence to support his theory. Obviously an extremely powerful ascendant had laid the curse down, then made it invisible to all senses, even ascendant sight. How and why that had happened was a mystery for the ages.

While Nym was standing there, a man walked by and gave him a weird look. Nym's nose twitched as the aroma following the man wafted past him. He now had two possible theories, both equally likely.

With a shake of his head, he reminded himself that he had actual business to attend to. The fight between the two Exarchs would happen about fifty miles southwest of Thrakus and would be remembered as the worst storm to ever rock the region. In actuality, it was barely more than a scuffle between the immortals, the ascendant equivalent of throwing a handful of mud at someone's back. But Myzalik would be there, and that was the important part.

Nym didn't think it was a good ambush spot. His target would be in an open sky, clearly facing Niramyn, and unless Nym managed to find a way to dual cast a spell he could barely do once at a time, whichever one of them he didn't target was going to tear him apart. If he could bring his total parallel processes up past forty or so, it might be possible to hit them both at once.

That would require him to get to at least the tenth layer, maybe the eleventh. Even then, he wasn't completely sure it was possible. Twenty-four was already pushing it. No, if he didn't want to spend five or six centuries as a hermit, he needed a scenario that let him come at Myzalik alone, with nobody else ever finding out it was him that had killed the Exarch.

Nym was about to go back to the sixth layer when his nose caught a familiar smell. Just down the street, a pair of entrepreneurial men had set up some kind of grill and were busy roasting meat on it. One was about the same age that Nym appeared to be, and the other was likely a father judging by the fact that he was in his late thirties and looked remarkably similar.

Nym strode over and eyed up the workstation they'd set up. "Steaks?" he asked, though he already knew the answer.

"Yes, sir," the younger one said. "Shield and a half will get you a nice cut."

He didn't have any money on him, of course. Nym had stopped caring about gold and silver the moment he ascended, but it was easy enough to cast a quick scry and confirm the shape of the coins, then create a few inside his pocket. He pulled out two shields and laid them into the waiting hands of the father.

"If this is half as good as it smells, you can keep the change," Nym said.

"Mighty generous of you, sir."

"Not at all. I think this is going to be worth every last shim."

"I hope you still think so in a few minutes. This one is almost ready."

Nym waited near the grill and made small talk while the meat sizzled. "Unusual to smell something this good just on the side of the road. I would have expected you to be working in a restaurant."

"I wish," the young one said while he poked at the steak. "Something of a dream for Pop 'n' me, you know? But, money . . ."

"Makes the world go around," Nym agreed. "What would you call the place if you did ever open your own restaurant?"

"That's a good question," the father said. "What was it you said last week, Baram?"

"The restaurant name? Hmm . . . I had a good one, what was it?"

Nym's breath hitched. If his guess was right, Baram would have a familiar idea. Oblivious to Nym's sharpened interest, the boy pulled the steak off the grill and plated it. "Here you go, sir."

Nym cut a bite off and put it in his mouth. It wasn't exactly like he remembered, but then, there would be at least six generations between now and when he came back to Thrakus in the future. That was plenty of time for things to change.

"Delicious," he pronounced. "Food this good brings back many fond memories. I might take another one."

The father of the duo let out a belly laugh and said, "I won't turn down the business, but maybe you should finish this one before you decide to buy a second."

"So what was your restaurant-name idea?" Nym asked as he cut off another piece.

"Slipped my mind," Baram confessed. "Something to do with horses, I think. Quarter-something."

"A quarter horse?" Baram's father asked.

"Might have been," the boy agreed easily.

"How about Quarterhouse instead? Don't want people thinking they're eating horsemeat," Nym said casually.

"Hey, that's not bad! Yeah, if we had a restaurant, we could call it the Quarterhouse."

"If we had the money," the father said. "Which, that'll never happen. So we have this grill setup instead."

"You make a lot of money off this thing?" Nym asked. He was really hoping the answer was yes.

"Nah. It's hard to gauge how much meat to bring, and if we overstock, we've got no way to store it. Most days we make a bit of profit, but a slow day will kill a whole week's worth of sales."

Nym chewed his steak thoughtfully, then said, "If that's the case, why do it?"

"That's my fault," Baram said. "I love to cook, but if I didn't sell them, we'd bleed ourselves dry off the ingredients."

Nym could fix that, if he wanted. A whole sack of gold crests would solve all those problems, but he had no idea how to just casually deliver that. He could hand it to them, but there would be questions there. Alternatively, he could hide it for them to find. They'd still have questions, but at that point he wouldn't be around to answer them. As long as they didn't connect their sudden windfall to him, it probably wouldn't screw with the timeline much.

Or he could just thank them for the meal and leave. The Quarterhouse did exist in the future, somehow, and would continue to do so regardless of his interference, unless of course the very reason it existed was because of his interference.

"What do you think the chances are of you ever being able to open your own restaurant?" Nym asked.

He already knew the answer, but his heart still sank a little when both of them just shook their heads. "It's a fun dream, but that's all it is," Baram's father said.

"That's too bad. I'm sure it would be a successful business, the way your son cooks."

Nym scanned through the future to see where the duo would return to at the end of the day and, after locating the farm, started checking for a good hiding place. There was no way he was risking the Quarterhouse not existing in his time. Eventually, he found a spot where the wall was going to collapse in three years when one of their goats smacked into the outside of the house. Smiling to himself, Nym deposited a sack of gold crests he conjured up inside it.

He flipped another shield over to Baram, who barely noticed it in time to catch it. "What's this?" the boy asked.

"Keep the dream alive," Nym said. "You've got talent."

He made his goodbyes and walked away. Even if there was no opening to get at Myzalik in this time period, it had been worth the trip.

The original Nym smiled to himself when he finished processing the past copy's memories. The Quarterhouse had been a staple of more than a few good memories. Without it, he might not have ever joined up with the Earth Shapers, which had arguably been some of the happiest weeks of his life.

Good feelings aside, he was a bit disappointed to learn just exactly how utterly unsuited for an ambush the encounter between Exarchs in the past was. Hopefully he'd get better news from the other two groups of Nyms, but neither had returned yet. He generously assumed that was because those conflicts were more complicated and there was more to investigate.

Then the future Nyms returned. Both of them had grim looks on their faces. "That bad?" Nym asked.

"It's pretty rough. We agreed it's a last resort situation, only if the other two possible attack sites are completely unsuited."

"We think there's about a thirty-second window, but we're going to have to majorly brush up on ward breaking if we're going to take advantage of it."

"Past Nyms already came back in," Nym said. "It's not possible to make it work there unless we get strong enough to dual cast the god-killer spell and hit them both at the same time."

"Let's hope present Nym comes back with better news then."

"Yeah, otherwise we're screwed for the foreseeable future."

CHAPTER SEVENTY-FIVE

Present Nym had ample evidence to prove his theory that the games the ascendants played were motivated by equal parts boredom and spite. There was no reason that Exarch Niramyn needed a silkworm colony. He could have conjured up all the silk he ever wanted with ease. He certainly hadn't established the colony to assist a middling merchant house.

Nym was pretty sure the only reason Niramyn cared was that Myzalik was backing a rival merchant house, and either Exarch would happily put the screws to the other if the opportunity presented itself. The silkworms provided product, which turned into capital, and the merchant house he was helping overpowered its rival.

Maybe that would have some far-flung effect in the future that Niramyn was angling for, but Nym was inclined to believe the Exarch didn't care. He'd checked Myzalik's play just because he could, because stopping his rival from achieving any of his goals was reason enough. Nym could scarcely believe the pettiness he saw in two immortal godlike beings.

It gave him a measure of hope though. They weren't infallible. They weren't above base emotions. They could be tricked, or surprised, or outwitted. They were, for all their power, still human at their cores. Thousands of years of experience had not altered that.

That did not mean it was going to be easy, but Nym didn't feel like his goals were impossible to achieve. He hid away, watching the two Exarchs maneuver around each other from their palaces, sending emissaries out into the world, manipulating events, feeding misinformation to the other side, and cheating outrageously when they thought they could get away with it.

Thankfully, the bulk of their effort was put into thwarting each other, so much so that neither bothered to look at anyone else. Other ascendants did whatever things they did and knew to stay away from time slots that the Exarchs fought in. Nym kept himself hidden and watched it all.

Now that he knew how the spell itself worked, and knowing what he did about what had happened in that fateful clash, Nym could make a few guesses about what was going to happen. Myzalik was going to be so focused on the spell itself that he wouldn't have the time to look anywhere else. If Nym could use that as an opening, he could get close.

He could prepare his own spell ahead of time and ambush the Exarch with it when he was distracted. It wouldn't allow him to hit Niramyn, but then, it would also prevent Niramyn from seeing what had happened. Thank God that Exarch Niramyn was the one ascendant who never left the core reality. That would make it easier to predict things, since Nym was going to need to do some guesswork. The timeline was thick with obscuring magic around the event. Myzalik had taken no chances with anyone reverse engineering his spell once he'd unveiled it.

He had enough information for now and didn't want to burn too much of his time here. Nym pushed himself out of reality prime and returned to the original to give his report.

He had two possibilities, neither of them great. If he did it right, he'd have a significantly wider window in the present time than the future, and the past was just out of the question. The only way that one worked is if he decided he was fine with Niramyn capturing him and forcibly taking the god-killer spell.

Since Nym *wasn't* fine with that, he had two possibilities left: present or future. Present worked better for killing Myzalik, but future gave him the opportunity to take out both Exarchs. It would just be far more difficult. At least if he used the future conflict as his staging point for the attack, Nym himself had better odds of not being shunted into an alternate timeline when the prime started fixing itself.

He'd focus on the future, he decided. In order to do that, he was going to need to break through some extremely potent defenses, which meant he needed to figure out a lot of stuff before he was ready to make his attempt. Nym did his best to hold back a groan; he was sick of the hermit life already.

Perhaps Abarach could introduce him to a trustworthy ascendant who wouldn't try to sell him out. Nym could disguise his interest as a fascination with building stronger and better defenses instead of breaking into them, which wouldn't even be a stretch. He was interested in that, after all. He was just also interested in all the ways they could fail or be broken.

He already had a thorough grounding in the field as far as mortal magic went, but ascendant magic teetered back and forth between being the exact same, only more so, and being so wildly different as to be unrecognizable. That wasn't even looking at all the spells that were only possible using outer-layer arcana, things like jumping around in the timeline or resurrecting the dead, or creating something from nothing. Reality didn't like that last one though, and it was ironically harder to make conjured-up items continue to exist than to time travel or bring back someone who'd died, at least as long as he still had the body.

Nym conjured up a message for Abarach, sent his copy out with it, and then settled in to wait. He busied himself by constructing wards using seventh-layer arcana and testing them to see how they compared to the sixth-layer versions he was more familiar with. He found that most of his designs didn't function very well, or at all, due to the amount of arcana bleed over from the physical runes being so close together.

It was possible he could streamline that process and find a way to minimize it, but it was also possible that he'd just need more physical space to accomplish the same thing. Part of Nym hoped that wasn't the case, since it would make it harder to construct wards with stronger arcana while simultaneously making them easier to break.

The other part of Nym hoped for the exact opposite, since his real goal was to get through any defenses Myzalik had set up. If wards became more and more impractical at higher layers of arcana, that might mean the defenses were within his range of skills already. Unfortunately, he hadn't had much opportunity to study how other ascendants did their setups while he was a guest in their homes.

Another open avenue of experimentation was trying to figure out what he needed to reach the eighth layer, but having just barely cracked the membrane to the seventh, Nym thought that might not be the best use of his time. If he had to go that route, it meant he was in for a long, long fight. The feud would probably be over long before he got close to that goal, which might actually be a good thing depending on who won.

He wasn't under any illusions that it was likely anyone besides Myzalik would win. Even without the ability to kill his opponents, something the other team sorely lacked, he was an Exarch with a powerful following. If and when Myzalik won, Nym would have no choice but to sever any and all connection to ascendant society.

At that point, he thought his best bet would be to cycle back to his original plan after building out more anchors if none of the three conflict points he had access to now would work. Hopefully that wouldn't be necessary, but he'd have to see if his ward-breaking skills could compete with an Exarch.

While he was experimenting, his copy returned with the answer. "I guess you could consider this good news," he said. "We already know the ascendant he's recommending we speak to."

"Who is it?"

"Pyoka."

Nym blinked. "The one with the weird shapes for a home? I suppose that makes sense. I hope those aren't an example of high-level ascendant wards though."

"Either way, she turned us away last time. What do we have to offer her now that we didn't then?"

"She was willing to take a favor later to assist us," Nym said. "We just rejected it at the time because we didn't want to get dragged into things."

"That's still true," his copy argued.

"If we're really lucky, she'll have something she needs done now. Otherwise we won't have much of a choice. I'm less concerned about owing her a favor if she can show us what we need to know to end the conflict."

"So we'll see her?"

"Well, you will. I'm staying here."

The copy snorted. "Why am I not surprised? You're kind of risk averse, you know. How are you expecting to pull this off if you won't take chances?"

"There's a difference between a necessary risk and a pointless one," Nym said.

"That's true. Still, we shouldn't let opportunities pass us by because we're afraid to act on them."

"I agree. That's why I'm sending you to go learn about ascendant-style warding."

"Right. Anything else before I go then?"

"Nothing I can think of. Actually, let's merge here so you can pick up everything I've experimented on while you were gone. I'll spin out a new copy."

Pyoka's physical form was every bit as eye-searing as he remembered, or rather, her new body was just as hard to look at as her old one. It was some sort of upside-down pyramid with glowing lines going through it. Pieces of the pyramid kept breaking off the bottom side, rotating around to the top, and reassembling themselves as everything fell.

"I admit, I wasn't expecting to see you again so soon," she said. Her voice was weirdly modulated, sounding like it came from far away, and with no discernable source in her anatomy. Nym tried not to focus on it too much; he didn't need the distractions right now.

"I'm a little bit surprised myself."

"Nothing has changed, I'm afraid," she told him.

"On your end. I am after more specific and important knowledge now, something I'm willing to owe a favor or two to gain."

"Oh? Interesting. What are you looking to find out?"

"I have been told that you are the ascendant to talk to if I'm interested in wards and defensive rune sequences."

"Ah, true. That is one of my specialties, though perhaps not the one I am most well-known for. I could provide you with access to my knowledge of initiate spell forms and . . . Hmm. You managed to break through already? That was fast."

"Er, yeah, I guess so?" He wasn't about to admit how much of an accident it had been.

"Very well, if you are capable of stealing arcana from the Crushing Void, perhaps I do have a few tasks you could undertake on my behalf."

That was theoretically better than a favor to be named later, though Nym wasn't entirely sure he liked the idea. For one thing, it would take precious time that he might need later, and for another, if it wasn't a task he was able or willing to do, that could halt the whole agreement right there.

"What are you looking to have done?"

"You are aware of our research labs, yes? Do you have access to any of them yet?"

"Research Lab Six," he said. "Why?"

"Perfect. Somebody needs to go charge the batteries in that one at around 1492 from the Fourth Cataclysm."

Nym did some mental calculations in his head. That would be about seven years after he'd ascended, six years or so after he and Rizin had drained the batteries. *Ha.* And they said they'd just leave it for the next guy to clean up.

"I think I can help with that."

"Good. It shouldn't take more than a day or two of your time."

"Yeah. I'm familiar with the process."

CHAPTER SEVENTY-SIX

Nym chose as late a date as he could, not that he liked anywhere in the time frame. There were multiple other ascendants in the core reality right now, moving against one another either indirectly or in open battle, and he really, really, really didn't want to get dragged into that. As far as he could tell, the majority of the fighting had ended by the time he popped into the core reality, so with a little luck, he'd be in and out after completing his chore.

"Hello, Exarch," Naera said when he entered the lab.

"Hi," Nym said. "Just here to charge the batteries again."

"Ah, thank you. They were starting to get low."

"Just the seventh-layer ones," Nym added.

"Those are the only ones that are dangerously low."

"Great. Lead on then?"

Naera escorted Nym through the lab, which looked exactly like he remembered it. "How'd our fox-breeding program do?" he asked when they passed the data archive.

"Very well. We produced three hundred viable samples, which were released into the wilds at your specified coordinates. The program was put on pause due to significant recent drains. Would you like us to restart it after the batteries have been recharged?"

"No, that's okay. I think it's done what I need it to. If I change my mind, I'll be back to let you know."

"Very well."

Nym already knew where to go, and he could get there ten times faster on his own, but he remembered the last time he'd gone in there, only to find a dozen research assistants waiting for him to come back out. One of them had even told on him to Baracia somehow. If possible, he wanted to avoid that, which no doubt meant that Naera would want to stay in the room just in case he needed anything.

"Has anyone else been through since the last time I was here?" Nym asked, curious to know who might have seen that the arcana batteries needed recharging but not been willing to do it.

"No, Exarch."

Nym probably should have corrected her on calling him that, but since he didn't really have legitimate access, he was concerned that any updates or changes now might bar him from the lab. After he got the batteries charged and got back to Pyoka, he was more than happy to wash his hands of the place.

Until that happened, he wasn't willing to risk getting kicked out. The golems might not be able to handle him directly, but if they removed his arcana print, there were plenty of automated defenses that he was not strong enough to beat. Besides, as long as there were no other ascendants there, it didn't much matter if Naera called him Exarch or not. He was scrambling the timeline anyway so no one would be able to tell who'd been there.

The more he learned, the less confident he was in that as a defense. The spell only worked in the primary timeline, which meant an ascendant of sufficient skill might be able to sort through various alternate timelines and, if not guarantee what had happened, watch enough other versions and make accurate assumptions. Nym hadn't figured that one out until he'd started working on the god-killer spell and realized the obvious weakness.

They reached the battery chamber, and Nym went inside. He was not surprised to see Naera come in right behind him and take up a position right next to the door. "Please let me know if you need anything, Exarch."

Nym closed his eyes tried not to sigh. "Of course. If you have any other duties to attend to, go ahead and take care of them."

"I have nothing as pressing as this," she said.

"Very well."

Nym had charged his share of batteries, though admittedly very few that had been designed to hold arcana from the outer layers, and not ones that held that arcana in the core reality. Outer-layer arcana functioned differently here, mostly in that it was used to permanently rewrite reality instead of to produce a temporary effect. The stronger the arcana, the more spectacular the new reality could be.

Eventually, of course, the arcana would run out, and the effect would collapse as reality rushed in to reassert itself. There were ways around that, depending on the goal. Usually it was best to change something in a way that could have happened, such as conjuring up a building that could have existed but didn't. As long as the spell didn't break in the middle of the process, reality didn't need to correct much once the arcana fueling the change was spent.

Arcana batteries designed to hold outer-layer arcana were specially reinforced to hold against that push of reality that kept trying to wipe them out, and in fact had to use some of their own charge to keep from disappearing out of existence. Since that conduit always had to remain open, at least enough for a trickle to empower the housing, it got tricky refilling them.

It was a bit like trying to pour water into a jug that had water pouring out at the same time, at least if he ignored other problems, like gravity. Fortunately, Nym had watched Rizin fill all of these up already, and he knew the trick. He had to stick a metaphorical finger in the spout to block the arcana coming out, then provide his own trickle to keep the arcana battery firmly anchored in reality, then channel a second stream of arcana through his finger plug into the battery.

It wasn't complicated, but if he screwed it up, the battery would flash out of existence and then he'd have to build a new one. He could do that, but it would take time he didn't want to spend, so he planned on being extremely careful. Before he did anything, he needed to open up a conduit to the seventh layer, which was slightly more difficult when his consciousness wasn't mainly on the sixth layer at the moment.

He took a second to synchronize his existence across layers, then cracked the membrane to the Crushing Void and started to absorb the arcana pressing down on his conduit bubble. Once he'd stabilized the connection, Nym took hold of the battery and began pouring arcana in. After half an hour, it was full, and he let it take over maintaining its own existence again.

Glumly, he stared down the hallway. One down, ninety-nine to go. At the rate he was going, it was going to take him the full two days and then some to fill them all.

"Fourteen to go," Nym said.

He was beyond tired. It wasn't a physical exhaustion or even really a mental one. It was just the pure drudgery of it. There was no thinking, no doing. It was just existing, holding still. He should take some sort of break, but he just wanted to get it over with, so he kept going.

He was about to connect to the next battery when Naera, who'd remained silent the entire time he was working, said, "Another ascendant is approaching the facility."

Nym paused and looked over at the golem. She was still standing at the door, but now there was a second golem with her. "Do you know who it is?"

"I'm afraid not, Exarch. Whoever it is does not have a registered arcana print."

"Anything you can tell me about them?"

It couldn't be Niramyn, otherwise the lab would have welcomed him in. Going by that logic, he could safely remove a dozen or so ascendants, almost all of whom were part of Niramyn's faction. That just left everyone loyal to Myzalik, Myzalik himself, or any of several dozen neutral ascendants. Whoever it was, it would be better for him if he didn't have to meet them.

"They have not breached the magic sealing the entrance yet," Naera said. "Though they have not really tried other than to cast one or two exploratory spells. I cannot guarantee the passive defenses will be enough to bar them entry."

"So switch to the active defenses then."

"Understood. Please relay the Exarch's orders," Naera told the other golem.

"Is this going to cause a problem with the recharge?" Nym asked.

"As of right now, no. The passive defenses draw from the eighth-layer batteries. However, if those are drained to critical levels, the defenses will shift over to using the seventh-layer batteries."

"Okay, I'm going to keep working then. Let me know the instant this ascendant does anything, even if it's just leaving."

"Yes, Exarch."

Nym got back to work, only now the otherwise dull task had an edge of nervous tension to it. It was possible that a random ascendant showing up had nothing to do with him, but one who didn't have access to Research Lab Six didn't have any reason to be there. It was too much of a stretch to say it was just a coincidence.

Even if the ascendant did nothing but sit at the front door, Nym would have to face them eventually. He couldn't jump out of reality prime while inside the lab, couldn't even teleport around. Maybe if he used the specimen-teleportation platform to exit, he could dodge the ascendant that way.

Two hours later, a crash shook the building. Nym almost lost his concentration on the battery but managed to keep it from vanishing. He severed his connection and glanced over at Naera, who looked worried.

"What was that?"

"I am not entirely certain, but I believe the containment space holding the lab has been breached."

"What about the defenses?"

"I do not know, Exarch. Would you like to go to the data archive and coordinate the defense?"

Nym had no interest in doing that. He wanted to charge the last ten batteries and leave, but he suspected he wasn't going to get what he wanted.

Failing that, it was probably best for him to at least keep up with what was going on. He obviously wasn't going to get any more work done, and if he had to fight, he could use a breather first. It was too bad he hadn't been able to spin off a copy to double his working speed, but seventh-layer arcana was still just too new to him. He considered leaving one behind to keep working though, but if he did, he'd be devoting too many processes to the copy and leaving himself without the resources needed to pull in that arcana for his own use.

"Okay, fine. Let's do that. We can at least see what's going on."

The halls were completely empty as they ghosted through them, Nym carrying both himself and Naera on rapid air currents to the data archive. "Where is everyone?" he asked.

"Defending the lab," she said. "We all have our assigned stations."

"Shouldn't you be at yours then?"

"Assisting you is my highest priority."

Nym would have rolled his eyes if the situation wasn't so dire. Even now, with a literal invader to the lab, she was still trying to stick to him. It was no wonder something as simple as routine battery recharging hadn't been able to shake her off.

"Get me to the data archive and show me what I need to know, then go do your job defending the lab."

"I . . . I am not sure— Can I . . . Forgive me, Exarch, but this order contradicts my directives. You can update my directives at the data archive if you wish to give me new ones."

Sometimes the golems were unnecessarily difficult to deal with. Most times actually.

The hallway split in two in front of him, like someone had snapped a stick in half. The part they were in shifted down, and the hallway on the other side of the split twisted up. Nym had just enough time to alter the air currents to throw Naera over the gap before he slid out into a landscape of swirling black and purple.

A man floated there in front of him, but not one he recognized. "So you're him then?" the man asked. "Nym, is it? You have no idea how much of a pain you've been. I lost years of time because of you."

CHAPTER SEVENTY-SEVEN

D o I know you?" Nym said. "Sorry, but I'm still new. Haven't met everyone in the club yet."

The ascendant snorted. "I watched your struggle against that giant ice worm. It was pathetic. Hard to believe you clawed your way so high from there. I think it's more likely that someone dragged you past the finish line. Niramyn? One of his lieutenants like that bastard Ferro? Well, I guess it doesn't matter. He won't be helping you ever again."

Nym did not appreciate the nasty little snicker at the end of that rant. Myzalik had probably done him an unintentional favor by interfering and killing Ferro when he did, but Nym wasn't giving him credit for any altruistic motives. And anyone who thought it was funny was all kinds of messed up.

"Who are you?"

"You may call me Abdun."

Ah, that explained a lot. "You were one of Myalik's bootlickers," Nym said. "Spent a year and some change trying and failing to find me. And then Ferro sucker punched you at the end and cost you a few years of time. That Abdun?"

Abdun's face contorted into a snarl, and arcana flared up around him. "I've been wanting to do this for a long time."

Nym wasn't exactly feeling confident about this fight, but of all the ascendants who could have confronted him, Abdun was probably the best. He was notorious for having been stuck in the sixth layer as an initiate for a long, long, long time, like an unreasonably long time, and with no breakthrough in sight. That meant he had an edge with raw experience but that Nym overpowered him in terms of what arcana he could summon up.

Whatever spell Abdun was casting, it wasn't harmful. Nym was tempted to reach out and try to break it, but he was curious what exactly the other ascendant was doing. Curiosity was overwhelmed by self-preservation though. Abdun was obviously hostile, and whatever he was doing wouldn't be in Nym's best interest.

He lashed out with raw arcana of his own, trying to break the spell apart before it was completed. Abdun showed his experience there and swept Nym's attempted sabotage aside like a fencer parrying an opponent's blade. It wasn't exactly an unexpected response, but Nym had never fought another ascendant and only had his own hypothetical scenarios to draw on.

He came in at Abdun again from four different angles at the same time, but the other ascendant easily blocked each attack while still forming his spell. "That's all you can do? I'm not even fighting back. You really are pathetic."

Then the spell finished forming, and both of them were pulled out of the swirling black-and-purple void into the core reality. They appeared next to the needle, Abdun hovering perfectly still in the darkness and Nym taking a fraction of a second to stabilize himself. He cast a quick perfect-vision spell and floated back up to face the other ascendant.

"Maybe you were wondering what took me so long to come fetch you," Abdun said. "Or maybe you just thought the lab's defenses were keeping me out. I can assure you, that wasn't the case. I just know better than to break expensive toys my Exarch wants left intact. So I had to lock this place down, just to make sure you wouldn't get away, before I went and dragged you out."

Nym didn't need to test that to know Abdun wasn't bluffing. He could feel it woven into reality around him, the same way it was inside the lab. He just hadn't quite recognized what that feeling was amid all the other differences between lab space and reality space. Now that he was away from the lab, he could clearly pick the teleportation- and reality-locking wards out of the background ambience. It seemed Abdun wasn't taking any chances with him getting away. By the time Nym found his way through those wards, he'd have given the other ascendant a hundred chances to take him out.

Losing a fight here would result in him blowing out at least one anchor, possibly more, and this wasn't the best time to lose access to a chunk of the primary timeline. Worse, it could mean capture and delivery to Myzalik, whom Nym did not want to see again except on his own terms. Preferably, that would be at the end of an ambush that resulted in him smiting the Exarch with his own spell and ending the threat permanently, all while making sure no one else witnessed it.

Abdun's body flared with arcana, and he began casting a dozen different spells. Nym recognized all of them at a glance, spells to paralyze and blind him, spells to break his own spells, spells to blast him with fire and lightning and ice, spells to attack his soul well. Those were mild inconveniences at best, mortal magic that would handicap him so that Abdun could hit him with the real spell.

Hidden behind all of it was a sixth-layer spell, but not one Nym knew. If he'd had a few seconds to study it in relative peace and without the screen of other spells being generated on top of it, he could have figured it out. Failing that, he was forced to react immediately. Nym attacked again, this time in an effort to break through the screen of weak spells and disable the reality-warping spell Abdun was weaving together.

His inexperience showed again, and he realized moments too late that despite being aware of the danger that sixth-layer spell presented, he'd allowed his opponent to direct his response by giving him a target and forcing him to focus on it. Most of Nym's attacks failed, and the ones that succeeded only did so because Abdun didn't contest the dispelling arcana. He didn't need to.

What Nym should have done was to completely ignore the weaker spells, take the hits if he needed, and go straight for the throat. He'd known it was too dangerous to ignore, but he'd stupidly torn apart the spells in front of him in an effort to figure out the best way to attack the spell that was important. If he'd just wielded his stronger seventh-layer arcana like a sledgehammer and broken everything instead of relying on finesse, he might have won the fight right there.

Instead, Abdun finished the spell, and Nym found himself being crushed under the weight of a reality that no longer recognized his presence. It was trying to force him out, but he was still caught in the dimensional lock. Magic ground him between the two and tore at his physical body, threatening to break him if he didn't do something soon.

For all Abdun's experience, he'd made a mistake. Nym was new as an ascendant, and that made his opponent underestimate him. Once he thought he'd snared Nym in his spell, he stopped to gloat again. "As I said, pathetic. I can't believe I lost so many years hunting you down. You're barely even an ascendant."

To be fair, the fight had lasted all of two seconds before Nym had been caught, from Abdun's perspective. It took another second for Nym to establish a connection to the seventh layer, and then one more for him to break Abdun's magic. His body unfolded back into its normal shape, no worse off than he'd been when the spell had started trying to push him out of reality.

Nym didn't waste a moment trading snarky quips. He just poured seventh-layer arcana into reality and told it that Abdun was being thrown all the way to the ground and that he'd be stuck there. Instantly, the ascendant was jerked sideways, then straight down. He broke free of the spell just as he was skimming across the rock, barely in time to avoid crashing.

Nym chased him down, already forming his own screen of spells and hurling them in a barrage to keep Abdun on the back foot. Even if all he managed was to destroy a mortal shell, that was enough for him to break the dimensional lock and escape. But Nym wanted more. He wanted to break an anchor loose and prevent Abdun from even coming back for months, maybe years if he was lucky.

So while he was tying Abdun up with lesser spells, he was preparing his own real attack. And since he wasn't aiming to capture, it was actually far easier. Abdun's gloating smirk had turned into a hate-filled snarl, and arcana blasted out in waves of pure force, breaking through every spell Nym threw his way. Most of them didn't even have time to fully form before they disintegrated under a wave of magical force.

The thing about an anchor-severing spell was that it was remarkably similar to one part of the god-killer spell. Breaking the safety nets ascendants used to maintain their immortality was one of the major steps in the process of erasing them from existence, after all. But while the god-killer spell had so much more going on, breaking an anchor was significantly simpler.

It was so simple, in fact, that Nym could do it five or six times at once. More specifically, five or six Nym copies could do it all at once. Abdun's eyes widened as multiple Nyms descended on him, blipping short distances through the air as they fought against the teleportation lock.

He blasted the first Nym with another reality-crushing spell. There was no resistance there, that Nym having existed as nothing more than a delivery method for the spell that would boot Abdun out of reality prime. But his attacks on the other Nyms fell short, too predictable or too slow.

Spell after spell smacked into Abdun, each one individually weak but also enough to rock his mind and shatter his concentration. Abdun howled in fury and upgraded his force magic to a wave of pure arcana that blew the crowd of Nyms backward but not quickly enough. Four of them had already delivered their payloads, and with them serving as an optical barrier and distraction, Abdun had just enough time to see the spell slam into him through the copies.

Nym watched with fascination as Abdun was jerked through reality. He could actually see the tethers connecting Abdun to his temporal anchors flex against the spell, then snap. One, two, and then a third all popped loose, and Abdun tore through the dimensional lock as reality spat him out of the timeline, leaving Nym alone once more.

It was a good thing Nym had that seventh-layer shot of arcana ready to go. Without that, Abdun's opening salvo would have caught him, and the fight would have ended without him ever getting a chance to defend himself. He couldn't rely on that again, especially since the number of ascendants still stuck in the sixth layer was vanishingly small. Abdun was very much an anomaly, from what Nym understood.

He approached the needle and let it pull him back into the lab. For the first time ever, the entry hall was completely empty, which, once he thought about it, didn't really surprise him. Nym glided through the halls on fast currents of air, eager to reach the back and get this job done with. If he was lucky, he'd finish it before any other ascendants got the bright idea to come after him.

He'd only kicked Abdun out of the mortal timeline for at best a year or two, maybe not even that long. Nym was no expert on judging how much damage he'd done. He was confident he had enough time to finish this favor for Pyoka though. What he wasn't confident about was how Abdun had known to find him. Pyoka might be a dead end, and he'd have to consider that carefully, but for now, he'd already done almost everything he'd promised to, so he might as well finish it instead of burning that bridge before he determined who exactly was to blame for that little ambush.

Nym got back to work charging the batteries, this time without Naera staring at him. He almost found he missed her presence. Almost, but not quite.

CHAPTER SEVENTY-EIGHT

Abarach was noticeably annoyed to see Nym again so soon, but he maintained a polite tone. "I really am quite busy," he said. "Surely there must be someone with less on their plate you can turn to for help."

"Well, I thought so, but you see, Pyoka sent me out to do something for her, and while I was working, one of Myzalik's men found me. So now I'm concerned about whether or not I can trust Pyoka to deal fairly with me. And since you recommended her to me, and I've already been burned by a Council-recommended ascendant once, I thought you'd be the best person to talk to about it."

"And what makes you so sure it's not just a coincidence?" Abarach asked, still stiff.

"I take great pains to obscure my activities as best I can. You may notice that even now, I'm maintaining various effects to make it difficult to find or track me."

The old ascendant took a moment to study Nym, then shook his head. "Your attempts are admirable, such as they are, but such workings can be countered. You are hardly as invisible as you seem to think."

"Duly noted," Nym said. "So you will vouch for Pyoka?"

"Absolutely," Abarach told him immediately. "You would be hard-pressed to find any ascendant who cares less about our politics and drama."

Nym wondered exactly what she did care about then, and whether or not it was something that other ascendants could use to buy information from her. Just because she wasn't likely to go out and fight another ascendant didn't mean she wouldn't sell him out to someone else who would.

"It's still suspicious that someone found me," Nym said, more to himself than to Abarach.

"Is it? It is well-known that new ascendants have a tendency to visit the same places over and over again during the time periods they would have lived as mortals. Eventually, they use all that time up and become much less predictable since they don't tend to develop new bonds in other time periods, but until that happens, an excellent way to find an ascendant who is taking steps to ensure that they are well hidden is to watch the timeline for them physically appearing in a place you know they like to go to."

"Oh, so you're saying because I've visited that place repeatedly, he knew to look for me there," Nym said. "But why wait so long?"

"Perhaps this other ascendant had already used his time in the core reality during your other visits," Abarach said.

That made sense to Nym. He knew that Abdun had been beaten soundly and lost a big chunk of time for the current conflict. Perhaps Nym had just gotten lucky and all his previous visits to Research Lab Six had taken place inside that block of time. That did mean that in the future, he would have to be wary of ever visiting the lab again, now that Abdun knew he could find Nym there.

"That is an excellent point," Nym said. "Thank you for taking some time to help reassure me."

"You are quite welcome," Abarach said, but in a way that made Nym feel very much like he was not welcome at all. "Now, if that's all, I really do have many other matters requiring my attention."

Considering that splitting off a copy was a spell that even a mortal mage could cast, and that new ascendants could make ten or twelve copies that acted simultaneously, Nym didn't feel too guilty about wasting a few minutes of the councilor's time. He'd raised a few good points Nym hadn't considered and perhaps shaken his confidence in his ability to hide.

Then again, if Abarach was right, the only reason Abdun had found him was because he was getting predictable. Baracia had found him in the same place too. The real lesson was to stay far away from Research Lab Six before it got him in trouble. He'd gotten lucky that Baracia wasn't aligned with either of the two warring factions, and then lucky again that the first hostile ascendant to find him was somehow still stuck as an initiate.

Next time, it might be Myzalik himself tearing him out of the lab. Nym didn't see any reason for it, since he was no longer Niramyn, but that hadn't stopped Abdun. The safe move was to just stay away and to send a copy of himself to everything he could reasonably send a copy to. They weren't as good as going himself in a lot of ways, mainly that for the more complicated spells, they were almost completely incapable of performing them. Anything that started requiring he run pieces in parallel processes in order to cast a single coherent spell was unlikely to be replicated by a Nym copy.

For basic fact-finding and exploration though, copies were fine. More importantly, they were disposable. As long as they made it back to him, he'd get all the knowledge as if he'd done it himself. He could even see through them, though after Ferro had shown up at his sanctuary, he was hesitant to use a scry link anymore. It was too easy to trace back to him.

That was precisely why he went through the laborious process of teleporting all over the place, dozens of times, before he returned to where the original Nym was waiting for him. The two merged back together, Nym took a few minutes to process the conversation and his copy's thoughts on it, and then, finding that he agreed with himself, he spun off a new copy to go talk to Pyoka.

He wasn't looking forward to absorbing those memories back in. The instruction would no doubt be useful, but Pyoka herself continued to give him headaches every time he saw her. While he waited for that Nym to come back, he occupied himself by creating an illusion of Myzalik's core-reality palace. There were a lot of gaps in the layout, places he hadn't been able to scry into.

In fact, most of the layout was extrapolation from the few places he had been able to look at. More than that, the scrying wasn't based in the same time that he planned on entering. Changes happened by the minute, and it was almost certain there had been some fundamental shifts in the decades between Nym's various scrying probes. His options were limited, and he was working with as light a touch as he could, only at times when he could confirm Myzalik wasn't actually present in his palace.

And he was still concerned that, for all the delicacy he was putting into the operation, the Exarch had seen him and knew about his intentions. Every single time one of his copies worked a spell designed to poke at Myzalik's palace, they wondered if this was the time the Exarch would come storming out and obliterate them. If they did, Nym would never even know what they'd done to tip him off. Worse, if that happened, he might never find another window where his target was vulnerable.

The backup plan at that point was to join forces with Niramyn. It would certainly be easier, but Nym suspected the first thing his progenitor would demand of him was the spell form for the god-killer spell. He could easily see Niramyn deciding to test it out on Nym to dispose of him, then using it on Myzalik himself.

It wasn't an ideal solution, as far as Nym was concerned. Sure, it was possible Niramyn would play it straight with him, but he didn't expect it. Taking that risk would be beyond foolish. Besides, his ultimate goal was to get rid of both Exarchs, though failing that, Myzalik was his priority target. As long as nobody figured out it was him who had done them in, he might finally be able to get a little peace.

The pessimistic voice in the back of his head laughed at him for thinking that. Even if he pulled it off, there would always be another problem. Every time he'd tried to just have a life, something had come up. The undead invasion from the tear in the veil had just been the first disaster. The ice-worm queen, the Collective kidnapping him, the chance meeting with Rizin, Ferro finding him—his life was just him lurching from one problem to the next.

Nym was tired of that. Even with all the subjective years he'd lived after ascending, he still felt mentally and emotionally exhausted. The long periods of enforced isolation hadn't helped either. He really just needed it all to be over with so he could finally unwind and relax.

A week or so after he'd sent a copy to Pyoka, that copy returned. He met it at the dummy safe house he'd constructed, absorbed its memories, and then returned to his real, somewhat more secure sanctuary. The Nym copy had a ton of new insights into warding, both setting and breaking them on a level that ascendants were accustomed to working at.

Whether it would be enough was another matter, but that was all he was going to get from Pyoka unless he wanted to run more errands, and she didn't have anything else available at the moment. So Nym settled in, started scrying through the future of the core reality, and ever so slowly teased his way through the defenses embedded in Myzalik's home. He spied on the guests, the servants, and the minions. He mapped the layout and its changes over hundreds of years.

Nym plotted, and he planned, all with the singular goal of finding a way through the twisted labyrinth of defenses so that he could take one single shot at the Exarch, just one surprise attack that Myzalik wouldn't see coming.

He thought he could do it, if he was bold and smart and lucky. Time would tell if he was correct.

Myzalik was annoyed more than anything. He'd kept about half of what he'd stolen from Niramyn during the two years or so when the other Exarch had been rendered powerless, but none of his people had actually been able to find his rival when he was trapped in a mortal body. If only they had, his victory would have been complete.

Now Niramyn was back and almost as strong as the day Myzalik had tried to kill him. What's more, he'd even inadvertently created some sort of sapient duplicate as a side effect of the temporal-breaking spell. That had been completely unforeseen, despite all Myzalik's testing.

So there was a new ascendant running around now, but thankfully Niramyn had treated him like he did everyone else, and his little doppelgänger had enough of Niramyn's personality that he hadn't taken it graciously. The fact that an Exarch had somehow lost track of what had been at the time a mortal archmage and failed to find him before he ascended and now still didn't know where this Nym was, well, Myzalik would have laughed if he wasn't so annoyed about Niramyn managing to claw his way back into power.

More than that, it seemed like everybody was trying to spy on him now. Fifty times a day, his wards pinged another attempt and activated his misdirection enchantments. Sometimes it was better to provide false information than to flat-out deny the intrusion. It was helpful to catch someone trying to act on their divinations after he'd twisted them to give him an advantage. The problem with that was if they managed to slip through, even once, it would tip them off that their information wasn't trustworthy.

But he wasn't an Exarch for nothing. In fact, he was the most powerful Exarch of them all, despite what Niramyn liked to think. His flying fortress island was impenetrable to mortals and immortals alike, and he dared any of them to be foolish enough to try assaulting him. He'd happily scatter their arcana across the infinite realities, an abject lesson to all who thought to test him.

CHAPTER SEVENTY-NINE

Nym was both impressed with and frustrated by Myzalik's defenses. The wards weren't that strong, by ascendant standards. Almost all the arcana used was sixth layer, with a few seventh-layer sections and a single eighth layer that he'd found so far. But they were so intricate and complex that Pyoka's lessons were much less helpful than he'd hoped.

That was to be expected, honestly. Wards just weren't a branch of magic that benefits greatly from excessive power. They were all about finesse, a quality an Exarch had in spades. Nym could barely figure out what the wards did, let alone how to disarm them.

Maybe if he'd been closer to Myzalik's palace, chronologically speaking, it would have been easier to decipher the warding scheme. Doing it from reality prime would also make it easier to examine, though any increased proximity to the palace also increased the risk he was taking. As it stood, it would be the work of decades to find a way through the defenses.

If it was just that, Nym could have dealt with it. He had literally an unlimited amount of time, after all. Unfortunately for him, the wards weren't a static defense. They were continually being updated, improved, or changed in some way. Sometimes, they just shifted as part of the defense. Even if he learned how to perfectly get through them in the time he was studying, that didn't mean they wouldn't be different seconds later.

It became an impossible puzzle, where he needed to not only sort his way through the wards, but then do it again a thousand more times just to make sure he wasn't caught by them minutes later. And that was only to pierce the outer layers of Myzalik's defenses. Even that much assumed he was never caught while he was teasing out a solution. If the Exarch ever became aware of Nym's attempts, he might take an active hand in his warding.

This was the reason his copies had told him he'd have at most a thirty-second window, probably less, to strike at Myzalik in a hundred years. There was also an unfortunate amount of risk of Niramyn getting involved in that scenario, which wasn't something he had a good way to mitigate. It could just as easily end in the same catastrophe that striking at the past scenario would.

Nym hadn't yet begun the process of figuring out Myzalik's personal defenses. His hope was that the magic itself would bypass most of those. It had worked on

Niramyn, after all. Theoretically, the spell would be recognized as beneficial and, more importantly, self-cast. That was one of the tricky things it did, he'd found. God-killing magic was based on age-reducing magic, which was impossible to use on someone else and seemed to ignore a lot of defenses because it tricked them into thinking the victim was the caster.

His main concern was that there would be other defenses Myzalik might have that Niramyn didn't. As the creator of the spell, if there was anyone who'd figured out countermeasures to protect against it, it was Myzalik. But, if that were the case, Nym's only remaining options were an endless existence as a hermit or to die fighting.

Given who he was going against, his death would erase him from existence. He supposed at that point, he wouldn't care either way. Nym certainly didn't want to die, but he wasn't willing to spend centuries or longer hiding, waiting for someone else to take care of his problem for him. There was nowhere left to run now.

Still, for all the problems arrayed against him, Nym thought he had a chance of winning. He was working on cracking the wards, the god-killer spell should account for most personal defenses Myzalik would have, and if not, it didn't matter. He was only going to get the chance to cast that one single spell anyway. If it didn't work, the final fallback plan was to turn the spell over to the Ascendant Council and, well . . . everybody.

If everybody could kill an ascendant, there wouldn't be anything special about him knowing too. They'd be just as mortal as the humans they looked down their noses at.

But first, he needed some help. Nym knew the weakest point in any warding scheme. He'd spent an inordinate amount of time trying to strengthen it himself. It was the spot where the ascendant looked out at the rest of existence. That, if anything, would be his entry point. At least, it would be if he could find the damn thing.

Nym decided he needed help from an infiltration specialist. Fortunately for him, he happened to know one. He had lost track of his acquaintance over the last century or so, but, well, finding him again shouldn't be too difficult.

Nym appeared in the sky over a familiar island and glanced down at it, searching. His eyes were keen enough to make out individual leaves from a mile overhead, but his magic was what did the heavy lifting in his search.

There was plenty of wildlife on the island but no people. Hidden by the shadows of the trees and also their own magic, the foxes skulked about. They hunted for prey or for one another in games of sport. All of them were intelligent, at least as smart as any human Nym had ever known. Truly, Rizin's project had borne fruit.

In a way, he was surprised that the island had existed for a hundred years without interference from so much as a single ascendant. Perhaps Rizin had found some way to hide the connection between the lab and his island. Or perhaps no ascendants had ever bothered to go look. It seemed to Nym that very few of them did more than casually glance in the lab's direction to check up on whatever projects were important to them, of which there were few.

Then again, he'd had the bad luck to encounter other ascendants there twice, including one who seemed to hold a grudge against him. Nym suspected there were some sort of fox-magic shenanigans going on, which suited him just fine. Fox-magic shenanigans were the reason he was there, after all.

He quickly found hundreds of foxes, but none of them were the one he was looking for. That didn't do much to deter Nym, since what he was really doing was making his presence known. Rizin would find him soon enough.

An hour later saw Nym feeling considerably more impatient about the whole thing. Either Rizin wasn't paying very close attention to his foxes, or he knew that Nym was there and was screwing with him. Or . . . something had happened to him in the last century. Perhaps the ascendants had been paying more attention than he'd given them credit for.

Nym was in the middle of skimming through the island's timeline, looking for any signs of Rizin, when he noticed one of the foxes watching him. She had pale-blue-and-white fur, and unlike the other foxes he'd found, this one had three tails fanning out behind her.

"Interesting," he said. She wasn't immortal, but she was on her way. He didn't know exactly how foxes went about the process, but it was obvious that she'd begun it. That might be Rizin's work there. It was at least a good place to look.

He teleported down to stand in front of her, scattering nearby wildlife with his abrupt appearance. The fox watched him calmly, unmoved by his magic. "Hello," she said.

"Hi. I don't suppose you could spare a minute to help me out."

"I could," the fox said. "I'm not sure that I will."

"Mmm, that's fair. It would be foolish to agree to something without first knowing what it is you are agreeing to."

"Precisely," the fox said.

"Then, let me tell you. I am searching for Rizin, a mystic fox I once knew a hundred years ago."

"I do not know such a being."

"I see. Interesting. Well, then, I guess I'll be on my way. Thank you for taking some time to talk to me."

"You are still no fun at all, even after all these years," a voice said from behind. "Or maybe it's just been a blink of an eye to you."

Nym felt power swell up behind him, something huge and looming and dark, and he rolled his eyes. "I see the project's going well for you. I was wondering if it was a coincidence that no other ascendants have ever appeared or if it's something you did."

"Little bit of both," Rizin admitted. "Aren't you going to turn around?"

"No."

"Why not?"

"Because you want me to."

"Considering that you're here to ask me for a favor, it seems like the least you could do is humor me."

With a sigh, Nym spun in place and looked up at Rizin, who was about thirty feet tall now. His fur had lightened to a washed-out, sun-bleached, pale red. He sported the same vulpine grin he always had. The big difference though, at least from Nym's perspective, was that he could see eight tails now. There was still space missing for one, but he suspected if and when he reached the eighth layer, he'd finally see that as well.

"I thought you were immortal," Nym said.

"I am! Why would you think otherwise?"

"Just noticing a bit of gray here and there."

"What?" Rizin yelped in outrage. "There's no gray!"

"Mmm, looks pretty gray to me." Nym looked over his shoulder at the blue fox. "What do you think?"

"I see no . . . new . . . gray," the fox said.

"New gray! You traitor!"

"Apologies, Father."

"Father, huh?" Nym asked.

Rizin shrunk down to a more reasonable size and said, "I am father to them all."

"As long as you don't try to insist I'm their mom," Nym said.

"Well, of course not. If anyone is, it would be your golem."

"Naera isn't really mine."

"That wasn't the point," Rizin said.

"Father, do you need anything else?" the blue fox asked.

"Hmm? No, thank you for the help."

With a nod of her head, the fox disappeared from sight. Nym could still see her outline inside the cloud of arcana she'd cloaked herself in, but he pretended not to as she slipped away into the brush. Rizin watched him with a grin, and said, "My protégée. Someday, in a few hundred years, she might become like me."

"Want me to check for you?"

"Nah, half the fun is in waiting to find out. Why skip to the end?"

"Well, if you're sure," Nym said. "So how has the last century been treating this place?"

Rizin circled around Nym once, then said, "You don't really care. Hmm . . . Not much has changed. You've made it to the seventh layer though. Congratulations. How many decades has it been since you've last seen me?"

"It's hard to keep track in the outer layers," Nym admitted. "No need to eat or sleep. No rising or setting of the sun. Really, no sun at all."

"Sounds awfully boring. I never could figure out why your kind is so obsessed with lurking out there, where nothing interesting ever happens."

"I'm starting to agree."

"But you're here now, so I'm guessing you have something exciting in mind."

"You could say that," Nym said. "I'm looking for a bit of advice on a project I'm working on."

"Interesting. Why don't you tell me what it is you're looking to know, and I'll tell you how much it'll cost you."

"Not here," Nym said. "I want to be behind as many wards as I can."

"Oh? You must be working against someone quite dangerous if you don't trust the hidden-presence spell."

"You have a new lair set up?" Nym asked.

"Of course. Come with me."

Rizin disappeared, leaving Nym just enough time to latch on to the arcana he left behind with his magic and follow it through space. He appeared next to the fox in a vast underground cave, right in front of the giant cushion he'd grown accustomed to finding the fox sleeping on.

"Now then," Rizin said, hopping up, "let's talk."

CHAPTER EIGHTY

That is a tough nut to crack," Rizin said after Nym finished explaining what he was trying to do. "And also, you're an idiot."

"Hey . . ."

"No, seriously. You're having trouble figuring out how to even reach this Exarch, and you think you're going to take a swing at him once you do manage to get in his face."

"I mean, it's more compli—"

"Which, even if you do connect, so what? He's going to hit you back so much harder, probably make your life miserable for decades, maybe centuries if he's the vindictive type. He is, by the way. I don't know a lot about specific ascendants, but Myzalik's got a reputation."

"I know all that. I have a plan," Nym said.

"And, just by helping you," Rizin continued, completely ignoring Nym, "that puts my projects at risk. I don't need a vengeful Exarch mucking with my life. My advice to you is to let this go. You are a long, long, long way off from having the strength to stand up to someone on this level. You have bitten off more than you can chew, and it is time to spit it back out before you choke on it."

"Stop," Nym said. "There's more I haven't told you about. If I can make contact with him, I can beat him."

"There is no way you can beat him," Rizin said. "The idea is laughable. You can't beat me, and I can't beat him."

"I just want you to know how much I appreciate your faith in me," Nym told him.

"It's not about faith. You're smarter than this. You know you can't— Wait a second. You *are* smarter than this. What are you not telling me?"

"I . . . would rather not say."

"Then I would rather not help you."

"Damn it. Fine. You know what Myzalik did to Niramyn about a century ago?"

"The act that created you, yes. And he's done it many, many times in the intervening years to other ascendants, with markedly more permanent results. Why do . . . No. You didn't."

Nym grimaced but kept silent. Rizin stared at him for a moment, a slow grin widening across his face. "You did, didn't you?" the fox squealed. "You figured out how he did it."

"Saw him use the spell," Nym admitted. "He didn't know I was there. Your hiding spells really are top-notch, by the way."

Rizin started cackling madly. "Oh, that changes things! You think that if you can make contact, you can hit him with his own spell. And it only has to work once, right?"

"Yeah. I would appreciate it if you don't go spreading around that I know this spell."

Rizin nodded along with Nym's words. "Of course, because you'd be their next target if the rest of the ascendants found out. And you're much easier to take care of."

"Pretty much, yeah."

Nym hadn't wanted to tell anyone, but he needed Rizin's help. Part of getting that help involved convincing the fox that his plan actually had a chance of working, and if there was anyone he could trust with that information, it was ironically an ally prone to lies, deception, and stealth. The mere fact that the god-killer spell was designed to work against ascendants automatically made it a nonthreat to Rizin.

It occurred to Nym that he probably ought to explain how it worked so that Rizin knew that. The last thing he needed was a powerful and immortal fox deciding that Nym needed to be handled to ensure his own personal safety. He doubted Rizin could do anything permanent to him, but he could severely inconvenience Nym and make it that much more difficult to take any actions in the core reality. Worse, he could tip off other ascendants and let them handle the problem for him.

"The spell works a lot like the standard age-reversal spell, except that it doesn't sort through alternate timelines to mix and match until it gets what it wants. It just turns back the clock, which breaks down connections and can actually split the target back into multiple discrete entities on separate layers of reality," Nym said. "It could turn an ascendant mortal, like what it did to Niramyn, or just completely erase them from existence if it's used long enough."

"How long is long enough?" Rizin asked. "There's a big difference between five seconds and a minute."

"For someone who's physical body is around thirty, maybe ten to fifteen seconds of exposure to completely wipe someone out of existence. Less to just turn them mortal and kill them the old-fashioned way. If it worked on someone like you, it would take a long time. You'd get progressively weaker as you were de-aged, but since all your time is linear and builds on itself, you'd be far less susceptible to the effect."

Rizin started laughing about halfway through Nym's explanation. "I appreciate you taking the time to reassure me, but I'm not concerned about you turning your god-killer spell on me. Although, let's talk about payment. There has been a pesky ascendant who's harassed me repeatedly over the last century. Capturing him and using this spell on him would be both a good test to make sure it works and a convenience for me."

The thought of casually executing someone because Rizin found them annoying didn't sit well with Nym. He could acknowledge the practical benefits of a test run of the god-killer spell before he had to use it on Myzalik, but at the same time, he ran the risk of alerting Myzalik that someone else had figured out the spell. Every other ascendant might just assume Myzalik had been the executioner, but he would know it wasn't him.

If they were going to do that, and that was a big *if* in Nym's mind, it would have to be done almost immediately preceding a strike at Myzalik himself. Otherwise, the risk of him noticing the missing ascendant and tightening his own defenses was too high. The only way Nym was going to pull this off was with the element of surprise. He had to come out of nowhere so fast that Myzalik never even saw what hit him.

"It's risky," Nym said. "Myzalik would know it wasn't him who killed an ascendant."

"It's risky not to make sure the spell works before you try it on an Exarch."

"Well, I mean . . . I can always try the spell on myself and just stop it after a second."

"Now that's just dumb," Rizin said.

"I didn't say I was going to! I just meant that it's an option."

They went around in circles about that for a little while, with Nym unwilling to make such a conspicuous move without having first ensured his access to Myzalik was secured and Rizin unconcerned with the fact that executing an ascendant might provide Myzalik advanced warning. To his way of thinking, if Nym was only getting one shot, seeing what Myzalik's defenses at their maximum looked like was a good thing. That assumed they could overcome those defenses, and in that regard, the fox was much more confident than Nym was.

"Either way, before we even consider this, we need to figure out how to get to Myzalik. The whole exercise is pointless if it doesn't result in taking out the Exarch who has more reason than anyone else to want me dead. Preferably, the plan would also include a way to take out Niramyn, and everyone else can just think they killed each other."

"A second Exarch? You don't ask for much, do you?" Rizin had hopped off his cushion at some point and was pacing back and forth. He stopped and gave Nym a flat stare when he found out about the second target.

"And it should be at a point where Niramyn doesn't see what happens to Myzalik, so we can maintain the element of surprise against him too. But also close enough in time that to anyone not there, it looks like they took each other out."

"I cannot even imagine the magnitude of the favor you'd owe me for this," the fox said.

"All I'm asking you to do is help me figure out how to crack some wards! I'm the one taking all the risks."

"You're still putting me in front of some very powerful, very scary, extremely vengeful immortals that, in the likely event you fail to pull off assassinating one or both of them, might decide to ruin my life."

"No risk, no reward," Nym said pitilessly.

"Too true. Well, let's get started then."

Nym showed Rizin where Myzalik's floating palace was in this time period and went over everything he'd learned about the ever-shifting wards. Rizin followed along easily and several times stopped Nym to ask a few questions clarifying how the wards shifted or interacted with other layers in the ward stacks.

"Okay, let me get my own look at them."

"I've been looking ten years into the future," Nym said.

"It's a lot harder for me to do that than it is for you. I'll be looking at them in the now and giving you my professional opinion. You'll have to apply that to whatever time you do actually act in."

Nym was silent for the next hour while Rizin worked, until the blue fox appeared next to him out of nowhere and asked, "How is he doing?"

Once he got his heart rate back down, Nym scowled at the smirking fox and said, "He's working. It's a delicate job, so I'm trying not to distract him."

"I see. Do you know when he'll be done?"

"Not a clue," Nym said, glancing at the big red fox. Rizin was sitting up front, as immobile as a statue except for his tail, which flicked back and forth regularly. If Nym took the effort to look, he could see the faint outlines of other tails waving about in the other layers of reality he had access to. Other than that, Rizin had given no indications that he was alive.

"I have been done for twenty minutes," the fox said without opening his eyes. "What do you need?"

"The families have assembled, Father."

"Ah, already? Very well, I'll be along in a minute."

The blue fox dipped her head, then disappeared in a burst of unstructured arcana. Nym examined the cloud curiously as it diffused and faded. It was nothing like what he knew teleportation to be and in fact resembled how he moved using sixth-layer arcana, just willing reality to accommodate him.

"That's a neat trick. I could not do that at her level of strength," he said. "Your magic really is different from mine."

"In some ways," Rizin agreed. "One moment while I send an avatar out to attend to this, and then we can go over what I've discovered."

A second Rizin walked out of the first, paced around in a circle once, then disappeared. Unlike the blue fox, there wasn't a whiff of arcana left behind. As always, Rizin's abilities in the field of stealth were unparalleled. Still, for there to be no arcana at all, Nym suspected that the second Rizin was fully illusionary.

"Alright, let's go over this and see how we can adapt it to the time frame you need to use it in," Rizin said. "First, I want to talk about how the ward stacking rotates. Did you notice the pattern on this? Look how the primary node shifts around here, then here, here, and here. Then it exits the stack, and a new ward scheme comes into play over here."

"Right, but the pattern shifts to a completely different path as soon as that new one comes in."

"Every twelve wards, yes. But every one hundred and forty-four wards, it goes back to repeating the first pattern again."

"Ah," Nym said, his eyes gleaming as he watched the illusion move. "So if he doesn't change this up, it's just a matter of figuring out the weakest points in the ward patterns. That's going to be difficult to do though, since there's an outer layer operating on its own pattern and timing and an inner layer past this one that I wasn't able to get a good look at."

"Yes, it's very complicated. Lucky for you though, I am who I am. Let me show you what I found in the next layer."

CHAPTER EIGHTY-ONE

In the end, they concluded that it just wasn't a viable strategy to try to pierce the wards. It wasn't that it couldn't be done, it was that it was going to be tremendously difficult even if they worked together and that Nym would need to focus all his attention on the god-killer spell to hold it ready. They managed to get a look around the palace, even managed to find a redirection ward so cleverly done that Rizin spent a whole afternoon just playing around with it, incorporating parts of the structure into his own magic.

What they didn't find was a quick way through. Lacking the power to smash the wards, their only option was the delicate process of bypassing them if they wanted to strike Myzalik from inside his own palace. Since Nym had never wanted to do that to begin with, it wasn't a huge loss for him. His plan had always been to take advantage of a moment of active conflict between Myzalik and Niramyn.

Unfortunately for Nym, his copies had been correct in their assessment that he'd have bare seconds at most to take out Myzalik before Niramyn arrived on the scene. Given how long he expected he'd need to get a second god-killer ready to go, it didn't look possible even if he executed everything perfectly.

"I think we're going to have to use a different time," Nym said. "I just don't see a way to make this work with the abilities I have now."

"I agree. Of course, I always thought that. There is a vast gulf between your power and those you intend to wield it against."

"And yet, you're still helping me."

"Well, yes, but only because I want to see you use this spell on that ascendant who keeps showing up to pester me every few years."

"Speaking of," Nym said, pausing in the scrying spell he was casting. "We should talk about that. I don't love the idea of killing a random person just to get some target practice. There are really only four ascendants, maybe five, I'm okay with taking out."

"Well I hope this one's on your list," Rizin said, projecting an illusion of a familiar face.

"Huh. You know what? He is." The ascendant who'd attacked Nym at Research Lab Six spun around in a circle, allowing Nym to view him from all sides. "That guy works for Myzalik. He's attacked me once already. Seems to have a vendetta against me for some reason. As long as we do it carefully and don't tip our hands to his boss, I am perfectly okay with testing out the spell on him."

Considering that if Abdun had found him, Nym's fate would have been to be handed over to Myzalik, the only other ascendant who could actually kill him, he felt fully justified in hitting back. He just wanted to do it smart, right before he took out Myzalik.

"So, the encounter a hundred years ago then?" Rizin asked, dragging the conversation back to the two Exarchs.

"The one that resulted in my creation," Nym said. "I wanted to avoid it for a couple reasons. I'm not sure how bad it's going to deviate the timeline if I take out Myzalik before he hits Niramyn with the spell. Also the whole thing has Exarch-level obscurement keeping anyone from looking at what happened."

"That could work in your favor though. It would prevent any other ascendants from discovering what you did when they investigated," Rizin pointed out.

"It could, and that would be helpful. It also prevents us from getting a good look at it and figuring out an angle of attack."

"Does it? If there's anyone who knows what happened in those few minutes of scrambled time, it's you."

"Me? Why would I know? I didn't even exist then."

"But Niramyn did, and you came from him."

"But I don't have his memories," Nym objected.

"No? Are you sure?"

Nym squinted at the fox, who looked unbearably smug. He knew something Nym didn't, and he was going to drag it out for as long as he could. If Nym let him, they'd be going around in circles for the next hour.

"I have never been able to access Niramyn's memories, even before I became Niramyn again. There were a few involuntary memories he planted in me with specific triggering conditions, but free access was beyond me."

"You're not going to let me have my fun with this, are you?"

"I was not planning on it, no."

"Fine. If you're going to be like that then. No, you don't have Niramyn's memories, and no, you can't access them, but you can serve as a focus to look into the past. You are close enough to what he was that with the right magic, we can pierce the shroud hanging over that section of the timeline."

"Do you know that magic?" Nym asked, suspecting he already knew the answer.

"I do." The fox grinned at him. "I'm sure you're familiar with mortal magic that uses objects with abstract ties to a person or event to look through the past."

"Psychometry," Nym supplied. "Or just token or object reading."

"Precisely. It can be done on people too, and you're a prime candidate. It would be better if you could cast the spell on yourself, but in the interest of saving some time, I'll try it on you first, and we'll see what it reveals."

"Before we do that, is there any chance that Myzalik will realize we broke through the spells he put on the timeline?"

"None at all," Rizin assured him.

The fox stalked around him in a slow circle, arcana flaring and billowing out into the air. At first, it was nothing but a cloud of mist that clung to Nym, but gradually it grew denser, and patterns emerged. Layer after layer of runes Nym didn't recognize cocooned him, and if he didn't trust Rizin quite so much, he would have bolted.

Nym was incredibly vulnerable, ripe to be incapacitated in some way if Rizin betrayed him. The magic was well past the point of fighting back though; he could only wait nervously while Rizin made ever-widening circles around him.

Finally, the arcana burned away, and the fox let out a satisfied sigh. "You're sixty-two years old, just so you know. Subjectively speaking, between the time you've spent here and the time you've spent in the outer layers, that's how long you've been alive. That's not counting all the years you've tacked on through making copies of yourself. I'm sure you already know not to do that in reality prime unless you want to age rapidly."

"You'd think I'd know what I was doing after that many years," Nym said quietly. "Sixty-two. Older than all my friends now, by a lot. And I still feel lost most of the time."

"Sixty-two is barely a puppy," Rizin said. "You're immortal. When you get into the thousands, come let me know."

"Right. It could happen in a blink, as far as you can tell. I could just flit off to the outer layers and not come back until I'm an Exarch myself." Or insane, which was far more likely. "Anyway, did you get a look?"

"I did. Behold."

An image was cast directly into Nym's mind, though it was more than just sight. He could hear the wind, feel the sunlight on his skin, taste some type of wine on his tongue. He could even feel the memory's eagerness for the upcoming show. He was looking forward to rubbing it in Myzalik's face.

The other Exarch projected a visage into his scrying room, as expected. And then things went horribly, horribly wrong. The god-killer spell was already primed; it struck him before he could react. He was overcome by rage and desperation, threw himself bodily from his own palace to break the spell's lock on him.

And then, still a hundred miles or more from the coast, he struck the water. The many enchantments woven into his clothes shielded him from a fatal impact, but his impromptu flight had already worn on them, and skimming through the water was doing him no favors.

He set up the spells that would hide him, mostly mortal magics used in inventive ways, and used the last of the arcana burning in his soul well, now too powerful for his newly mortal body to contain, to weave the strongest protections. The last thing he remembered was sand on his cheek and cold water lapping at his ankles.

Nym snapped out of the memory and shook his head to rid himself of it clinging to his thoughts. "Exarch Niramyn's last moments," he said softly.

"So it would seem. It tells us exactly when Myzalik attacked."

"We could hitch a ride on the connection between his true body and his visage,"

Nym said. "It would bypass practically all his wards. I might not even need to do that. God-killer itself could target Myzalik through the visage. It worked from his end to cast the spell into Niramyn."

"You would have a minute at most between Niramyn's defeat and your own birth," Rizin cautioned him. "At that point, you'll be ejected out of the core reality."

"Right, because that's time I've already used as Nym. Okay, still workable, and it even has the benefit of making sure I don't end up the product of a deviated timeline that never exists in the primary."

Rizin stared at him for a moment. "That's not how it works."

"What?" Nym asked. "Why not?"

"Every alternate timeline is as real as this one. They are all self-correcting, and they all merge together where they can and separate when they must. Regardless of what you do or don't do, you already exist and will continue to do so. That is what makes your spell so dangerous, that it rips its victim out of every possible timeline and reverts them into nothingness. It leaves an ascendant-shaped hole that time itself rushes in to fill."

"Yes . . . That is how it all works," Nym agreed, his face blank.

"Ugh. You're still a baby. You'll figure this all out on your own someday. For now, I think we have a viable target and time frame. There are two components that need to be addressed."

"Niramyn and Abdun."

"Precisely. I'm sure it won't be difficult for you to find out the next time Abdun is going to show up and be here to meet him. From there, we'll proceed directly to crashing your birthday party. What about Niramyn though?"

"Preferably, he would disappear at the same time, but I actually have a thought about that," Nym said.

"Oh? Do tell. I don't think you'd have enough time to recast the spell on Niramyn to finish him off before you're kicked out of the timeline."

"No, you're right. Even knowing exactly where he's going to land, I effectively begin to exist the moment Niramyn seals his memories inside that cube. That's a hard wall for me, and I need the time he spends casting those spells to take care of Myzalik. There's no way to get them both if we let Myzalik strike first before ambushing him."

"So then, you'll need to repeat this whole setup but focused on Niramyn. You are of course aware that he is considered the more powerful of the two Exarchs."

"Yep, I know. But there's a spot where he's vulnerable. It's going to be tricky, but I think I can exploit an open window at a different moment in the timeline. I might need your help."

"Hmm. That would mean bringing me up to speed in the past, which you clearly didn't do, else I'd remember it."

"I did say might," Nym said. "If I do it right, I can do it on my own."

"Well, tell me what you have in mind then."

With a grin, Nym started laying out his plan.

CHAPTER EIGHTY-TWO

Nym waited in terse silence while Rizin lounged lazily. In two hours, Abdun would show up and try to screw with Rizin's island. It seemed the ascendant knew he couldn't actually face Rizin in an open battle, but Rizin lacked the ability to sever any meaningful number of anchors, and Abdun made it his goal to avoid the fox for as long as possible while he killed the mortal foxes living there.

Rizin's prophetic magic wasn't precise enough to know exactly when Abdun would appear, but Nym didn't have that problem. He knew down to the second when the other ascendant would show up. The trap had been laid, and Abdun wouldn't be escaping the island this time.

He went through his checklist again. The wards were primed. They just needed to be activated, and it would become impossible to teleport or step to another layer of reality. If Nym could tag Abdun with the spell, he'd set up a spatial anchor too that would prevent the ascendant from moving more than five hundred feet from the center of the island.

It would be up to him to work to counter any magic Abdun performed, to keep the foxes living on the island safe. He didn't need to go on the offensive, that being Rizin's job, but he did need to disrupt any and all spells of any significance. Rizin didn't want his new home to be reduced to a barren rock jutting out of the sea. Abdun had tried that several times already, especially when he was ready to give up and needed a nice distraction to keep Rizin from pursuing him.

Really, Abdun wasn't that smart. It was no wonder he'd been stuck at the sixth layer for centuries now. Nym was morbidly curious just what series of events had resulted in the man's ascendance and had to assume he'd had a massive amount of help from some other ascendant to get there. It wasn't an easy mountain to climb, but if someone had guided every step of the journey, he thought it was possible Abdun was just tenacious enough to succeed.

He could just picture whoever had held Abdun's hand the whole way waiting anxiously to see if he managed to form his new body in the outer layers and being half-surprised, half-relieved to see that the man had pulled it off. Nym wondered what had caused that mysterious benefactor to stop assisting the ascendant after he'd managed to cross the threshold.

Perhaps Abdun simply lacked the willpower to withstand the seventh layer, even if he knew exactly what he needed to do. Perfect technical knowledge did not translate into ability, after all. At some point, it no longer mattered if he knew the answers unless he had the power to act on them.

Either way, Abdun had a grudge against Nym and was working to actively kill him, so he was the perfect research specimen. They just needed him to show up. It wasn't like Abdun was late or anything, but Nym was tired of waiting.

"Just skip ahead," Rizin said.

"I considered it, but I don't want to have to deal with accidentally setting off any of the traps designed for him. If I triggered something, I wouldn't be able to get it set back up in time."

Rizin had been waiting for this for three years. Nym had only been in this time frame for about six hours, but he'd overestimated how long it would take him to set everything up. Or rather, he had underestimated how much Rizin had already built in preparation for Abdun's next visit. Everything was ready, and they knew the plan. If it all worked like Nym expected it to, he'd be moving directly from executing his first ascendant to his second and third.

He went over his preparations again, not just for capturing Abdun, but for what came next. His biggest concern was casting god-killer three times in what would be, for him, less than five minutes. Knowing that he had absolutely no margin for error was stressful, to say the least. Once Abdun was gone, he couldn't stop, or retreat, or try to rethink his strategy. If any part of the plan failed, he would need to adapt on the fly.

"One hour left," Rizin announced some time later.

Nym glanced up at him, then went right back to worrying. Over and over again, he played out each step. Over and over again, he considered what might go wrong. Worst case, Myzalik saw him coming and obliterated him before Nym could react. That shouldn't happen, if for no other reason than that the spell did take some time to put together, and he would have just used it against Niramyn. That didn't mean the Exarch couldn't use other magic that was far swifter to cast though.

Even if he got the spell off and hit Myzalik with it, there was still the possibility that the Exarch would do the same thing Niramyn had done and outrange the spell to break it. Or he might know a counterspell or have some other sort of defense. If that was the case, then there had never been any hope of success, no matter what Nym did. The only way to find out was to proceed.

Ironically, he was less worried about Niramyn. There was very little room for error there, but if something went wrong, he was more confident in his ability to recover from it. Getting over the hurdle that was Myzalik was what concerned him the most.

"Ten minutes," Rizin said. "Time to get ready."

Nym opened his conduits up and filled his soul well with a mix of third-, fifth-, sixth-, and seventh-layer arcana, heavily weighted toward seventh. Anything else he could stream practically endlessly, but seventh-layer arcana was still hard enough to connect to that he wasn't so confident about holding an open conduit while he was midfight. It was easier to keep a reservoir of it available if and when he needed it, not that he expected to.

"You want to go over the plan again?" Nym asked.

"Not really, no. Would it calm your nerves if we did it anyway?"

"No," Nym admitted.

"Then no. Spend your time casting prebattle spells instead of reconfirming what you already know."

Nym did just that, not that he expected to need them. He layered spell effects on himself, one on top of another. By the time he was done, he was all but immune to any spell cast using mortal arcana. He couldn't be drowned or suffocated, not even if he was hurled up past the sky to where the air vanished. He couldn't be burned, shocked, frozen, crushed, or cut apart. His mind was fully shielded from all sorts of tampering. Nym could drop into the middle of a battlefield and stand there for days while both sides tried uselessly to break through his barriers. He even had a layer of extrarealness just to reinforce his own personal reality and make it harder for Abdun to change him.

He had to admit, he was still afraid it wouldn't be enough. He'd only won the first confrontation with the other ascendant by taking advantage of being underestimated and through the use of seventh-layer arcana like a sledge. It didn't seem likely that Abdun would make that same mistake twice. Then again, it was Abdun.

Either way, he had Rizin to help this time, and that should be enough to make the difference. But he knew that Abdun would know the powerful fox was there, and he might have taken measures to protect himself.

"Stop worrying so much. It's getting annoying," Rizin said. "Besides, it's time."

Nym nodded once, took a breath, then teleported into the open air above the island. All the foxes below were safely holed up in various sanctuaries Rizin had set up for them, magical shelters that should keep them safe from stray spells and incidental damage. It was actually kind of touching how protective he was of those foxes, especially that blue one who sometimes visited. Nym had eventually learned her name, Sohu.

Reality popped, and Abdun appeared in front of him, right where Nym had predicted. Before the ascendant could say so much as a word, the first spell hit him. Nym had been holding it, primed and ready, and he successfully tagged Abdun with the spatial lock. The other ascendant appeared surprised, but then he laughed.

"To hold me here? Why, so I can't chase you when you run away?"

Nym shot a flurry of weaker spells at him, his opening salvo designed to distract his opponent. Abdun responded immediately, and arcana flowed out into the world between the two of them. Nym's advantage was soon overturned when Abdun showed his centuries of experience and began systematically cutting Nym's spells away before they were even fully formed.

The longer the fight went on, the harder Abdun pushed Nym back. He laughed the entire time too while sixth-layer arcana built up around him. "What's wrong?"

he taunted. "No seventh-layer arcana this time? I know you've got it; I can feel it. Was that all you could hold? Too hard to get it on your own? Have to beg for scraps from other ascendants?"

Nym wasn't sure exactly what he was talking about there. He hadn't realized it was possible to take arcana he was unable to gather on his own from a donor source. If he'd known that, maybe he'd have gone about things differently, but it was too late now either way.

They traded more spells, some of them detonating with explosive results, but usually they would manage to crack open a spell form before it could be completed or shear off an important section that rendered the whole thing useless. Nym almost felt like some sort of giant squid grappling with another one deep underwater, their arcana flowing out of them like tentacles that thrashed around and broke apart anything they came in contact with.

Now that the fight was on, time seemed to stand still for him. He was painfully aware of each passing second, but somehow it took ten times longer than it should have. In the brief minute they sparred with each other, they covered the entire length of the spatial lock a dozen times and cast hundreds of spells.

Enough power erupted out of them to level mountains, wipe cities off the map, and boil seas. For the most part, it didn't look that impressive. Anyone unable to see arcana would have thought they were just dancing around each other in the air. Nym played it that way on purpose, to give Rizin the time he needed to spring his big trap while minimizing damage to the island.

And then the fox's teeth closed around Abdun. Arcana, previously invisible, lashed out of nowhere and snared the ascendant. Abdun fought back, his own magic surging through him to break the spell, but Rizin had built it right, and he'd done it using eighth-layer arcana. It was too dense for Abdun to shatter, and it dragged the ascendant down to the dirt.

Nym landed nearby and added his own bindings, ones designed to prevent Abdun from snapping back to his outer-layer body. They were redundant spells, hopefully unnecessary with the wards that Rizin had stealthily activated one at a time once Abdun had arrived. Given the stakes they were playing for though, Nym was fine with a bit of redundancy.

The other ascendant's face was slack, and his eyes were fogged over. Rizin appeared, at full size for once, and loomed over the apparently comatose ascendant. "Yes, good. He's been trapped in the illusion. This should hold his mind and allow us time to work the magic. Come, let's get him behind the wards and confirm that your spell works."

"Yeah, and then . . ."

"And then, the rest of this business."

"One way or another, live or die, it's going to end today," Nym said.

CHAPTER EIGHTY-THREE

A large majority of their efforts had gone toward making sure Abdun couldn't escape. Those might have been redundant, considering that the actual fight itself was mostly just them breaking apart spells as quickly as the other could form them. Nym wasn't sure that Abdun had ever even tried to flee, and if he had, Nym had broken the spell form without realizing what it was.

He'd found it was faster to break a spell than to try to figure out what it was and decide if it was worth the effort. By the time he'd determined that, he could have just broken it anyway. With so many spells flying back and forth, with dozens forming every second between the two of them, and especially with him spending most of his efforts on neutralizing Abdun's magic instead of going on the offensive, he'd opted to just treat every spell as necessary to defuse.

The strategy had worked, but only because Rizin was there to take advantage of Nym's tactics. If and when he got into a fight with another ascendant, he'd need a completely different strategy. With luck, that was many decades or even centuries away. Without luck, he might be fighting an unwinnable battle against an unbeatable opponent in the next few minutes.

Abdun was still conscious, but bound by Rizin's traps, he was unable to do anything. He was sunk up to his neck in a cube that looked like glass but was hard as stone that they'd conjured up for the express purpose of holding him. Arcana flickered and sputtered around his head as he tried to shift it to produce a spell effect or to bend reality to the shape he desired. His lack of ability to use seventh- or eighth-layer arcana really hurt him there, but neither Nym nor Rizin had any sympathy for him.

"Ready?" the fox asked, after Nym had taken half an hour to recover from the fight. He was going to need to be in top form for what came next.

"Maybe we should knock him out, just in case."

"I hardly think it will matter in a few minutes."

"It will if it doesn't work right," Nym argued. Abdun watched them both, his eyes narrowed and calculating.

"Just do the spell behind him. As I understand it, your ability to see arcana is strictly limited to what you can actually see."

That was a surprisingly simple solution, but Nym couldn't actually think of a rebuttal to it. Shrugging, he walked around behind the cube, took a breath, and started. It was just like practicing with the butterflies. The spell formed, all twenty-two pieces of it emerging out of raw arcana simultaneously over the next few minutes, connections linking each piece together and regulating how it functioned, all of it just waiting for a target to be pointed at.

Nym knew from experimenting that once he reached this point, he had about fifteen seconds before the whole thing started to destabilize. He could extend that another five seconds if he actively worked to hold it together, but past that point, the spell either failed completely or it went off but didn't work properly. The results of an improper cast were . . . unpleasant, even when it happened to an insect.

The spell didn't require him to touch Abdun, thankfully. He had a range of about fifty feet from the source, which could be him or a theoretical copy if he could have spared a process to pilot it. In this case, he wanted the spell to be cast through a visage, a kind of projection connected back to him. It was thankfully much less intensive to cast than making a copy.

Nym didn't need it here, but he would for Myzalik, so he cast the spell to project a visage off to the side. Immediately, his perception shifted to the visage, and the god-killing spell jumped across that connection. Though he was completely insubstantial, he could still direct his own magic, and he did.

The spell leaped from him to Abdun in a flash of light, and his victim let out a brief, strangled cry. In the first second, he went from looking like a grown man in his thirties to a younger, more slender man in his early twenties. In the next second, he reverted to a teenage body, similar to Nym's own age. The connections anchoring him to the timeline started to unravel, not snapped, but simply vanishing into nothingness.

In the third second, Abdun's existence flattened out. He no longer had a presence in the outer layers, and his physical form was that of a boy. Nym guessed this was the point in the spell where Niramyn had finally escaped its effects, as it was similar to how Nym had started his own life. Abdun was mortal again.

Even if the spell ended there, he could be snuffed out by any of a thousand spells designed to kill. Had he not been disabled, Abdun would have been able to fight back, perhaps as a weaker version of an archmage with all the required skills but lacking a full-size soul well. In that sense, with all his memories intact, he was still stronger than Nym had been when he'd first opened his eyes.

But the spell didn't end there. Abdun tried to flail about, to drag in arcana to defend himself with, to do anything at all, anything to escape the fate he'd recognized the moment the spell hit him. Rizin's trap prevented all of that, prevented him from even moving. The glass cube constricted around the former ascendant as his body physically shrunk.

By the end of the fourth second, Abdun was a baby, no longer capable of even using magic. Nym could have let the magic go there and then. Part of him thought that he should, but he was well past the point of no return. Just because Abdun wasn't a threat now didn't mean he wouldn't grow back into one. How exactly his brain handled all the knowledge he had wasn't something Nym had fully considered, and he wasn't keen to find out.

Five seconds. The glass cube was empty now. No one had ever been in it. In fact, it had no reason to exist. Nym and Rizin stared at it for a moment, then looked at each other. "Guess it works, and faster than I was expecting," Nym said.

"I suppose so." The cube vanished, and Rizin paced around it. "Not even a trace of his smell left. He really never did exist. What happens to the timeline now, I wonder. Will we forget about him as it corrects itself? Or will it simply be like he died, his accomplishments and the memory of him remaining but him no longer able to act. If you travel into the past, would you find him there?"

"The timeline will correct itself as it sees fit, I guess. But no, you won't find Abdun anywhere in the past. No one will ever see him again; no one ever has seen him."

"A strange paradox. This spell is . . . dangerous. It would be best to limit its use," the fox said.

"Two more times, and I'm done. Speaking of, I need to move on to the next step before Myzalik has a chance to become suspicious and alter things."

"Go," Rizin said. "I'll . . . Well, not clean up here. There's nothing to clean. Just go. Good luck, my friend."

"I'm afraid I'm going to need it."

Nym disappeared, pulled back into the outer layers so that he could step a hundred years into the past. He arrived four minutes before Myzalik attacked Niramyn, with just enough time to prepare himself, cast the spell, and launch his own attack.

He was calibrating his timing based on how many seconds he had until he was forced back out of the core reality, literally counting seconds to start the spell back up. It was harder to cast this time, but not so much that he was afraid he'd botch it. He was just more worn out, more nervous, more afraid.

"You got this," he muttered to himself. "Two minutes, forty-eight seconds."

The spell came together again, just like the first time. It was nerve-racking building it, knowing that the slightest mistake would mean complete and utter failure. At best, he'd spend the rest of eternity in hiding. At worst, he'd trip at the very end, alert Myzalik to his presence and his knowledge of the god-killer spell, and spend the rest of his life running from an Exarch who would no doubt personally feel the need to track him down and execute him.

So far, so good. The spell was forming at speed. As long as he timed this right, Myzalik's visage would be appearing in twenty-six seconds. He needed twenty-four to finish the spell, plus one additional second to form his own visage after, and then he had a three-second window to project the visage to Niramyn's palace.

Of course, if he mistimed things, he'd either miss the visage completely and lose his window to attack Myzalik, or he'd appear too early and expose himself to Niramyn. This was the part he had to take on faith. Rizin had pulled the time frames for him using spells Nym wasn't capable of replicating.

The god-killer spell finished forming, whole and perfect, just like the last hundred times Nym had used it. He held it steady and cast the spell to form a visage that he'd project his magic through. The spell started to come together, and god-killer flickered. Panicked, Nym immediately devoted more mental processes to keeping it stable, and the spell form for visage started to unravel.

Nym shored it up, but he lost a second. Mentally cursing, he transferred god-killer into his visage, then projected it outward. Despite the setback, he thought he'd make it in time. He hoped he'd make it in time.

"Please let me make it in time," he whispered.

The visage didn't cross the physical distance, but it still took longer than he'd expected to reform. He should have practiced casting it out across long distances into warded locations. Even though his destination was a room specifically designed to communicate with the outside world, he hadn't even thought to test if it might impact the speed at which the visage formed.

The room snapped into focus. Myzalik's visage was there, looking smug as he watched his rival Exarch succumb to his magic. Niramyn himself looked like a man in his early twenties, and then in a flash, he was gone. Nym blinked away a blurry line in his vision where Niramyn had shot past him out into the open sky and focused on the other visage.

Myzalik hadn't noticed him yet, so that part at least was going to plan. He'd come in just in time. Another few seconds at most and the other Exarch would have dismissed the visage, and Nym wouldn't be able to use its connection to send his own visage back toward his target. He did still have those seconds though, and he was determined not to waste them.

Nym's visage jumped again, this time following that thin thread of arcana between Myzalik and his visage. When he materialized a second time, the Exarch was standing alone in a room filled with pillars made of marble trimmed in gold, with a shallow pool of crystal clear water in front of him. Nym examined the rune sequence etched across the bottom of the pool just long enough to ensure it wouldn't interfere with what he was there to do, then shifted his focus.

Myzalik was alone. Good. He was distracted, no doubt trying to track Niramyn's progress as he fled across the ocean. That was even better. Nym would never get a clearer shot. Before he could second-guess himself, he selected the target for the god-killer spell he was holding.

For the second time in less than five minutes, he cast the spell that would end the life of an immortal.

CHAPTER EIGHTY-FOUR

Myzalik whirled in place, eyes wide and his mouth twisted into a horrified grimace, just as the god-killer spell struck him. Nym watched through his visage for that first tell-tale physical change. Something, anything at all, was all he needed, proof that the spell had taken hold. He looked for hair thickening on Myzalik's head or his skin getting smoother, his shoulders narrower.

There was nothing, and Nym knew his worst fears had come to pass. The Exarch who'd invented the spell was protected from it in some way. All Nym had accomplished was giving the man a good scare and painting a massive target on himself. Any second, Myzalik would obliterate his visage and appear to deal with Nym in person.

But then he saw it. The fine lines around Myzalik's eyes stretched tight and vanished. Unlike Abdun, Myzalik could still fight back, and he did. Arcana lanced out around him, and though Nym couldn't match its quality, he could still work against whatever spell his victim was trying to cast. His own arcana poured out, mixed sixth and seventh layer, and attacked Myzalik's spells. He pried the spell forms open, dispelled the Exarch's magic where he could, slowed it down where he couldn't.

He didn't have to win this. He just had to hold on for four more seconds. Even weakened by the god-killer spell, the Exarch was still easily overpowering him. Forty different spells blossomed in the aura of arcana around him, and Nym managed to break at most five of them. He slowed down the formation of six more.

Myzalik shuddered and grabbed at his chest. Spells twisted around him and shot through, coming out into other realities and even alternate timelines as he tried desperately to forge new connections to replace the ones god-killer was erasing. Nym did his best to hinder those spells, but Myzalik protected them with a screen of other magics designed to focus Nym's attention, spells that if ignored would sever his own anchors.

If he lost his access to this time frame, his plan would be unsalvageable. Desperately, he fought back against the magic, dodging or deflecting it as best he could. It was only the fact that almost all Myzalik's attention was on fighting off the effect of his own god-killer spell that Nym survived for even an instant.

Since that was the situation, however, he found himself up to the task of fighting off a bare sliver of Myzalik's attention. Three seconds had passed since he'd struck the Exarch, and far from being reduced to a child, he was still holding strong as a grown man. He was definitely younger but at barely a fraction of the rate it had affected Abdun.

Nym caught something strange in the arcana storm around Myzalik. All his spells had been forged with arcana from the outer layers, but then in the middle of that was a sliver of magic from the Astral Sea. It started to shape into a spell he recognized, and Nym's breath caught.

If Myzalik got that teleportation spell off, he'd break the link between the visage and the god-killer spell. Nym lashed out with six different limbs of arcana, all focused on attacking that spell before it fully formed. Barriers of solid arcana blossomed between him and Myzalik, each one heavy with power and actually strong enough to draw Nym's own arcana toward them.

He resisted the pull, slipped three of the limbs past the makeshift walls, and dug into the teleportation spell. It was too late to pull it apart, but he could and did slice off the part of the spell that specified a target destination. With nowhere to go, Myzalik merely blinked in place without moving.

God killer was moving faster now, and the Exarch appeared to be in his early twenties or late teens. His soul well started to contract as his body regressed, and the many, many augmentations he'd made vanished. His ability to fight back was weakening, and Nym started keeping up with the various spells Myzalik wove.

He saw the exact moment the Exarch accepted his fate. If he could have trusted the spell to do its work, Nym would have fled then and there. But without his interference, Myzalik would escape the radius of the spell. His options were limited now that his immortality was broken, but he could escape the same way Niramyn had if Nym wasn't there to stop him.

Myzalik realized it too, but it was too late. If he'd fled the moment the spell hit him, Nym suspected he'd have successfully escaped permanent damage. He might not have been an Exarch anymore, but he would have still been immortal. Whatever power he'd lost could have been recovered.

Perhaps it was because he was used to being unchallengeable, to never losing to anything but another Exarch, but Myzalik hadn't run. He'd fought and, without Nym's interference, might even have beaten his own spell. Immortal they might be, but they were still humans, as prone to errors in judgment, petty jealousies, and irrational compulsions as anyone else.

Myzalik appeared to be a boy now, seven or eight years old. He was still struggling to draw in arcana, to escape in some way. The spell had run for fifteen seconds, more than three times as long as it had taken to destroy Abdun, and it still hadn't completed its work. It was impressive, in a way.

Nym lashed out with arcana designed to daze Myzalik, to interrupt his thoughts and leave him vulnerable. It would not have worked against any ascendant, or even some mortals. For his purposes now, it was more than enough.

Myzalik stopped struggling.

The magic took him.

Nym killed an Exarch.

The visage vanished, and Nym drew in a deep, shuddering breath. His heart slammed against his rib cage repeatedly, and his hands shook. Sweat covered his brow, and he sat down heavily, collapsing onto the ground without even making the effort to conjure up anything to sit on.

He hadn't thought his mortal body could even have reactions like that anymore. It was unpleasant and reminded him of his early days when everything had been so overwhelming that he'd basically shut down instead of dealing with it. And as much as he wished it was over now, there was more work to be done.

Reality pushed against him suddenly, hard and absolute, and he found himself back in the sixth layer. Laughing helplessly, he shook his head. He'd been so focused on finishing off Myzalik that he'd stopped keeping track of the seconds. It was a good thing the spell had ended when it did. Another few seconds, and he'd have been forced out of the core reality before he had confirmed the Exarch's death.

Niramyn had let go, relinquished his body to the Nym persona that had grown into a whole new existence, and reality wouldn't stand for there being two of him at the same time, not even if one was immortal and the other not. Nym was forever locked out of the next few years, having already lived them once.

He needed to move quickly, but he took a minute to recover his strength. This next part should be easier in a lot of ways, but the timing was going to be even tighter. Worse, they hadn't been able to pull the memory of him to plan it out down to the second. All their attempts to scry during the moment in question had been unsuccessful. Nym was going in blind, and it would be all on him to make sure he pulled it off.

He knew roughly what was going to happen but only from memories formed when he'd been subsumed by Niramyn. Everything from that time was jumbled and overwhelming. Nym didn't trust them to be accurate, and he couldn't plan a strategy around what he thought might have happened.

That wasn't to say he had no advantages. He knew exactly where and when he needed to appear. It was just what he needed to do once he got there that was still in question. Niramyn would have some spells to defend himself with, and Nym wouldn't have time to construct the god-killer spell again. If everything went right, he wouldn't need it, not right then.

He was under no illusions that things were going to go as easily as they had with Abdun. There was no time to prepare, and Niramyn, despite his massive ego, was many, many times smarter than Abdun had been. Worse, he wouldn't have Rizin to help. Still, it was his best chance.

The goal was to subdue Niramyn and transport him to another time, then execute the onetime Exarch before he could regain his power. If he could have constructed the god-killer spell while in the sixth layer and brought it with him when he appeared in the core reality, everything would have been so much simpler.

That wasn't an option though, so he'd be doing it the hard way. Nym had reviewed this plan repeatedly; he knew which spells to cast, what order to cast them in, and how to make sure Niramyn didn't shake them off. He'd given himself a few precious minutes to reaffirm that his plan was sound, and now it was time to implement the last phase.

Nym prepared every spell he could, and then he slipped back into the timeline a second after he'd activated Niramyn's memory cube. He could see his body, now controlled by the immortal ascendant, already reaching for sixth-layer arcana somehow, that connection restored with the recovery of his memories.

Nym unleashed spells designed to lock Niramyn down spatially and temporally. They surged out, stuck themselves to Niramyn, and were resisted by the former Exarch's own magic. The gate below Niramyn's feet flared to life as the runes lit up, and Nym knew he had only a single second to tag his target with the locking spell before he missed his window.

The lock snapped closed around Niramyn and started to pull him back out of the gate. The gate itself provided an unexpected resistance to the magic, but Nym's spell was still strong enough to overcome it. Niramyn wouldn't be saved by just that. All it did was buy him a second.

Nym knew he had caught Niramyn, and he knew he'd failed. Some fragmented shard surfaced in his thoughts, and he watched what happened next with a sort of grim horror. It played out exactly as he knew it must.

Arcana slapped against Niramyn, the locking spell that would keep him from slipping into his sanctuary. The gate itself pushed back against the spell, tried to force it out, slowed it down just enough for Niramyn to unleash his own spell.

Niramyn's counterstroke blew the spell form apart. The spatial lock was destabilized so badly that the whole thing disintegrated on the spot, despite Nym's attempts to hold it together. The trap broke, and Niramyn resumed his descent through the gate. There was nothing Nym could do to stop him.

Just before the Exarch disappeared, he let out one final spell, the one that had thoroughly foiled Nym's attempts to catch him. A pulse of arcana rippled out into the timeline and scrambled it. It was weak, as far as ascendants were concerned, only sixth layer. But it only had to wash out a handful of seconds, and it did.

That arcana pulse was what had prevented Nym from scrying this scene and forced him to rely on the faulty, fragmented memories he'd barely retained when he'd been severed from Niramyn's being. If not for that, he would have planned it better, would have known what he needed to counter.

Instead, the Exarch had broken through the spatial lock and fled into his sanctuary, where he would recover and emerge much stronger, too strong for Nym to fight.

He had failed.

CHAPTER EIGHTY-FIVE

Nym allowed himself a few seconds to just stare at the now-closed gate. When Niramyn came back out, he was going to be far stronger than Nym, too strong to defeat. If he could find a way into the sanctuary, maybe he could attack Niramyn before it was too late, but Nym didn't think he had the ability to do that. This sanctuary had been set up by an Exarch at the height of his power, after all.

Maybe he could trick the gate into letting him in. It wouldn't be the first time he'd taken advantage of Niramyn's credentials. Catching his opponent in the middle of some delicate operation could make for an easy victory, especially if he did it quickly enough.

The runes were hideously complex but also intimately familiar. He may not have been Niramyn, but he'd literally learned from the Exarch's own memories. He was as close as anyone was going to get. When it came to doing magic, Nym knew how Niramyn thought. He understood the logic behind Niramyn's choices because they were the same choices he would make.

The rune sequences were too sophisticated to be easily tricked. There was a key spell needed just to activate them, something of Niramyn's own devising. He'd been in the midst of casting it when Nym had appeared. Unfortunately, Nym hadn't caught the entire spell, but he could reverse engineer it from the final result. The question was whether he could do it fast enough.

Whatever he was going to do, he needed to make a decision quickly. Niramyn's timeline-scrambling spell was already fading away, and with it went Nym's cover. He had at best a few minutes of core-reality time. But then, he knew exactly what he needed to figure out. There was no need to stand in front of the gate to do it.

Nym stepped back into the sixth layer and found as he transitioned across that he could see the connections between the gate and the sanctuary. It was a simple matter to follow the lines of arcana through the sixth layer and appear just outside what amounted to a room-sized box. It was a featureless cube of gray draped with wards, very similar to the ones Nym himself had set up. The major difference was that it lacked his hidden-presence spell or the prophetic wards he'd integrated into his own designs.

So there were some things Nym could do that even the mighty Niramyn didn't know about. Nym wondered if there was a way to use that to his advantage. That would come later. First, he needed to crack the rune sequence on the gate or, failing that, tear right through the wards protecting the place. They couldn't last forever, or even very long. In fact, now that he looked at it, they would fail in less than a week if they maintained their current use of arcana and Niramyn didn't do anything to strengthen them.

Nym could use that time to prepare himself. He would need to figure out the exact moment the wards failed if he was going to prepare an ambush. No, it would be better to figure out when they were weak enough that he could force them to fail. If he could get Rizin to help him prepare the field, they could do the same thing they'd done to Abdun.

Excited now, Nym started working on deciphering the warding scheme. It was as complex as anything Myzalik had used but so much easier to sort through. Nym knew the weaknesses in such a design, knew where he could poke holes in it.

The plan came together in his head. There were risks, certainly. The biggest one was spending a week in the core reality, vulnerable to other ascendants interfering with him. But if everything went well, he could recover from his miss with Niramyn. Hope wasn't dead, not quite yet.

Nym dipped back into the core reality, to a time about a month before the initial cast of god-killer on Niramyn. He appeared in the sky above the ice fields of the frozen north and sought out Rizin.

"No," the fox said. "And also, how are you *again* in my den? Do you just go around cracking my defenses every few decades for the fun of it?"

Oh, right. Nym had forgotten that in this time period, Rizin didn't know him yet except for that brief conversation they'd had a hundred years earlier. He hadn't developed the friendship he held with the fox in a hundred years yet, and Rizin was rightfully distrustful of him.

"Would you change your mind if I said we became good friends in a hundred years?" Nym asked.

The fox snorted. "I'd say to leave the lying to me. I'm better at it."

That ruined the bulk of Nym's plans. Rizin couldn't jump through time with him, and the one in the time period he needed wasn't willing to help. The clock wasn't going to stand still for him while he tried to change Rizin's mind either. Nym was going to have to do it without help.

Or did he?

"Fine, my apologies for intruding then. I'll see you in . . . oh, sometime in the next two years or so."

"No, you won't," Rizin growled at him. "I've had enough of you."

"Please, for the chance to mess with me at our first meeting? Back when I was still mortal? I'll be seeing you."

Nym stepped back out of time.

* * *

"Did you succeed?" Rizin of a hundred years into the future asked.

"No. I missed my shot. I think I can get a second chance, but the you in that time period was—"

"Uncooperative," Rizin said. "Yes, I remember. From my point of view, you were just this annoying ascendant who kept popping up and breaking through all the spells I'd laid out to keep my den hidden. I had fully intended to eat you that day you first met me on the trails until I realized you were half an ascendant at that time."

Nym just stared at him for a second. "Oh."

"In my defense, you were incredibly annoying, and a security threat besides."

"But you don't feel that way now," Nym said.

"I don't think there's much I personally can do to help you in this fight," Rizin said.

"Hey, you don't think I'm annoying now, do you?"

"But maybe there is something that could help you," the fox mused.

"Rizin . . ."

"More amusing than annoying anymore," Rizin admitted. "Still a security threat."

A cloak pin with a fox head on it materialized in front of Nym, who reached out to grab it. "What is this?" he asked.

"Fox magic. It will make it harder to keep track of you, both physically and magically. It can also project illusions, ones that should fool even an ascendant's sight. It won't save you from an area bombardment, but it might give you enough of an edge to tag Niramyn with your god-killing spell. That's the best I can do for you."

Nym conjured up a cloak and pinned the fox head on it. "Thank you," he said softly.

"You're welcome. Good luck. I hope you survive. It has been . . . surprisingly nice having a peer of sorts to talk to."

"Thanks. I've . . . I've got this." He hoped.

Nym skipped backward to where he'd left the timeline outside Niramyn's sanctuary.

The wards started to crumble. Niramyn had to know what was going on inside his sanctuary, but he didn't appear to fight back. Nym left them in a state of collapse, one shove away from shattering completely, and began his preparations.

There wasn't a lot he could do, not if he wanted to have god-killer primed and ready to go. More than that, he was counting down the seconds to rip Niramyn out of the sanctuary. Every moment that went by only saw the Exarch growing that much closer to his former power.

He obscured the timeline with everything he knew to use, laid out his locking spells to keep Niramyn from escaping, wove together the god-killer spell. It took all the focus he had to prepare that spell and still reach out to tug that last thread that collapsed the wards and tore open the wall into Niramyn's sanctuary.

Immediately, Nym projected an illusion of himself, or at least of a powerful, brash, overconfident ascendant, charging into the breach. The fox-head pin's arcana started draining, far faster than he'd expected. He shouldn't have been surprised by that, he knew. It was a tool designed for an ambush, barely good for more than a single use.

Something materialized in the breach, something both dark and light, blinding in its brilliance and in its unknowable shadows, something that hurt Nym's head to look at. It caught his lifelike illusion and banished it before disappearing itself.

Nym held the god-killer spell perfectly balanced, ready to strike. But it would only keep for a few seconds. If Niramyn didn't appear, Nym would have no choice but to go in after him, which was something he wanted to avoid at all costs. Technically, the sanctuary hadn't been located on reality prime, and god-killer wouldn't function inside it without the stabilizing framework that Nym had no way to recreate.

Of course, with the wards breached and the core reality reasserting itself over that space, it was possible the spell would work just fine now, but Nym had no plans on testing that if he didn't have to. He'd expected the Exarch to come barreling out as soon as the decoy had taken the hit, secure in the knowledge that he'd defeated whatever upstart ascendant had taken a swing at him.

Niramyn appeared in the air overhead, and the spatial and temporal traps snapped down on him. They were strong, but Nym could tell at a glance that Niramyn had advanced to the ninth layer. He was too strong to be held for long, but maybe long enough . . .

Nym let loose god-killer for the third time. For the third time, it struck home.

Abdun had gone through a steady regression, becoming young again by about six or seven years every second. He lacked the experience or power to fight the spell, and it had taken him smoothly. Myzalik, by contrast, had fought it all the way. He'd gotten younger in spurts, all the while fighting Nym off. He'd lose a year or two of age, then nothing for a few seconds, then a whole decade all at once.

Niramyn wasn't like either of them. The instant the spell hit, he regressed from late twenties to eighteen. The arcana held in his soul well practically exploded out of him, suddenly far too much for him to hold on to. The next instant, before Nym could even begin to follow up, the Exarch snapped the spatial locks and vanished.

Nym teleported after him, determined to end the fight. If not for those locks, he would have lost. Niramyn would have teleported immediately. But Nym had placed the locks, and the god-killer had gotten him one last time before he vanished.

Niramyn didn't look eighteen anymore. He looked fourteen or fifteen at the oldest. Maybe less. He wasn't going to suddenly pull in ninth-layer arcana and obliterate Nym's temporal anchors with it. He wasn't even going to use eighth layer, or seventh, which Nym could probably have defended against, at least for a second or two.

If Nym was right, Niramyn wasn't even going to use sixth-layer arcana because he couldn't. The spell had broken a few seconds short of killing him, but the reason it had worked so quickly was simple: Niramyn had artificially inflated his age with some sort of magic, and the spell didn't care about that. It knew that a week ago, he'd been a teenager, so it rewound him by one week and took all those fake years he'd packed on away.

And then it had gone one step further back. Niramyn had all the knowledge of an ascendant, but he was mortal. Nym didn't need god-killer to slay a mortal.

He just needed to catch Niramyn before he escaped to a new hiding place. Nym wove the magic, locked onto the teleportation, and jumped after him.

CHAPTER EIGHTY-SIX

Something was wrong, but Niramyn couldn't figure out exactly what. He recognized a timeline deviation when he saw one, but how exactly it had deviated escaped him. The fact of the matter was that Niramyn had been the anchor to the primary timeline for thousands of years, and if things were going to change, they changed to his will, not the other way around.

It stood to reason then that this new ascendant, one he didn't even recognize, was the result of Myzalik's meddling. There was something off about the man though, some sort of magic he was only passingly familiar with. It was another annoyance, something he understood as wrong but couldn't quite figure out why.

Whatever it was, it had strong elements of misdirection in it, with notes of illusion and darkness. It was magic for hiding, an assassin's tool for striking from the shadows. Now that the mystery ascendant had blown his opening attack, Niramyn was confident he could escape defeat. It would be difficult, with that damnable age-reversing spell once again robbing him of a portion of his strength. At least he wouldn't be forced to go to such drastic measures to regain it this time, though the fact that he'd immediately lost practically all the work he'd put into the last week or so within moments of stepping back out of his sanctuary was infuriating.

When he figured out how Myzalik had crafted such an impossible spell, he was going to torture the Exarch with it for a thousand years. And he was going to kill every single ascendant who knew it, even if that meant he was the last one left. He was already alone at the peak, a god among immortals, so what difference did it make if he had to wait a few hundred years for new ascendants to start showing up? At least they'd know their place.

Before that though, his pursuer needed to be dealt with.

Niramyn had been regressed far enough to become mortal again, but that was a momentary problem. He still had enough of the body enhancements that idiot Nym had managed to scrape together to reach back to the sixth layer and ascend for what he could scarcely believe was the third time. At least the second one had been nothing like the first. It was more like putting the pieces to a puzzle he'd solved a long time ago back together. It was easy, comforting, familiar. Best of all, it happened outside of mortal time, in the in-between space. His pursuer wouldn't be able to stop him.

A bolt of solid arcana slammed into Niramyn and hurled him toward the ground. He was so surprised by the attack that it took him a second to dispel the magic, start his divinations to find his assailant, and right himself in the air. Even before the divinations came back, he was casting new spells, both to defend himself and to prepare his counterattack.

It was frustratingly slow to only cast at most three or four spells at once and, even then, only if they weren't terribly complicated. He was used to his mind being an entire legion of mages working in concert, not just a single partner. For all the handicap that represented though, he still found the ascendant who'd attacked him quickly enough and launched his own attack.

Despite the magic hiding the other ascendant's presence, some sort of mystical-fox spell, he now saw, his attack homed in unerringly and struck his pursuer. It was nothing so crude as elemental fire or earth—lightning had already been his preference for that tier of combat anyway—or even solid kinesis like the force bolt he'd been struck with. No, even as limited as he was Niramyn still had all the knowledge and skill of the strongest of all the Exarchs.

He struck the ascendant with a spell designed to fracture a soul well. It was no simple arcana injection, oh no. His spell would actually break away the augmentations the ascendant had made, sever the connections between nodes, and cast them about randomly to fully destabilize the structure of the soul well itself. It would cripple the ascendant for weeks, complete overkill when Niramyn needed only moments to escape.

Satisfied that he'd escaped the age-reversal magic and incapacitated the pursuing ascendant, Niramyn turned his attention back to ascending. It would take only a second, and this game would be over. There was nothing anyone could do to stop him now.

Nym was more surprised that Niramyn had spotted him through the shroud the fox pin had cast over him than he was by the former Exarch's choice of attacks. A soul-well breaker was exactly Niramyn's style: excessively brutal and guaranteed to incapacitate the target with physical pain while simultaneously crippling his ability to do any sort of magic. Even as an immortal ascendant, he was vulnerable to having his soul well tampered with.

So he was surprised, and also a little insulted.

Nym recognized the spell even as it formed. Admittedly, he couldn't have formed it that fast himself, not even now, but that didn't stop him from defending against it. The spell struck him and shattered against his own arcana. Nym barely even acknowledged the successful deflection of the attack though. He was too busy attacking Niramyn himself.

A storm of arcana whipped up in the sky over the prairie they'd ended up teleporting to. Spells sparked in the air and struck at the former Exarch, perfectly timed to hit one after another and negate his every attempt to craft new magic.

This was no time to underestimate his opponent though. Niramyn was mortal, vulnerable, but still an Exarch in mind if not body. Nym had a hundred different ways to attack his target, and he planned on using all of them. No doubt Niramyn would defend against some, but without the dozens of parallel processes, unlimited stamina, and the practically bottomless soul well a powerful ascendant had that let them cast twenty or thirty spells at the same time, every second, for hours if needed, he would be overwhelmed before he could do anything else.

The air ignited into flames around Niramyn, and shards of stone materialized out of nothingness next to him, already moving forward to drive themselves into his mortal body. Arcana assaulted his body, trying to lock his muscles in place, trying to smother his senses, to still his heart or rupture his organs. Creatures made of pure ephemeral darkness phased into existence, blackening the skies around Niramyn and sending questing tendrils of arcana into his mind.

It was too much for any mortal to defend against, and that was only the ones meant to actively harm Niramyn. Nym devoted a considerable portion of his mind to keeping Niramyn from running again, everything from spatial locks for denying teleports to dispels that attacked the flight magic holding Niramyn aloft. There was no single strategy for victory, no clever combinations that would slip past Niramyn's defenses.

Nym was stronger, if not more skilled, and he intended to leverage that and bury Niramyn in so much arcana that the sheer weight of it would collapse the now-mortal Exarch's defenses and snuff him out. He couldn't even see his target through all the spells currently active. That didn't stop him, of course. He had several scrying spells feeding him information and two processes currently devoted to nothing but parsing that. There was no way he was losing Niramyn now.

But just to be safe, he started reinforcing the various denial spells he was already laying down. He wanted there to be no way Niramyn escaped that cloud of death, no split-second teleport out of the way, no stepping into another layer, no summoning anything and swapping places with it.

He knew something was wrong immediately when his scrying spells reported that Niramyn was still alive somehow, and he knew exactly what it was that was wrong an instant later when he felt reality flex inside the storm of deadly arcana covering the sky. Either some other ascendant had come to Niramyn's rescue, or he'd managed to ascend back to the sixth layer immediately after being knocked back down to mortal status.

Nym didn't see another ascendant anywhere, and his area denial-spells were still functioning at full strength. Somehow, Niramyn had ignored them and managed to ascend, again. Nym hadn't realized he could do it so quickly, in barely an instant. He'd already been too late to stop Niramyn the moment he'd deflected the soul-well breaker, well before he'd woven together his first attack.

Nym had to admit, that wasn't ideal for him. It meant he needed to use the god-killer spell to end this now, which would tie up so much of his spell-casting ability that he'd be hard-pressed to keep up with Niramyn even before he'd ascended again. Now that his opponent had regained his access to sixth-layer arcana, Nym's new top priority was keeping him anchored in the core reality.

This was the only place god-killer was going to work, and even with everything that had gone wrong, this was still his best chance to kill Niramyn. Maybe if Nym somehow managed to stretch his own anchors back far enough, he could eventually visit the time period that Niramyn had ascended from, but he doubted it. No one else knew when Niramyn had ascended. He'd just always been there, a fixture of reality for as long as time had existed.

It really was now or never.

Niramyn had been reasonably sure he could reascend despite the various locking fields the other ascendant had layered across the area. If it had been his first time, he might have been in trouble, but in this case, it was much closer to opening a conduit than trying to step through to the sixth layer.

That still left him stranded here, of course, and at a severe disadvantage in terms of absolute strength. But whoever this mysterious ascendant was, he wasn't a match for an Exarch. Already, Niramyn could think of a few different ways to break the locks and escape, though they unfortunately relied on him waiting for an opening to execute his plan.

The battlefield wasn't the place to make changes to his mind, but he needed those parallel processes up and running. Being limited to a few spells at a time was no way to win a fight of this caliber. To that end, Niramyn's first order of business was to stall and distract.

"You've missed your shot," he said, his voice carried by his magic to the other ascendant. Even if the man was physically deaf, he'd still hear Niramyn clearly. "Not that I'm surprised, an amateur like you. But tell me, even if you'd succeeded, then what? You know that Myzalik isn't going to leave you alive with knowledge of his spell, don't you? You were dead the moment you learned how to cast that."

It wasn't that he expected to gain any useful information from the ascendant. It was just that Niramyn needed about twenty seconds uninterrupted with having to defend himself to increase the number of processes he could run up to six. That was still far too few, but it was better than what he was currently working with. Once he got those up, he could devote half to defending himself and the other half to continuing to modify his mind.

Tricky but possible. It was about as far from ideal circumstances as it could get, but Niramyn needed to learn the identity of this ascendant, and he needed to escape this fight in one piece. Anything else was a bonus.

Once he'd regained his power, again, he was going to find his assailant, torture the bastard until he revealed how to cast the age-reversal spell, and then kill him with his own weapon.

Then something twisted inside him. Reality itself fought against Niramyn, tried to push him to the outer layers. That wasn't possible while he was caught inside the area-denial fields the other ascendant had put up, but reality didn't care. It just kept pushing, grinding against him. Niramyn needed to break the denial field, or else he'd be torn apart.

CHAPTER EIGHTY-SEVEN

Nym could feel something twisting in reality, something he couldn't quite place. It was familiar but, at the same time, strange. It didn't originate from him, was in fact hanging off of Niramyn, but it worried him. It was a variable, a powerful one, and it could alter the entire course of the battle. At best, it would help him do what he could accomplish on his own. At worst, it'd give Niramyn some new edge and allow him to snatch victory from Nym.

Whatever was happening, it had distracted the Exarch sufficiently that he didn't even react when Nym doubled down on his spatial and dimensional locks. He built a cube out of solid arcana, a thousand feet to a side, just to prevent anyone else from interfering by means of physical locomotion or Niramyn from flying away to get out of the range of the lock spells. Then, preparations complete, he attacked again.

Now that Niramyn had regained his immortality, Nym needed to subdue him the same way they'd taken out Abdun. However, without Rizin to help, without a prepared battlefield littered with traps, and against an opponent who might be technically the same rank as Abdun but significantly smarter and more experienced, he didn't have a lot of hopes of the same strategy working.

He would be going with a more brute-force approach.

Nym ignored the Exarch's barbed words. Either they were an attempt to stall and buy himself more time, or they were the arrogant rantings of a twisted psychopath. Whichever was the case, Nym wasn't interested in banter.

He was wary of getting too close, but it seemed whatever was twisting reality up into a knot was working against Niramyn after all. He barely parried the first few spells Nym threw at him, and when Niramyn tried to assert his will against reality to break Nym's magic, it was easy for Nym to counter him.

It seemed victory was within his reach, but something about the twisted knot of reality surrounding Niramyn still worried him. It shouldn't be happening, and he couldn't shake the feeling that it was going to blow up in his face.

His eyes widened as he realized what was going on. The paradox of Nym's existence had wracked Niramyn's body. Nym only vaguely remembered the end result, when Niramyn had realized what had happened and been forced to form a new body for Nym to occupy, to separate them into two different people.

It was happening again now, and as soon as Niramyn figured out what was wrong and splintered off a new Nym, one of them was going to be forced out of the core reality. Considering that the Nym Niramyn would be forced to create was mortal, it seemed to him that reality would force the ascendant version out so that he couldn't relive that time. All of a sudden, he was on a clock with an unknown length of time. He had however long it took Niramyn to figure out why reality was attacking him and correct it to finish this fight.

Subduing Niramyn was no longer an option. He needed to be destroyed while Nym still had the ability to do so. If a new Nym entered the timeline now, it would block Nym from reaching Niramyn for more than enough time for the Exarch to get back up to full strength again.

Nym immediately devoted the bulk of his mind to casting god-killer. Doing it in front of Niramyn was a terrible idea, but the fox pin still had some arcana left in it, and he used it all to shield himself while spinning off a copy to engage Niramyn directly. With only a single process to run it, he doubted it would be all that effective, but he didn't have enough left over to add a second copy. Hell, he wasn't confident that he could even keep the first copy going while he cast god-killer. He never had before.

Two minutes was all he needed. Surely his copy could hold out that long. Surely he could manage with one less mental process. All the locks were already in place. Niramyn wasn't leaving. Nym just needed to keep him busy and distracted until god-killer was finished.

Two minutes was an eternity for the copy of Nym. Niramyn would have overwhelmed him in seconds if not for the fact that reality itself was trying to push him into the outer layers. That helped Nym now, but if reality broke through the dimensional lock, Niramyn would escape. If Niramyn figured out what he needed to do to appease reality, Nym would end up banished.

Two minutes.

Nym flew forward, bolts of lightning thundering around him as he fired them off, one after another. Niramyn didn't even bother dispelling them, opting instead to create a lightning catcher, something like the ones Nym himself used, though far more advanced and made of fifth-layer arcana.

If lightning wasn't going to do it, there were plenty of other elements to tap into and no reason to limit himself to low-level spells. Nym pulled in his own fifth-layer arcana and shaped it into a destructive beam of liquid sun, bright enough to sear the vision from his eyes and hot enough that the temperature inside the cube immediately spiked to the point that he needed magic to protect himself.

Niramyn didn't try to dodge. He just let himself fall while casting his own spell. The beam of liquid sun tracked him, only to be swallowed by a whirling black circle of gravity so strong that not only did it eat Nym's spell, it pulled him toward it.

He lashed out with raw arcana, unaffected by the gravity of the black circle, and tore open the spell form supporting it. It flickered, then cracked and vanished just before Nym reached it. He couldn't celebrate though, not with a hundred lances of some sort of shimmering green light thrumming through the air to skewer him.

One minute, fifty-five seconds remaining.

Nym teleported, just a short hop that he barely managed to cast due to Niramyn's interference. Six of the lances struck him anyway, three in his back, two in one arm, and one in his leg. His arm was sliced off cleanly, and pain surged through the stump of his shoulder. Nym bit off a sharp cry, spun out more arcana, and killed his sensation of pain. It would do him no good anyway, not as a copy with a life span that could be measured in seconds.

At the same time, he attacked the elemental-air magic Niramyn had woven to keep himself from splattering against the ground below. The fall itself wouldn't kill him, not now that he was immortal, but everything Nym did was just a distraction. Each spell was calculated not to do the most damage but to buy the most time.

One minute, forty-five seconds remaining.

Niramyn was winning the fight, and he had to be wondering why. Or maybe he already knew. It didn't matter, since the fox pin had enough arcana left in it to hide the original Nym still. At least, he assumed it did since Niramyn was focusing all his efforts on the copy. Even distracted by his fight against reality itself as it tried to expel him despite the dimensional lock, he was still quickly overpowering Nym.

Spells flew through the air or materialized next to their targets. Nym got the worst of it, though Niramyn took a hit or two as well. Part of that was that Nym was far more willing to accept damage in order to dish it out, but most of it was just that Niramyn was a better mage than him. All things being equal, Nym with only a single mind to cast spells couldn't match Niramyn.

One and a half minutes left.

Niramyn fought against reality with everything he had. If he didn't, he'd be crushed between it and the area denial that kept him trapped in place. Despite everything, he managed to give himself two extra processes for spell casting. It wasn't what he'd been going for, but he'd done the best he could with the considerable handicaps he'd labored under.

The enemy ascendant had sent out some sort of copy to distract him while he hid behind a veil of fox magic. Niramyn knew a dozen ways to strip it away, but all of them required immortal arcana, and his was tied up contesting reality's attempt to eject him. Even if it wasn't, with his downgrade from ninth layer to sixth, he didn't have access to more than one or two options.

Once he took care of the pesky simulacrum, he'd be free to hunt down the original. With their arena being so small, it was merely a matter of exerting the effort to find the ascendant, fox magic or not. After the first minute of combat, he reconsidered his plan. Breaking the area denial and retreating might just be the better course, loath as he was to lose track of the ascendant without first learning who he was.

Oh well, there were plenty of other ways to learn the man's identity once he'd fully recovered. Other than Myzalik himself, who had specialized in time magic to a ridiculous degree, there was nobody who could obscure the timeline well enough to keep him from peering into it.

Niramyn deflected a fifth-layer spell from the copy, one that would have boiled the blood inside his body to the point that he started sweating it out of his pores, and frowned. He knew why the copy wasn't using sixth-layer or higher spells. It could damage the area denial and force Niramyn out of the battlefield, but something about the spells he had chosen to use bothered Niramyn.

It was too close to his own preferred spell repertoire. Was the copy deliberately doing that, or was it a coincidence? Before he could chase that line of thought down, another spasm of reality rippled through him and dragged him across the dimensional lock. That was painful in a way that mortals didn't have words for, an agony of the mind more than the body, but he endured.

He was Niramyn. He was an Exarch. The Exarch. The most powerful of them all. His will wouldn't be denied by the weak fabric of reality prime, and it certainly wouldn't be blocked by an ascendant barely into the seventh layer.

Five seconds left.

Nym's copy was a sliver of itself at this point. Only the fact that he was actively channeling sixth-layer arcana to contest reality's insistence that he was dead kept him from falling apart. Even that was a precarious connection. But he'd almost done it. One more salvo of spells to distract Niramyn would be enough. Even if he was obliterated in the counterattack, he'd bought the original enough time.

As it turned out, he didn't even get a chance to do that. Niramyn diverted enough of his own sixth-layer arcana to lash out at the copy, broke his hold over his personal reality, and allowed the core reality to overwrite him. Nym's body turned to raw arcana and unraveled, his existence burned out before he had a chance to dictate any other possible reality.

Niramyn's mouth curved up into a grim smile. Now that he was done with that, he just needed to find . . . There. The ascendant who'd been hiding didn't seem to realize that the fox magic had run out. He'd been too distracted by the monstrously complex spell he was putting together.

Niramyn looked at it curiously. He didn't recognize it, and that almost never happened. There were many, many familiar pieces though, with only a few new ones. His eyes widened. The ascendant was casting the age-reversal spell again!

And now that the fox magic had burned away, Niramyn saw him clearly. It was . . . him, but not him. Nym. That little mortal existence he'd briefly been forced to—

That was it! That was the problem. His existence was a paradox right now, two discrete entities in one body. He just needed to expel his version of Nym out to stop reality from trying to shove him into the outer layers. It would even banish the ascendant Nym at the same time.

A single spell was all he needed to cast to end this fight. He could have done that a few minutes back. Mentally scolding himself for his own foolishness, Niramyn reconstituted his Nym into reality.

Nym felt reality pushing against him, that same feeling that told him he was running up against an immovable wall. For all the ways ascendants could twist reality to their desires, existing in two different places at the same time was not one of them. At least, not like this, not as two separate beings.

He had seconds before he was ejected, but the spell was ready.

He released it, watched it arc through empty air to strike Niramyn, watched the shape of a young man coalesce into existence, an empty shell about to be filled with everything left inside the Exarch that was still Nym.

God killer struck.

Nym felt the push of reality vanish, and Niramyn's body skipped backward through time again. His mouth open in a scream of rage and denial, Niramyn became mortal again. This time he couldn't run, physically or magically.

Niramyn looked like a ten-year-old boy, the twin to Nym the day he'd woken up on that beach. And then a bolt of lightning struck him, and he became a seared and smoking corpse falling through the air to crash against the earth below.

Wearily, Nym descended to the ground to examine the body of his fallen foe, to make sure it was really over.

CHAPTER EIGHTY-EIGHT

He felt . . . hollow, empty, without purpose. For so long, for sixty years, if Rizin was to be believed, Nym had been struggling to escape from under two titans before he was crushed in their struggle. Now it was finally done, and he couldn't believe it.

He cast god-killer on the corpse one last time to pluck Niramyn completely from reality. Then he reshaped the prairie to erase the damage from the fight, scrambled the timeline of the last few minutes, and left. Even without the new Nym that Niramyn had tried to create during their fight, he only had about ten minutes left before he bumped up against himself anyway.

The deviation to the primary timeline there was going to be migraine inducing for those ascendants who cared enough to follow it. No doubt they'd be very curious about the exact cause of Niramyn's death. Nym had faith in hidden presence to keep him safe though. It had been strong enough to work against Myzalik, and the cloak-pin version of it had worked against Niramyn to an extent even when the Exarch had been right in front of him.

Now that he thought about the pin, he realized Rizin would probably want to know how everything turned out, and Nym needed to return it since he was done with it. That would come later though. For now, he just wanted to exist for the first time since his own ascendance without fear driving him to push forward. Just for a few minutes, he stared out at the world and thought about the fact that he could go anywhere, do anything he wanted, and that he didn't owe anybody anything.

He was truly, finally, free.

He was without purpose, and that was fantastic. It meant he had room to find new purposes, ones that he wanted to work toward, not that he was forced into. He didn't know what those purposes were going to be, but finding out was going to be an adventure in and of itself.

The minutes ticked by, and soon he felt the pressure of reality building up, ready to force him out to keep him from reliving time he'd already spent. He allowed himself to be pushed back into the sixth layer just long enough to take a step forward into his future and appear on Rizin's island a hundred years in the future.

The fox was beside him immediately. He gave Nym a single, swift appraising glance, then nodded. "What now?" he asked.

"I have no idea," Nym said with a smile. "Anything I want."

He removed the pin, held it out to Rizin, and let the cloak he'd conjured up break apart into arcana. Rizin eyed the pin for a moment, then said, "Keep it. It's not like I need it."

"You sure?" Nym asked. "Trusting me with this fox magic. It's not like we had any sort of agreement."

"Sure we do. If I need your help, you'll help."

Well. That was true.

"What could you possibly need help with? Aren't you supposed to be a big bad fox with . . . quite a few tails?"

"I'm sure I can find a use for you," Rizin said.

"You do always seem to have something you want done but are too lazy to go do yourself," Nym agreed.

Something that felt suspiciously like a tail swatted Nym in the back of the head, but there was nothing there. He side-eyed Rizin, who just smirked back at him. None of his tails had moved, not even the invisible ones that Nym could only see in other layers.

For all that Nym had achieved, he still was far from the strongest thing around. That was fine though. All the strong things that had been interested in hurting or killing him were gone. He wondered how the landscape of ascendant society was going to change now that Niramyn and Myzalik had both vanished.

He suspected change would be slow to come about. It could take years, decades even, before they accepted that their Exarchs weren't coming back. Perhaps the fighting would continue until both sides realized there was nothing left to fight for. Perhaps even that wouldn't be enough, and they'd rally behind new banners. Nym didn't know, and he found that he didn't really care. As long as they left him alone, they could do whatever they wanted.

"I think I'm just going to live a mortal life," he said finally, "at least once. I only got a couple years as a regular person before I ascended."

"I hardly think *regular* is a word that described your life prior to that point."

"Well, no, probably not. And it might not be the right word for the rest of it either, but at least that'll be my choice."

"You're going back a hundred years, to when we first met?" Rizin asked.

"I am, yeah."

"That will be the first point in time anyone looks for you," the fox warned.

"It's not like I'm done growing. I am still an ascendant, after all. But after all of this, I'm confident I can find a way to defend myself. I just don't expect to need to. I am well hidden, after all."

"You're welcome for that."

Nym made a show of looking around the island. "You're welcome too," he said.

Rizin laughed and leaped into the air. His body started to fade away, and all that was left was his voice, saying, "Go on. Go see your friends and family again. Come back to visit occasionally. I'll pretend to be entertained by your dull stories of acting like a human."

Then Rizin was gone. Nym just shook his head and laughed. It wasn't hard to read between the lines there: Rizin was going to miss him and wanted him to come around more often. He'd have to check in on him from time to time in the decades leading up to the current year.

For now though, it was time to go home.

There were many things Ciana liked about her new life. For one, she was insanely wealthy, at least by her standards. She hadn't been shy about spreading that money around either, though she'd been surreptitious enough that nobody suspected her of having a whole bagful of crests. She kept a modest apartment by their standards, but compared to that shack on the coast, it was absolutely lavish.

She had comfortable furniture, good food, new friends, and a lovely little garden she shared with her next-door neighbor to keep her busy. They worked hard on that one, as neither the soil nor the climate were ideal for growing. Space was at a premium in Abilanth too, so gardens were a rarity. It had been the envy of the street, and when one of the neighbor kids had tried to pilfer food from it, the whole neighborhood had come down on the little brat.

For all of that, there were some things she missed. The smell of the sea was one of them, as were her old chores, the crab traps and snares that she'd checked regularly. Privacy was also a lot harder to come by in the city than it was out in her old home. She even missed that one stupid shark that was always following her around whenever she took Nym out with her to check the traps.

She was walking along, a bag of supplies for the garden held in one hand, when a man appeared in front of her. She bumped into him, sending both of them staggering, and quickly grabbed hold of his arm to keep him upright. "I'm so sorry," she said. "I don't know how I didn't see you there."

"Well, I guess I'll forgive you this time," the man said, turning to grin at her. "But I'm going to get you back."

"Nym," she breathed out. "You . . . You're so tall."

"Don't worry, you're still my big sister," he told her. "Even if you aren't taller than me anymore."

"You jerk!" she said, throwing her arms around him and pulling him into a hug. "Just abandoning me here for so long. I didn't know if you were ever coming back."

"Well, you know, I had some things to take care of. Actually, I do still have a few odds and ends to wrap up, but one thing at a time and all that. You're the one I wanted to see first, now that all that other business is taken care of."

"So you're . . . You're safe now? It's over? We can go back home?"

Nym shrugged. "If you want to. Or anywhere else in the world. Nothing is really off-limits. I've got some friends I want to introduce you to later."

A door in a nearby house opened, and an older man stuck his head out. "Everything alright, Miss Ciana?" he asked.

"Just fine, Mr. Cleef," she said. "This is my brother, Nym."

"Oh yeah? Nice to meet you, son," the man said, coming fully out of his house and grabbing Nym's hand to give it a vigorous shake. "Your sister's had nothing but good things to say about you."

"Well, mostly good things," she said. "I may have mentioned some of the mischief you got up to when you were younger."

"What in the world makes you think I stopped getting into mischief?" Nym asked.

Ciana let out an exaggerated sigh and shook her head. "It's good to see you again."

"You too. Now, how about we go grab something to eat? We can catch up and figure out what we'll do next."

"Oh, sure. There's a nice restaurant not too far from here. Mr. Cleef, could you maybe give this to Semara for me?" Ciana asked, holding out the bag.

"Garden stuff?" he asked. At her nod, he laughed and took the bag. "You gotta stop spoiling my wife like this. That little project of yours is all she talked about all winter. She just couldn't wait for the snow to melt to start it up again."

"I know," Ciana said. "I can't wait either."

The man took the bag, bid them both a good day, and disappeared back into his house. Nym and Ciana went to eat at a cute little place where the staff all knew her by name. The food was delicious, and the company better. When they were done, Nym whisked her away to her old ocean-side home to visit. That was only the first stop of the afternoon.

Nym took Ciana to meet the rest of his friends and was pleased to see the generally positive reaction he got on his return. Kazie gave him a few tight-lipped glances when she thought he wasn't looking but refrained from bringing down the general mood.

While the others were mingling and chatting, Nym went over to sit down next to her. "Still don't like me?" he asked.

"It's not about that. I'm sure you're a fine person," she said.

"But I shouldn't have come back," he finished for her.

"No, you shouldn't have."

"If it sets your mind at ease, there won't be any trouble following me. It's all been taken care of."

"You sound so sure of yourself," Kazie said. "I guess only time will tell."

Nym laughed. He couldn't help himself. "I guess so. Maybe you'll think better of me in a few years."

"As long as you don't hurt them, I think you're just fine."

"I think the two of us will get along alright. I don't want to hurt them either."

"Hmm. We'll see." The two lapsed into silence for a few moments. "Your sister seems nice."

"She is. She's just . . . She's a good person. The best, really."

The two of them watched Ciana sit down next to Analia, who glanced at her once, then went back to staring at her shoes. "How is Analia doing?" he asked.

"Ophelia says she's getting better, but it'll be a long process. It could be years. I don't know what she was like before, the poor girl."

"Happy," Nym said. "Carefree. A bit bossy. She knew what she wanted and wasn't afraid to go after it. Terrible taste in desserts though. Nobody's perfect."

Kazie barked out a short laugh. "If that's the worst you can say about her . . ."

Nym smiled and leaned back in the chair. All around him, his family chatted, snacked, and played. Life was good, and a few lingering shadows weren't going to demolish the happiness he saw in front of him.

"Nym!" Bildar called out. "More custards, my man! We've run dry!"

"By God, this shall not stand!" Nym bellowed. Arcana surged through his soul well, and he materialized a new plate of desserts.

"Unbelievable," Nomick said, sliding into the chair next to Kazie and slipping an arm around her. "The power of the gods, and this is what you use it for. I'm sure you could find something more important than this."

"You're such a hypocrite," Nym said.

"What? Why?"

"I watched you eat the last custard not two minutes ago. And I saw you sneak another one just now."

"It would be wrong of me *not* to eat them," Nomick protested.

"Whatever helps you sleep at night, man. Besides, you're wrong."

"I am?" Both Nomick and Kazie looked at Nym curiously.

He gestured at the table where the rest of the Earth Shapers were engaged in a three-way battle to claim the most custards off the new plate. "Nothing is more important than this, not to me."

EPILOGUE

Twenty years later . . .

Nym sat cross-legged on the floor across from a little boy, barely ten years old. He had curling blond hair and bright-blue eyes that gleamed with excitement and an infectious smile. Currently, his face was pinched in concentration as his conduit quested out through the first layer and brushed up against the membrane blocking off the second.

Nym watched silently and made no moves to help. Eriam needed to learn to do it himself, after all. Nym had shown him how, and he'd proved he could do it. He just had a bit of anxiety now that someone was watching. A few feet away, standing next to a barrel of sand, was his earth-magic teacher. Professor Ophelia had been personally tutoring him for the last year but had requested Nym sit in on a lesson to offer some additional help.

Eriam's conduit punched through the membrane. Immediately, second-layer arcana flooded his soul well. "I did it!" he said.

"Very good," Ophelia told him. "Now, just focus on the sand and cast the spell like we talked about."

That was . . . a little bit painful to watch. Watching mortal mages learn new spells was like watching a blind man write a letter. They learned the individual shapes and what order to put them in, but nothing ever quite lined up right, and the words meandered across the page. New mages just wrote their spells over and over again until they got it right, then tried to remember what that felt like.

Not for the first time, Nym was glad he could actually see arcana.

Despite that handicap, Eriam was actually doing quite well. Of course, he had private tutors, copious amounts of time to practice, the resources of a noble house backing him, and the occasional assistance of an actual ascendant, though Nym limited himself severely in his help. It wouldn't mean anything if he just did it for Eriam, and the boy wouldn't thank him for the interference in the long term.

After about twenty minutes, Eriam managed to get all the pieces lined up, and his terrakinesis spell triggered. A blob of sand rose up into the air about a foot, leaking out of the bottom at a decent rate. It only took about three seconds before enough of the sand had fallen out of the blob that there was practically nothing left.

"Excellent work!" Ophelia said. Oh yeah, she'd definitely gotten her teacher voice down. Eriam seemed to appreciate the encouragement at least. "I think we'll stop there for now. We've got to go get ready for the party."

"Okay," Eriam said. He let go of the spell, and the rest of the sand fell into the barrel. Nym swept up all the loose grains to clean up the room, then floated the lid over and pushed it down while Eriam watched him, eyes wide. "When will I be able to do that?"

"Soon enough, I'm sure. Just keep practicing," he said.

"Don't measure yourself against Nym," Ophelia warned. "That's just going to set yourself up for disappointment. You're doing very well for your age."

Nym smiled but said nothing. Eriam was one of the few people who could measure up against him, one day. But that would ruin the surprise. "Come on, let's go find your mother so we can all go."

Analia looked up from her desk when her son ran into the room, followed closely by Nym and Ophelia. "All done?" she asked.

"For today," Ophelia said. "Eriam is doing very well."

"I got the sand to move with my magic today," he said.

"Good job," she told him. "We'll make an expert mage out of you yet."

"I'm sure he'll be one of the best," Nym said, a soft smile on his face. He knew . . . something, but he refused to say what, no matter how much she pestered him. Considering how easily he could look into the future, it could be anything. She trusted that if he'd seen anything bad though, he would take steps to prevent that.

"It's time to get going," Ophelia said. "A bit past time, actually."

"Ah, right. One moment." Analia finished jotting down a note to herself for when she came back to finish her work, then stood up. "Shall we?"

Nym's magic swept over the four of them and whisked them a thousand miles away to a large hall they'd rented out for a party. As expected, it was already full of people. Bildar was there, of course, as it was his retirement party. His beard was almost pure gray at this point, and his belly was considerably bigger than it had been when she was a kid, but he was still an active man with a vibrant personality. He was busy talking to Monick about something when they arrived and didn't notice them right away.

Nomick and Kazie did, or rather, their little girl did. "Look, Mom!" she said. "Can I go play?"

Kazie glanced over and smiled. "Of course, dear. Stay in the room, please."

Eriam and Cari ran off together, with the boy excitedly telling her about the new spell he'd learned to cast. Analia made her way over to Cari's parents to exchange pleasantries. "Where's your husband?" Kazie asked after.

"Still working on that trade agreement with the Kolquidst Consortium. They've been bickering about the shipping costs for a week. I'm about ready to just build the teleportation platform myself just so I don't have to hear about it anymore," Analia said.

"He works too hard," Nomick said. "We're supposed to be celebrating today."

"I know. I told him, but he had meetings all day to get to."

"His loss," Nomick said. "Did you know Nym got the Quarterhouse to cater the party? They don't even do that. I have no idea how much he paid them to agree."

"I did not know that," Analia admitted, "but now that you can mention it, I can smell the food from here."

She turned to look toward the smell, which was emanating from an open doorway with a small crowd of people she didn't recognize loitering near it. "Are those the new hires?"

"Yep. Monick picked them. With Ophelia gone and Bildar retiring, he had to hire four earth mages to replace them. I think Bildar helped vet them. The business is all those two talk about anymore."

"Well, I suppose some introductions are in order. Come on, you can make them."

Everyone else had wandered off in one direction or the other, but Nym sat down in a random chair among a row of empty ones pushed up against the wall. "I didn't think you were going to come," he said.

"I wouldn't have, except there's something I wanted to talk to you about," a voice said from the chair next to him. Though it appeared empty to anyone who didn't know how to look, Rizin sat there, his body in the shape of a human man.

"Another problem with Research Lab Six?" Nym asked, trying not to wince. It would be the third time he'd had to go in there and correct an issue.

"Oh no, nothing like that. It's just a message I was asked to pass on."

"Really? That's a bit unexpected. Who would be sending me a message through you?"

"That snow-wolf patriarch you go hunting with sometimes somehow got hold of my ring. Apparently, someone taught him how to channel arcana into it."

"Cold Paw? Ah, well he's a clever guy. I'm not surprised he managed something like that."

"I regret not eating you when we first met," Rizin deadpanned.

"No, you don't."

The fox sighed, then admitted, "Well, it has been an interesting few decades. Anyway, the wolf wants you to come visit soon. He's got something time sensitive he wants your help with. And now that I've delivered that message, I'll be off."

Rizin's presence disappeared from the hall, and Nym relaxed into his chair. He only got a few minutes of solitude before Ophelia walked over, one arm held out for Archmage Veran to hold. He'd looked old when Nym first met him, but he was positively ancient now. He was a bit slower than he used to be but hardly needed the help. Not for the first time, Nym considered adapting his age-reversal spell to work on mortals. It wouldn't even be that difficult. The only reason he hadn't was that it was suspiciously similar to the god-killer spell he'd used on precisely three ascendants, then done his best to forget ever existed.

"You're looking well," the archmage said by way of greeting. "I appreciate the invitation."

"Of course," Nym said, gesturing for him to take the seat next to him. "How have you been, sir?"

"Thinking about retiring in the next year or two," Archmage Veran told him bluntly. "It's all just getting to be a bit too much to keep on top of anymore. Ophelia has been a lifesaver, but she has her own classes to teach and can't spend all her time helping me."

"Maybe we'll have to throw you a retirement party next," Nym said, nodding his head toward Bildar, who was still discussing work stuff with Monick across the room while Nomick loudly bemoaned that they were ruining the party by refusing to shut up about business. Both of them ignored the man.

Laughing softly, the archmage sat down in the chair Rizin had recently vacated. "I suspect it would be somewhat less rambunctious than this one. Though if the smells coming out of the kitchen are any indication of the upcoming meal, I would hire this catering company again."

"It does smell good," Nym said.

"Indeed. Now though, I assume that little boy playing over there is the one you wanted to introduce me to?"

"Eriam is his name," Nym said. "He'll be starting at the Academy soon."

"I see. You know he won't receive any special treatment from me just because he's from a noble family, right?"

"I'm not asking for any special treatment for him. I have a vested interest in him though, so I would like to be kept updated on his progress."

"A vested interest," Archmage Veran said, his gaze sharpening. "Am I to assume . . . ?"

"Almost certainly," Nym confirmed.

"Assume what?" Ophelia asked. "Are you saying he's going to be, you know . . . like you?"

"Nobody knows what the future will hold," Nym said. "But I've got some pretty good guesses. It's very, very possible. We won't be telling him or his family, of course."

"Hmm," Ophelia said. "Analia would probably like to know. Then again, with everything her own father did, maybe not."

Nym glanced over to the woman, who was talking to the new earth mages Monick had hired. She was a lot quieter than she'd been as a kid, more reserved. Time had helped, and he thought confronting her father had helped as well, but he had no doubt that she was a very different person than she would have otherwise grown to be if not for the geasa she'd suffered under.

Nym had never asked what she'd done, but Jaspar Feldstal had died less than a week after that meeting, his heart giving out, and with there being no nearby healer to save him, that was that. It was a strange way to go for someone still so relatively young and in good health. There had been suspicions, but as far as he knew, they'd never amounted to more than that.

"I think we'll just keep this to ourselves for now," Nym said. "It'll be easier for everyone, and nobody needs to be put under the pressure to succeed at a task that big. If he decides he wants to try for ascendance when he's older, we'll help him. If not, that's his choice."

"But you think he will," Archmage Veran said.

"I think he's a very bright young man, and he'll do great things."

The archmage watched the little boy play with his friend. "Interesting. I'll keep an eye on him."

"Thanks," Nym said. "Now, I think I hear them plating our meals. Let's go find some seats at the table."

"That is a most excellent suggestion. Here, help an old man up."

Nym pulled the archmage to his feet, and together, they went to join his friends and family.

One hundred years later . . .

"I cannot believe you just let yourself age like that for a century," Rizin said. "You're all saggy."

Nym smiled and said, "I know. It was totally worth it."

"To live a mortal life? It's overrated."

"No, it's not. But yes, I am ready to feel young again."

"When will you do it?"

"Soon. Analia's funeral is tomorrow. After that, I think it's time to take a step back from the mortal world."

"Well it's about time," Rizin said.

"I wasn't in a rush," Nym said. "I would think a fellow immortal could appreciate that."

"I have no problem with the number of years you took. I just can't believe you took no steps at all to keep yourself young."

"That's part of a mortal life," Nym said.

It had been too. He'd grown older with his friends, helped them raise the next generation, and watched, one by one, as they'd passed on. Finally, only the two youngest of their group remained, Analia and him. And she'd let go of her hold on life too. As far as he was concerned, that was the end of it. All the children had grown, had children of their own, and lived their own lives. His time as a mortal was over now.

It was time to try something new, to truly be the immortal he'd spent a hundred years pretending not to be. "I think it will be an interesting few decades," Nym said.

"Not as interesting as the last time, I hope."

"Well, I guess we'll see. I've got to get going. Next time you see me, I'll be young and fit again."

"Good," Rizin said. "And get rid of that stupid cane."

Nym frowned and looked down at it. "What's wrong with my cane?"

"You are a godlike being. Act like it."

Nym rolled his eyes and smiled. "See you soon, old friend."

"Yeah, yeah. See you soon."

About the Author

EmergencyComplaints grew up reading fantasy and tried his hand at writing his first novel on an old MS-DOS text editor program when he was seven years old. That story didn't pan out; maximum character limits were a thing back then. Undeterred, he kept writing on other platforms, reading full-time, devouring JRPGs, and playing *D&D*, and he is now the author of the God Machine and Ascendant series. Check out his most recent work on Royal Road.

Podium

DISCOVER
STORIES UNBOUND

PodiumAudio.com

Milton Keynes UK
Ingram Content Group UK Ltd.
UKHW020050061124
450708UK00006B/705

9 781039 446878